Dandy Gilver and
the Unpleasantness in
the Ballroom

The Dandy Gilver Series

After the Armistice Ball

The Burry Man's Day

Bury Her Deep

The Winter Ground

Dandy Gilver and the Proper Treatment of Bloodstains

Dandy Gilver and an Unsuitable Day for a Murder

Dandy Gilver and a Bothersome Number of Corpses

Dandy Gilver and a Deadly Measure of Brimstone

Dandy Gilver and the Reek of Red Herrings

About the author

Catriona McPherson was born in the village of Queensferry in south-east Scotland in 1965 and educated at Edinburgh University. She divides her time between Scotland and California.

www.catrionamcpherson.com
Twitter: @CatrionaMcP

CATRIONA McPHERSON

Dandy Gilver and the Unpleasantness in the Ballroom

HODDER &
STOUGHTON

First published in Great Britain in 2015 by Hodder & Stoughton
An Hachette UK company

1

A CIP catalogue record for this title is available from the British Library.

Hardback ISBN 978 1 444 78610 1
eBook ISBN 978 1 444 78609 5

Typeset in Plantin Light by Palimpsest Book Production Limited,
Falkirk, Stirlingshire

Printed and bound by Clays Ltd, St Ives plc

Hodder & Stoughton policy is to use papers that are natural, renewable and
recyclable products and made from wood grown in sustainable forests.
The logging and manufacturing processes are expected to conform
to the environmental regulations of the country of origin.

Hodder & Stoughton Ltd
Carmelite House
50 Victoria Embankment
London EC4Y 0DZ

www.hodder.co.uk

To Rosalind and Malcolm Smith, with love

Acknowledgements

I would like to thank: Suzie Dooré, Francine Toon, Becca Mundy and Jessica Hische; Lisa Moylett; my friends and family; and Sam Hood, who taught me everything I know about ballroom dancing.

I

Mrs Woolf and I are hardly kindred souls taken all in all but on a room of one's own we agree. My sitting room, in the south-east corner of the house, has long been my favourite part of Gilverton. Bright in the morning, cosily lamplit by teatime, looking out over lawns towards the park beyond the ha-ha, it is papered in yellow silk, rather greyed now around a few restful pictures, carpeted in the palest shade of grey-blue, terribly thin these days but still beautiful, and draped and littered with damask curtains and cushions so faded that one has to peer into the folds to see from whence – blue or yellow? – their journey to greyness began. It is as restful as a lily pond and my only sanctuary in that house of mahogany, leather and blood-red velvet. That house of *men*. Particularly after the telephone was installed at the advent of my detecting career and, more lately, after one of the long windows was turned into a garden door, I used to think I could live there quite contentedly, dining off trays the maids brought me and reading by the fire with my feet up on a stool.

Now, as I sat at my desk and listened to the empty silence, the tick of my Dresden clock on the chimneypiece only making it seem quieter still, I had never felt less happy to be alone. My eyes strayed, as they were wont to fifty times a day, to the pale blue chair, now without its blanket since now without its dog. I could feel my eyes pricking as I rose and walked over to run my hands over the cool nap of the seat and remember her.

Bunty. She had clambered into that chair as a leggy puppy

three months old, as soon as she was able, and nothing would ever persuade her back to her basket on the hearthrug again. I smiled to remember the way she would curl up when newly asleep and then gradually unwind until she was sprawled with her paws waving and her head hanging down, like one of the carousers in a Hogarth tavern scene. Then, at the sound of the door, she would awaken, flop and lollop herself right side up again and sit up on the chair, nose quivering and half of her body wagging along with her tail.

The maids had done a good job and there was not a single one of her stiff white hairs left anywhere in the upholstery. I knew because I had sat there and looked for them, weeping like a ninny, in the first few weeks. I was better now. I had taken her collar and lead down from the coat hooks at the garden-room door and had moved the short set of steps back to the library where they belonged, away from the side of my bed where Bunty had used them to help her retire for the night once her hips had started troubling her.

She had a wonderful life, I told myself sternly. A good innings and more adventures, I would wager, than any Dalmatian since the days they actually ran alongside carriages and bit highwaymen. All of this was true but I was still sitting there when the door opened and Pallister, our butler, prowled in. He looked first at my desk, where I am usually to be found; and then, glancing over and seeing me in Bunty's chair, he nodded very faintly and tilted his head about ten degrees to one side in a manner that looked a good deal like sympathy. I had to catch my lip and hold my breath so as not to dissolve into sobs at such a display of emotion.

'A letter, madam,' he said, proffering the salver. 'It came by special messenger just now.' I nodded, lifted the envelope and set it down on my lap. 'Shall I fetch your opener over, madam?' I nodded again. 'Rather showy stationery,' he went on, as I slipped my paperknife under the flap and slit the envelope open. I looked, to be polite, and nodded a third time. It was thick vellum the colour of buttermilk and had a crest stamped in gold on the back. 'No one I've come across before, madam,' Pallister said. 'Perhaps it's from a "client". Perhaps there's a "case" coming your way.'

Even with the rather deafening quotation marks, this was amazing. Pallister's usual tack – through letters, calls on the telephone, appointments with clients, visits from police, press attention, the arrival of witnesses to be hidden and the departure of paperwork to be burned – was to affect perfect oblivion. Gilver and Osborne could not be countenanced and so did not exist. His aptitude for ignoring unpleasantnesses rivalled that of my grandmother Leston; and she had lived for ten years in India without seeing a single shoeless child.

'Perhaps,' I agreed faintly.

As Pallister withdrew, I undertook what amounted to an impromptu séance; I called upon the departed spirits of my mother, my Aunt Hortensia and Nanny Palmer herself to help me re-square my shoulders and re-stiffen my lip. Then I shook open the sheet of writing paper with a sharp crack, prepared to forget Bunty and apply myself to whatever adventure was calling me away from her memory and into the lonely future without her.

The return address, which was "Balmoral", Manse Road, Bearsden, Glasgow, held out little promise of adventure, it is true. The name of the letter's sender, which was Sir Percival Stott, almost wrenched a groan of dismay out of me. The first line, which mentioned a beloved daughter and the need for discretion, came within a whisker of causing me to cast the letter into the fire. Such humdrum affairs, I feared, could not put a dent in my grieving.

I could hardly have been more wrong. Not only did the Stott case – a murder case as it turned out to be – take Alec and me into a world of glitter and glamour, a world steeped in human depravity and conscienceless evil such as we had never encountered before, but it also brought me Bunty the

Second, who – as I read Sir Percy's letter that morning– was four days old, tiny and mewling and tucked under her mother's flank along with all her littermates, as unaware as I was that she would spend her life with me.

2

'I've never been to Glasgow before,' said Alec Osborne as we drove sedately through the streets of villas which make up the westerly suburbs.

'The second city of the Empire?' I said. 'That's a shocking admission.' I was teasing. One of the things I hold in highest affection about Alec is his cheerfulness in the face of any amount of teasing. He is most unlike other men in that regard. Besides, he had not been ignoring Glasgow for long; he had only lived in Scotland for a little over eight years, moving there at the close of our first adventure.

It had started out with all the appearance of a jewel theft – the Case of the Duffy Diamonds – but really it had been a murder and, as is often the case when death strikes, there was an inheritance. Alec had ended those few turbulent weeks down one fiancée, but up a Perthshire estate and with a devoted friend and colleague thrown in. I dare say it was a net loss but he seems reconciled to it. He was chuckling even now.

'Shocking indeed,' he was saying. 'Never been to Liverpool either for that matter.'

'Well, gosh, I've never been to Liverpool,' I said. 'Why would one have gone to Liverpool?'

'To catch a boat to Ireland,' Alec suggested.

'Why on earth would one have gone to *Ireland*?'

'Horses?' said Alec vaguely. 'Anyway, I expect it's just the same as Edinburgh, isn't it?'

'Don't let the denizens of either hear that,' I said. 'There'd be a riot. Oop, there it is.' A discreet sign heralded our arrival at the Manse Road turn-off and I wrenched the wheel of my little Morris Cowley hard left, catching it just in time.

Alec whistled through his teeth. The trim villas we had been passing for the last ten minutes were replaced, on Manse Road, with out-and-out mansion houses, some of them almost as stately as Dunelgar and Gilverton, respectively Alec's home and mine, albeit set down in grounds of only an acre or two and without a gate lodge to their names.

'I smell money,' Alec said. 'Let's hope for a nice, juicy, time-consuming case and a good dollop of Sir Percival's loot.'

'You are disgusting,' I said, for it was easier on my conscience if neither of us said what we were both thinking.

'It's going to be Mr Birchfield all over again,' said Alec, rubbing his hands. 'And about time too.'

Mr Ernest Birchfield, fish merchant, of Aberdeen was the last client to make any significant contribution to Gilver and Osborne's coffers. Since the conclusion of that case we had been scraping by, our services sought either by supplicants from the working classes too poor to pay us the going rate but too desperate for us to turn away or – which was worse – supplicants from the upper classes, too feckless to pay us and too likely to be encountered at parties to be refused. The cheek of some of them could hardly be believed: one old pal had even had the gall to try to pay for a week's investigation of household pilfering by offering to take my elder son to London and wheel him about while she got her daughter launched. As though single young men of good family were not hen's teeth and welcome everywhere.

'Ah, the middle classes,' Alec said, sitting forward and peering to right and left, looking out for Balmoral. 'So punctilious at paying their bills and so anxious to have their indiscretions tidied away. Perhaps we should compose an advertisement or two especially for them, Dandy. Plenty of veiled hints and assurances, nothing vulgar.'

6

'Here we are,' I said, spotting the glint of gold lettering on a gatepost. 'Balmoral.'

'What can he have been thinking when he chose such a name?' said Alec. 'He can't possibly be a sensible man.'

'"Great hopes of finding him quite the reverse", eh?' I said.

But, as ever when I quote Miss Austen, Alec merely grunted and we rolled up the short drive of raked gravel in silence. He was right about the money, I thought to myself, looking around, for the lawns were as carefully swept as the drive was raked, and the roses growing in crescent-shaped beds cut into the turf on either side were lovingly tended; not a speck of rust nor a spent bloom to be seen, and not a single petal lying on the dark earth below them, which is well-nigh impossible in June unless battalions of garden-boys keep vigil. Certainly the rose gardens at Gilverton had been carpeted in a kind of brown confetti, holding open house for any aphid who cared to drop by. My husband, Hugh, mounted the odd dawn raid with a nicotine gun but only when he remembered and never when salmon, stags or grouse were in season.

'Tobacco lord, do you think?' said Alec as we drew to a halt at the front door. It was freshly painted in a bright sunflower yellow which clashed with the brass work and with the pots of orange and pink begonias ranged on the steps leading up to it. Still, it was a cheerful prospect and went some way to counteract the gloomy elevation of the house overall. I have been more than twenty years in Scotland now, longer here than in Northamptonshire, which shall always be home, but still I miss those low, spreading cottages of ochre stone and the cosy glitter of their little windows. Scotch houses like this one, gaunt and majestic, stare down at one like a minister in his pulpit, their windows so very much taller than they are wide and so very blank and dark, reflecting the cold northern skies.

'The tobacco lords are long gone,' I said. 'They're all living on their estates. Sir Percival is probably a—'

The door was opened before I could hazard a guess and we were ushered in by a pretty young maid in black and white. Lady Stott, if she existed, rose in my estimation. It is becoming harder and harder to get girls into a cap and cuffs, even in Perthshire, and I imagined it would take a forceful personality to carry the day here in Glasgow.

She showed us into a sumptuous morning room where a coal fire was leaping in the grate even though the day was so warm that the windows had to be opened to let out the heat. The room had a close-fitting carpet in a most impractical shade of peach and a collection of plush and satin armchairs arranged around a low table where the latest issues of every imaginable magazine were laid out in fans, everything from *Woman's Weekly* to *Popular Aviation*. The *Vogue* made my fingers twitch; I had stopped taking it because it gave Grant, my maid, alarming ideas.

Alec gave a look of recognition to something called *Parisiana*, and leafed through it briefly, before returning it to the bottom of the pile and sherlocking around the room instead, scrutinising the photographs ranged on the piano – 'I'm pretty sure that's Haile Selassie' – and the spines of the books on the tiny oak bookcase behind the door: 'Scott and Kipling. Sir P is not a scholar.' I sat with my hands folded and my gloves in my lap, cursing Nanny Palmer although unable to escape her training.

The Stotts arrived just in time to stop Alec from opening the writing desk and reading letters. Sir Percival was a dapper man of sixty-odd, very correct in his morning coat and striped trousers, although rather more fidgety than a man in his own house should be. His lady was about as fidgety as an ocean liner and just as magnificent. She sailed in, her long skirts sweeping the plush carpet and continuing to eddy about her feet even after she had drawn to a halt before us. She held out a hand, stiff with jewellery; she had to have been wearing seven rings as well as a collection of gold and ivory bangles, a gold and pearl brooch fashioned in the shape of a basket of lily of the valley and what was either two entire triple strands of pearls or a sextuple strand, if such a thing existed. My heart instantly melted. Whatever trouble the Stotts had found themselves in, they were clearly quite at sea and utterly terrified to have called upon Alec and me. They had decked themselves out in all their finery to try to face us down and I only wished I could throw my arms around both of them and tell them, 'There, there.'

Alec, as it happens, is Gilver and Osborne's specialist brow-mopper and he went to work right away.

'Sir Percival,' he said, 'and Lady Stott. I hope you will forgive me for plunging in, but I can see how distraught you are and I want to set your minds at ease before another minute passes. Whatever is wrong, whatever is troubling you, we are here to help. We are one hundred per cent confidential, one hundred per cent dedicated and – forgive me, but it must be said – one hundred per cent unsurprisable.'

I watched them closely while he worked off all this and for a minute I thought he had over-egged the pudding. Assurances that one cannot be shocked do rather suggest that, somewhere near at hand, there is something shocking. In the end, however, relief won out over dignity and Lady Stott plumped down into one of the cushiony armchairs and let out an enormous sigh.

'It's our daughter,' she said. 'Our only one. Our darling girl. We're so very worried about her.'

'Eunice,' said her husband mildly. 'Perhaps you'd let me.' He himself sat then, with a tweak of his trouser legs and an expert flick of his coat tails to stop them from being trapped underneath him.

I am always reminded of my younger son, Teddy, whenever I see this; it took him years to learn the ways of a tailcoat, years and years before he could sit without threat of strangulation. 'The coat grabs on to the waistcoat, Mummy,' he would say. 'And the waistcoat sticks to the shirt which is buttoned to the collar, so when you anchor the coat to a chair with your behind, it gets you right in the windpipe. Why must I wear it?' I would tell him that generations of Etonians had worn them every day and survived, and would advise him to watch Daddy, but it was not until around 1922 and those accursed dropped waistlines that I ever experienced the sensation for myself and truly sympathised.

'Now then,' said Sir Percival, once he was settled. 'You come highly recommended, although by someone who wishes his name to be withheld, but I have a few questions to ask before we begin. If we begin.'

'Bounce!' said Lady Stott for some reason.

I tried to look unsurprised and I saw Alec struggling with his eyebrows.

Sir Percival ignored her. 'You have no formal training in investigation,' he said. 'Is that right?'

'We are not police officers,' said Alec, 'if that's what you mean.'

Lady Stott raised a fluttery hand to her six strands of pearls and Sir Percival swallowed so hard that the knot of his tie moved at least an inch down his neck and then up again.

'Actually,' I said, 'I'm a Special Constable of the Edinburgh Constabulary. And have been since 1926.' It was true; I had been sworn in during the General Strike and, through over-sight more than anything, had never been sworn out again. 'But we answer to no one,' I went on. 'Except you, our clients, and Him, our maker.' I had a hunch that rigid respectability was the way to go.

Sir Percival nodded slightly.

'And we have solved a good many crimes of every size and seriousness from petty theft to murder,' said Alec.

Sir Percival swallowed again and Lady Stott lay back in her chair with a creak of whalebone.

'Tweetie,' she breathed.

This time I know that my brows knitted as I tried to understand her and Alec chewed his lip for a moment or two while he sought a rejoinder.

'Eunice!' said her husband, rather more sharply than the first time, before turning back to Alec and me. 'And how did you fall into this line of work?'

Alec and I shared a glance and he nodded imperceptibly. I was to take the lead, he meant to say. I knew what was wanted for, while Alec is our silver tongue, I am our archivist. It is not a role that comes all that easily but I do what I can; it would be unseemly, given what is in our archives, for Alec to attempt it.

'Our very first case came about when a dear friend of mine was being threatened by a scoundrel,' I said. 'I stepped in to help and discovered an aptitude for investigation. Mr Osborne here, on the other hand, could hardly help becoming involved. The threatener killed his fiancée.' No matter how matter-of-factly one recounts it, this fact always startles. Today, it was rewarded with a gasp from Lady Stott and a twitch from Sir Percy. Alec stared straight ahead.

'I hope you will accept Lady Stott's and my condolences, Mr Osborne,' said Sir Percy.

'When was this?' said Lady Stott.

'Nine years ago,' I said. I could see her checking his hands for the kind of signet rings gentlemen sometimes put on their little fingers when they marry. She was aquiver to ask if he had replaced the fiancée and embarked on his intended bliss after the disruption.

'Since you mention a fiancée,' said Sir Percy. He cleared his throat. 'I did want to ask, as a matter of fact . . . I was surprised to hear that the Gilver of Gilver and Osborne was a lady, if I might be so frank as to speak my mind. And we wondered, Lady Stott and I, if "Mrs" is a courtesy title. Like a cook.'

Alec snorted but managed to turn it into a cough.

Lady Stott shot upright again with another creak in her rigging. 'We did not!' she said. '*You* might have. Mrs Gilver, I must apol—'

'Not at all,' said Alec magnanimously on my behalf. 'If the case concerns your daughter, Lady Stott, I quite see that your husband would want to exercise the utmost caution.'

'I am flattered, Sir Percival,' I said. 'But the truth is that I have been married to Mr Gilver, of Gilverton in Perthshire, for more than twenty years and have two grown-up sons. Young Mr Osborne here is our neighbour and friend and my professional partner.' Alec preened himself rather to be described that way and I looked forward to kicking him when we were alone.

'Two sons,' said Lady Stott. 'You're a mother? She's a mother, Bounce.'

'Percy, please,' said her husband, flushing. 'I'm in rubber,' he added, for Alec and me. 'Started out in ladies' foundation garments and expanded into dampeners. These days we grow our own.'

I might have managed to contain myself, had not Alec asked in a studious way, 'Grow your own what?'

I whinnied and coughed. 'Dam—' I managed before I was overtaken. I tried again. 'Dampeners?'

'Is something the matter?' said Sir Percy.

Alec's mouth was beginning to twitch.

'I keep telling you,' said Lady Stott. 'I keep telling him. I was brought up with my father saying he travelled in marmalade and never understanding why people tittered.'

'Dampeners for motorcar engines,' said Sir Percy. 'We did so well out of them that I bought into a plantation in British Malaysia.'

'Oh!' said Alec. 'Grow your own *rubber*.'

Lady Stott started to giggle then and, although her husband continued to look far from pleased, the ice was broken and the decision seemed to be made that Gilver and Osborne were employed by the Stotts to look into their troubles for them.

A minute later the neat maid came back with a coffee tray.

'It's our daughter,' said Lady Stott again, while pouring. 'Our darling Theresa. Someone is making her life rather unpleasant.'

'And she's too stubborn to do the sensible thing,' said Sir Percy.

'She's too principled to let herself be intimi—' said Lady Stott, interrupting him.

'She's too spoiled to forgo her whims—' Sir Percy cut in.

'She's come too far to give up just becau—'

'Perhaps!' said Alec. 'You should fill in some of the more factual details.'

Both Stotts gathered themselves. Sir Percy's gathering was completed first and he resumed speaking.

'Our daughter Theresa is engaged to Julian Armour.' He paused, apparently for reaction. 'Of Armour Ely.' He paused again. 'One of the city's most prestigious firms of solicitors. His father started it up in eighteen hundred and ninety-two.'

I knew that some appreciation was in order. While it would have been heartbreaking for a daughter of mine to attach herself to a Glaswegian lawyer, Sir Percy was clearly delighted. 'How lovely,' I said.

Sir Percy, mollified, went on. 'Her wedding is in July and if we can get her there, she has promised to settle down and be a credit to us.'

'But?' said Alec.

'But,' said Sir Percy, 'in the meantime, there are "the Championships". Theresa, despite her upbringing and all her advantages and despite Julian and the good fortune of her engagement, has got herself mixed up in . . . *dancing.*'

I let go of the enormous pent-up breath I had been holding. 'Dancing,' I said.

'Not ballet dancing, which would be bad enough the way they flit about in their nighties,' he said. 'And not good Scottish country dancing either.'

'She likes a dance!' said Lady Stott. 'It's a bit of harmless fun.' Sir Percy snorted. 'And, besides, Julian knows nothing about it.'

'That seems rather risky,' I put in. 'What kind of dancing is it exactly?'

'The Charleston,' said Sir Percy, with some venom. 'The paso doble. The black . . .' He stalled.

'Bottom,' said Lady Stott. 'But I keep telling you, Bounce – I keep telling him – that the Scottish Professional Championship covers the waltz, the quickstep, the foxtrot and . . . Well, yes, the tango, I'll grant you.'

'Professional?' I said. Sir Percy swept his arm out towards me in a grand gesture, supposed to show to his wife that I agreed with him in his horror. To be fair, I rather did; at least, I wanted to hear more about it.

'It doesn't mean anything,' said Lady Stott. 'Some of the *other* professionals run dancing schools and some of them work in hotels and on the pleasure boats, but Tweetie just practises and competes and lives quietly at home between times.'

'Quietly!' said her husband. 'She's out every night at that dance-hall—'

'Tweetie is Theresa?' said Alec.

'Tweetie Bird,' said Lady Stott. 'Oh, you should see her costumes, with the feathers and the little wings on her head-dresses. She's as pretty as a picture. And trips around the floor like a little fairy in Roland's arms.'

'*Roland!*' growled Sir Percy.

'Roland's a lovely boy and so discreet,' said his wife. Sir Percy snorted again and looked, briefly, as though he had caught a sudden whiff of something nasty. 'He's a clerk in Julian's office. That's where Theresa met him, don't you know? But he never says a word out of turn and he knows it's only until the wedding.'

'He's got her twisted round his little finger,' said Sir Percy, his voice rising. 'She couldn't pull out now even if she wanted to. *Roland* could destroy her with a word. One word in Julian's ear and—'

'Dear me,' I said. 'Are you saying that Theresa would like to withdraw but that her dancing partner is threatening to expose her to her fiancé?'

For the first time both Stotts were in complete agreement. 'No!' they chorused.

'It's much worse than that,' said Sir Percy. 'Someone is really trying to frighten her.'

'What has this person been doing?' asked Alec.

I was not sure at all that I wanted to know.

'Well,' said Lady Stott, but before she could go on, we heard a sudden commotion at the front door. It was flung open and then there came the sound of soft but hurried footsteps crossing the hall and the morning-room door was flung open too. A young girl stood there, framed in the doorway, with her head hanging down as though she were exhausted and her chest heaving with ragged, panting breaths.

'Tweetie?' said her mother.

'It's happened again,' said the girl. 'Worse than ever.' And very elegantly, dropping her handbag and her wrap on the way, she sank to the floor in a faint.

3

Alec lifted her and laid her on one of the plush sofas, then he and I stood looking down at her while her father chafed her hands and kissed her forehead and her mother ran to the bell pull.

She would have been a remarkable sight anywhere, as true beauty always is, but in that solid Glasgow morning room she was astonishing. Her face, pure white at the moment, was heart-shaped and framed by soft dark hair which fell across her forehead in a fan, echoed by the fans of soft dark lashes which fluttered against her cheekbones. They were quite an inch long but looked real to me. She wore no make-up or jewellery and actually very little at all. Her slender body was dressed in a single floating garment of pale blue crepe and she had a pair of peculiar little low-heeled shoes, fastened with elastic on her bare feet.

'Send for Dr Mackie!' commanded Lady Stott when the maid answered the bell.

The girl's eyelids fluttered even more, the extraordinary lashes batting up and down on her pale cheeks, and she groaned.

'Mother?' she said very faintly. 'Mother, is that you?'

'She's coming round,' said Sir Percy. 'Bring a glass of water, Mary.'

'Ring the doctor!' said his wife.

'Get the water!' shouted her husband.

'Father?' said Theresa, half opening her eyes and smiling wanly. Then she saw Alec and me for the first time and suddenly her eyes were as round and wide as two blue marbles, and her cheeks flushed deep pink. 'Who are you?' she said, sitting up. 'I don't need a doctor and I'd rather have a cup of tea than water, Mary please.'

'These are the people we've got to help you, Tweetie,' said Lady Stott, coming over and taking her hand. 'Now, you must sit quietly – none of your leaping about – but you have to tell them everything.'

'But who *are* you?' said the girl. In one smooth motion she tucked her legs up under her and laid one of her bare arms along the sofa back.

'Private detectives,' I said. 'I'm Mrs Gilver and this is Mr Osborne. Your parents have engaged us to find out who's been upsetting you.'

She did not gasp or gape or even so much as blink. She merely grew very still while she considered it.

'I hardly know what to say to that,' she offered at last. 'It makes it seem much more real somehow. Private *detectives*?'

She sounded very different from her parents. Their voices swooped and soared in true Glasgow fashion, which always sounds to my ears like a music-hall tune, romping along and trembling on the high notes. Theresa had either had elocution lessons to iron matters out or had been sent away to school to be worked on by packs of girls. This latter was more likely, I decided, because she spoke in an off-hand manner, halfway to the languid drawl of my own sons, and elocution lessons do tend to leave their recipients rather careful.

'Just tell them, Tweetie,' said Lady Stott.

Theresa drew in a huge gathering breath as though about to start singing. 'I thought at first it was nothing,' she said. 'It's a very competitive world and there are bound to be little jealousies, especially once a couple starts to win things. So when I found the first "wee giftie", I laughed it off.'

Lady Stott rose and went to the writing desk in the corner

of the room. She sat, with a great deal of creaking either from the dainty chair or from the undergarments containing her considerable person, and opened one of the many little drawers.

'It was tucked into my slipper-case in the ladies' cloakroom,' Theresa went on as her mother returned. 'And it was so pretty it took me a minute to understand. A pretty picture of a rose bush, I thought. How lovely.'

It was a prayer card, I saw, as Lady Stott handed it to me and Alec leaned over to see better. I had had an aunt who went in for such things when I was a child and so I recognised it at once. Deckle-edged and gilded, and illustrated with all the sentiment that high Victorian taste could summon, which is a great deal, its import escaped me until I read the verse printed below the picture. 'He sees each little sparrow fall,' it said. I took a closer look and there, below all the tumbling pink roses, in the shadows, was the tiny form of a small brown bird.

'Are you sure . . . ?' Alec said.

'And then another,' said Lady Stott, handing him a more substantial item.

This was a booklet and once again it was familiar to me. Alec recognised it too, I concluded from the curl of his lip. Perhaps his nursery days had been spent, like mine, trying not to weep over it while an older brother teased him for being a ninny.

'*The Death and Burial of Poor Cock Robin*,' said Sir Percy. 'There's no other way to understand that than as a threat to our darling girl, is there?'

'There doesn't seem to be at first glance,' said Alec. He leafed through the little book, holding it carefully by its edges.

'Fingerprints?' I asked, from the care he was taking with it.

All three Stotts squeaked. At least, Lady Stott and her daughter did; the noise emitted by Sir Percy was more complicated although hardly more manly.

'We don't want the police involved,' said Lady Stott.

'Well, we certainly don't want anything public,' said Sir Percy. 'Anything that might attract the so-called gentlemen of the press. Not after last time . . .'

'Last time?' I said.

'Hush, Bounce,' said his wife. 'It's not that at all. It's just that we don't want dear Julian to . . .' What she could not bring herself to say was 'get wind of a scandal and be frightened off before the wedding'.

'Theresa,' said her father. 'Why, for the love of everything sacred, can you not just be done with it? It's only a month until your happy day and then you can please yourself for the rest of your life. Parties, balls, cruises; you can dance every night if you've a mind to.'

'With Julian,' said Theresa. Her voice sounded like the toll of a passing bell. 'I shan't be bullied, Father. *I shan't*. And when you see the latest, maybe you'll agree. Mary?'

The maid had been standing quietly in the background, in that way that maids do, trying to turn herself into a lamp so that she missed none of the news. She started forward with only a little flush of colour in her cheeks.

'Miss?'

'Bring me my bag, please?' said Theresa, unfurling an elegant white hand. 'And a sheet of writing paper from the desk.'

The maid bustled to and fro while the rest of us gathered around the couch. Theresa laid the writing paper on her lap and then opened the clasp of her little round bag, one of those rustling, crocheted affairs which always remind me of a dish scrubber. She took out a handkerchief and used it to cover her fingers, then she reached inside the bag again and as daintily as someone choosing a sandwich from a tea-stand she drew out a small dead bird and laid it on the white paper.

Lady Stott shrieked, although the hands she had clapped to her mouth muffled it nicely. Sir Percy gasped so sharply it set him off coughing. Even Mary gave a little cry and looked down at the hand she had used to touch the bag. Alec drew nearer to look more closely.

'Good heavens,' he said, bending over the paper and peering at it. He picked it up and turned to the light from the tall windows, then glanced at Theresa over his shoulder. 'No chance that it just flew in the window and died of old age in the bag then.'

Curiosity piqued, I went over and stood behind him.

'Oh my,' I said. It was a pitiful thing, as a dead bird must always be, so impossibly tiny and frail-looking, its little claws clenched as though in pain and its little beak open as though it were panting. Its eyes were half open too and rather dull in the usual way of death, but its eyes were not what arrested me, for, reaching down in a peak between them, and all over its head, like a cap, were stuck coloured spangles or sequins of some kind. The same sequins, iridescent and twinkling, edged its wings and its tail feathers too.

'They're off one of my dancing gowns,' said Theresa.

Alec and I did not need even to look at one another to know that we were of the same mind. He nodded slightly to tell me to take first bash at the work of persuasion.

'Lady Stott,' I said. 'I cannot impress upon you strongly enough how serious this is. I really do think you should consider contacting the authorities.'

She was shaking her head before the words were even out of my mouth, and so Alec took over.

'This is a crime,' he said. 'It's a clear threat to kill and it's illegal.'

'Hardly clear,' said Theresa. 'I mean, unmistakable. But hardly clear.'

'The Act of 1847,' Alec said, as he loved to do, 'has been used time and again to cover threats much more oblique than this one.'

Sir Percy was nodding along and looked relieved to have

things so baldly stated. Lady Stott on the other hand gave every indication of being about to fly into either a panic or a temper at Alec's words and Theresa had turned even whiter than when she was unconscious, dark smudges under her eyes, her lips showing almost blue. She sat back carefully, gazing at us but saying nothing.

'And where was Jeanne?' said Lady Stott, almost loud enough to be classed as shouting. Temper it is then, I found myself thinking. 'She's supposed to be your companion and your protector. Where was she when some grubby little so-and-so was sneaking around, leaving filthy things in your bag?'

Theresa opened her eyes very wide and put her hands to her mouth in a gesture which, for the first time, showed her resemblance to her mother. She, however, did not shriek behind them. She giggled. Her eyes sparkled with merriment and she gave a definite little laugh. 'Oh, yes. Drat the circus rat!' she said. 'I forgot her.'

'What do you mean?' said Sir Percy.

'I saw the thing' – she waved at the bird in Alec's hand. He was busy trying to form the sheet of paper into a little box around it – 'and just grabbed my coat and fled. I drove home as fast as my little bus would take me. I didn't even think of traffic policemen, much less *Jeanne*.'

'Your maid?' I said, hazarding a guess.

'My cousin,' said Theresa.

'My brother's girl,' said Lady Stott. 'An orphan. Her father died in . . . well, it was a dreadful thing, and her mother died five years ago so we took her in. It was neat timing with Tweetie needing a companion.'

'Mother!' said Theresa. 'Rather heartless. And I didn't "need a companion". You thought I needed a chaperone.' Her mother began to reply but Theresa held up a finger, rather rudely, and cocked her head. 'Hark,' she said.

Right enough, when I listened closely, I could make out

21

the sound of footsteps on the gravel outside, then the front door opening and someone crossing the hall.

'That was quick,' said Theresa, as a young woman entered the room.

She was dressed rather more conventionally than her cousin in a pearl-grey gabardine coat and matching felt hat with shoes chosen for comfort rather than style, but she had the same slim figure and the same lovely line of jaw and cheek.

'What happened to *you*?' she said, taking in the scene.

Her voice was something else again, hardly a trace of Glasgow, but none of Theresa's flapperish affectations either.

'Did you catch a cab?' said Theresa.

'All the way from Sauchiehall Street?' said Lady Stott. 'I'm not made of money.'

'I took the tram,' said Jeanne. 'Are you ill?'

'I've had another delivery,' Theresa said, nodding to Alec.

Jeanne walked over to him and peered into the cup of paper he had fashioned around the bird. 'Is that a wren?' she said. 'It's not a sparrow anyway.' She put her head on one side, looking rather bird-like herself. 'It's not often you get the chance to study one at leisure.'

Lady Stott was rendered speechless by this. She was still on her feet and she simply lifted her hands and let them fall to her sides with a soft clap. Alec, after a glance under the brim of Jeanne's hat, studied the bird with more attention than he had shown before. I concentrated on not letting my thoughts show on my face. After another minute, Jeanne wrinkled her nose and turned away.

'I'm going to change,' she said. 'The tram was terribly smoky.'

Then she turned on her heel and left us. We listened to her footsteps crossing the hall and beginning to mount the stairs.

'Well!' said Lady Stott.

'Poor Jeannie,' said Sir Percy. 'She cannot abide the smell of pipe smoke.'

'Oho!' said Lady Stott. 'Twenty feather beds to cushion a pea!'

'She's a thoroughly sensible young woman,' said Sir Percy. '*She's* not swooning and fainting all over the place.'

'*She's* no call to,' said Lady Stott. '*She* saw nothing.'

'But last time,' said her husband. 'When she did.'

Lady Stott shook both her hands at him and shushed him very loudly, more like someone shooing chickens into a henhouse that someone trying, discreetly, to stop a conversation going in an undesired direction.

'Your father's right,' she said to Theresa. 'Jeanne's a good girl.'

'And you shouldn't have left her stuck there in Sauchiehall Street without a word,' Sir Percy said.

I would have expected Theresa to be stung by her father's taking a cousin's side against her own, but she merely looked amused. Her mother, in contrast, turned on a sixpence and drew herself up so sharply that her pearls rattled.

'If she had been looking after Tweetie properly as she should have been, she couldn't have *been* left behind,' she said.

'She can't be in two places at once,' said Sir Percy. 'If she was sticking to Tweetie like flypaper she couldn't have been in the cloakroom guarding her belongings, now could she?'

'She could have been sitting at the side of the dance floor, *holding* her belongings,' said his wife.

'I wouldn't want my coat crushed by Jeanne clutching it all day,' said Theresa. 'In fact now I think of it . . .' In a fluid movement, she rose to her feet. It was a kind of unfolding, quite unlike the way most of us, even at twenty, clamber up from a couch. She glided over to the doorway where she had dropped her coat and executed a graceful sideways dip to snatch it up again. Then she twirled it like a matador's cape and settled it around her shoulders. And tiresome as she was, even on our short acquaintance, as I watched her I found myself hoping that while we were in the Stotts' employ we should get the chance to see Tweetie Bird dancing.

4

We finagled a minute alone, walking around in the gardens, by telling the Stotts that an immediate *synthesis* of the *elements* of the case was a crucial step if we were to start off on the right path.

'I don't know how you can say it with a straight face,' I told Alec once we were out of earshot of the house. 'Synthesis, indeed. What does it mean?'

'No idea,' Alec said. 'Barrow's reading is as broad as it is modern.'

Barrow was Alec's valet-cum-butler, a very superior young man who offset the horror of suddenly being dragged to Perthshire by knocking the household into a particular and somewhat peculiar shape. Alec was wont to say Barrow was sublimating and repressing and that we should be glad of it, but I did not find the explanation helpful.

'So,' I began. 'How are we going to find out what happened when they're all so determined not to tell us?'

'What, you mean "last time"?' said Alec. 'When the press came sniffing around and Jeanne was so splendid?'

'It might not be connected, of course,' I said. 'So, leaving it for the moment, what do you think of the current troubles?'

Alec took his time answering and for a couple of minutes we simply strolled along. We were passing between two herbaceous borders of a length, depth and abundance that would have reduced Hugh to seething envy, not to mention my mother in her day. This early in June, the rigging of nets and rings and stakes was still visible amongst the vegetation and its sturdiness was a testament to good planning and a steely nerve. I, had I ever had the kind of clout that could direct gardeners, should never have been tough enough to order what had been done here: to dig up, chop apart and prune to the ground the fledgling plants each spring and then to overlay them with a superstructure which put one in mind more of Mr Brunel spanning a gorge than of stopping a few hollyhocks from flopping over. I had a sudden vision of Lady Stott in her bedroom in the morning before her frock and jewels were added, cinched and buttressed and perhaps, if she were loyal, held together with Stott's patent rubberised fastenings.

'I don't know why you're smiling,' said Alec, breaking into my thoughts. 'There's something pretty nasty going on here, if you ask me. One doesn't want to display finer feelings than a young woman, not in front of witnesses anyway, but I couldn't really share in Miss . . . We haven't heard, have we? In Jeanne's detached interest. That bird gave me the willies, if I'm honest.'

'It was *Cock Robin* that made me shudder,' I said.

'And three times,' said Alec. 'Surely a dancing school must have a fair amount of bustle. If Miss Stott broadcast her plight – and I can't imagine her being stoical, can you? – then everyone there – the other dancers or students or what have you and the instructors – must have been on the lookout. Someone must have seen something.'

'If there was anything to be seen,' I said. Alec nodded. It is always gratifying the way he understands me.

'Indeed,' he said. 'That occurred to me too. Perhaps the items were slipped into her bag before she left home. An inside job, as it were. With plenty of possible suspects.'

'I can't see Sir Percy sticking sequins to a wren,' I said. 'But Lady Stott? She passionately wants "Tweetie" to pack it in before Julian finds out and takes fright. She might well have decided to do it this subtly.'

'And then there's Jeanne,' said Alec. 'There's no love lost there. Poor thing.'

I filed this remark away. It is always interesting to see a woman, apparently perfectly ordinary, who exerts an unaccountable influence over men, whether charming them, terrifying them or, as in this case, wringing sympathy out of them like sponges.

'She didn't strike me as the sort,' I said. 'She's rather too forthright. And wouldn't she have put on more of a show of concern?'

'Besides,' Alec said, 'if we're speculating about jealousy, we should really find out if "Tweetie Bird" is any good and who her rivals are, shouldn't we?'

'She mentioned winning prizes,' I said. 'But you mean envy, not jealousy,' It was one of Hugh's many little peculiarities to insist on the correct use of these two terms and, as was often the case, it had rubbed off on me. 'Although there is jealousy too. We need to talk to the lovely and discreet Roland who is a clerk in Julian's office. And we should probably try to talk to Julian. Perhaps he *does* know.'

'If he doesn't and we alert him, we'll get sacked,' Alec said. 'Again.'

'Then we must proceed with the utmost caution.'

'But why would Roland jeopardise his own chances of winning the trophy?' Alec said. 'And why would Julian not just chuck her? You really are off on a flight of fancy this time, Dan. We've never even met these people.'

'We can remedy that,' I said. 'Now, let's go back and put the Stotts out of their misery, shall we?'

They were assembled en masse when we re-entered the morning room. Sir Percy had taken off his coat and was resplendent in waistcoat and watch chain, and Lady Stott I could just see, although she tucked her feet under her chair in an attempt to hide the fact, had eased out of her uncomfortable shoes. Tweetie was back on the sofa in a silk jersey so fine it looked oily and a pair of trousers with legs wide enough to make a skirt easily as bountiful as that of her mother. Jeanne was neat in tweed, with a jersey that looked to be hand-knitted and indeed she had a knitting bag at her side right now and was clicking away industriously without looking, pulling the wool out of the ball with a jerk of her elbow in a way that made me think unaccountably of a bird with a worm.

'Thank you all for your patience,' Alec said. 'Now, we'd like to get started right away while memories of this latest incident are still fresh. Miss Stott, do you feel well enough to be interviewed?'

She did. She provided us with the dates of the two earlier incidents, ignoring her mother's clucking and tutting, and was able to describe in painstaking detail who had been there each time, what dance they had all been practising, what every one of the young women had been wearing and what she thought of the young men's 'hold', 'frame', 'rise and fall' and 'sway'. Alec grew owlish with boredom and even I eventually gave up jotting down notes and simply nodded metronomically.

'This morning,' Theresa went on, 'it was the usual crew. Big Beryl was there. In her pinafore, looking like a nursing sister. I tell you, she only needs a fob watch pinned to her breast. Well, I dare say if I had her figure I wouldn't want to be in anything too clinging either, but why she wears rehearsal clothes that force her to keep going to wipe her neck with a flannel, you tell me!'

'Now, now, don't be coarse,' said Lady Stott mildly.

'And she and Beau were dancing a waltz, of course. Of course they were, when everyone else had asked for a foxtrot and it was a foxtrot being played. "I don't mind," she says. "Don't mind me." It's all for show – all to let us know that she can dance a three-four with a four-four playing. As though that proves anything except that she doesn't have an ounce

28

of musical feeling in her. And anyway, it's poor Beau who has to keep time. It's poor Beau who has to shut his ears and recite cricket scores to himself to stop his feet following the music. Or it would be if Big Beryl wasn't the worst lady leader in the whole of the league. She drags him around like Christopher Robin with Pooh.'

'Don't be catty now, Theresa,' said her mother.

'Anyway, they were all there. I put my things in the cloak-room when I arrived and the first time I went back – to fetch a peppermint, actually – there it was. There it jolly well was. I can't really tell you any more than that. Not today, anyway. You must forgive me.' She touched her brow with the back of her hand in a delicate show of weariness and then rested her head against the cushions and smiled bravely across at Alec and me.

'You should rest, Miss Stott,' Alec said.

'Perhaps you'd even take a day or two off to recover from your ordeal?' I said. 'Might we ask that you take them? If you were to stay away until Wednesday that would give us ample time to settle ourselves in Glasgow and be available to accompany you.'

'I can't take days off now,' said Theresa. 'The Championship is on Friday. Roly and I must practise every hour we can.'

'Oh, Tweetie!' said her mother.

'Of course, we really *are* just practising now,' Theresa went on, looking rather sly. 'We're not receiving instruction. All we need is a floor.'

'Oh, Bounce!' said his wife. 'We were unlucky that last time. Couldn't you—'

'No,' said Sir Percy.

Theresa was giggling and even Jeanne wore a small smile as she glanced down at her knitting.

'Roly and I were practising in the ballroom here, before the Easter friendly,' Theresa said, 'and Julian turned up uninvited. Poor Roly had to be spirited away!'

'Unexpected, Tweetie,' said Lady Stott. 'Your fiancé doesn't need an invitation to your home. But he's very busy at work just now, Bounce. I'm sure it would be fine.'

'I will not have that creature in my house behind Julian's back,' said Sir Percy.

'As you wish, Father,' said Theresa. She blinked innocently. 'In that case, I shall be returning to the ballroom tomorrow, Mrs Gilver. With Jeanne. If you want the job you'll have to take up your task by then.'

'Theresa,' said her father, 'you are over-tired or you would hardly be so rude to our guests.'

'Guests?' Theresa retorted. 'Employees, surely?'

But even her mother took exception to this. As for me, my hand twitched to smack her legs as it had not twitched to smack anyone's legs since my elder son, Donald, had taken his feather eiderdown out into the garden and left it there in a thunderstorm.

'We certainly don't want to tire you further,' Alec said. 'We can ask Miss . . . ?'

'McNab,' said Jeanne, without looking up from her pattern.

Alec inclined his head in thanks which went unnoticed. 'We can ask Miss McNab for as many of the more mundane details as we can, now that you've provided the most crucial information.'

'What?' said Theresa, sitting up again. 'Jeanne doesn't know a thing about it. How do you imagine she can help you?'

'Oh, merely by giving us names and addresses,' said Alec airily. 'To save you. You've had a shock after all.'

Apparently, he had just delivered another one. Her eyes once again grew round and she shook her head slightly as she spoke.

'What names?' she said. 'What do you mean?'

Her mother was paddling the ground like a restless horse in a loosebox. The click of Jeanne's knitting needles made much too sprightly a sound to accompany such expressions as all three Stotts now wore.

'Only the dance-hall,' I said. 'The owners and employees. The names of the others who were there.'

'It's not a *dance-hall*,' said Lady Stott.

'See the impression you're giv—' said Sir Percy to Theresa.

'The Locarno, one of the grandest ballrooms in all of Glas—'

'The grandest ballroom is still no place for our daughter, Eunice. The grandest public house, the grandest dog-racing track—'

'I keep telling you – I really do keep telling him – dancing is harmless fun that does wonders for your health and yet he turns round and accuses his own daughter of drinking and gambling.'

'It's not harmless fun, Mother,' said Tweetie. 'It's very serious.'

'I must apologise,' I said. 'Ballroom, of course. I meant nothing by my unfortunate mistake and I don't doubt for a moment, Miss Stott, that your interest in dancing is as harmless and healthy as hunting and skiing and everything that any young girl might do to turn her father's hair white with worry. And I think it's marvellous that you apply yourself to it seriously. We should always do our best in every endeavour, shouldn't we?' I stopped just short of babbling. I had mollified all three Stotts, though, even Sir Percy, and they each beamed at me.

Then Jeanne spoke up. 'It didn't do much for Leo Mayne's health,' she said.

'Who?' asked Alec.

'No one at all,' said Sir Percy.

'Don't be naughty, Jeanne,' said his wife, rising and making for the servant's bell at some speed. 'The detectives don't need to hear your nonsense.'

'Lady Stott,' I said, 'please don't worry about wasting our time. We'd far rather know too much than too little.'

'Was Leo Mayne injured?' Alec said.

Lady Stott was tugging on the bell rope like a navvy.

'Injured?' said Jeanne, smirking. 'That's hardly the word I'd use.'

Then Mary answered the bell and all but hustled us out. If she had taken a broom to our heels we could hardly have landed back on the gravel with more of a thump: Sir Percy said we should let him know our terms; Lady Stott invented an entirely fictitious and entirely unconvincing luncheon date; Theresa dragged Jeanne away, whispering furiously. Then the yellow front door with its shining brasses slammed shut behind us.

'Right then,' said Alec. 'The Locarno Ballroom in Sauchiehall Street, I think. Don't you? To ask after the health of Leo Mayne.'

5

Sauchiehall Street is to Glasgow what Princes Street is to Edinburgh, and Bond Street is to London. It spoke volumes about the Locarno Ballroom's claims to respectability that it was situated there. And when we rolled up and parked the motorcar outside twenty minutes later we saw a façade sufficiently grand to do away with my lingering worries about what we might be getting ourselves into. I had been imagining telling Hugh that I had spent the day in a Glasgow dance-hall and not been enjoying what the imaginary Hugh had to say.

'Rather swish,' said Alec, craning out of the side window at three storeys of good red Glasgow sandstone, pillared, pedimented and porticoed, and at the gilt paint of the sign – quite five feet tall and ten feet long – which proclaimed that there was *DANCING!* nightly. There were gold posts and gold tasselled ropes, drawn aside in the daytime but clearly intended to give the impression of a ballroom in a mansion in Berkeley Square. There was even a rolled-up carpet there too, its woven backing facing out but the brilliant red of its pile showing like the jam in a pudding.

'But oh my goodness!' I said. 'Look at that. Do you think the Stotts know?'

In the curved windows flanking the grand entrance to the ballroom, like the playbills in a theatre's foyer or the 'posters' (as they are called by those in the know) which entice audiences into cinemas to see the latest moving pictures, there were enormous tinted photographs of the

Locarno's attractions. On one side, 'Miss Beryl Bonnar and Mr Beau Montaigne' were captured in the midst of a spin, their feet crossed at the ankles and Miss Bonnar's head thrown back and to the left at such an extreme angle that I winced to see her. On the other side, looking straight out at us, clearly engaged in a tango – for why else would they be joined at cheek and hip that way – were 'Miss Tweetie Bird and Mr Roland Wentworth'. Their front shoulders were hunched up and their joined hands were driven down in an attitude which was no doubt thrillingly dramatic as part of that most dramatic of dances. Caught in stasis by the camera, however, they looked as though they were trying to share a golf club during a tricky putt. And their raised front legs, no doubt caught in the process of unfurling with all the sultry grace of a panther about to strike, nevertheless made me think a little of dogs begging for biscuits.

'I take it dear Julian's office is nowhere near here,' Alec said.

I shrugged. 'He probably wouldn't recognise her. I shouldn't have, if we'd happened just to walk past.' For Tweetie Bird in full feather bore almost no resemblance to Miss Theresa Stott, even in her practice clothes. The fan of black hair was concealed under a close-fitting cap and the pretty face under lash-black, kohl pencil, rouge, lipstick and a beauty patch which had been coloured in bottle green to match the spangles on her dress and to echo the peacock feathers and paste emeralds on her headdress.

'She must be good,' said Alec. 'And there must surely be some rivalry with Big—'

'Alec!' I said.

'With Miss Bonnar,' he corrected himself.

There was nothing in the photograph – large as it was – to explain the nickname Theresa had bestowed upon Beryl Bonnar. She was not a sylph but she was far from the plough ox I had begun to construct in my imagination, after hearing

34

about the striped pinafores and the way she reportedly steered 'poor Beau' around the floor. In fact, or at least in photography, she was a fine, handsome girl of a type one encounters often in Scotland and rarely so well executed. That is to say, she had abundant sandy hair, waved and shining, and soft pale skin, milky and dimpling on her arms and shoulders, plump and rosy on her cheeks. Her eyes had been tinted brown by whatever photographer's assistant had set to with his paintbox on these enormous portraits and I looked forward to finding out if such an unlikelihood could be true.

We stepped down from the motorcar and prepared to enter.

'I'll mind your car for sixpence,' said a voice behind us and I turned to see two children of about eight and six, the boy in shorts and jersey with a large cap on his head, the smaller girl in a cotton dress with a shawl pinned over it and a knitted bonnet tied under her chin. I was silenced by the sight of them.

'Tuppence then, if you're short,' the boy said.

But he had mistaken the reason for my pause. It was their feet which had rendered me dumb. They were bare, filthy and blue with cold this chilly morning, when the barometer defied the calendar as Scotch barometers so often do.

'I accept your original terms,' said Alec. 'Sixpence each it is, when we come out again.'

The boy showed no sign of his surprise at the sudden doubling of their fee, for of course the price had been for the job and not for the labourers. The girl, younger and less poker-faced, was unable not to beam with pleasure.

'Can we sit inside?' she asked. I took a swift look under the edge of her bonnet at the curls, dark and dull with dirt, and managed to squash my sentiments. I had had a flea or two in my time and had not enjoyed them.

I opened the boot and drew out a picnic rug, which could be washed in Lysol if need be.

'Sit on this,' I said, spreading it on the pavement. I tried not to notice how gratefully they wrapped themselves up like two little caterpillars in a shared cocoon.

Inside, the Locarno Ballroom was as dowdy as any place whose life is lived in the evening always looks in the cold light of day. The walls, papered in a kind of figured velvet, showed every scuff and the glass chandeliers above us in the foyer and stair were dull under the dust. Even the carpet, plum-coloured and once sumptuous I am sure, was flat and dark in the middle of the steps where countless feet passed every night. As we ascended, we could hear a piano being played very loudly, with great emphasis on the marked beat and none at all on phrasing or melody.

When we were almost at the double doors into the ballroom itself, the music broke off to be replaced by the sound of laughter.

'Well, don't look then!' called a woman's voice.

'I can't dance with my eyes shut,' called another. 'Not waltzing anyway. I get that dizzy.'

'You're swooning in my arms,' said a man's voice and the laughter broke out again.

When it had quieted, Alec knocked on one of the double doors and, not waiting for a reply, swept it open. We entered to see, in that enormous echoing space, the very last of a swift movement. I filed it away for later; one of the two young couples in the room had sprung apart when they heard someone coming.

'Mr Lorrison!' shouted one of the young men. He was dressed very oddly in some kind of knitted long-sleeved vest, enormously wide trousers with yellow braces and very shiny shoes.

'Can I help youse?' said one of the women, after glaring at him. She had her hair tied up in a scarf and, standing foursquare with her hands on her hips, she looked very different from the spinning elegance of her picture in the window. The striped pinafore over a plain navy-blue jersey, however, told me that this was Beryl Bonnar. She grinned at us. 'Are youse after lessons?' she said. 'We're sort of closed today. Getting ready for the Champs. Youse can watch, but, if youse promise not to listen to the language!'

The other young woman, a pretty little fair-haired thing, put up a hand and tittered behind it.

'I'm sorry, Beryl,' she said. 'I just can't get my feet to do a forward change after a double reverse and swearing helps.'

'Mr Lorrison!' shouted the same young man again. 'Customers!' He was standing beside Miss Bonnar, actually with one hand still at the small of her back and I deduced that this must be poor Beau, even though he looked as unlike his posed and tinted picture downstairs as did Miss Bonnar.

'Ordinarily, I'd love to watch,' I said. I saw each one of them note my voice and make their adjustments to me. It is a perennial irritation that I cannot smooth away the history of my life when I am detecting. Of course, it is splendid to have the patrician tones at my disposal. Sometimes they draw out exactly the obedience and eagerness to comply they used to when my mother or even I was a girl. More and more, however, in these changed days, it would be marvellous to sound like a schoolteacher or a farmer's wife or even a typing clerkess, to meet other teachers, clerks or farmers on level ground where they are all beginning to feel they have some God-given right to be.

I suppressed a sigh – it was not an effort, for I am no snob – and took note of what adjustments the four young people made when they suddenly found a lady in their midst. Miss Bonnar's partner narrowed his eyes as though at something unsettling. The other young man swallowed and darted a quick look over to the girl who had sprung away from him. She simply drank us in as though we were exhibits, on show but unseeing, giving me a sweeping look from hat to shoe-soles before turning to Alec and doing the same again. Beryl Bonnar looked neither aggrieved, alarmed or agog; she acknowledged the oddity with a little cock of her head and then stepped forward, holding out her hand to shake mine.

'But what can we do for you today?' she said.

Before I could answer, a door banged open and we all turned. At one end of the ballroom, there was a half-circular stage for the orchestra and in the middle of its flat back wall, in a doorway, stood a tall thin man dressed in a loudly striped suit, with a soft hat on the back of his head.

'Whit?' he said, spitting the word across the space between him and the rest of us.

'Visitors,' said Beryl's partner.

'I thought you said customers,' said the thin man. 'If they're customers they can come back when we're open. If they're not they can get lost.'

'Mr Lorrison?' said Alec. 'Are you the owner of this establishment?'

'I'm the manager,' he shot back, 'and the owner's not to be fashed no matter what youse are after. It's not for sale, it's come one come all and we're closed today.' He turned as though to leave again, but Alec stopped him.

'We are here as the representatives of Sir Percy and Lady Stott,' he said. 'Mrs Gilver and Mr Osborne. And we're private detectives, actually, which probably puts us in the category of visitor and the subcategory of "unwelcome". We're investigating the series of threats suffered by Miss Stott here at the Locarno. We haven't contacted the authorities yet and we'd be delighted if we managed not to. We thought if we interviewed everyone who was here earlier today we might bring something to light that'll solve the puzzle.'

'You . . . you . . . ?' said Mr Lorrison. He walked rather distractedly to the front of the stage and leapt down, showing great agility for a man of his age, which I took to be over sixty. Perhaps he had been a dancer in his youth and had never lost his edge.

One could forgive the manager of any going concern for

being nonplussed at the sudden appearance of professional nosey-parkers, threatening him with police. What was interesting were the reactions of the others in the room. The fair-haired young woman who had been drinking us in blushed deep pink with excitement and pleasure. Drama had announced itself in her life and she was delighted. The young man who stood alone went through another bout of darting looks. Poor Beau rolled his eyes, sighed, and gave a pointed look at Miss Bonnar. Miss Bonnar herself blinked once or twice, shook her head and then took another step forward.

'Interview *me?*' she said.

'Beryl, I can give you my word of honour,' Mr Lorrison began.

'Interview everyone, Miss Bonnar,' I said. 'You included, if you would be so kind.'

A frisson, whispers perhaps or maybe just pent-up breaths let go, ran around the room. Beryl grinned and shook her head again.

'Youse know my name then,' she said. She giggled. 'Aye, g'on yourself. Interview away. Why not, eh?'

6

There was a little room to the side of the main dance floor – a ladies' withdrawing room, I should have called it, if it had been anywhere except in a Glasgow dance-hall – and it was to there that Miss Bonnar led us. We were not, it appeared, in charge of who was to be interviewed first, although we did manage to impose our authority as far as preventing Mr Lorrison from tagging along.

When we were settled into three of the shabby armchairs and had lit our cigarettes, Alec – at a glance from me – relenting in the matter of his pipe for the room was windowless and hardly ten feet square, Miss Bonnar gave us a steady look, smiling and open. I met it with another the same and drew out my little notebook and propelling pencil.

'Miss Bonnar,' I began. 'Won't you begin by telling us what you know about the distressing events?'

'Distressing?' said Beryl. 'Tweetie loved every minute.'

Her words summed up so perfectly the swooning and sobbing that Alec and I could not prevent a chuckle.

'I only heard about the prayer card after the wee book turned up,' she went on. 'So I can't help you with that.'

'Starting with the "wee book" then,' I said.

Alec cleared his throat and sat forward. 'You sound rather different, Miss Bonnar,' he said.

I flushed for I should have noticed. Beryl did not flush, not even the slightest heightening in her milk and roses colour, but she twinkled and blew out in a little carillon of short puffs as though smoking were laughing.

'Ah'm fain tae git aboon ma freens,' she said.

Alec frowned and I, feeling my stock rising again, translated for him. 'One doesn't care to be above one's company,' I said. 'But back to *Cock Robin*, Miss Bonnar. It was nicely judged, was it not? Nursery terrors are so very persistent.'

Miss Bonnar twinkled again. 'But I won't pretend to be what I'm not either,' she said. 'I never had a nursery. I for sure never had a book!' Neither Alec nor I managed to fill the pause which followed and Miss Bonnar took pity on us and returned to the business at hand. 'It was a Thursday afternoon, our practice day. Mondays is Beginners' Competitive, Tuesdays is Beginners' Social, Wednesdays is the open tea-dance, Fridays is Advanced Competitive. Saturdays is the ticketed tea-dance. Closed on Sundays – officially anyway, but we need all the practice time we can get coming up to the Champs. Theresa found the wee book on a Thursday. Definitely.'

'And who was there when it happened?' I said. 'Assuming that no one who had been at the tea-dance the day before could have left it. It was in a bag Miss Stott brought with her on the day, wasn't it?'

'Aye, but . . .' said Miss Bonnar. She screwed up her nose and gazed off to one corner of the room, thinking hard. 'There's people in and out in the mornings when the lessons are held.'

'Forgive me,' said Alec. 'I assumed that Beginners' Teas and the rest of it *were* lessons. I'm not with you.'

Beryl stubbed out her cigarette, only half-smoked, and took a compact and lipstick out of her pinafore pocket to effect repairs. It was done without self-consciousness or simpering.

'They're classes,' she said. 'Beginners, Advanced and the dances. The lessons are private. A lady might pay for an hour of Bert's time or a gent might pay for an hour of mine. Or more than likely a couple'll pay for both of us to knock both of them into shape. By the hour. Theresa doesn't do it.'

'I see,' I said. 'Yes, I see. The classes are for fun and the lessons are for serious competitors. I see. It seems rather churlish of Miss Stott not to lend a hand to her fellows when presumably she benefited from the system when she was rising through the ranks.'

'No,' said Miss Bonnar, smiling wider than ever, 'none of the young contenders could afford a private hour with Bert and me. The competitors come to the classes. The lessons are for anyone who can pay for your time and wants to spend an hour in your arms.'

Alec, mid-smoke, coughed suddenly.

'And now I've shocked you,' Miss Bonnar said. 'But nothing of that sort goes on at the Locarno. I can't answer for every backstreet hall in the city or every young couple who'd do anything for a regular booking.'

'You've certainly explained why Sir Percy and Lady Stott are so very worried,' I said.

'But you say Theresa doesn't offer lessons,' said Alec. 'So presumably she arrived with her slipper bag after the departure of the pupils.'

'She doesn't,' said Miss Bonnar. 'Her father would have a fit. The clubhouse would come down on his head like the walls of Jericho.'

'Doesn't your own father mind?' I said.

'It's mostly ma faither's freens Bert and me end up teaching,' said Beryl and I noticed that her Glasgow tongue sprang back into her mouth as she spoke of him.

'Oh, well then,' I said. 'That's all fine. Now, who is this "Bert" you mention?'

'My partner out there,' said Beryl.

I frowned and turned back a few pages in my little notebook to where I had jotted down what I could while Alec drove us here from Balmoral. 'I thought your partner's name was Beau?'

'Beau Montaigne it says downstairs,' said Alec.

'Herbert Bunyan just doesn't have the right ring to it,' Beryl said. 'Beryl Bonnar's bad enough without that! I thought on a fancy name, thought long and hard, but there's a good side to being yourself. And you can end up sounding a wee bit daft if you're not careful.'

No one spoke, but the words 'Tweetie Bird' were ringing in all three of our heads.

'So,' I said, marvelling to myself how difficult it was to keep Miss Bonnar applied to the matter at hand, 'Miss Stott arrived after the departure of the private pupils. Who was here? You, Miss Bonnar. Mr . . . Montaigne. Who else?'

'Roly and Tweetie,' said Beryl. 'And Jamesie Hodge – he's a promising young dancer. His partner Alicia – that's her out there on the floor today, waiting for him to get off his work at the bakery. And that's it. Well, Mr Lorrison was in his office and he might have had some of the boys in, but they come and go by the back close. They're never anywhere near the floor or the cloakrooms.'

'And what about this morning?' said Alec. 'The same people?'

'Mr Lorrison wasn't here,' Miss Bonnar said. 'He was away at the races at Ayr for the weekend and I think it took him a wee while to get ready to face the day. And Alicia didn't get here until after Theresa had left. It was a piece of luck that Roly stayed back to work out some choreography and was still here when she arrived. There's nothing on earth like dancing with a better partner to help you improve. Roly dances with Alicia and she'll take what she learned back to Jamesie and there's another couple coming up to Champs standard.'

'So, it was just the four of you competitors this morning?' I said, rather interrupting her. 'No private pupils?'

'Not this close to the Champs,' said Beryl. 'They've opened right up since Cecelia Bristow and Alex Warren retired. We're hoping—'

43

'And Jeanne,' said Alec, like me, sensing that he would have to jump in to stem the flow.

Miss Bonnar opened her eyes very wide and nodded. 'That's awful,' she said. 'I completely forgot about Jeanne. Yes, just the five of us. That's right. Poor Jeannie.'

'And the pianist,' said Alec.

Anyone who did not know him would have missed it but I could tell that he was proud of having thought of this when all around, by which I mean me, had forgotten it. I groaned inwardly, nodded outwardly and turned my attention to Miss Bonnar to see what she would say.

'Miss Thwaite,' she said. 'Right enough, she was there and now you come to mention it, she'd be best placed to see if anything happened that shouldn't have. She sits opposite the big doors, facing the cloakrooms and she always looks over the top of her piano so she can tell if she should keep playing or stop. She'd see someone slipping in and out again, even if the dancers missed it.'

'But is that likely,' I said, 'since, at any moment, one of you must be facing that way?'

'Well, you spin so fast in the waltz you can't really see anything.'

'And I dare say you're looking down at your feet a lot too,' said Alec.

Miss Bonnar turned incredulous eyes on him. 'Never,' she said. 'Look at our *feet*?'

'While you're learning,' Alec persisted.

'Never. *Never!*' said Miss Bonnar. I tried not to smirk. 'Is that what *you* do? Who taught you? Look, come through and I'll show you the difference it makes.'

'I hardly—' Alec began.

'Don't mind me,' I said. 'I'd like to study the layout of the room and make a little sketch or two. I know how impatient you get with me for sketching, Alec dear.'

He gobbled and muttered for another minute but Miss Bonnar was standing over him, with her hands on her hips, clearly not going to take no for an answer. When he was on his feet, she put a hand in the small of his back and propelled him back along the short corridor to the ballroom or, as I was beginning to notice the professionals called it, 'the floor'.

The pianist – I ground my teeth to think that I had heard piano music and not deduced her existence – was pounding out another waltz when we re-entered and the three dancers were engaged in a most peculiar activity. Roly and Alicia were dancing, but Bert, looking very Beau Montaigne-ish with his head high and an elegant arch to his back, was right beside the other man, like Peter Pan's mischievous shadow, copying his movements.

'Oh, I see now,' said Alicia as the curious threesome broke apart. 'Thanks, Bert. I really do see.' She turned to face us. 'Who's next?'

'No one for a minute,' said Miss Bonnar. 'Slow fox, Miss Thwaite. This one thinks he can dance looking at his feet!' She rubbed her hands together and approached Alec, looking more like a cricketer going to bat than a dancer. 'Right then.'

I slid into one of the chaperone's seats which ringed the dance floor and prepared for great enjoyment.

'Hold me,' said Miss Bonnar, as sweet strains began to drift softly over the room from the little upright piano. This was far better playing than the rumpity-thump we had heard up to now.

Alec stepped forward and took Miss Bonnar into a firm but polite grip, the typical attitude of an English gentleman on those occasions when, try as he might, he cannot escape dancing.

Alicia tittered. The two men cast critical eyes at Alec's feet, hands and middle.

'I've not got nits,' said Beryl and she pulled Alec into such a close embrace that had she not embarked on a series of sharp commands I might have accused her of flirting.

'Head right,' she said. 'More, more, more. And drop your

45

shoulders. Bend that arm. Curl your fingers in. Bend your thumb back. Drop your wrist forward. And close your hand on my back. It's like a bunch of bananas; I can feel it. And lift it, lift it. Under my shoulder blade. Ready, Miss Thwaite?'

Without missing a note, the playing turned from sweet music back to the bald rhythmic thumping. I craned to see over the piano top. Miss Thwaite, from this angle, consisted of a felt hat with some tufts of grey hair peeking out from under its brim and a pair of large spectacles.

'And right foot forward. Slow walk,' said Miss Bonnar. 'I'll squeeze your hand to keep you straight.'

I left them to it and went a-wandering. The cloakrooms were on either side of a short corridor opposite the dais where Miss Thwaite sat at her piano. Inside the ladies' room were two rows of coat hooks with hat shelves above and low stools underneath for sitting on while changing shoes. There were hand basins with mirrors behind them and two short wooden doors open at top and bottom. I pushed on each one in turn, finding only what Nanny Palmer called 'necessaries' and no window large enough for even the slimmest figure to crawl through. The men's cloakroom was identical, except that there seemed to be rather a lot of light around the wooden doors at the far end. I hesitated. If there was a large window there, someone might have climbed through it to put the bird in Tweetie's bag. I did not want to check but there was no point in snooping unless one did it thoroughly.

I stepped at a brisk pace along between the two rows of coat pegs and nudged one of the doors open. The window was indeed bigger, but there were bars across it. I turned back to face the room.

'Looking for someone?' said an amused voice. He had outdoor shoes on, great solid boots, and was at least six feet tall and rather burly with it, yet I had not heard him approaching.

'Mr . . . Hodge?' I said, making a guess from his dusty appearance that this was the baker at the end of his shift.

'Looking for *me*?' he said. As his eyes opened wide in surprise, I saw that there was even flour in the creases around them. 'Aye, I'm Jimmy Hodge. Can't decide between Hawtry and Halliwell, so it's Hodge for now.'

'Mrs Gilver,' I said, striding forward and offering my hand. 'Of Gilver and Osborne, private detectives. You've missed some excitement this morning.'

'Is that right?' said Mr Hodge. He sat down on one of the low stools and untied his laces, then eased off his boots.

'I was just carrying out a "recce",' I said.

He stood, wiggled his stockinged toes, removed his coat and loosened his tie.

'There's been another prank played upon . . .' I began and then, as he started to unbutton his waistcoat, 'What are you doing?'

'Stripping to my semmit to get a wash,' he said. He was in his shirtsleeves and undoing his collar studs now.

'I'll just . . .' I said and ducked out. I leaned against the wall of the corridor and tried to recover my sangfroid. Had he really been about to take off his shirt and start sluicing himself in a basin with me just standing there? It had seemed so.

I did not regret my foray, I decided as I re-entered the ballroom. I had learned that no one could have got into the cloakrooms without being witnessed. Whoever was threatening Tweetie Bird was here right now, either Hodge or one of those swishing and dipping around the floor like seaweed in a tide pool while Miss Thwaite kept time.

I blinked. The shock of Mr Hodge and his shirtsleeves had distracted me but I remembered now and my mouth dropped open. One of those fronds of seaweed, tripping around with Miss Bonnar clasped in his arms was Alec. I watched in stupefaction and then jumped for the second time in five minutes. Someone – Mr Hodge – had taken hold of me around the waist and grabbed my hand.

'You're not cut out for a wallflower, my girl,' he said and, driving me backwards by some means as subtle as it was unavoidable, he stepped onto the floor and we started dancing.

7

Mr Hodge's broad face was shining from its cold-water wash and his damp hair was combed back in furrows but he still smelled faintly of bread and sugar and the overall effect was rather overwhelming. He held me startlingly close, my front pressed against his front and his legs brushing mine as he moved them.

'I, I,' I said. He checked himself, then spun around causing me to take a few skippy little steps to keep up. I thought I was about to fall over my feet or at least turn an ankle, but I managed not to, caught up again and then set off in a different direction, flying along so fast that the walls of the room began to blur. I tightened my grip on his shoulder but he shook his head and laughed at me.

'I've got you,' he said. 'You've no need to hang on.'

'I, I,' I said, although it did feel rather delicious, and surprisingly weightless, considering how solid a young man he was. I obeyed his instruction and we floated away.

'Swaps!' he shouted after another minute and, as suddenly as it had started, it ended again.

Alec stood opposite me, swaying gently, while Miss Bonnar and Mr Hodge spun away across the floor.

'Blimey,' said Alec. 'I can't imagine what takes sets of lessons, an hour each, can you? Miss Bonnar has just taught me to dance in ten minutes.' He stepped forward and grasped me, his grip confident to the point of some discomfort.

'On three,' he said, squeezing my right hand to indicate which foot to begin with. We waited for the music to catch up with us and set off. I banged my knee, Alec stood on my foot, we knocked heads, and then we stopped again.

'Hmph,' he said. 'Oh well.'

'They're awfully good, aren't they?' I offered.

'Let's go back to what we do best,' said Alec. 'Who's next?'

'Roland,' I said. 'He must know Theresa best out of this lot, wouldn't you say?'

Mr Roland Wentworth was even more beautiful in the flesh than in his posed and tinted photograph downstairs, and with a style of beauty currently much in vogue. His corn-coloured hair fell in waves from a peak upon his high, smooth forehead, his eyes were hooded, his cheekbones severe, and his mouth sulky and full. Yet, for all that, he was less attractive than the cheerful and ruddy Hodge; anxiety is always rather off-putting.

He gazed at us as though we were snake-charmers while we dragged every syllable out of him.

'Enemies?' he said, swallowing. 'No.'

'Rivals then,' said Alec. 'No little jealousies?'

'No,' said Mr Wentworth.

'What about Miss Bonnar?' I put in. 'She and Miss Stott would have to be rather remarkable not to feel any friction.'

Mr Wentworth shook his head so fast it was almost shivering. 'No,' he said. Then, after licking his lips, finally he offered a little more. 'Don't you go saying I told you things.'

'Saying to whom?' said Alec.

He swallowed hard before answering. 'My work!' he said at last. 'I'm begging you. Don't go blabbing to my work.'

'About Miss Bonnar?' I said, genuinely mystified.

'About anything. About Tweetie and me dancing. Mr Armour knows nothing about it.'

'Of course not,' I said. 'We wouldn't dream of such a thing. I take it you really do believe that Mr Armour hasn't guessed the secret or found out in some other way?'

'How could he?' said Wentworth. 'Who would tell him?'

'Well, there's a rather large photograph downstairs,' I said.

'He's never been here!' said Mr Wentworth. 'He's never seen that! Why are youse going on and on about Mr Armour?'

'My dear Mr Wentworth,' I said, 'it was you who brought him up.'

'Taking another tack, then,' said Alec. 'Did Miss Stott say anything after any of the discoveries?'

'Not to me,' said Mr Wentworth.

'And I don't suppose you noticed anyone going into the cloakroom during the morning.'

'Nobody,' said Mr Wentworth. 'No one. Not once.'

'Not even Miss Bonnar?' I asked, remembering that Theresa had mentioned Beryl wiping her neck with a flannel.

'I never said that,' said Mr Wentworth. 'Don't put words in my mouth. I said nothing of the sort. So don't you go and tell on me.'

At that we took pity on him and let him go. He ducked out of the room with one last glance behind him and left a distinct handprint on the dull green paint of the door.

'What's he so frightened of?' Alec said. 'Who does he think we're going to blab to?'

'Most peculiar,' I said. 'Now then: Mr Bunyan? Or shall we call him Montaigne? Then we'll have the set.'

Mr Herbert Bunyan swept into the room, Montaigne much to the fore. He offered his cigarette case to us then sank into one of the grubby armchairs and slung one long leg over the other.

'So who called you in?' he said. 'Tweetie?'

'I think we already mentioned,' I replied, 'that we have been retained by Sir Percy.'

'She's got *him* round her pinkie,' he said. 'And she'll not mind having detectives making a fuss of her.'

'Many a young lady has a taste for theatre,' Alec conceded,

although how he would know such a thing was beyond me, 'but Miss Stott was quite genuinely distressed this morning.'

'Not as if the wee thing could harm her,' Bunyan said.

'Now then,' said Alec, 'we shall ask you what we asked the others: does Miss Stott have any enemies or rivals who might want to upset her?'

'What wee thing?' I said.

'What?' said the young man. He looked as cool as ever, but he took the next puff of his cigarette directly after he had breathed out the last one.

'Did Miss Stott tell you what was left in her bag today?' I said. Mr Montaigne took a third puff. The air around him was growing quite blue with smoke.

'It's the same do again, isn't it?' he said. 'More wee pictures and poems.'

'Were you in the cloakrooms after she arrived this morning?' said Alec.

The young man took his time answering. He looked in a measured way from me to Alec and back again. 'I can't remember when Tweetie turned up today,' he said. 'I'm nothing to do with her. And you'll have to ask somebody else if you want my movements.'

'We shall,' I said. 'You haven't told us whether you think Miss Stott has enemies, Mr Bunyan. But I suppose if she's beneath your notice, you'd hardly know that either, would you?'

Miss Thwaite gave a surprisingly sharp rap on the door for such a bird-like little woman, but I suppose one's hands and wrists must be kept strong by pounding out dance tunes on a piano all day.

'You looked good out there, the pair of you,' she said shyly as she entered and sat. She had brought her handbag with her and clutched it on her knee, peering at us over the top of it in much the same way as she had peered over the top of the piano earlier. I eyed her thick spectacles glumly. She might be in the position to see everything but I would not imagine that she could discern much in the way of fleeting expressions passing over faces.

'Not once we were a pair we didn't,' said Alec.

Miss Thwaite tittered. 'It's like a magic spell, isn't it?' she said. 'Mr Hodge often takes me for a twirl at the end of the day and leaves me quite giddy. I've got two left feet if I try on my own at home with the wireless on.'

'Miss Thwaite,' I said kindly. I had warmed to the little woman right away. She was English and even though there was a dollop of Lancashire or some such in her speech, set against that dreadful Glasgow burr she was quite the sound of home to me. 'We're investigating this rash of silly pranks played upon Miss Stott. But we're not getting on very well. Something was left in her bag this morning and we're stumped as to who might have put it there.'

'What something?' said Miss Thwaite.

'An object decorated with green sequins we believe to have come from one of Miss Stott's gowns,' I said.

'Her sea-green pleated,' said Miss Thwaite. 'She wore it at Easter for the big friendly but never since.'

'And so we are concerning ourselves with means, motive and opportunity,' said Alec very grandly. Miss Thwaite turned admiring eyes on him. 'Anyone might have got his hand on the object,' he went on. 'But the sequins are a different matter.'

Miss Thwaite, however, was shaking her head. 'Tweetie had got behindhand,' she said. 'And I was busy taking in Bert's waistbands. The weight's been dropping off him lately and the judges come down on poor tailoring like a ton of bricks. So she pasted the last of them on.'

'And anyone at the dance might have snatched them off?' I guessed.

'They were falling like autumn leaves,' said Miss Thwaite. 'The floor was littered with the things. Miss Bonnar slid on them in the cloakroom and nearly went over.'

'Really?' said Alec. 'That's very interesting.' He nodded at me, telling me to note it down.

'As to motive,' I said, for I had written down *BB slipped – angry?* already, 'does Miss Stott have enemies? Mr Wentworth thought not, but although his loyalty does him credit . . .'

Miss Thwaite was shaking her head. 'I'm not saying everyone loves her,' she said, 'for she's full of nonsense like a lot of girls that age and she's been spoiled her whole life, but she doesn't have enemies.'

'Rivals, then,' I said.

Miss Thwaite took her time to answer that. 'If I denied it, would you believe me?' she began cautiously. 'But I don't want to give you the wrong impression. Beryl loves to dance, loves the dancing world through and through. It's an escape for her and she wouldn't do anything to spoil it. She never questions a score, never argues if she's knocked out. So yes they're rivals, but Beryl Bonnar – despite everything – is as honest as the day is long.'

'And opportunity,' said Alec. 'We've heard conflicting stories about this morning, Miss Thwaite. Miss Stott reckoned someone might have gone into the cloakroom, but Mr Wentworth didn't think so.'

'They all went,' said Miss Thwaite. 'Their coats were in there for one thing.'

'But once the practice was under way?' said Alec.

'In and out all morning,' said Miss Thwaite. 'Same as ever. They go for drinks of water, to change their shoes, powder their feet, mop their brows after a fast dance, dab at perspiration all over, I expect.'

'You're saying that Miss Bonnar, Mr Wentworth and Mr Montaigne all visited the cloakrooms while Miss Stott's bag was in there.'

'And Tweetie herself too,' said Miss Thwaite. 'In fact, there was one moment when they were all in there and I got to play for pleasure for nearly three minutes. I got through my favourite section of Chopin's Nocturne in C minor.'

'Yes, I noticed your two styles,' I said. 'It must pain you if you're a musician.'

'Oh, I'm no musician,' said Miss Thwaite. 'I'm a seamstress. I make the costumes. I just help out on the piano for practice sessions. It's Wally Walton and the Wallflowers that play for the dances and Champs. Mr Lorrison would never have an old woman the likes of me on his stage when the punters are in.' She smiled, seemingly without rancour. 'But he does pay me, so I'd better get back to it, if you're finished.'

She rose and made for the door, opening it and standing half behind it as though to shield herself.

'What was the object, if you don't mind me asking?' she said.

'It's not important,' I replied, meaning that we would rather keep the information to ourselves, for Mr Montaigne-Bunyan had already tripped himself up most usefully.

'It wasn't . . .' Miss Thwaite hesitated. 'You'll think me fanciful, but it wasn't a creature of some sort, was it?'

'Now what,' said Alec, 'makes you ask that?'

Miss Thwaite looked from one of us to the other and her thin cheeks paled. 'It was, wasn't it?' she breathed. 'It was an animal.'

'It was a dead bird,' I said, swiftly changing my mind and deciding that we would learn more from telling a little. 'With the spangles stuck to it.'

Miss Thwaite put one hand up to cover her mouth, pressing it hard against her face until her skin whitened around her fingers. 'Just like poor Leo Mayne,' she said.

But despite our pleading, despite Alec's urgent assurances of confidentiality, despite my leaping to my feet and practically shaking her, she refused to say any more. All we got out of her as she scuttled off was a look of despair and a muttered: 'Dear Lord above, not again.'

55

8

Mr Lorrison, seen at close quarters in his office, was no more appealing than he had been across the dance floor. It always perplexes me when someone takes the trouble to be dapper, without taking the trouble to be clean. In this case, an unfortunate suit was paired with a stridently patterned tie and some very pronounced braces, not to mention his cufflinks, which looked like polished jade but which were surely onyx (or even Portsoy marble). Yet, for all that swank his hair was stiff with old pomade and his cuffs were grey along the edge. When he turned his head one could hear the rasp of a badly shaved jaw scraping against his soft collar and a look at it – frayed at the seam – told one that this must happen most days.

'I don't want any trouble,' he said when we entered after knocking.

'And yet trouble you have,' said Alec. 'Miss Stott's troubles are yours if they befall her here, wouldn't you say?'

Alec is usually adept at meeting his company on their level, winkling information from carters and cottagers with his easy talk of farming troubles. He even made himself at home in a coalminer's kitchen once and secured his welcome with a gift of pipe tobacco. I wondered if he was unaware that he was putting Mr Lorrison's back up or if he simply found the fellow so unsavoury that he did not care. Certainly, the curled lip and narrowed eyes could not be misunderstood. Mr Lorrison thought Alec was a fop and despised him.

'If Tweetie Bird's not happy at the Locarno, there's plenty

more would be glad to step into her place,' Lorrison said. 'I'm not running a finishing school for young ladies.'

'I see,' I said. 'Sink or swim, is it?'

He inclined his head as if to salute one who shared his understanding.

'I take it Leo Mayne was one of the sinkers?' I went on, then took an involuntary step backwards as Lorrison rose to his feet and leaned across his desk towards where we stood.

'I'll have none of your snide hints here,' he said. 'You're on thin ice, if you only knew it. Very thin ice. That was an accident. It could have happened anywhere.'

'And what exactly did happen?' said Alec.

But Mr Lorrison was shaking his head and walking round his desk towards us. 'Out,' he said. 'Out you go. I'll need to see about this. I'll need to see what I think before I let youse back in here to spread rumours. Go on, sling your hooks, the pair of you.'

'Shall we go to a tea shop and see if we can get ourselves thrown out of there too?' asked Alec when we were back on the pavement again. 'We might as well try for the hat-trick.'

I ignored him, for something had caught my attention. A pair of girls in shop overalls were standing in front of the large picture of Beryl and Bert and scrutinising a small bill pasted at the bottom of the window. I sauntered over to them and eavesdropped shamelessly.

'It's Friday, I'm telling you,' said one. 'Today's the first and that makes Friday the fifth. They never have the Champs on a Saturday, when it's professionals. They don't have to.'

'Are you dancers?' I asked them.

They started a little for they had been attending so closely to their discussion that they had not noticed me.

One of them giggled. 'We're not bad,' she said. 'We don't disgrace ourselves.'

'Are you competing?'

This brought gales of laughter.

'In a pig's ear,' said the other. 'Naw, we're coming to watch if we can get tickets and time off.'

'And who is your favourite?' I said. 'Who would you put your money on?'

'My da would kill me if I placed so much as a penny bet,' said the first girl. 'But my favourite is Beryl and Beau. Oh, they're just lovely!'

'And how long have you been following professional dancing?' I asked.

Alec, who had been looking perplexed, finally cottoned on. 'Were you there last year?' he said.

The girls nodded and one clasped her hands under her chin with a sigh. 'Beryl was that elegant,' she said. Then she continued in a more determined tone: 'She deserved her win. She would have won anyway.'

'Even if . . . what?' I said.

'Even if Leo and Foxy had carried on,' said her friend.

'Leo Mayne?' I said. 'We keep hearing his name but we don't know the story.'

Of course, that was irresistible to them and led to a measure of drawn-out, dramatic hinting.

'It was hard to credit it really,' one began. 'The way they glide about – and some of the quicksteps so tricky.'

'And yet they never put a foot wrong.'

'I still can't believe it.'

'Me neither. Beryl's my favourite but I wish Leo and Foxy were going to be dancing again.'

'You're quite sure they won't be then?' said Alec.

Both girls turned scornful looks upon him.

'What?' said one. 'Listen to what we're telling you!'

'You haven't told us anything,' I said, 'except that the dancers glide about without losing their footing.'

'Aye,' said the other. 'And then Leo Mayne goes to walk

down the self-same stairs he walks up and down ten times every day of his life and bang!'

'From top to bottom like a sack of coal.'

'During the competition?' said Alec.

'Right in the middle of the Champs. Right before the tango.'

'Straight down the stairs and stone dead at the bottom.'

There was a moment of silence after that.

'Dreadful,' I said.

'Awfy.'

'And now here it's come round again.'

'Still, no reason to expect that anything will go wrong this year,' said Alec, completely mistaking their mood.

They threw him a cold glance, as befitted one who had spoiled the fun, favoured me with a significant, conspiratorial look, since I had not, and took themselves off.

'Well,' said Alec, gazing after them.

The children huddled in the rug against the wheel of the Cowley were getting understandably restive, and so, digging in my purse for sixpences, I went to dismiss them and start the journey homewards. Despite the fact that the boy had cheek enough to bite down on the coin, testing it, I told them they could keep the blanket and they bore it away wrapped around themselves like a cloak.

'Do you think they'll pawn it?' I asked Alec, watching them go.

I have grown so used to Hugh's sanguinity regarding my detecting affairs that, when I told him of our latest engagement and he banged down his wineglass and dropped his fork on to his fishplate with a clatter, I honestly believed that he had swallowed a bone or looked through the dining-room window and seen a poacher.

'A Glasgow dance-hall!' he said. 'Dandy, have you gone quite mad? I don't expect you to know about it, Osborne old chap, because you are not Scottish—'

'*I'm* not Scottish!' I retorted.

'You are a Scot by marriage to a Scot and the mother of two more,' said Hugh. 'And you have been reading the *Scotsman* every day for twenty years.'

I did not disabuse him. In fact, I had been having the *Scotsman* laid on a table in my sitting room for twenty years but I do not think I had ever glanced at the thing. Donald, who knows this, giggled and then buried his nose in his glass.

'Know about what?' said Alec.

'Gangsters,' said Hugh. 'Glasgow is rife with gangsters and dance-halls are their lairs.'

'What rot!' I said. 'Gangsters are an American invention, Hugh. I don't suppose they've got as far as London yet, much less Glasgow.'

'Rival gangs with knives and razors marauding around the city and fighting in the dance-halls,' said Hugh. 'You must have seen the newspaper reports, Dandy.'

'Actually, Mother,' said Donald, 'I saw something on a newsreel at the Regal and I think it was Glasgow. I wouldn't like to think of you getting mixed up in anything like that.'

'When were you at the Regal?' I asked, for I had never known either of my sons to show an interest in moving pictures. Donald blushed to the tips of his ears and bent his head over his plate again, concentrating like a surgeon on removing some minuscule bones from his turbot. I took this to mean either that he had developed an interest in some Hollywood glamour puss and was sneaking into the Regal to gaze at her or, less ridiculous but more worrying, that he had formed an attachment to some girl who would not be coming to dine here with her parents and at whose home we should not be going to dine either and whom he had therefore to meet in Dunkeld and take to the pictures. I glared at Hugh, telegraphing an instruction to draw Donald aside and get the name out of him, only praying that the name he got was Mary Pickford.

'The Locarno is not a gangsters' lair, Hugh,' I said. 'It's the venue for professional dancing championships and the people there are perfectly respectable.' I squashed down a mental image of Mr Lorrison and his green cufflinks as I said so.

'What are you two doing there if they're so respectable?' said Hugh, rather nastily and quite unfairly. The first case I ever took was amongst our set, the second too and, although I have since been mixed up with shopkeepers and school-mistresses, the number of truly disreputable individuals with whom Alec and I have had dealings is tiny.

'It's a matter of jealous rivalry,' said Alec. 'Sabotage at most. I think there's a woman's hand behind it, don't you, Dandy?'

'Some of the women are as bad as the men,' said Hugh. 'I'd be a lot happier if you wrote to these people and gave your apologies.'

I shook my head at him in disbelief. 'My dear Hugh, if you would like Sir Percy and Lady Stott to be informed that I'm throwing in the towel because you think they and their daughter might set upon me with knives then *you* write and tell them.'

'Who?' said Hugh.

'A baronet with plantations in the Indies,' I said. 'Now, let's talk about something else, for heaven's sake.'

'What did you see?' Alec asked Donald.

'*The Blue Angel*,' said Donald, blushing again.

'Ahh,' Alec said, sitting back and smacking his lips like someone tasting a new bottle of port. 'Miss Dietrich, eh?'

'Who?' said Hugh again, for he only reads the gloomy pages of his gloomy newspaper and never the reviews.

I drafted my letter to the Stotts after dinner, accepting the commission and quoting a reasonable daily fee to see us through the days leading up to the Championship and the day itself. I had just started writing out the final copy in ink on good headed paper when Alec joined me. He looked at the blue chair, gave a great sigh and sat opposite it.

'Hugh and Donald in the billiards room?' I asked.

'Donald's gone home and Hugh's busy with this river weed thing,' Alec said.

I nodded as though I knew what that was. Hugh is forever busy with some dreary calamity or other somewhere on the estate and since we bought the neighbouring one for Donald he has twice the fun. Donald himself marches about dutifully enough with his father or his steward but he has never shown any true zeal.

'He needs a wife,' I said. 'He shouldn't be sloping off to the Regal and mooning over German sirens.'

'He's twenty!' said Alec, whose own efforts at making a match were still rather desultory as he headed towards forty.

'Where shall we stay in Glasgow?' I asked. 'I don't have any friends there, obviously. But there must be a decent hotel somewhere near the Locarno, don't you think?'

'The Central at the station, I expect. Presumably that will be quite near the library too.'

I had to hide a smile. If I am overly fond of my little notebook and pencil then Alec's weakness is the clippings collection of the nearest library. It started in Edinburgh once when he was poring through back copies of the *Evening News* looking for a wedding announcement for a case of suspected bigamy and the librarian in charge, tired of his endless huffs and sighs, asked if perhaps the clippings would be more convenient for sir.

The clippings were of no use at all to sir in the matter at hand but he fell instantly under their spell anyway. He even rang me up from a kiosk across the street to regale me.

'They've got everything in there,' he had said. 'All gathered together by subject matter and catalogued by date. Everything, Dandy. This is going to change our world. Transport, council meetings, weather reports. You name it.'

'Gosh,' I remember saying. 'Council meetings and weather reports.'

'Criminal stuff too,' Alec assured me. 'Theft, burglary, assaults. Everything gathered together and indexed.'

To tell the truth, I thought I would rather miss the quiet afternoons sitting at one of the large library tables, turning the pages of years' worth of bound newspapers, hunting that elusive pip of information that might crack a case.

'What do you think the papers will tell us about Tweetie Bird and the Locarno?' I asked now.

'Nothing at all about Tweetie,' he said, 'but I was hoping for something about Leo Mayne. I know those two girls on the street said it was an accident and I can understand it not being Lorrison's happiest memory, but why did Jeannie McNab drop his name into the conversation in that sly way and why did Miss Thwaite bring him up when she did? Why would a dead "creature" make her think of a young man falling downstairs?'

These were excellent questions. I mulled them over again as I went upstairs to bed a little later but had made no progress by the time I reached my room.

Grant, my maid, was there before me and judging by the way she stood like a totem-pole in the centre of the carpet upon my entrance, she had been mourning again and had snapped out of it when she heard me coming.

'I just can't get used to it at all,' she said. 'It's so quiet. And she wasn't even a barker. I had no idea what a hole she'd leave, had you?'

'Oh, I knew very well,' I said, thinking back to Flasher, my childhood terrier, and the large ginger cat which used to live in the kitchen and whose death had left our cook sobbing and shaking in her Windsor chair for two days while the family dined off ham sandwiches and apples. Flasher's death had been the end of childhood for me and even that was as nothing compared with the loss of Bunty. For Bunty, quite simply, was the dog of my life.

'I keep looking for her,' said Grant. 'And listening.' She

bent her hand into a claw shape and tapped her fingertips on my dressing-table top. It sounded uncannily, horrifically, like the sound of an elderly dog's toenails on a parquet floor and tears sprang into my eyes.

'Grant, for heaven's sake,' I said.

'Sorry,' she replied. 'Madam.'

I sat at the dressing table and turned my back to let her undo my necklace clasp.

'What's in the offing?' she asked. 'I know the signs when you're gone all day and then Mr Osborne stays for dinner.'

'It's a curious case,' I said. She was taking the clips out of my hair ready to pin it close to my head for the night but her eyes were on mine in the mirror. 'A Glasgow ballroom dancing professional being threatened with harm in a particularly underhand way. And odd murmurs about the death of a dancer last year.'

'Ballroom dancing?' said Grant, perking up.

'Do you know anything about it?' I asked her. 'It seems to be quite a world of its own.'

'I don't know much more than the next person,' said Grant. 'I did hear that the proponents of the Argentine Tango were going to approach the IDMA to get some of their steps recognised for competitions.'

'The ID what?' I said.

'The International Dancing Masters' Association,' said Grant. 'They're trying to amalgamate all the older bodies, but I heard Mr Silvester at the Imperial Society is having none of it.'

'Not much more than the next person,' I echoed. 'Do you actually know the dances, Grant?'

'The usuals, madam,' she said as I stood and slipped my unbuttoned frock down to my waist. 'Waltz, quickstep, foxtrot. Both tangos. The rumba.' As I turned she was holding her arms towards me.

'The rumba?' I said, reaching out and taking her hands.

64

She lifted an eyebrow. 'Your dress,' she said.

'Quite, quite,' I said, letting go again and wriggling out of the skirt part. 'Well, then, Grant, I should think you'd be an asset, don't you?'

'I'll be where I'm needed most, madam,' she said. 'Either Glasgow to help with the case or here to start packing away for the change of season. Whatever you tell me to do.'

She was working hard to be convincing but I could not miss the way she moved over to my wardrobe and back again with a little catch, almost a skip, in her step. Nor did I miss the tune she was humming under her breath as she bore my soiled linens away to the basket.

'What time are we leaving?' she said from the door.

'Bright and early,' I said. 'I should pack tonight if I were you.'

'We'll see,' she said. 'I've got a bit of sewing to do first.'

Ten other mistresses would have taken that to mean that the conscientious Miss Grant could not contemplate leaving behind any undone mending as she set off on her spree. I knew better. She was planning to turn some outfit of her own into one grand enough for a starring role in the forth-coming adventure. I smiled to myself as I switched off the lamp. Then, curling my own hand round, I tried to reproduce the sound of Bunty's toenails on the wooden top of my bedside table. It was nothing like them. It was more like someone dropping a box of tapers on a marble hearth. Just as well, I told myself, for I would do it if I could and it promised only misery for me.

9

Glasgow's Grand Central Hotel was certainly grand and it could hardly have been more central, crouched there as it was on top of the railway station at the heart of the city, with bustling streets around it in every direction. They teemed with people – costermongers, delivery boys, newspaper sellers, crowds of neatly uniformed schoolgirls and scruffily uniformed schoolboys – and the roads were jammed with carts and buses, trams and taxicabs, carriages and motorcars, as though every street in the whole of Glasgow met here and shook hands as do all Parisian streets at the Arc de Triomphe; so unhelpful when one is hurrying but such a blessing when one is lost.

I instructed one of the hotel garage-men to keep the motorcar handy and watched the doorman pile bags into a heap to take them upstairs. There were more than I could account for and I suspected Grant of packing either for a longer stay than I expected or for a more varied itinerary than we had agreed was likely.

She had come on ahead on the train and when I arrived at my rather sumptuous room was deep in muttered discussion with the bellboy. I was interested to see that rather fewer bags came into the room than had left the motorcar.

'Have you brought mending *with* you?' I said.

'I'm just keeping our options open,' said Grant. 'Barrow too.'

'Barrow too what?' I said. Alec had decided to bring his valet for once. Not from laziness or vanity but to head off trouble between valet and cook if they were left at Dunelgar together and the master away. For Mrs Lowie, tired of Barrow's superior ways, had recently staged something of a coup. She had persuaded Alec that since he kept no housekeeper, her title should more properly include that rank. Alec saw no reason to disagree and cook-housekeeper she duly became. As soon as the first pay packet was in her hands, though – for of course there was a raise commensurate with the improved standing – Mrs Lowie laid out her manifesto. A butler, she argued, was on equal footing with a housekeeper but a cook outranked a valet by some way. Therefore, she concluded in a way that would have made Aristotle proud, a cook-housekeeper outranked a valet-cum-butler. Mr Barrow's days of rule at Dunelgar were, she explained, over.

Then began a rumpus the like of which the house had never seen in all its days, or at least not since the Jacobites were passing. Mrs Lowie reorganised the servants' accommodations, stirring the few maids and even fewer men around in the cavernous attics for no reason at all. She moved the linens, she moved the flower room to an old dairy and then, for sheer spite, she emptied, relined and restocked the silver cupboard, undoing Barrow's pet system and almost breaking his spirit.

Alec had watched it all in helpless wonder, since his attachment to Barrow was as deep as it was unaccountable but his attachment to Mrs Lowie's cooking gave it a good run for its money and was easier to explain. Her steamed pudding with caramel, her cream ices and her raspberry cake were beginning to show in Alec's silhouette, such was his enthusiasm for them. He would never let her go even if it meant Barrow accompanying him everywhere.

As I thought that there was a rap at my door and Alec strolled in.

'Grant,' he said, nodding. He has charming manners. Then he threw himself down into a chair and laid his head back.

'He's brought white tie,' he groaned. 'God help me.'

Grant smirked and left us.

'Ring for some coffee, won't you, Dan?' Alec went on. 'And then we can stop in at the Mitchell on our way west.' We had arranged to collect Tweetie immediately after luncheon and Alec was determined to fit the Mitchell Library into our day even if we starved.

The Mitchell was even grander than the Grand. It rose in honeyed splendour out of the hubbub of the city street and, walking up its many steps to pass between the pillars and in under the dome, one might almost have been in some great European gallery, come to see the Old Masters. It was an effect which lasted until the porter hailed us just inside the door.

'Whit are youse wanting?' he said, hitching his britches and ambling over on bow legs.

'Press clippings about Glasgow life,' said Alec.

'Ah, Glasgow,' said the porter and munched silently for a while, working his false teeth into a more comfortable position. 'Well you might ask about Glasgow life. For it's a city as full of life as any of the great capitals of the world. The cradle of the Empire, the engine-house of all our prosperity and the heart of Scotland.' What he meant was: not Edinburgh.

'Oh, quite, quite,' said Alec. 'And where are the clippings held?'

We were sent on our way and it was not long until we were each settled in a little wood and leatherette chair at a table made for two, opening bound volumes of press cuttings which were stamped 'Dancing and dance-halls 1929–1930' in gold upon their spines.

'Good grief,' said Alec. 'Hugh isn't far off the mark, is he? It says here: "Police called to Lorne Hall, seven arrests and thirteen in hospital".'

I swallowed hard, for the story I was reading was even worse. There had been a razor stabbing at the Tower Palais during a dance in October. 'No witnesses came forward out of the one hundred and fifty patrons who were present,' the article said in primly outraged tones.

'But not a breath of scandal about the Locarno,' I said. I flipped to the contents page, written out in a librarian's crabbed handwriting in very pale brownish ink. '"Locarno, Ballroom, the". "Scottish Professional Dancing Championship 1929, 1930". "Visit from Victor Silvester, see Silvester, Mr, Victor". And "Christmas party". That's it.'

'Odd that the death of Leo Mayne doesn't get its own entry,' said Alec. 'Since the visit of Victor Silvester gets two. Who is Victor Silvester anyway?'

I shook my head for I was puzzling over something much more troubling.

'It's not in here,' I said, looking up at last. Alec raised his eyebrows. 'The write-up on last year's competition doesn't mention Leo Mayne. Not by name and not even by noting that one of the dancers died. Nothing.'

'Perhaps . . .' said Alec, but then stopped, unable to come up with a reasonable explanation.

'And it's not as though they're protecting the good name of the dance-hall, is it?' I said. 'They went absolutely to town on the other places when the fights broke out. His name's in the starters published the day before,' I went on, leafing back a few pages. 'Trotter and Mayne, couple number eleven. Bonnar and Montaigne, couple number four. Hodge and Christie, couple number nine. Christie must be Alicia, don't you think?'

'Why are you reading out lists of names?' said Alec, turning forward several pages again. 'You're right though. Not a peep about them in the results. First place, couple number four, Bonnar and Montaigne. Second place, couple— Sorry,' he said, catching my look.

'It's very odd,' I said. 'Everyone knows what happened. The Stotts and Miss Thwaite, certainly, those girls we spoke to, too. But not a word.'

'Well, it's not strictly dancing news, is it?' said Alec. 'And if it was a simple accident, it's not strictly news at all.'

The librarian sitting behind the enquiry desk was watching us and looked poised to come over and shush us if we made much more noise. I bent my head even closer to Alec's and murmured in his ear.

'But if it was a simple accident, why would Jeanne mention him and why would Miss Thwaite be reminded of him when you told her about the dead bird?'

Alec nodded and rose to meet the librarian who was stalking over to remonstrate with us, her block heels making ten times as much noise on the polished floor as my whispers could have done.

'Might I have the *Glasgow Herald* for June last year?' he asked her as they met.

She shot a look at the bound volumes of clippings and then glared at him.

'If it is for private consultation,' she said. 'Even shared private consultation. But not' – she paused dramatically and her words rang around the room – 'if it's for further discussion. Silence is essential.' The sibilants in this last bit were hissed so loudly that the only other patron, an elderly gentleman poring over some maps, looked up and blinked.

'What on earth?' said Alec after she had stalked off.

'I rather think asking for the whole newspaper when you've tried the clippings might be rude,' I said. 'Casting doubt on the legitimacy of their archive.'

When the newspaper was brought to us, however, we found nothing with which to reproach the skills of the Mitchell staff. We read from miscellaneous items for sale on page one to the lowliest of the third division association football scores on page eighteen and there was not so much as a word about the sudden death of a young man that day, nor even the report of a tumble which might have become death later in a hospital bed; this despite an inch-long story about a private

70

motorcar which had broken down in the middle of the street and been dragged off by a milkman's horses, then another about a child who had climbed a tree in Kelvin Park to retrieve a kite and had suffered a broken arm and cut head when the tree limb broke under him.

'Let's look at the next day,' I murmured, one eye on the librarian, who had both eyes on us. 'The death notice might be in by then.' Another day, however, yielded nothing. We closed the volume, rose, thanked the librarian, who shushed us vigorously, and left, descending the grand steps between the pillars and back into the sunshine.

'Don't tell me there's nothing fishy about this,' said Alec. 'Someone died at the Locarno, during the competition last year, and it's been swept right under the carpet.'

'But our task is to make sure Tweetie doesn't join him,' I said. 'Let's get out there and see what she's got to say for herself today.'

The shining yellow door, pots of begonias and neat maid were all as before at Balmoral but the Stotts had reverted to their real selves, Sir Percy in loud tweed knickerbockers and a moss-green jersey and Lady Stott in a house dress of very limp and shiny bombazine with a cap over her hair. It aged her by twenty years but she was so much more comfortable-looking that the overall effect was a pleasant one.

'Welcome, welcome,' she said. 'Mary, run and get a round of sandwiches each for the detectives and a pot of tea. Can you eat tongue? There's a lovely tongue.'

Alec and I assured her that tongue would be fine. I quietly determined to nibble at the crust of mine and lay it aside.

'And what did you unearth at the Locarno?' said Sir Percy.

'Rather little,' I said. 'We've come today in hopes of interviewing Miss McNab at greater length.'

The Stotts, very ostentatiously, did not look at one another.

'You're not to upset her dragging up old worries,' said Lady Stott.

Sir Percy nodded along. He even mouthed the last word in time with his wife. They could not have made it more clear that this was a rehearsed formulation if they had sung it in close harmony.

'We wouldn't dream of it,' said Alec, just as ostentatiously not looking at me.

It was an extraordinary feat, one my mother herself would have been proud of, to take a day-old memory of Jeanne's sly hint and our being hustled out of Balmoral before we could ask her to say more, and to turn that into a story of poor Jeanne being distressed by the brutal detectives making her speak of painful matters.

It backfired rather spectacularly too, only rendering Alec and me more determined to get to the bottom of the mysterious Leo Mayne, and to glean all our information from the dancers at the Locarno so that Sir Percy and his lady would never know what we were up to. To Jeanne we did not so much as mention his name.

'Miss McNab,' Alec began, when we were settled with her. She was upstairs in what Lady Stott had called 'the sewing room', surrounded by half-made costumes hanging from the picture rail in muslin bags, some of them with sketches pinned to them. In the middle of the floor there was a hamper, thrown open, its stuffing of feathers, beads and tassels bursting out of it. Jeanne herself sat at the window carefully stitching each of these in turn to a floor-length gown.

'Good afternoon,' she said. 'Can you find a perch? I'm happy to talk to you but I can't stop working.'

'Is that for Friday?' I said, thinking it rather late in the day.

'She's always the same,' said Jeanne. 'Changes her mind up until the eleventh hour and everyone's to jump. This is for the Latin. Heaven knows what she's got in mind for the waltz.'

'We spoke to Miss Bonnar and Mr Bunyan yesterday,' Alec said. 'And Mr Hodge and Miss . . . Christie?'

'Mrs Hodge to be,' said Jeanne. 'Although she might keep her own name for the sound of it. It's very common for married couples to compete as dancing partners, or dancing partners to end up married. Well, you can understand that, can't you? The romance of it all, being swept round the room in a chap's arms as the music swells.'

Her wryness, added to the memory of my two minutes in the arms of Mr Hodge the day before, made for uncomfortable listening.

'And we took in Mr Lorrison and Miss Thwaite too,' Alec went on.

'What a treat that must have been for you,' said Jeanne. She finished stitching on a tassel and rummaged in the open hamper for another.

'To meet Miss Thwaite?' I said, wondering how the little woman could have earned such disdain.

'To commune with Lorrison,' said Jeanne. 'He's a dreadful man, isn't he?'

'He's unappealing at first glance,' I said and my understatement was rewarded with a smirk from the girl. 'But do you know anything solidly wrong about him? Do you think he might be behind the nastiness?'

'Not a chance,' said Miss McNab. 'Anything for a quiet life is Lorrison's way. He'd never risk the wretched Champs being taken away because of a scandal. There are at least three other ballrooms in Glasgow just as fit to hold them, more so even, and Lorrison knows it.'

'He's lucky to have been chosen then,' I said.

'We make our own luck in this world,' said Jeanne. 'Or so my mother always told me. I often wonder where I went wrong.' Once again, she gave the wry grin which seemed to be her favourite expression.

'Was your mother Lady Stott's sister?' said Alec, showing

a young man's usual lack of recall for genealogy. Even our nine years of detecting had not changed that about him.

'Good gracious no!' said Jeanne. 'Heavens above! Lady Stott's sister and my mother have absolutely nothing in common whatsoever. My mother was a teacher and a Sunday school teacher too. She met my father, Lady Stott's brother, when she took the children in her class to the baths for their swimming lesson. He ran a boys' club in the East End, right in the slums. He went down amongst them, you understand? He needn't have. He didn't come from that world and didn't belong there. He was a printer.'

Her pride was as unmistakable as it was unaccountable. A teacher and a printer, even if they did trouble themselves with good works for the poor of the East End, were nothing much to brag about when set against Balmoral and the rubber plantations that built it. Some of this must have shown on my face for Miss McNab continued.

'Lady Stott was working at the Crown when she met Sir Percy,' she said.

'A pub?' I said, unable to stop my voice rising.

'A tea-room,' admitted Jeanne. 'Sir Percy went every day for his mutton chop and treacle pudding.'

'Ah,' I said. 'Well, a pretty waitress who brings you chops is quite appealing, I dare say.'

'Lady Stott was never pretty,' said Jeanne. 'My father got all the good looks of the entire family and still he chose his wife for her fine mind and her Christian living.'

Now it made perfect sense. The teacher no doubt felt rather above the waitress and had passed her sense of superiority on to her daughter. That daughter, poignantly enough to onlookers, now sat in the sewing room of the waitress's mansion, stitching her cousin's frocks like an unpaid skivvy.

'And what's Lady Stott's sister's station in life?' I asked. 'Not a teacher anyway, you seemed to imply.'

Miss McNab opened her eyes very wide and closed her

mouth very tight, until her unpainted lips all but disappeared.

'A respectable widow living alone,' she said when she had unpursed them. 'What does that have to do with the threats?'

I surmised that while *she* might denigrate her relations I was not to allude to their shortcomings even in the most oblique way.

'Nothing at all,' said Alec. 'You are quite right. Detecting does make one horribly inquisitive. The threats, then. What do you think it's all about, you who have a ringside seat at the dance-hall?'

'That's what the Stotts would like and so that's what Theresa and I tell them,' Jeanne said. 'But I'd be screaming with boredom if it were true. In fine weather I take pictures. I'm rather keen on photography, as a matter of fact. If it's raining, I go to the art gallery some days, some days to the reading room on St Vincent Street and sometimes I look around the shops. Although, to be honest, that's almost as dull as watching Theresa dancing.'

'So you weren't there on Monday?' I said.

'I wasn't there for the dramatic moment,' said Jeanne. 'I arrived about ten minutes later and heard all about it from Beryl.'

'Which makes it all the more remarkable that you got home on the tram so quickly after her,' I said.

Jeanne bowed her head slightly in acknowledgement of my perspicacity. 'Yes, I *did* take a taxi,' she said. 'I was worried about what Theresa might blurt out.'

'Oh, I shouldn't think you've got much to worry about on that score,' said Alec. 'Miss Stott managed her shock and fear without any loss of control.'

Jeanne laughed out loud at that and I could not help a smile, remembering how elegantly Tweetie had fainted and how neatly she recovered at the threat of a doctor. The additional thought occurred to me, however, that in lying so effortlessly to her aunt and even adding the detail about how smoky the tram had been and how she needed to change, Miss McNab had showed herself to be equally on top of things. Just as I had noticed the physical resemblance between the cousins, now I saw their mirrored characters too.

'But you do stop in at the Locarno first?' said Alec. 'Is that the drill? You drop Miss Stott off, go shopping or looking at statues or whatever, then pick her up again?'

'That's it,' said Jeanne. 'We've found that works nicely. And I often have sewing to give to Miss Thwaite or gowns to collect from her.'

'Couldn't Miss Stott take care of that?' I asked.

'Oh no,' said Jeanne. 'That would never do. She tells us what she wants and then she has nothing more to do with it until it's time for the fittings. Theresa couldn't bother herself with patterns and linings when she's consumed with her art.' She had almost finished applying another feather, but suddenly instead she wrenched it off the gown and looked down at the resulting tear without a glimmer of expression on her face. I tried to keep mine equally blank.

'So you can't actually help us with who went where and when,' said Alec evenly. 'Not to worry. You can still – I hope – tell us who you think might have a motive. Miss Bonnar is the obvious suspect.'

'I shouldn't think Beryl worries much about Theresa,' said Jeanne. 'If it were the other way – if Beryl was being threatened – that would be much less of a mystery.'

'Ah,' I said. 'Beryl is the Queen and Theresa is the young pretender?'

'That sums it up quite neatly,' said Jeanne. 'Beryl's position is unassailable. Everyone except Theresa seems to know that. It would be amusing if it weren't so pitiful.'

'And yet,' said Alec, 'Miss Stott's picture is right there in the window just like Miss Bonnar's, just as large.'

'Oh, I'm not saying Theresa isn't a good *dancer*,' said Jeanne.

'She's an excellent *dancer*. But Beryl has something that she never will.'

She was coolly amused by her own cryptic words, which was rather annoying, and even more amused by the way Alec and I were scrutinising her, both of us frowning, trying to decipher them.

'Miss Bonnar is certainly the more mature,' said Alec. 'Dressing so sensibly to rehearse, for instance. And using her own name even if it's rather unmelodious, instead of dreaming up "Tweetie Bird". What does the dance world make of that I wonder?'

'Oh, no one can resist Tweetie Bird,' said Jeanne. Then she cocked her head and held up one finger; Theresa's very gesture from the day before.

When the door opened Theresa stood framed there, striking a pose just as dramatic as that she had chosen for her entrance the previous day, although where *it* had been bathed in pathos and suffering *this* was triumphant. Both her arms were above her head and one of her feet was thrust forward and pointed. She looked the personification of a great hurrah! and she was, from head to toe, glittering. Some unfortunately glamorous species of bird had clearly been hunted in dozens, chased through the jungles of its tropical home and plucked of its finery, all to turn Tweetie into the vision before us. The feathers were not green, nor were they blue, nor were they purple; instead they shimmered with all three colours and more and – if such a thing were possible – they twinkled.

Certainly, her headband twinkled, for as well as feathers the circlet had a fringe of amethyst droplets She had somehow managed to make her eyelids glitter too – dulling the blue of her pretty eyes with the harshness of paste sapphires above them; a memory of the way the sequins were glued to the little dead wren made me shudder.

Even her cheeks glittered. Georgian ladies of questionable virtue used patches black as soot and shaped like hearts and clubs but Theresa's – just to the side of each eye, were green diamond-shaped jewels making her appear as though she were crying emerald tears.

She twisted this way and that and the gems on her golden shoes winked and dazzled.

'Mummy told me you were here,' she said. 'What do you think? And what do *you* think, Jeanne? Even you must admit it's rather marvellous, isn't it? I had given up all hope of these arriving in time. I tacked them on just to get an idea.'

'You can't seriously think you've got time to sew something that elaborate before Friday,' said Jeanne.

'Not me!' Tweetie said. 'Not me alone.' She pouted. 'But look at how beautiful I am. We've got to try. It's not as if you've got anything else to do.'

I half expected Jeanne to fly at her and rip the glittering feathers from her back, but to my great astonishment she simply pressed her lips firmly together and gave a curt nod.

Tweetie fluttered over, kissed Jeanne on both cheeks and then floated away.

10

She did not go to the Locarno in the entire get-up, since apart from anything else she needed to relinquish the frock to have it properly stitched, but she kept the extraordinary face-paint on and took the shoes to give an impression.

'There would be no need for you anyway, Jeanne,' she said blithely, 'since I have Mrs Gilver and Mr Osborne to look after me. Make sure it's all very securely fastened.'

Jeanne said nothing, merely nodded.

As the three of us trooped away from the sewing room, I took the chance to set matters straight with Theresa.

'We might not be with you the whole time, Miss Stott. If we need to take off after a lead then you'll be alone there.'

'What lead?' said Theresa. 'Surely if one of you sits in the cloakroom and one of you sits at the side of the floor then no harm can come to me?'

'We're not nursemaids,' said Alec.

We were crossing the main landing, and a little creature on her knees polishing the edges of the stair risers looked delighted to have overheard the young mistress being spoken to that way. I imagined her in the servants' hall at dinnertime regaling the rest of the staff and so I gave her a little more material.

'Nor are we watchmen,' I said. 'I am not prepared to sit in the cloakroom simply so that your coat can be stowed on its usual peg. Miss Thwaite can keep an eye on your things and Mr Osborne and I will do as we think best to fulfil our agreement with your parents.'

The maid sat back on her heels and beamed. Luckily, Theresa did not see the look of delight upon her face.

'How do you know Miss Thwaite?' she said. 'And what makes you think you can trust her?'

She had reached her bedroom door and she stood half behind it, clutching it and looking like a siren.

'We interviewed her along with everyone else yesterday,' I said. 'And of course it wasn't her who hid those things among your belongings.'

'What?' said Theresa, coming back around the door.

'I think the others would have mentioned it if Miss Thwaite had stopped playing and disappeared, don't you?' said Alec.

'You went to the Locarno?' Theresa's eyes, already made to look enormous with the paint and lash black she had applied, seemed now to grow even larger. 'If you've spoiled things for me, I shall never forgive Mummy and Daddy. If Lorrison bars me or Roly sacks me or if Big Beryl flexes her muscles and gets rid of me, I shall never forgive any of you!' She turned smartly on her heel and stalked into her bedroom, slamming the door behind her.

'For two pins,' I said. Alec did not understand the phrase, which was just as well since it was a saying of Nanny Palmer's concerning the putting of little girls over her knee for a spanking and one does not wish to be thought of as a brute. Brutal or not, however, it had worked wonders on me when I was a child and I could not help thinking that Theresa Stott had been ill-served by not having a Nanny Palmer of her own.

She kept up her grumbling all the way to Sauchiehall Street, sitting in the back seat of my motorcar, inspecting her painted face in her compact mirror and berating us and her parents.

'One week,' she said. 'Just one more week and then I'll be a good dutiful daughter and a good dutiful wife for the rest of my life.'

'But surely our being there will rather help you get through this one last crucial week,' said Alec.

'Mr Lorrison doesn't like trouble,' said Theresa. 'If I cause it I'll be out on my ear and if I lose my place at the Locarno, I shan't be a professional and I shan't be eligible for the Champs. Do you see?'

'We've no intention of causing trouble,' I said. 'Rather of preventing it, as Mr Osborne just told you.'

'Detectives!' said Theresa. 'Even just having detectives there is like saying there's something wrong.'

'But there *is*,' said Alec. 'What's happening to you is unmistakably wrong. I really can't understand you.'

'Oh, Mr Lorrison wouldn't care about that,' said Theresa. 'As long as Beryl's happy.'

This did chime with what the man had said, placating Miss Bonnar but brushing off Theresa's troubles. Perhaps Miss Bonnar was the big draw; she was certainly friendlier than Theresa, and if she taught private lessons presumably she was of more use to the Locarno financially too. It was all faintly depressing and suddenly my appetite for any of it was gone. When we arrived, I held Alec back as Theresa stepped down.

'We shall join you in just a minute, Miss Stott,' I said.

When she was out of earshot, I tried to explain. 'We're making something out of nothing. Why don't we do what Theresa wants us to: just chaperone her through the Championship, keep our eyes peeled, then deliver her back to her parents and dear Julian.'

'And let whoever it is just get away with it?'

'Yes, frankly.'

Alec took his pipe from his mouth and knocked it out against the window frame of the motorcar. I bit my lip. I had asked him many times not to, but I did not want to annoy him just then and have him disagree with me for the sake of it.

'I suppose you're right,' he said. 'Very well.'

We both got out and I was pleased to see the same two small children strolling towards us again.

'Mind your car, missus?' said the boy.

'Sixpence each, wasn't it?' I said. 'But you must sit on the ground because I can't throw in a daily blanket.' It was milder today and the sun was hitting the car broadside on so they had no need for it anyway.

Upstairs on the dance floor Beryl and Bert were in full flight. It was a waltz, I rather thought, but so much faster and with so much more spinning than any waltz I had ever seen that I could not be sure. I watched for a long moment, listening to the click and thump of their dancing shoes on the boards and not noticing what was missing until Theresa came up and stood beside me.

'All right for some,' she said. 'Beryl and her party piece.'

'What do you mean?' I asked her.

'Lorrison has sacked Miss Thwaite. So there's no accompaniment until we track down a gramophone.'

'Sacked her?' I said. 'Why?'

'He won't tell me,' said Theresa. 'But this is the last straw. Roly and I are going back to practise in the ballroom at home and if Daddy doesn't like it he can throw us *both* out. Come on, Roly! We can catch a cab. It *would* be the one day I don't drive myself.' She gave me a sour look, as though my driving her about the city was some kind of mean trick, and then swept out, with Mr Wentworth trailing after her.

Alec and I mounted the stage and headed for the little door which led to Lorrison's office, pausing to look down on Beryl and Bert as they twirled on and on, covering the whole of the floor in dizzying circles.

'It is rather remarkable that they can dance in perfect time to silence,' I said. 'Poor Miss Thwaite.'

Lorrison did not share even a scrap of our sympathy. He was sitting behind his desk looking more unkempt than ever, if that were possible, his eyes hooded and dark and his cheeks pale as though from sleeplessness.

'Mr Lorrison,' I said, 'I hear Miss Thwaite has left you.'

'She's only got herself to blame,' Lorrison said. He shook a cigarette out of a packet, placed it between his lips and lit it with trembling fingers.

He was either hungover or suffering from some kind of shock, I thought. Either way, it was not an attractive sight, all that twitching and sniffing.

'Was it anything to do with us?' I asked innocently.

'I'm not discussing it,' Lorrison said. 'I want no more trouble.'

'But surely sacking your accompanist days before the competition is going to put your dancers at a severe disadvantage,' I said. 'Wouldn't it be better to help them all in their final preparations?'

'Beryl and Bert don't need a wee woman at the keys,' said Lorrison.

'But what about the others?'

'Tweetie and "Roly"?' said Lorrison with a sneer that showed the entire top row of his ill-fitting teeth.

'And young Jamesie and Alicia,' I said.

'Oh well,' said Alec, in a voice which might have sounded casual to one who did not know him, but which rang all sorts of alarm bells with me, 'we shan't press you if you don't care to dwell on it.' Then he put a firm hand under my elbow and drew me away, back into the corridor.

'Mayne,' he whispered when the door was closed. 'I know how to find him.' Then he went on in his usual voice: 'We're free, are we not, since Theresa has gone home to her family?'

'I suppose so,' I said, as we emerged back into the ballroom, 'although if the Stotts ask us what we're up to while they're paying us a daily retainer, I'm not sure what I would say.'

'You've missed Tweetie,' said Beryl. She and Bert had come to a stop in the middle of the floor. 'She's away.'

'And we're off too,' I said, coming back down the steps from the stage. 'We shan't be hanging around disturbing you. But can you answer a question, Miss Bonnar? Why was poor little Miss Thwaite sacked? Was it because she said something to us that she shouldn't have?'

Mr Bunyan gave us a sharp look. 'How?' he said. 'What did she say to you?'

'She mentioned Mr Mayne's unfortunate accident,' said Alec. 'And then she seemed to think perhaps she shouldn't have.'

The effect was extraordinary. Bert grew very still until the only thing about him that was moving was the smoke curling up from the cigarette he held pinched between his thumb and fingers. Beryl muttered something about a glass of water and walked off towards the cloakroom. With a glance at Alec, I followed her.

She was standing at the sinks, right enough, but she had not poured herself any water. The tap was off and the basin was dry. She was looking at herself in the mirror and shifted her glance to my reflection as I approached her.

'It's all very puzzl—' I began.

'You should just leave it alone, Mrs Gilver,' she said. 'This is our world. My world. It's not something you'd understand so why not just leave it alone, eh?'

'Are you threatening me, Miss Bonnar?' I said, caught between the pleasant tone in her voice and the unmistakable import of her words.

'No,' she said, almost groaning. 'No threats, no insults, no favours, no "accidents". I don't want anything to do with it. I'm done with it. I just want to dance. If we win, we win fair and square and if we lose we'll be back next year.'

'I don't understand,' I said again.

'Good,' she said, her cheerful face back to normal. 'Count yourself lucky.'

The stewards of the motorcar were distraught to see us returning, until they realised that they would be paid the same rate for a few minutes' work as for half a day.

84

'I'll drive,' said Alec. 'Since I know where we're going. You see, I've had a brainwave, Dandy. We were looking in the newspapers for the death of "Leo Mayne". But death is an official business. If it was Beryl's partner who'd died the death would be announced of "Herbert Bunyan", not "Beau Montaigne".'

'Good heavens, you're right,' I said. 'What suddenly put you on to that?'

'Lorrison reminding me of Sir Percy,' said Alec. 'He said "Roly" in just the same way Sir Percy said "Roland". In quotation marks. Now, it's back to the Mitchell with us to track down Billy Boggle or whoever who died during the competition last year. And if there's nothing in the notices under his real name we shall go to Register House and look up all the deaths by date until we find him.'

Thankfully, there was no need to. The librarian was not pleased to see us returning but when we asked for newspapers covering the same dates as last time, she smirked as she walked away. Evidently we had revealed that we had missed what we were looking for and that evened the score after our insult to the press clippers.

'Right,' said Alec as he opened his enormous volume flat on the table at the date in question, and I opened mine.

'Ssshhh,' said the librarian, predictably.

There was nothing even remotely likely that day, not in the *Herald*, the *Evening Times* or the *Record*. Everyone who died in Glasgow on 11 June 1930, be they gentlemen, professionals, tradesmen or common folk, died in a bed of their own or one in a hospital and at the age of sixty at least, except for one poor child of three who was carried off by a fever.

'We'll keep looking,' said Alec. But the next day's budget of newspapers was as unfruitful. More dowagers and pensioners and only one young man, who had been scalded in a shipyard accident.

Alec turned to a third day with a brave smile which did not quite reach his eyes. He ran his finger down the column of names in the *Herald* as I ran mine down the shorter column in the *Evening Times*. We both stopped at the same moment.

'Eureka!' Alec said, then gave an anxious glance at the desk. The librarian, however, had gone to help a patron decipher the card catalogue.

'I've found him,' I said.

'So have I,' said Alec. 'Peter Dooley. That would be a terrible name for a dancer.'

'Len Munn,' I said.

'Mine's twenty-two.'

'Mine's thirty-eight,' I conceded, 'but it's not as though they're acrobats.'

'Peter Dooley died suddenly of an accident on Monday the fourteenth of June,' said Alec.

'Len Munn died after an accident too,' I said, swivelling the volume so that he might read it for himself.

'It could be either of them,' said Alec, ignoring it. 'We should look into both.'

'Oh come off it,' I said. 'Len must be short for Leonard and so is Leo. Munn practically *is* Mayne.' Alec looked mulish. I swivelled the volume back. 'Does yours have an epitaph?' I asked.

Alec nodded. 'Taken too soon.'

'I win then,' I said. 'Len Munn's says "Waltzing with the angels".'

Alec sighed. 'Touché,' he said reluctantly. 'Now how do we find someone who knows him and hasn't been told not to talk?'

I considered the question while rereading the notice of death. 'Suddenly at home, following an accident, on the 14th day of June, 1930. Len Munn (38) of Glasgow, beloved husband and son. Funeral ten o'clock, St Peter's Church. "Waltzing with the angels".'

86

'I wonder who's the nearest undertaker?' I said. 'They must keep a ledger with addresses, mustn't they?'

'But we couldn't get near it for a king's ransom,' said Alec. 'Undertakers are notoriously punctilious. Well, I suppose one would be glad of it when it came to oneself really.'

'There must be some way,' I said. I could not take my eyes from the little entry in the newspaper. There was an idea somewhere in the back reaches of my brain, struggling to come to the fore.

'Mrs Munn must be a fanciful sort of woman,' I said.

Alec knows when I am truffling after a useful notion and merely nodded and watched me. The librarian, finished with her customer, came stalking back on those block heels and settled herself behind her counter again. She bent her head until she could not be seen behind the vase of peonies which sat there.

'Florist!' I said. The librarian looked up in great umbrage at the outburst but I waved a hand at her. 'It's all right. We're going. If you would just be so kind as to tell us in what part of town St Peter's Church is to be found.'

It was almost too easy to give any sense of satisfaction. We found our way to Partick, following the instructions the librarian shied at us more to make us leave than from genuine helpfulness and, from St Peter's, set out in all four directions, crawling along and peering up and down the side streets.

It was a comfortable and prosperous-looking corner of town, far from the dazzling heights of Bearsden but equally far from city slums. The tenements were set back behind railings, with narrow strips of garden in front, allowing laurels and hydrangeas to soften the line of the ground-floor windows, and they rose only three storeys high in total, letting some light into the streets between them.

After a few forays, we found a short shopping street, where the tenements had painted banners between the ground and first floor and large plate windows giving straight on to the pavement. There was a dairy, a Co-operative Society Baker, the obligatory Italian fish and chip restaurant, and finally what we were searching for: Dainty's the Florist, only a stone's throw from the church where Len Munn had been sent on his way. I crossed my fingers as we entered.

The smell of a florist's shop is a curious mixture. There is the scent of the hothouses where one spent such swathes of one's girlhood, taking exercise in foul weather and attempting to find quiet corners to talk to suitors during one's season: the warm damp of the sprinkled water; the rich fragrance of soil and moss; the flowers themselves, rank lilies, spicy roses and the pungent reek of hyacinth. As well as these comforting smells, though, there is always that of wet news-paper and floor soap too to stop one's reverie.

The door, which had clanged as we opened it, clanged again as we let it close and a middle-aged woman in a stout green apron came bustling through to the counter from a back room.

'Help you?' she said.

I scanned her person quickly, looking for signs of the best approach. She wore no wedding ring and so might still be a romantic soul despite her decades. Before I could turn that thought to account, though, Alec had taken charge.

'I hope so,' he said with a huge sigh. 'We're at the end of our resources, to be frank.'

'If it's a rush job I'll do what I can,' the florist said.

'It's not a job at all, strictly speaking,' said Alec. 'It's this. We're trying to track down a Mrs Munn who lives near here. Mr Munn died last year – young chap. And the only thing we know is that you did the flowers for his funeral.'

'And how did you know that?' said the woman.

'I asked,' I said when I sensed Alec hesitating. 'During the service I couldn't help whispering to my neighbour in the pew. They were so very beautiful.' I took a wild guess. 'White is such a restful colour—'

'They were purple and yellow,' said the florist, making my heart sing.

'And yet for a chap as original as Leo, it was exactly the right thing to do.'

This mollified her, as well it might for I could only imagine the ruckus purple and yellow funeral flowers must have caused.

'And now you're looking for her? Why?'

'News to her advantage,' said Alec. 'But we've had no luck finding her.'

'Are you from a solicitor's, sir?' said the florist, with a dubious glance at me, for I was inexplicable in those terms.

'We're from the SCDM,' I said, thinking nothing ventured nothing gained, and sure that some of these initials must be the right ones. 'We've set up a memorial cup and it's due to be awarded for the first time later this week at the Championship. We'd like so much for Mrs Munn to know. She might even wish to come and see the cup awarded.'

The florist clasped her hands together under her bosom as though about to sing and a beatific smile spread over her face. 'That's just lovely,' she said. Then she frowned. 'Don't any of Mr Munn's old pals at the dancing know the address?'

I swallowed. Thankfully, Alec took over.

'It's a delicate business,' he said. 'Rivalries, you know. And superstitions too. It's a world apart.'

This was vague to the point of senselessness but the florist did not want to admit how far outside the dancing world she lived by revealing her puzzlement. She nodded slowly with her lips pursed, then reached under the counter and drew out an enormous tome of a ledger, bound in half-calf and much mended with plaster linen. She heaved it open, flicked back and forward a few pages, and then stopped with her finger tapping the page.

'Mrs Leonard Munn,' she said. 'Yellow snapdragons, yellow Turk's bonnets, purple iris and purple mock orange.'

'*Purple* mock orange?' I said.

'My own patented dye,' the florist said and turned the book to let us see what was written there.

'Now?' said Alec, back out on the street again.

I looked at my wristwatch. 'It's past teatime,' I said.

'I don't know what that means,' said Alec. 'Infra dig to go visiting, or you're too hungry to think straight?'

I considered loftiness, but in the end admitted the truth.

'I'm ravenous. But besides that, I could do with some time to work on a line of questions that won't get us shown the door.'

'To the Grand then,' Alec said. 'And we'll start afresh in the morning.'

I I

Hugh loathes to stay at hotels and will dredge up the most tenuous acquaintanceship with a nearby house whenever he is forced to travel from home, ending up unwelcome and uncomfortable but always unbowed. He then has the cheek to complain to me when our hosts exercise the right to pay the return visit if headed north.

'But who *are* these people?' he demands, glowering down the breakfast table at me.

'The same people they were when you were passing through Gloucestershire last spring,' I say. 'I said we should press on to Bath and the Royal Crescent, if you recall.' This usually puts him firmly back behind the *Times* and lets peace, or at least silence, reign.

I, in contrast, like nothing better than a night or two in a cosy hotel room. Choosing dinner at dinnertime, rather than just after breakfast with Mrs Tilling complaining about the fishmonger, is always a delight to me. And Grant makes friends wherever she lands and is usually so taken up with them that she pares her attentions back to a minimum and is a great deal less bother than when she is bored.

That night in Glasgow's Grand Central was a treat. We dined downstairs, sure that no one we knew would see us and stop to chatter, and then had coffee and brandy up in my room planning for the next day. When I went to bed, after a delicious bath in a toasting warm bathroom with a carpet upon the floor, and lay listening to the traffic – a perfect cacophony of horses' hooves, motorcar engines and the thrum of the tramlines even at ten o'clock – I could not have been more content. I even missed Bunty a little less there where she had never been and went as far as to imagine her back at Gilverton curled on the blue chair or down in the kitchens being treated to milksops and leftover gravy.

The next morning we took up the reins of the case, refreshed and determined.

White Street, where the Munns had lived and where we hoped to find the widow Munn still in residence, was only minutes away from the florist and we left the Cowley outside the little run of shops there, thinking that a visitor in a motorcar was unusual enough to interest a whole tenement and put Mrs Munn on her guard in fear of neighbours gossiping.

And this was exactly the sort of respectable place for interfering neighbours. We had to pull a brass bell beside her nameplate outside and wait to be admitted through the front door of the close and ascend.

'Try to look harmless,' I said to Alec, 'in case she's checking from the window. No, don't look up!'

Either Mrs Munn was trusting enough to open the door to all-comers or she had peered down at us and liked what she saw, for in only a moment the door clunked, the latch sprang open, and Alec and I entered a tenement for the first time in either of our lives, the first of many times in that most peculiar case.

A long narrow corridor lay behind the door, stretching back into the heart of the building. The floor was painted stone and the walls were tiled to shoulder height with bottle-green tiles so dark they were almost black, and painted above shoulder height in a cold pale grey, an attempt to help what little light crept into the stairwell and passageway from the windows above the flats' front doors.

Mrs Munn was out on the landing, the door open behind her. At first I assumed that we had found Leonard's mother, rather than his widow – 'beloved husband and son' the notice had said, after all – for she looked well into her forties and if someone had told me she was fifty I should have believed him. She was still slim, with fine wrists and ankles and an attractive way of holding her head on her slender neck, and was dressed glamorously in a silk wrap and long earrings, with her red hair piled high. Her face, though, was the face of a Scottish matron, less weathered than many although as unpainted as all, and so ordinary as to seem familiar, a face one had encountered a hundred times on any walk along any street in a Scottish city.

'Mrs Munn?' said Alec. She nodded, politely quizzical. 'We're here to talk about Leo Mayne. We need your assistance with something.'

She took a step back before she could help it, then she checked herself and drew up.

'Who's sent you to my door?' she said grandly but not managing to hide her fear. 'As if I didn't know.'

'We came off our own bat,' I said. 'Might we come in?'

Mrs Munn turned and walked back into the flat leaving us to follow her and shut the door.

Inside was a remarkably well-fitted-up little house of sorts, rather surprising when one has only ever looked at tenements from the street and imagined slum life to be going on in there. There were half a dozen doors and although some of them must lead to cupboards it appeared that Mrs Munn's style of living was equal to any of Hugh's tenants and was probably superior to most of them.

We were taken into a parlour overlooking the street, with a bay window and a yellow-tiled fireplace, empty and with its polished grate gleaming.

Mrs Munn sat down on the edge of a dark velvet armchair and waited, her poise unmistakable.

'We've been trying to form a clear view of how Mr Munn died,' I said, 'and we keep running up against a brick wall.'

93

'But who are you?' said the woman.

'Private detectives,' said Alec.

'But who's sent you?' she asked again. 'Who would want to be investigating Leo's death now?'

'We can't divulge that, I'm afraid,' I told her. 'But we're very interested to know why it wasn't reported in the newspapers.'

'I couldn't have kept it out of the papers,' Mrs Munn said. 'There's no use looking at me.'

'And can you tell us what exactly happened?' I asked.

To my surprise, she plucked a handkerchief from the sleeve of her dressing gown and pressed it against her eyes.

'Poor Leonard,' she said from behind it. 'I relive it every day.'

'You were actually there?' said Alec.

'Of course I was there,' said Mrs Munn, drawing the handkerchief away. 'We were competing. Couple number eleven, Foxy Trotter and Leo Mayne.'

'You,' I said. 'You were his dancing partner?'

'His partner in everything,' said Mrs Munn. 'And yes – I see the looks on your faces – I was a little older than my husband, but we were a true match.' She rose to her feet and opened a door beside the fireplace. I thought she was leaving us to enter another room, but behind the door lay a shallow shelved cupboard, from which she took a purple and yellow velveteen album, tied along its spine with yellow tasselled silk. She set it on the large table in the bay window, opened it and then brought it over to lay it across Alec's lap and mine as we sat side by side on the little horse-hair studio couch.

'There,' she said, pointing.

I felt sure this was the original of a photograph like those that adorned the foyer windows at the Locarno. The tinting was the same and the backdrop was similar. What was different was that even though this couple – Leo and Foxy – were quite still, frozen in their pose for the camera, there somehow seemed to be something of the dance left about them, almost as though the figures in the photograph were still spinning.

'What happened?' said Alec gently.

Mrs Munn took her seat again and this time she eased back until she was comfortable.

'He fell down the stairs,' she said. 'It was right in the middle of the competition, still in the knock-out rounds, and we were dancing the tango.' She gestured to the album. 'We would never have won a tango round,' she said. 'It was our weakest competition dance. I could never get the movements sharp enough. It's supposed to look as much like a fight as a dance, properly. But in Leo's arms I melted. Look for yourself.'

I found the photograph of them in the throes of a tango and it looked aggressive enough to me. They were glaring daggers at one another, drawn back like vipers about to strike.

'Far too mushy,' said Mrs Munn. 'Look at my top line! I'm like a shepherdess sitting on a tussock. Anyway, we thought we'd get through it and whatever marks we dropped there we'd make up for in the foxtrot.'

'From where you got your name,' I said, smiling.

'No,' she said, smiling back, 'but the foxtrot suited Leo and me. Suited our style of dancing. We weren't too shabby at the quickstep and waltz either.'

'But what happened in the middle of the tango?' I said. She was as bad as Beryl Bonnar, just as single-minded when it came to dancing.

'Leo was taken ill,' she said. 'He said he needed some air. I went with him, meaning to go down to the street, and at the top of the stairs he just tripped and went top to bottom.'

She was staring straight ahead as she spoke and from the stricken look on her face it was very clear that she was playing the scene over again as she described it. She even reached out, clutching at nothing, then let her hands drop into her lap.

'And was his death instant?' said Alec.

'No,' said Mrs Munn. 'We got him home.'

'From the hospital?' I said.

For the first time she looked uncomfortable as well as anguished. 'He wanted to come home,' she said. 'I brought him home, put him to bed and sat with him. I called the doctor late the next night when he seemed to be slipping in and out. But it was too late.'

'What did the doctor say?' I asked her.

Her voice was a ragged whisper now. 'Bleeding on the brain. He'd cracked his skull when he fell down the stairs and his brain was bleeding. I knew something was wrong. His eyes were getting bloodshot. There was nothing anyone could have done. Even if I'd taken him to hospital. He would have died in hospital with strangers around him instead of here at home with me holding his hand. There was nothing to be done about it. As soon as he tripped at the top of the stairs, his fate was sealed.'

Something about what she was saying was troubling me but I could not put my finger on it. I turned to Alec for help and saw him looking equally troubled.

'Was the doctor able to say what might have been ailing your husband?' he said.

'What?' said Mrs Munn, a sharp stab of sound. 'What do you mean "ailing"?'

'Earlier in the evening. You mentioned that he was feeling ill.'

'Oh,' she said. 'I see.' She put a hand up and patted at her hair, tidying a few strands back into place. It was flame-red hair, helped along surely at her age, and although it suited her pale complexion well enough ordinarily, just at that moment it clashed rather horridly with a sudden flush. 'I can't remember if I even mentioned it to him,' she said, trying for an airy tone. 'It was a moment of extreme distress, as I'm sure you can imagine. It didn't really matter why Leo left the dance floor, did it, not by then. It was tripping at the top of the stairs that did it. Hitting his head. The doctor signed the certificate and that was that.'

That appeared to be that again. I could not think of a single additional question to ask her, even though nothing she had told us made any sense of Jeanne's sly comment about Mayne dying, or of Miss Thwaite's sacking when she mentioned his name. I closed the album, with a last look at the tango picture. Again, a faint idea stirred in me, something about the way they were glaring at one another, this pair of married lovers, with the husband coldly smouldering and the wife gimlet-eyed. I shook my head, for the thought would not form, and rose to leave.

'Wait a minute,' said Mrs Munn. 'You never said why you were asking.'

'Mr Munn's name came up once or twice in the course of quite another matter,' I said. 'We're investigating a case of poison-pen letters being sent to one of the Locarno dancers.'

'Poison pen?' said Mrs Munn. 'Who's been getting *them*?'

'Miss Stott,' said Alec. 'We're working for her parents, Sir Percy and Lady Stott – I don't expect you know them.'

'Oh, don't you?' said Mrs Munn, drawing herself up.

'We know you know Tweetie,' I said.

'Well, you're wrong,' she said, ignoring me. 'I do know the Stotts.'

'I apol—' said Alec, but she cut him off.

'I'm not received in their drawing room, of course. I don't move in the right circles for Sir Percy Stott and his *lady*. I'm just a dancer, an artiste. And no one's ever accused a Stott of *that*.'

We discussed this last, rather puzzling remark on the way back downstairs to the street and had not finished discussing it by the time we had arrived at the motorcar. I was happy to chalk it up to Mrs Munn – Foxy Trotter – feeling very keenly that she was not a lady, despite her poise and the soigné robe and the elegant world in which she used to live, with her devoted swain. Alec tended towards a much wilder idea.

'Didn't Sir Percy's scorn for dancing seem a little overdone to you?' he said. 'Almost as though he's covering up something even more unseemly.'

'No,' I replied. 'I think Tweetie being mixed up with Lorrison and Beryl is unseemly enough by far.'

'And wouldn't you say that Foxy felt more scorn for the lady than the gentleman?'

'Granted. There is a type of woman who always does.'

'Ah, yes,' Alec said. 'That's the question. What "type of woman" is Foxy Trotter?'

'Well, not *that* sort,' I said, unable to stop my jaw from dropping open. 'Good grief, Alec.'

'Would you know a woman of "that sort" if you met her, Dandy? Listen, hear me out. Beryl said it was men of her father's generation who had money to pay for lessons, didn't she?'

'I have no idea what you're getting at,' I said, staring at him over the bonnet of the motorcar.

'She knows the Stotts but not from being admitted to Balmoral.'

'Go on.'

'And Lady Stott and Mrs Munn are of much the same type except that one is a little younger than the other and has sent the pudding trolley away a good deal more often.'

'What does that have to do with anything?'

'I've had a flash of inspiration,' Alec said. 'It doesn't happen often and I'm always very patient when you have yours as you do with sickening regularity. So don't be mean, please.'

'I'm never mean!' I said.

'I think Sir Percy is down on Tweetie like a ton of bricks about her dancing because . . .' he paused dramatically '. . . she might run into his mistress.'

'That's ridic—' I said, before remembering the promise he had extracted from me.

'It would explain the flap about Leo Mayne,' Alec said. 'Since he's her partner.'

'It wouldn't explain Miss Thwaite's "flap",' I pointed out.

'Let's go to Balmoral, drop her name and see what happens,' Alec said.

When we arrived, however, we found it impossible to think of anyone except Tweetie. The whole house was reverberating to the strains of an orchestral gramophone record being played very loudly but not loudly enough to cover the sound of thumping footfalls.

'No need to ask if she's in,' growled Sir Percy, when we had been shown into the morning room.

'There's no pleasing some people,' said Lady Stott. 'He wasn't happy when she was out and he's not happy that she's here.'

'In the arms of a young man who is not her fiancé,' said Sir Percy.

'You admitted Roland then?' I said.

'Roland!' scoffed Sir Percy. 'His name is Ronald Watt.'

'He's never tried to hide that fact, Bounce,' said Lady Stott. 'You needn't sound as if you've caught him out at something underhand.'

'What could be more underhand than dancing with his boss's fiancée behind his boss's back?' Sir Percy asked her.

'Come to think of it,' said Alec, cutting in as we were learning to do when the Stotts started quarrelling, 'why is he not at work? I don't quite understand how he can practise on a Wednesday morning if he's a clerk in an office.'

I saw an opening and pounced upon it. 'Different if they were taking hourly pupils,' I said. I watched Sir Percy carefully as I said the next bit, wondering if he would blanch or redden. 'As Miss Bonnar's partner does and Miss Trotter's partner used to.'

I need not have worried. One did not have to have a magnifying glass trained on either of the Stotts to notice the effect of my words. Their argument was quite forgotten as they turned fearful eyes on each other, Lady Stott flashing a plea and Sir Percy unmistakably flashing a warning.

'Miss Bonnar,' said Lady Stott, 'is not a person we choose to know.'

'And she has nothing in common with our darling Theresa,' said Sir Percy.

'I wish her no ill,' said Lady Stott, and her husband spluttered in his eagerness to echo her words.

'Good heavens, no. No ill at all. She has done very well for herself, lifting herself out of the circumstances of her birth and by all accounts she's a nice enough girl. We needn't talk of her, though. We needn't let talk of the Bonnars into this house.'

I was kicking myself. Now, even if they admitted they had been flustered, they could say it was Miss Bonnar with her pinafores and her bookless childhood who had rattled them and not talk of the ever more mysterious Leo and his widow.

We left them there, still ruffled though calming themselves with extra cups of coffee, and followed the noise of the gramophone upstairs and out along a passage to a set of double doors, which led to the usual ballroom wing, built out on top of the billiards room wing, I supposed, and for a while every householder's pride and joy.

I had wondered how a gramophone could possibly be so loud but when I saw the size of the trumpet on it, I began instead to wonder that we had not heard it driving along the street, and also slightly to wonder why it did not topple over and dent the floor. It was a fearsome thing, elephantine compared with Donald and Teddy's, which one can take out on the loch in a rowing boat for picnics if one has a mind to. This would sink any rowing boat I have ever seen and would put many a tug below the Plimsoll line too.

Theresa and Roland, owing to the racket coming out of

the gramophone, did not notice us. They were doing the quickstep, I rather thought; at least, they were dancing something we had not yet seen and dancing it very fast indeed, ripping across the floor like smoke flares until in unison they groaned and broke apart.

'Sorry,' Roland said and as he turned away to wipe his brow with his handkerchief he saw us.

'You again,' he called over the din. 'What do you want now?'

Theresa had been too nicely brought up to be quite so rude as all that, but she gave us a look no less welcoming.

'All serene, Miss Stott?' shouted Alec.

'Did you manage to get Lorrison to give Miss Thwaite her job back?' said Theresa, coming over. 'It's jolly unhelpful to me for her to have gone.'

She was utterly self-centred, not a thought in her beautiful head about how unhelpful the sacking would be to Miss Thwaite. While I was gobbling and searching for an answer that did not sound too governess-like, she dismissed us by turning away and clicking her fingers, actually clicking her fingers, in Roland's face.

'Put the needle back to the slow section and we'll try to get those syncopated steps,' she said.

Roland to his credit took none of it. 'I've got them,' he said, 'and if you'd let me lead, you'd have them too. But aye, all right, let's practise from here to the end of the record and then once more straight through.'

Theresa screwed her face this way and that while she considered arguing but in the end she simply walked back into his arms and they re-started dancing. It was rather impressive the way they picked it up again in perfect time, no waiting and no counting. They seemed to be perfectly attuned to one another and for a moment I forgot the case, the mystery of poor Leonard Mayne, and the irritation of Theresa's rudeness, and simply watched them as they tripped and skipped across the floor, building up to what I believe is called 'the big finish'.

We could not help clapping as they held the final pose like a tableau in a music-hall show, while the needle ran round and round, scraping on the paper middle in that way which sets my teeth on edge as does little else in this world.

They had just broken out of their stance and Alec and I had just stopped clapping when there was a shriek from downstairs and the sound of thunderous footsteps approaching.

'Tweetie!' came Lady Stott's voice. 'Tweetie! Julian is here! Julian is walking up the steps right this minute.' She burst into the room, panting hard, her bosom heaving like a jam pan on a rolling boil. 'Tweetie, come away,' she said, 'and put a frock on, and some stockings for the Lord's sake and you!' She turned on Roland. 'You stay here and don't you dare make a sound or move an inch if it takes till midnight.' She turned to us. 'You two, keep him up here or you're sacked.' Then she clamped a hand on Theresa, who was giggling and tossing her hair like a schoolgirl, and stamped out.

12

The three of us were left standing rather witlessly staring at one another, until I broke away to rescue the gramophone record from the ravages of that endless needle.

'Put it back on if you like and we'll have a turn,' said Roland.

'I think gramophone music wafting through the house might excite suspicions in the visitor, don't you?' said Alec.

Roland laughed. 'Aye, no doubt you're right there,' he said.

He appeared to be very far from anxious, despite the potential catastrophe of his boss being in the house. It was quite puzzling when one considered the lather he had been in at the Locarno, jumping like a rabbit at the man's name, barely making sense.

'Instead,' said Alec, 'let's see if we can shed any more light on what's been going on, shall we?'

'Please yourself,' said Roland brusquely. He swaggered over to one of the windows and hitched himself comfortably on to the sill, then took his cigarettes out of his pocket and lit one.

'Which way does that wall face?' I said, joining him. I glanced out and saw the back gardens of Balmoral, terraced lawns and a tennis court. 'Well, I don't suppose Mr Armour will go outside. There's no French window that gives on to this side of the house, is there?'

'By jings, you're keen to keep your job,' Roland said.

'We both are,' said Alec. 'Our cases can be dull enough usually but this is one I'd like to get to the bottom of. Wouldn't you?'

He shrugged. 'I can't see what difference it makes,' he said. 'A wee bit of paper and a wee bird can't stop you dancing.'

I wondered if he realised that to be so sanguine was to draw suspicion on to himself.

'What are you going to do for a partner after Miss Stott's wedding?' I asked. 'Isn't she rather leaving you in the lurch?'

He shrugged again. 'I'll find someone,' he said. 'There's always more lassies than laddies wanting to dance and I can train one up easy enough.'

'That does make one wonder why you got mixed up with your boss's fiancée at all,' said Alec. 'If girls are ten a penny and easy to "train up", as you put it.'

At last, we had found a chink in Mr Roland Wentworth's suit of insouciant armour. He put a finger inside his collar and eased it away from his neck before he answered.

'She wasn't his fiancée then,' he said. 'Nobody could have seen *that* coming.'

'Forgive me, Mr Watt,' I said, no longer disposed to flatter him with his choice of name, 'but Miss Stott getting engaged to a solicitor is a great deal more predictable than her deciding to go dancing with one of his clerks.'

This stung him. 'Naw, naw,' he said. 'This might be Tweetie and me's first Champs but we've been dancing longer than that. It was a good year with me before she ever clapped eyes on Julian. If it hadn't been for me she'd never have met him and she'd not be getting married at all.'

'What?' I said and I shared a look of astonishment with Alec. 'Lady Stott told us she came to the office to meet Mr Armour and fell in with you there.'

'Naw, naw,' he said again and, to be honest now that I considered it, I did not understand how that could be. 'She came to meet me from my work one night when we were all getting a bus together to a dance out Lomond way, and Julian saw her sitting there.'

'Ah,' I said. 'I see.' He gave me a very searching look then, wondering what I saw, I supposed. There seemed no reason not to tell him, in hopes of shaking out something useful, as one would bang a pepper pot hard on the tabletop to dislodge its contents. Life in a damp Scottish house had taught me many such tricks. 'She was yours first then, was she?'

He blinked and then, when he realised what I was hinting, he laughed and took an exuberant drag on his cigarette, making the gesture very cocky somehow.

'That's right,' he said. 'She's broke my heart latching on to a good match and leaving me to pine. Aye, you've cracked it. I'm sending her wee birds to pay her out for it.'

His amusement was obviously genuine and was easy to understand. His relief – for relief there was – was much harder to account for.

'So you're not punishing her for betraying you,' said Alec. 'And you're not punishing her for leaving you with the task of finding a new partner. And since her place in this competition is your place too you're not trying to nobble her. Unless – you're not trying to get rid of Miss Stott *before* the Champs because there's someone better, are you?'

'Less than a week out?' said Roland. 'Talk sense. It takes time to get used to a new partner. If I had wanted a new lass I'd have had to start a fair sight before now.'

I wondered if I believed him. The couples in the Locarno looked just as much like twined ribbons of silk fluttering and billowing over the floor when they swapped partners as when they danced with their own ones. But I supposed there were arcane details which made all the difference to the trained eye, although invisible to mine. I remembered Foxy Trotter disparaging her 'mushy top line' whatever that might be and concluded that he was telling me the truth.

'Very well, Mr Wentworth,' said Alec, clearly of the same mind. 'You are officially in the clear.'

Roland saluted him with his smoking hand, another cocky gesture.

'And therefore,' Alec went on, 'you have nothing to fear from answering all our questions.'

It was neatly done. Roland's smile dimmed a little and he put the cigarette in the corner of his mouth and crossed his arms.

'Who do you think is behind it?' Alec said.

Wentworth shook his head very slowly and deliberately, while keeping eye contact. It was the most definite refusal to comply that one could imagine.

'I'm saying nothing,' he said.

'Very well,' said Alec. 'I shan't press you. But who *do* you think is behind it? Just think about it for yourself – you don't need to say anything. What do you *think*?'

He was unused to much thinking, I was sure. He was young and handsome, what my grandmother – in a fashion which always disgusted us as girls – used to call a fine physical specimen: broad of shoulder, narrow of waist and long of leg. He wore his clothes well and had arranged his hair carefully. He was the sort who would get through life on looks and charm and never need to think very hard about anything. Charged with the task, he grew very still and solemn. After a moment, he frowned and looked up at us.

'It doesn't make any sense,' he said. 'I thought I knew who it was, but how could she do it without being seen? The door and the cloakroom and . . .'

'She couldn't?' said Alec.

Roland shook his head. 'No way,' he said. Then he leapt to his feet and held out a trembling hand, pointing to us, accusing. 'I never said anything. Youse told me I could just think it out and never say a peep. So I never. Don't youse go tricking me.'

'Our lips are sealed,' I said. 'We shan't allude to it again.' Inwardly I was cheering. 'Whether it's Miss Thwaite or Miss Bonnar, we won't breathe a w—'

'You dirty cheats,' he said. He was backing away from us

now towards the door and he got as far as to fumble with the handle before Alec loped over and held it firm against him.

'Don't be hasty,' he said. 'Remember if Mr Armour sees you, you lose your job and you're out of the competition too.'

'How?' said Roland, that curt, belligerent bark of sound. There was umbrage and injury in it, a peevish demand to be answered. It came to be a sound I dreaded in the course of the Locarno case; it came to seem like an emblem of dull thinking and the hard scrabble of desperate individuals clawing their way to what they wanted, no matter whether they had earned it or what it would cost others to give it to them.

'Because,' said Alec, 'Miss Stott is only being permitted to carry on with it since her parents so keenly want to see her settled with Mr Armour. If the wedding were to be called off, she would have no bargaining chips left and the "Champs" would be a fond memory.'

But this was far too intricate for Mr Ronald Watt and he threw it off with a toss of his head.

'Backtracking a little,' I said. 'If Miss Stott didn't meet you at Armour Ely, how exactly did she come to be part of the dancing world?'

He spent another frantic moment deciding on an answer and finally blurted out: 'Jeanne's mammy taught her.'

We knew better than to pay attention. It did not seem at all likely that Jeanne's sainted schoolmistress mother had led Tweetie down the primrose path. Had it been so, then Sir Percy, in one of his public jousting matches with his wife, would have raised it. Hugh still blames my sister Mavis for taking Donald to Brighton five years since and letting him watch dancing girls. Such nonsense, because Donald chased little girls at birthday parties as soon as he could toddle after them without falling over.

Still, it was probably worth another visit to Jeanne in her

sewing room. The pepper pot method of interrogation suggested that if I reported Mr Watt's assertion she might blurt out something useful to us in her outrage.

'Might I leave you to look after Mr Wentworth, Alec?' I said. 'I shan't leave the house, but I'd like to pay a visit.'

'There's one just over there on the right-hand side,' said Roland.

'One what?' I asked before I realised what he meant and turned – I knew it from the flood of heat – deepest red from hat brim to collar button. I do not even think he meant to be coarse; he was merely helping.

'By jings,' he said. 'You'd never do in a single-end with a stairheid cludgie.'

I had not the faintest idea what that meant and even less intention of finding out, so I left them.

I never arrived at Jeanne's sewing room, though, for as I made my way back along the passage to the landing I was rewarded by the sound of fervent whispering coming from the hall below and I peeked over the banister to see Lady Stott, sitting at the small table set up for the telephone apparatus and speaking fiercely into it.

'I've no need of reminders,' she was saying. 'For who would know that better than me?' There was a silence. 'Well, what am I supposed to *do* about it?' Another silence. 'You maybe think you're being helpful, but all you're doing is making more worry. Unless you can tell me who's behind it, you're not telling me anything I don't know. I haven't got time! I've got to get back to them. Now don't go ringing up again unless you've something to tell me.' She banged the earpiece back into the cradle and stared at the instrument, chewing her lip and ruminating furiously.

'Lady Stott?' I said, a clear measure of how far I have come from where my careful upbringing left me, where eavesdropping is beyond anything except perhaps cheating at cards and even accidental overhearings are so shameful that one automatically starts to sing, stamp and whistle whenever one is drawing near the spot where a telephone is known to be. And if one cannot avoid catching a snatch of another's conversation one simply pretends not to have. How I have sunk, now that I can tiptoe up close enough to listen and then boldly ask questions about what I have heard.

'Mrs Gilver, you're supposed to be looking after—' She shot an anguished look at the library door as I came tripping downstairs.

'Mr Osborne is taking care of matters,' I said. 'Who was that?'

'I beg your pardon!' she said. 'I can't see that it's any of your business whom I speak to in my own home.'

'Only I wondered if you were discussing the topic in which we share a mutual interest.'

'I was not,' she said stoutly.

'Unless you can tell me who is behind what?' I said.

'It's nothing to do with' – she shot another look and lowered her voice – 'Theresa. That was a private family matter, quite separate.'

'It sounded urgent,' I said.

'Yes,' she said. 'A family crisis, I suppose you could say. But no concern of yours. Now, I must go back to dear Julian. He'll be wondering what's happened to me.'

'And I'll go back to the task in hand,' I said, but she was looking at me very speculatively.

'You could come and meet him,' she said, looking me up and down. 'I'm sure he wouldn't mind if you were introduced to him.'

My affront made me brusque. 'On the contrary, he would find it startling. You don't introduce women to men, Lady Stott. You present men to women.'

'Is that right?' she said. 'Even a detective such as yourself and a lawyer like him?'

'Even a duke and a shop girl,' I said. 'The only male person

109

I have ever been presented to in my life was His Majesty the King.'

She had started across the floor towards the library but that stopped her in her tracks.

'You never have!' she said. 'Really and truly? You've met the King?'

'At court, when I came out,' I said. 'And once more at a ball, but there were so many people that evening, it was simply a sea of faces for the poor man.'

'Well, I never,' she said. 'Come and let me present Julian then, even if he's not what you're used to.' She set off again and made it another few feet before she stopped and wheeled around. 'You've got your confidentiality clause stopping you saying anything you shouldn't to him.'

'How are you going to explain my presence?' I asked.

'Why would I need to?' she demanded. 'Why shouldn't Sir Percy know Mrs Gilver? And anyway, dear Julian is far too courteous to ask questions. He was beautifully brought up.'

With me firmly put in my place as to both rank and manners, then, we entered the library. It was a monument to the newness of Sir Percy's wealth. The yards of unread books in red binding not only matched all the other books but also the curtains, the background colour of the carpet and half the stripes on the wallpaper. The leather chairs were new enough still to have a scent about them and they squeaked like wet balloons when one sat down or shifted more than an inch. The desk across one corner was fitted up with exquisite pens in ivory stands and inkwells quite dry and unmarked by a single spot. Even the blotter was fat with unused sheets, as plump as a feather bed.

As to the paintings: they were far from the usual portraits covering hundreds of years of the family, prosperous gener-ations corresponding with enormous full-length oils, horse and dogs thrown in for good measure, lean times during the stewardship of rakes and gamblers showing up in the form of watercolours, ink sketches and even paper silhouettes worked by the unmarried sisters of the house.

The Stotts had had their own portraits done first, one assumed. The two large pictures showing Sir Percy and his lady sitting solidly in chairs, staring outwards, were hung in pride of place above the chimneypiece. Then, it seemed, pleased with the results, they had gone to an auction house somewhere and bought enough of the same to fill the walls above the bookcases all around. There were two more couples – solid and staring – and three stout and bewhiskered men in chains of office, all painted within the last forty years and all looking rather startled to have found themselves in this library together. It looked like nothing so much as the senior common room of a rich Oxford college which can afford to have every chancellor commemorated and must inevitably then find wall space for them.

Lady Stott cleared her throat and I came back to attention.

'Julian, dear,' she said, ignoring what I had told her, 'may I present our friend Mrs Gilver, who is visiting? Mrs Gilver, this is Mr Armour.'

'Sorry,' I said. 'I was wool-gathering, admiring your pictures. How do you do, Mr Armour.'

He had leapt to his feet as we entered and remained standing while Sir Percy plumped back down into his squeaking armchair. As he came forward I thought I detected a smirk in response to my mention of the pictures, but he was perfectly composed as we shook hands.

'How do you do,' he said. Then there was an unmissable pause while he tried to fit me into the Stotts' circle somewhere and failed.

'Mrs Gilver is visiting from Perthshire,' said Sir Percy.

Mr Armour nodded, but Perthshire was no sort of explanation at all and the quizzical look deepened. He was a handsome man, and I found myself thinking that his and Theresa's children would be angels, if the sons caught their father's height and chiselled bones and the girls their mother's delicacy and soft sweetness. Of course, it can just as often go the other way and Theresa and Julian, if they were very unlucky, might end up with soft puddings of sons and great galumphing carthorses of daughters, and be lumbered for life with the lot of them, despite Sir Percy's money.

'Whereabouts in Perthshire are you?' said Julian.

It was a perfectly acceptable opening gambit but I did not miss Theresa's small sigh or the fact that she had a magazine open upon her lap and that she turned a page while he spoke. She was either very sure of herself or she was quite indifferent.

'Oh, the middle of nowhere,' I said, sitting. 'Between Pitlochry and Dunkeld. The village is called Gilverton.'

The Stotts looked very impressed at that and it was lucky that Mr Armour did not notice because if I were really their friend they should have known it of old.

'Are you related to Hugh Gilver?' said Julian. Usually when one goes a-hunting acquaintanceship upon meeting a stranger, one is pleased or even relieved to find some. In this case, Julian began to look troubled. His dark brows lowered and he turned his head as though he could see me more clearly if he did not look straight on.

'I'm his wife,' I said, and the frown deepened.

'I'm sure we've never met,' said Julian, 'and yet I seem to have an idea . . .'

One could have bottled the electricity in the room and taken it camping to boil a kettle. Theresa was turned to stone, more still than she had been when she lay in a faint. Sir Percy and Lady Stott suddenly looked as blank as their portraits on the walls behind them, only the shiver of her jet beads and the wink-wink of his watch chain showing that both were breathing fast and shallow. I tried hard to return Julian's gaze with an open smile as though I could not imagine what he was thinking of.

'Are you a rose grower?' I asked, supposing I had probably sat through enough of Hugh's enthusiasm to put on a creditable show of being another. He shook his head. 'And you're the wrong age to have been up at school with my sons,' I went on.

He nodded and was almost ready to let the troubling memory go when Lady Stott stepped in and ruined everything.

'Well, that's a mystery,' she said and Julian's eyebrows shot up into his hair.

'Mystery!' he said. 'You're the lady detective, aren't you?'

Sir Percy put his head in his hands and groaned. Tweetie fired a look fit to drop a stag her mother's way.

'What's this?' said Lady Stott with considerably more presence of mind than her husband.

'Oh, dear,' I said, simpering at Julian. There was really no other word for it. 'I'm afraid I hadn't yet admitted my recent exploits to my old friends. Yes, I confess it's true. I've been making a bit of pin money by running a sort of enquiry agency. Are you terribly shocked?'

Sir Percy had recovered. 'Ocht, there's all sorts doing all sorts these days,' he said. 'Everything's changed since the war.'

His wife nodded but Theresa spoiled it by giving her father a murderous look, understandable since it must have been sickening to hear him so philosophical about my doings when he would like to keep his daughter in a tower.

Besides, Julian would not have been mollified if Theresa had pulled off an act worthy of the West End stage. He was beyond noticing anything that was passing in the rest of the room. He was horrified. His cheeks drained of colour, leaving his complexion yellow and revolting. It was not helped by the sudden sheen of sweat which appeared as a film on his lip and as beads – actual droplets of moisture – on his forehead.

'Heavens, Mr Armour,' I said, 'I didn't expect the news to cause such consternation.'

The Stotts were carrying on a whispered disagreement of their own.

'Consternation?' said Julian in a voice of great wretchedness, quaking with fear. 'Not at all. I'm simply . . . Not at all.'

'One almost wonders what you've been up to,' I said. I do not often look forward to advancing age, but I do relish the prospect of the day when I can be grand, plain and simple, and do not have to worry that in trying to appear playful I end up sounding like some superannuated coquette.

Julian did not answer. Slowly but surely all three Stotts had noticed his distress and there was a long empty moment of sheer wriggling misery for everyone, which no one could bring to an end: not the poor Stotts, certainly; not Julian who was so pale and waxy that I started to look around for a receptacle should his stomach give way completely; not Theresa for all her careful education; and heaven knows not me.

I could not say how they managed it. I never found out. I bolted.

13

'Well, I think I shall just slip upstairs and see dear Jeannie,' I said, standing. I sauntered out of the library, then picked up speed and flew upstairs, grateful for the thick carpet which deadened the sound of my flight.

'Alec!' I said, bursting back into the ballroom, where he and Mr Wentworth were whiling away the time, sensibly enough I suppose, on dancing practice, Alec leading and Mr Wentworth dancing the lady's steps. 'Go downstairs and see what you make of Julian Armour. I think it's *him*. I'm sure it's him. He found out I was a detective and he almost passed out.'

'What?' said Roland. 'How?'

But Alec was off already, shrugging himself back into his coat as he went.

'How?' Roland said again. 'Why would Julian send things like that to Tweetie?'

'If he found out about the dancing, nothing would be less surprising,' I said. 'Not many men could watch you and Miss Stott dancing and believe it was a purely professional partnership.'

'You've no idea what you're talking about,' said Wentworth. 'How could he get into the Locarno unseen?'

I opened my mouth to argue but then considered that he was right. Before I could try another tack, though, I heard Alec returning. I should know his footsteps anywhere.

'He's gone,' he said. 'And the Stotts are down there looking like walking wounded. Dandy, what on earth's going on?'

'Right then,' said Roland. 'If he's gone I can get back to work.' He went to the door, leaned his head out and whistled as though hailing a cab.

'I'm coming,' said Theresa's voice in the distance. 'But I'm not a sheepdog.'

Wentworth grinned and swaggered back over to the gramophone, where he wound it furiously and then set the needle down. I jumped at the blare of sound just as Theresa re-entered the room, kicking off the buttoned shoes she had put on for Julian and slipping out of her cardigan.

'Mrs Gilver,' she said, 'since you have blotted your copybook completely, you might make it up to me by finding Jeanne and telling her to bring me my dancing shoes.'

'Miss Stott,' I said, bristling. 'I was invited into the library by your mother who is not only a snob but also a show-off. And I fail to see how shaking clear proof of guilt out of your fiancé is blotting my copybook in the slightest.'

'Guilt?' she said. 'Julian? What rot.'

I became aware of Alec's hand on my arm and turned to see him giving me the impish look with which he tells me he has thought of something. I looked back at Theresa.

'Very well,' I said, 'I shall give your message to Miss McNab.'

But Theresa and Roly had already withdrawn their attention from me. At a particularly complicated little run of notes in the gramophone record they locked eyes with one another, nodding along in time and tapping their feet.

'I think you're right,' said Watt. 'If we go into it out of a featherstep instead of a fishtail there's probably just time. It's a difficult run to get out of too, mind you.'

We left them to it.

As we crossed the landing I could hear the Stotts well into one of their bickering matches. This one sounded heartfelt, as well it might after the recent debacle, but I thought the familiarity of it would soothe them.

'Jeanne's in cahoots with Julian,' Alec said. 'If you're right that he knows about Tweetie dancing then he has motive but she has the means. She's playing tricks on his behalf, I'll bet you.'

'In which case,' I said, picking up speed, 'she should be undone or at least discomfited to hear that her accomplice has shown his hand. Oh Alec, if you'd seen the creature! He looked as grey as a peeled prawn.'

'Don't, Dandy,' Alec said. He spoke quietly, for we were now in the narrow corridor leading to Jeanne's room. 'We can't all be brave, strong and true. The poor chap must have thought he'd walked right into a trap.'

I stopped dead and stared at him. 'Poor chap? Sending nasty messages and threats to his own fiancée? Death threats, Alec.'

'Perhaps he had a bad war,' Alec said. 'There are plenty walking around looking fine who're actually sicker than any old soldier in a bathchair.'

'I am beyond astonishment,' I said. 'A poison pen and a bully.'

'Perhaps uncharacteristically, though,' Alec said. 'Perhaps he needs Sir Percy's money so he's got to stick with Theresa even when she's making such a fool of him, thinking he doesn't know. And so he pays her back.'

I did not answer, for I was shocked to hear such callousness and, more than that, I was troubled to find Alec and myself so far adrift in our view of the matter. I filed it away to pick over later and knocked on Jeanne's door.

Perhaps I knocked too hard, rapped even, taking out my annoyance on blameless painted pine. Certainly, when we entered it was to find Jeanne sitting up very straight with a startled look upon her face.

She was in the late stages of making a brown-paper parcel, tying it securely with stout twine. Immediately my mind flew to the idea that there might be evidence to be got rid of. I have never been able to think of a better way to do it than to send a parcel off into the world with a fictitious return address and plenty of postage. Jeanne, however, tied off her knots very calmly and made no attempt to shift the parcel out of sight.

'Mr Armour was just downstairs,' I said, by way of greeting.

'Asking for me?' said Jeanne.

'Why should he do that?' Alec chipped in. But I could tell already that she had the better of us.

'I'm sure I can't imagine,' she said, 'but if not then why did you tramp all the way up here to tell me?'

'Do you know him well?' I asked her. She shrugged. 'You've never gone to his office on any of your days in town when Miss Stott is dancing?'

'I've no need of a solicitor,' said Jeanne. 'I have no property, nothing in trust, no inheritance.'

Either she was choosing, wilfully, to misunderstand me or she really could not imagine Julian the man rather than Mr Armour the lawyer, but she seemed sincere. Alec's neat theory began to dissolve before our eyes.

'Actually, I'm glad to see you,' she went on. 'I was thinking of coming down and trying to find you.'

'To tell us something?' said Alec. He sat down opposite her at the little table and had the cheek to nod at my bag, where I carried my much maligned notebook. I was to record the details for his later consideration it seemed, while he concentrated on extracting them.

'To share an idea, anyway,' said Jeanne. 'I've been thinking more about the threats, sitting up here alone.'

I could not say whether she meant to inject pathos over her reduced station in life into every single line of her conversation, or whether it had become a habit over the years since her parents died, but it was hard not to roll my eyes as she served up another slice of it.

'We'd be delighted to hear it,' said Alec, either oblivious to the annoyance or hiding it well.

'I've been thinking about who might be behind them, you know,' said Jeanne. 'Mr Hodge, Miss Christie, Miss Bonnar or Mr Bunyan.'

'Or Lorrison or Wentworth,' said Alec.

Jeanne shook her head. 'I can't imagine that Roland would put his own chances in the Champs at risk by upsetting his partner and Lorrison would push his own grandmother off a cliff before he made any more trouble for the Locarno.'

This did not quite chime with what Lorrison had told us, for he had seemed unconcerned by Tweetie's plight, sure that he could replace her.

'Now, Jamesie and Alicia weren't there every time something happened,' Jeanne went on. 'So that counts them out. And leaves Beryl and Bert. Either of them is capable of the wren. It's not a very sophisticated matter, is it? To take a real bird and dress it up to evoke the idea of "Tweetie". Anyone might have done that.'

'And what about you?' I said, remembering how unflinchingly she had bent over the dead wren as Alec held it that first day.

'Oh, indeed,' she said. 'But the book is another matter. I can't see Bert Bunyan knowing of such a thing, can you? I'm sure he's heard the rhyme but would he really think of it's being a book and go out to buy one? He would not. And he'd be too young to have had that edition of the book lying around, left over from childhood.'

'Unless it belonged to a parent,' I said.

Alec raised a hand a little, telling me not to interrupt in case I stemmed the flow, but Miss McNab welcomed my contribution.

'Exactly,' she said. 'My parents or your parents. But Bert's parents? Never.'

'Nor Miss Bonnar's, from what she told me,' I said.

'Ah,' said Jeanne. 'Well, we don't have to take Miss Bonnar's word for it, thankfully. Because even if a little girl from her family might have treasured *Cock Robin*, there's the prayer card.'

'It was pretty girlish too,' I said.

'It certainly was,' said Jeanne. 'But what it wasn't was ecumenical. Beryl wouldn't have had such a thing in her possession. She wouldn't dare. Her father would kill her.'

Alec said nothing; he is an innocent in these matters.

'I see,' I said, nodding. Then I put on my most guileless face. 'That really does just leave you then, Miss McNab, doesn't it? A girl brought up in a bookish house who need not view the prayer card as an out-and-out tinderbox. Is this a confession?'

Jeanne turned on a sixpence. 'The threats were a deliberate campaign,' she said. 'The culprit might well have procured the card and the book. You spoke as though they were used because they were lying around handy.'

'We both did,' I agreed. 'And, given that, you are the only likely person.'

Jeanne, after another sixpence, smiled triumphantly. 'You've forgotten someone,' she said. 'A female of the right sort who was there every day.'

'Miss Thwaite,' said Alec. 'But wouldn't the dancers have noticed if she had left the room? That's what we concluded.'

Miss McNab snorted. 'The *dancers* wouldn't notice if Miss Thwaite burst into flames,' she said. 'So long as she's there playing when they say stop and back when they say start again, she could turn cartwheels around the floor in between times and they wouldn't see a thing.'

This accorded perfectly with what we had seen of the dancers, of their concentration and their oblivion to all around.

'And now she's gone,' Alec said. 'I suppose Mr Lorrison might know where to find her, but he's not the most helpful chap I've ever met.'

'She hasn't really gone,' said Miss McNab. 'That is, the

pianist has gone but the seamstress wouldn't dare. Not when dear Miss Stott has just changed her mind about every bit of her silly costume days before the show.'

'Do you know where she is?' I said, sitting forward with great eagerness.

Miss McNab smiled her sly smile and pushed the brown-paper parcel across the table towards us.

'Not only do I know,' she said, 'but I have to get this frock and trimmings to her this afternoon. I don't suppose you'd like to deliver it for me?'

We were well on our way, with Alec driving and me clutching the parcel like a puppy, before we began to wonder if we had been . . .

'Played like a pair of trout,' Alec said, after searching for the right phrase a while. 'What was the great revelation about the prayer card, by the way?'

'Denomination,' I said. 'It must have the name of a church stamped on the back. Did you notice, by any chance?' Alec had taken charge of the items of evidence and they were currently in the dressing table in his hotel room, where Barrow had been instructed to place them.

He shook his head. 'It seemed the least interesting of the three exhibits,' he said. 'The sort of ten-a-penny little oddment one might find anywhere.'

'That's because you're English,' I said, 'and you very rightly imagine that all Christian churches are part of the same communion.'

'Whereas you are Scottish by marriage to a Scot and mother to two more,' said Alec.

He does not often tease Hugh, for he continues to feel a bond of brotherhood with him based on nothing more than their being men. It is that much more delicious to me, therefore, on those occasions when he reveals that he is really *my* friend and ally; kind to Hugh, but mine.

'We should have studied all three immediately,' I said. 'Holmes would be disgusted with us.'

'Holmes would have dusted for fingerprints too,' Alec said. It was becoming a theme with him. He had been pestering our friend Inspector Hutchinson for months for some training and a shopping list of equipment. Hutchinson, with his usual pith, had said: 'Leave the smudges to us.'

'Let's go over them with a fine-toothed comb as soon as we get back tonight, shall we?' I said. 'Rather late in the day.'

'And in the meantime, Miss Thwaite,' said Alec. 'If we ever find her.'

We were a long way from Balmoral now, and even from Partick and the good red sandstone streets where Mrs Munn mourned her lost love. This was Springburn, high on a hill looking down over the engine works towards the shipyards on the Clyde, and the tenements here had no railings, laurels, or brass pulls at the door. They were flat cliffs of soot-blackened stone, even the windows filmed over by the endless smuts and smoke that poured out of the chimneys to the south.

But the same bustling Glasgow life went on around them. There were fewer carts, since the women of Springburn carried their own shopping home in capacious baskets instead of waiting for grocers to deliver, and there were no motorcars at all besides ours, so that the streets were host to great tribes of children playing undisturbed at their mysterious games. They stopped open-mouthed and gawped at my Cowley, then fell into step behind it and made a procession as we went along. We had had no thought of a stealthy approach to Miss Thwaite and it was just as well because, by the time we neared the heart of the district, there must have been forty little followers.

None of them was barefoot, and none so ragged as the pair who had accosted us outside the Locarno. The boys were in jerseys and long stockings, rather thick for June except that most of them had pushed their sleeves up to their elbows and their gaiters down to their ankles or at least had become thus dishevelled in the course of play. The little girls were neater, with rough pinafores over their dresses, pinny strings tied in bows and dress cuffs buttoned, and their long black stockings were evidently fastened to something under their skirts. Not corsets, I trusted, judging from the way they ran and sang and tumbled over only to pick themselves up again.

Miss Thwaite lived halfway along a short street which led to a dead-end at the railway line. There was a grocer's shop on the corner and we came under the gaze of a handful of women who had congregated there to pass the time of day on their way to or from their shopping.

'Fine day,' said the boldest of these.

Alec tipped his hat, causing an outbreak of giggles. Some of the women could hardly have been twenty, despite being dressed in the same headscarves and house-aprons as those three times their age. It was only the hair rollers peeping out from under the scarves which spoke to their youth.

'Are youse lost?' shouted another woman.

'We've come to see Miss Thwaite,' I called back. And my accursed voice caused the usual ripple of interest and amusement.

'Oh my, my!' said the bold one, swishing her skirts and thereby mocking me.

'Ignore them,' said Alec grimly. He hoisted the paper parcel into his arms and marched from the car to the close mouth. Inside, there was no floor paint nor china tiles. The steps under our feet were bare stone and the walls were distempered, brown to shoulder height and cream above. It was less gloomy than the approach to Foxy Trotter's house, however, because here there were windows on the stairway, one at every half-landing, and someone had stretched net across the bottom halves of these and had hung cotton curtains too – rather old and faded, but neatly hemmed to just the right length and gathered into precise folds with tucks along the top. I guessed at a seamstress's hand.

The same hand had done a great deal to make the best of the little house. It was rather cramped, the hall being no more than a square of four doors and no room even for an umbrella stand. The facing door led merely to a cupboard, where Miss Thwaite stowed Alec's overcoat and hat, and I surmised that there was just one room to the front and one to the back. It was to the back room, the kitchen, that Miss Thwaite ushered us.

'I hope you'll excuse me,' she said, 'for my sewing is laid out in the parlour and if you would have wanted a cigarette I couldn't allow it.'

We assured her that the kitchen was fine and seated ourselves. It was more than fine, in fact: cosy from the fire burning in the range under the high mantel; smelling of lavender water from the ironing which was draped over the dolly above; and lightly spiced from a tray of scones cooling under a tea cloth on the table. The furnishings were mean enough, to be sure, a deal table with two wooden chairs, a painted sideboard and just one armchair near the fire, but Miss Thwaite's talents had provided many comforts. There were embroidered cushions anywhere one might come to rest and a little wooden footstool had been transformed with tapestry and horsehair stuffing. On the table and sideboard and on the shelves beside the sink there were doilies and lace-edged lining panels and the very curtain that hid the sink legs, and no doubt a pail or two, was as nicely tucked and hemmed as the curtains out on the stair, and as well-judged as to length. When Miss Thwaite opened a drawer in the table to take out a tray cloth I saw a pile of more than a dozen in all colours and all pressed into neat sharp rectangles. My own maids would have been proud to make such an even stack of cloth, for a maid worth her salt is much pained by oddments. I learned this when Becky explained the need for more linens to keep all the piles the same height in the cupboard and prevent it looking untidy. Hugh had queried the bill from the haberdasher's; it being one of the greater annoyances of life at Gilverton that we have never had a housekeeper and that Hugh therefore has a hand in such things.

'We were very sorry to hear that you lost your position,' I said to Miss Thwaite. 'Very sorry indeed if we had a hand in it.'

She considered this for a while before she answered. She was at the sink swirling hot water around in a teapot while the kettle came back to the boil. I found myself hoping that some of the spiced scones would be coming our way, for this case was turning out to be as badly catered as Alec had feared and my insides were beginning to pinch.

'It's as well,' she said in the end. 'It was convenient for picking up sewing and dropping it off again but I'm better off out of it.'

'And now that you are "out of it",' said Alec, 'do you think you can say a little more about what it is?'

She dashed the water down the sink and set the teapot on the board to the side. Then she came and sat down in the armchair. Alec and I had taken the wooden chairs at the table and were higher than she was, looking down. She seemed smaller than ever and childlike too.

'I will,' she said. 'I think I must.' The teapot was forgotten and the scones lay abandoned under their cloth as Miss Thwaite began to speak.

'It started the same way with Foxy,' she said.

'What did?' I prompted her.

'A note and a little book and then the fox itself.'

'A dead fox?' said Alec.

'A fur,' said Miss Thwaite. 'But made to look like it. Nasty, you know? Like the bird with the spangles. Nastier than you can explain unless you've seen it.'

'Which we have,' I said, 'and we agree with you – it was horrid.'

'And then he fell down the stairs,' said Miss Thwaite. We nodded. 'But that's not all. He was unwell beforehand.' We nodded again. Foxy Trotter had told us this much. He had left the dance floor feeling ill. 'And he fell down the stairs,' Miss Thwaite repeated. Her brow was drawn up in worry and she chewed at her lip. She was so very close to saying what was troubling her but something was getting in the way.

'Do you mean that he was so anxious about the threats to Foxy that it made him ill?' I tried.

She shook her head.

'Combined with nerves?' added Alec. 'I should imagine every dancer would be light-headed on the day itself.'

'No,' she said. 'He really was ill. But he was *made* ill. He was made too ill to dance. And that's what led to him dying.'

'That's it!' I said. 'That's what was bothering me when Mrs Munn was speaking about it, Alec. She let the doctor believe that he simply tripped and fell. But, for one thing, there's nothing to trip on at the top of the Locarno stairs. The carpet is close-fitting and there's no rug. And what those two girls on the street said is true: sure-footedness was his stock-in-trade.'

Miss Thwaite was nodding. 'He fell,' she said, 'but he didn't trip. He fell because he was faint and he was faint because—'

'Someone slipped him a powder?' said Alec.

Miss Thwaite gave Alec a look of gratitude that lit up her wrinkled little face and showed us a flash of the girl she was once. 'Yes,' she said. 'At least in a manner of speaking.'

'Who?' I could not help asking.

But Miss Thwaite shook her head. 'I can't say any more than that,' she said. 'But someone needs to warn Tweetie and Roly. I don't want one of them to go the same way but I don't want to get mixed up in it. I wouldn't have got myself mixed up in it last time except I wasn't thinking straight that night and I've ended up in possession of something I shouldn't have and I don't want and I don't know what to do about it.'

Alec and I were now as still as cats stalking a bird on the lawn. Neither of us wanted to be the one who spoke and sent Miss Thwaite fluttering off into the trees out of our reach. Alec, in the end, gave in first. And thank goodness he did because I had assumed that what she had come into possession of was unwelcome knowledge and what she might do with it was tell us.

'Give it to us to take care of, Miss Thwaite,' Alec said. 'And we need never tell a soul who we got it from.'

Even then I thought perhaps he might be speaking figuratively, as of a mental burden she could pass to us to carry.

'Someone might guess,' she whispered. 'Or there might be fingerprints.'

I tried hard not to let my astonishment show upon my face. I did not understand exactly but I knew enough to be sure that we were just about to come in for a bona fide clue.

'I'm not going to give it to you,' Miss Thwaite went on. 'But I shall show it to you. To convince you how real my fears are.'

She got to her feet and went over to the sideboard, then knelt in front of it and, opening one of the doors, reached far back into its innards. I could see stacked sets of china and some of the flat cardboard boxes which contain tea napkins and cake slices. Miss Thwaite reached past them and pulled out a small toffee tin. She picked at the lid with her fingernails and pulled it off, then showed us the contents.

'It's a handkerchief,' she said. 'Leonard's handkerchief. He dropped it on the landing just before he fell and I picked it up. I thought he had tripped on it and I didn't want anyone else to, so I picked it up and tucked it into my pocket. I thought no more of it but when I heard that he died, I admit I wept. I took out the handkerchief, put my face in it and wept. And I knew someone had deliberately killed him.'

'How?' I breathed.

Miss Thwaite lifted the handkerchief and buried her face in it briefly, then looked up at us again.

'I can't prove it,' she said. 'And without proof I'm not brave enough to tell you.'

'My dear Miss Thwaite, if you knew the things people had told us over the years,' Alec said. 'We are quite used to keeping secrets. There's no need for bravery.'

But she shook her head and folded her arms and there was no shifting her.

'Well, how tantalising and yet how ultimately pointless,' I said as we clattered back down the stairs to the street moments later. 'I really thought we were going to learn something, not . . .'

'. . . be shown a piece of the true cross,' Alec said. 'I know.' Then, after another moment's musing, he went on: 'Do you think she's protecting someone? Or just frightened?'

'Everyone's frightened in this case,' I said. We were back on the street and I stared up at the tenement front wondering which window was Miss Thwaite's. 'Theresa, for obvious reasons, the Stotts likewise, Lorrison, poor Roly – at least, he's frightened when he's at the Locarno. Julian Armour is petrified. Foxy Trotter too.'

'Everyone except Jeanne and Beryl,' said Alec, climbing into the motorcar. 'We should go back to Foxy now that Miss Thwaite has revealed all about the threats and ask her whom she suspects.'

'After we've taken another close look at the card, the wren and especially the book,' I said. 'I didn't care for Jeanne having more to say than us on the subject, did you?'

'To the Grand,' Alec agreed. 'Supper on a tray and an early night? Try Foxy in the morning?'

I turned the motorcar in the direction of Union Street, little knowing that we were far from done for the day.

14

When we opened the door to Alec's room, it was to find a remarkable sight, which put the prayer card's origins quite out of our heads. Barrow in his shirtsleeves was standing in the middle of the carpet – and there was a good deal of carpet to stand in the middle of, for the furniture had been pushed back to the walls – and was holding the limp body of Grant at an acute angle, just her feet on the floor, her arms trailing down and her head flung backwards, like a lily wilting on its stem.

'Grant!' I squeaked.

'Barrow?' said Alec, sounding flabbergasted.

Grant turned her face towards us and spoke quite normally, utterly as though she were standing upright as expected and not at all as though she were being held off the ground by Barrow's strong arms in their rolled-up sleeves.

'We're practising in case we need to help out,' she said. 'Madam. You've just missed our tango.' She put her arms around Barrow's neck and he lifted her back on to her feet and stepped away.

'How unfortunate for us,' I said. 'What are you wearing?'

'It's what they're all wearing now,' she said. 'These are called floats.' She flapped her arms up and down like a swan trying to take off from a lake and the wisps of gauze attached around her arms on bracelets fluttered up and down.

'And the rest?' I said, for the arm wisps were not the half of it. Grant was in nothing but wisps from neck to knee, except that because the wisps grew wispier at the edges, her neck and her knees were not so much clothed as decorated. I was surprised that Barrow could look at her without blushing.

'Quite a standard sort of frock for the Latin dances,' she said.

I opened my mouth once or twice but inspiration did not strike and so nothing came out of it. Grant did, it is true, aid us in a recent case by carrying out the sort of impersonation known as 'going undercover' and gave, it is also true, an outstanding performance which helped us no end. But I saw no necessity for the rigmarole going on in Alec's bedroom now.

'Put the furniture back, Barrow,' said Alec, apparently agreeing with me, 'and we'll say no more about it.' Barrow had already unrolled his sleeves, buttoned his cuffs and slipped back into his coat. He swept his hair back with the palm of one hand and nodded curtly.

Alec went over to his dressing table and opened the top drawer to take out the pieces of evidence. The wren was now inside a tea caddy in case it made its presence felt although, in my experience, creatures as small as wrens and even shrews and field mice never become noisome.

'Need I open this?' said Alec.

I shook my head but was distracted by an idea I could not quite bring into being.

'You've got that look again, Dandy,' Alec said. 'What is it?'

'Will you never learn!' I burst out. 'I've told you over and over again that that look means I'm trying to grab hold of an elusive thought and asking me what it is chases it off completely. I keep telling you.'

'You sound like Lady Stott,' said Alec. He was studying the prayer card and I joined him, squinting to make out the name embossed on the back of it.

'St Andrew's East,' he said. 'Catholic? Since it's a saint.'

'I shouldn't think so,' I said. 'Patron saint of Scotland after all. Grant?' They were almost finished with the furniture now,

Barrow wiping away handprints from the edge of the writing table and Grant straightening the fringes of the rug which had been rolled up while they were dancing. 'Have you made any friends among the hotel staff yet?'

'Oh yes, madam,' she said. 'The day-shift housekeeper is a bit of a card. The stories she can tell.'

'Excellent. Is she Glaswegian?'

'I think the whole populace could go on the halls with a comedy turn,' said Grant.

'Could you ask her about this church for us – discreetly? We'd like to know whether St Andrew's in Alexandra Parade is Catholic or Protestant. It won't be Anglican with that name.'

'Certainly, madam,' Grant said and, sensing the chance of a cosy chat over the amusing housekeeper's tea table, sanctioned by her mistress and counting as work no less, she took off.

'I'll go and see how they're getting on with your travelling clothes, sir,' said Barrow. 'I left strict instructions with the boot boy downstairs but he didn't seem to be listening.' As he left he gave a sort of bow with an accompanying heel click that owed more to Gilbert and Sullivan than to a valet.

'He's getting more and more eccentric,' I said. 'And he's hardly thirty. One never thinks of eccentric youngsters somehow.' I took the prayer card out of Alec's hands and turned it over and over in mine trying to decide if there was any more it could tell us.

Alec was doing the same with Cock Robin and it was his study which bore fruit.

'How interesting,' he said. 'Look at this, Dandy.'

I peered at where he was pointing. On the inside cover of the little booklet was a very smudged purple oval stamp of the kind used by subscription libraries to prevent theft. It had not been successful in this case, evidently.

'What does it say?' I said. 'It's terribly unclear.'

'It starts with a G,' said Alec, 'and the second word starts with a B.'

'Great Britain?'

'There's a third word. C . . . ?'

'Great British?'

'Too long. It might be "Girls". "Girls and Boys"?'

'That makes sense anyway,' I said. 'Since it's a children's book. Do you think if we decipher it it might lead us straight to the culprit? Someone who attended St Andrew's Church and frequented a Girls' and Boys' library there, perhaps?'

'It seems a bit of a stretch,' said Alec. 'The card and book might both have been bought at a jumble sale for all we know.'

There was a knock at the door then and assuming that it would be Grant returning with news from the comical housekeeper I distractedly called for her to enter without looking. It was Alec who turned first and saw Mrs Leonard Munn, Foxy Trotter herself, standing there.

'Forgive me,' she said.

'How did you know where we were staying?' I asked her. Then I shook the distraction out of my head and drew her in by her free arm. She was carrying a large carpet bag in the other hand and whether from the weight of it or from some other distress she was grey-faced and swaying.

'I'll ring for some tea and perhaps some brandy too?' said Alec as I ushered Mrs Munn into a chair and took the carpet bag from her.

'This has gone on long enough,' she said. 'If I can help put a stop to it I must do so.'

'I'm so very glad you've come to us voluntarily, Mrs Munn,' I said. 'Because we've heard from other quarters about the threats you received last year.'

'Other quarters?' she said. 'I thought everyone at that Locarno was too scared to say peep.'

'Miss Thwaite is made of stern stuff,' I said. Mrs Munn's eyes widened. 'And she has something from that dreadful night. A keepsake, I suppose you'd say. She saved it. Almost by accident, but it seems to have made her feel personally connected to the tragic events.'

Mrs Munn nodded. 'I wondered about that,' she said. 'I never knew where it had got to. I hate to think of poor wee Miss Thwaite worrying and fretting. And too scared to speak.'

'As we said, Mrs Munn,' said Alec. 'It's speaks well of you that you came.'

'Oh, call me Foxy,' she said. 'Everyone always has from when I was a wee bit thing and I don't want to be the Widow Munn who'll never dance the foxtrot again.'

'Childhood?' said Alec.

'That's right,' said Foxy. 'There were three of us. I was Foxy for my red hair, my big sister was Puddy because she was such a wee round dumpling and my brother was Goldilocks because of his flaxen curls. It started as a joke but he got Goldie until the day he died. Puddy stamped hers out once she was grown.'

'I'm not surprised,' I said.

'Not that her christened name is much better,' said Foxy. Then she came back from her childhood reverie and, blinking only a little, she lifted her chin and prepared to face us.

'As you've heard, I was threatened,' she said. 'First there was a card.' She dived into the carpet bag at her feet and drew out a small envelope, the kind ladies use for day-to-day correspondence.

I took it and removed its contents. It was a Christmas card of old-fashioned design, a gold lozenge containing a coloured picture of a wintry hunting scene, pink coats and horses flying over hedges, while in the foreground a bushy red tail disappeared into a thicket. I turned it over and read what was written on the reverse in thick black ink: 'Look out, little fox!' I showed it to Alec.

'How unsettling that must have been,' he said. 'Rather nasty, that exclamation mark, isn't it. As though it were a friendly greeting. Might I see the envelope?'

'Oh, it didn't come in the envelope,' said Foxy. 'I just put it in there to keep it.'

I nodded and once again I could feel an idea shifting inside me, lumbering forward in my brain, but still too far back to be hooked by me.

'Go on,' I said. 'What happened next?'

'Next the book,' she said and dipped into the carpet bag again. '*The Tale of Mr Tod*. About a fox, you see.' It was the familiar little white book, without its dust jacket as all nursery books tend to be, and bearing that beloved picture of the gentleman himself climbing the stile.

'This isn't quite as . . .' I tried hard to think of a different word but failed '. . . nasty as Cock Robin, though,' I said. I was very well familiar with it for my sons preferred the manly exploits of Mr Tod and Jeremy Fisher to the domestic travails of the bad mice or Miss Moppet and I had read it and then listened to each of them read it many times. I was sure that the final score of the wrestling match between fox and badger was left to the reader's imagination.

'Look at the last page,' said Foxy, handing it to me.

I turned to the end of the story where the Bouncer family are safely in their burrow having dinner. On the facing page was more of the thick black ink but this time it had been used to draw the crude outline of a gravestone. Written upon it were only five letters: 'F.T. RIP'.

'Did you not think of making a report?' said Alec.

Foxy Trotter shook her head. 'There was only a week to go to the Champs,' she said. 'I didn't have time to think about anything except practice and my costumes and trying to find out if it was true that Mr Silvester himself was going to be there from London. That's what everyone was saying and the excitement was nearly too much! But then just two days before, I found the last thing,' she said. She kicked the carpet bag with her toe. 'It's in there.'

Alec obligingly got down on to his knees and peered inside

the bag. Then he lifted out a paper parcel. I remembered, with a flash, Jeanne tying knots in the string around another.

'I wrapped it myself,' said Foxy, dispelling that idea. 'I didn't want any mess to get on my bag lining.'

Alec had spread the paper flat on the floor and in silence all three of us looked at what it contained. It was one of those fox furs with its head still attached, which is fastened by means of a clever little clasp hidden in the fox's mouth, allowing it to snap on to its own tail around one's neck. My aunt had one which Edward and I thought was a marvel (while Mavis predictably found it frightening; she is such a ninny). They had never struck me as macabre before but somehow, looking at this one gave me the shudders. It was probably at least in part because *this* snapping jaw had drawn blood.

'I take it that's cochineal,' I said, crouching down beside Alec and poking a finger at the stiffened spikes of fur, that had dried dark.

'Something like that,' said Alec. 'Where was it exactly, Mrs— Foxy?'

'In my dress bag,' she said. 'Ruined my dress I was going to wear for the quickstep.'

'Why didn't you tell us immediately?' I asked her.

There was an unmistakable flash in her eyes.

'What are you frightened of?'

'I'm frightened of Theresa being hurt,' she said, deliberately misunderstanding. 'I can tell you that for nothing. Why won't she just give up?'

'How do you know she hasn't?' I said. 'I thought you had severed all connections with the dancing world.'

'And why is it Theresa you fear for, rather than Roland?' said Alec. 'Since it was Mr Munn who met his end no matter that you were the target of the threats.'

She swallowed hard and held her hand out for the card which I was still holding. 'I shouldn't have come,' she said. 'I had better go.'

'Why didn't you take Mr Munn to hospital?' I asked. 'And why didn't you tell the doctor he felt ill?'

'I just didn't want any trouble,' she said. 'I still don't. But I can't stand by and watch Tweetie be hurt. Len was up to high doh with the threats. He was ill with the strain of it. Then he just . . . swooned at the top of the stairs. He just . . . fell into a faint.'

'He didn't trip,' I said. 'You're admitting it to us now.'

'Look, never mind all that,' said Foxy. 'Can you not try to get Theresa to see sense and pull out?'

'We are doing everything we can,' said Alec. 'Mrs Gilver and I and her parents too. But if just one person would come completely clean about what happened last year perhaps it would be easier to prevail.'

'Has Miss Thwaite not guessed?' said Foxy. 'Didn't she put two and two together when she found my headdress?'

For once in my life, I managed to bite my tongue before blurting. More than that I could not achieve, though, and so I left it to Alec to be clever.

'Did it come off as you followed Mr Munn?' he said.

'I'd taken it off already,' she said. 'It was digging in and I snatched it off as we left the floor. I must have just chucked it down to try to grab Leo. And then in the confusion I forgot all about it.'

'And you think Miss Thwaite might have guessed something significant using your headdress as a clue?' I said.

'If she did then whatever she's guessed must seem like something to keep quiet about. Like I kept quiet about the earlier threats. Look, I've done what I can. I'm a woman of my word and I'll not break promises I've made. I'll leave this lot with you to show to Tweetie if you think it'll help. Please, please take care of her, won't you? I don't have any children of my own and she's the dearest thing to me. As close as a daughter even if I don't see anything of her these days.' Then she put a hand over her mouth, either to stop herself from talking or to hold in a sob.

'You've been more helpful than you know, Foxy,' Alec said.

'Try to make her see sense and, if you can't, at least try to keep her safe,' Foxy said, then she gathered herself, picked up her empty carpet bag and left, passing a maid in the doorway.

'Brandy?' said Alec, taking the tray and closing the door behind him with his foot.

'A cup of strong tea with sugar will do me.'

'Could you make sense of the "headdress"?'

I thought hard about it but could not.

'I wonder if there were photographs,' he went on. 'If we were to see it, it might help.'

'We could ask Miss Thwaite to describe it,' I said. 'If she made the costume presumably she'll remember.'

Alec nodded and swallowed his glass of brandy in one gulp.

'And here's an idea,' he said. 'Send her a telegram and make it official.'

I began to drink my tea rapidly, but he gestured to me to slow down.

'I need to stash these,' he said, nudging the fox fur with his toe while he slipped the Christmas card back into its envelope. 'I don't want a chambermaid to come in and get the vapours.'

And just like that, the fog cleared. Somehow, the combination of his using that word while he replaced one of the items where Foxy had kept it served to jolt the idea into my head. I felt the smile spreading over my face.

'What?' said Alec.

'An envelope is the natural place to keep a card,' I said. 'But a toffee tin is a very odd place to keep a handkerchief, don't you think?'

'Now that you mention it.'

'Think of what she said, Alec. She put her face in his handkerchief and wept. And then she knew he had been deliberately harmed.'

'I cannot bear it when you do this, Dandy,' Alec said. 'Out with it, for God's sake.'

'Miss Thwaite picked up Leo's hankie. It can't have fallen out of his pocket for no reason. He must have had it in his hand.'

'If he wasn't feeling well, perhaps he was mopping his brow or perhaps he had it over his mouth.'

'My money's on that,' I said. 'He had it over his mouth. And then he fainted.'

Realisation spread over Alec's face and he gave a long low whistle.

'Oh, my sainted aunt,' he said. 'She put it in a toffee tin because it was airtight. She hoped to preserve the evidence. What do you think it was?'

'Chloroform,' I said. 'I'm certain of it.'

'And Foxy knew,' said Alec. 'That's why she was so careful to keep him away from doctors and hospitals until the effects had worn off. Even though it cost him his life.'

'I'm not sure that's fair,' I said. 'She knew, but if he'd cracked his head and injured his brain a hundred doctors in a thousand hospitals couldn't have made it better.'

'But why did she not tell the police?' Alec said. 'Why was she not shouting from the rooftops that someone had murdered her husband?'

'I've no idea,' I said. 'She's terrified. They all are. As we said before.'

'Except Beryl and Jeanne,' said Alec. 'Jeanne, if anything, is trying to help us think it all through and Beryl seems merely amused.'

We sat for a moment staring at one another, sorting the facts, looking for answers.

'I'm stumped by the headdress,' said Alec. 'She did say it was pinching. "Digging in" were the exact words. You don't suppose . . .'

'What?' I asked, almost laughing. 'Poisoned barbs? I hardly think so. Still, I'd like to find it and examine it. It must be somewhere.'

Alec quickly re-wrapped the monstrous fox fur and locked it, along with the other items, in a drawer.

'We need to tell the Stotts that Leo was killed,' he said. 'Tell Theresa and bring her to her senses. This damn thing is in two days.'

I nodded, considering it.

'But don't you think they already know?' I asked him. 'Isn't that why we were bundled out of there so unceremoniously when we mentioned Leo's name?'

'Well, then we need to tell this bally Scottish Imperial Battalion of Dancers we keep hearing about. Get the whole thing shut down. Go straight to Mr Silvester himself if we have to.'

'What makes you think *they* don't know?' I said. 'It got kept out of the papers, didn't it? And I can't see Foxy Trotter wielding that kind of influence with the press.'

'But surely Roly doesn't know the whole story,' said Alec. 'He'd be mad to carry on.'

'But they are mad,' I said. 'Dance crazy. They're worse than hunting fanatics and *they're* bad enough.'

'What the hell are we going to do if she won't withdraw or if Victor Silvester and the might of the SC Whatsit won't call a halt?'

'Solve it before Friday,' I said. 'We've got two suspects, haven't we? Jeanne and Beryl. We pick one and prove it.'

'And if we can't?'

'We must,' I told him. 'There's no other way.'

15

The first job on Thursday morning would be to revisit the Locarno and shake it hard to see what fell out. I had taken to the pepper pot detection method with the zeal of the neophyte. We were armed with Foxy's revelations and were emboldened by the knowledge that Tweetie was safely at home and could come to no harm, no matter who we angered and how much by our meddling. All in all, there was plenty to think of as I lay drifting towards sleep.

There was the ticklish question of how to ask about religion, of course. That prospect held no attractions. Grant had returned from communing with the housekeeper and delivered her news most succinctly.

'Prods,' she said.

'Grant!'

'Who prods?' said Alec. 'Prods what?'

'She means that St Andrew's is Church of Scotland, not Church of Rome,' I supplied. 'But really.'

'That's what Mrs Dolan said when I asked her,' said Grant, wide-eyed but fooling no one.

I ignored her.

'We must find a subtle way to ask Miss Bonnar where she worships,' I said to Alec, 'and we can take it, I suppose, that Jeanne is not RC? I mean her father can't have been or Lady Stott would be too and so would Theresa, but we'll have to ask about the schoolmistress. Wasn't there a Sunday school connection somewhere?'

'We should ask everyone,' Alec said.

'Or no one,' said Grant. 'I don't see why a Catholic couldn't use a Protestant prayer card as a threat, sir. I don't see that at all. It would add insult to injury. Or it might sit better to use a card the sender thought was already debased. Less blasphemous that way.'

'Or even, as Miss McNab suggested, the card might have been chosen with no thought to such matters at all,' Alec added, with no loyalty whatsoever.

'I disagree,' I said. 'Cock Robin and the poor dead bird might have been sought by pretty much anyone. But one would have to search for the prayer card with an expectation of finding it. One would have to know of such things and Protestant Glasgow would know nothing. Do you see?'

All in all we ended the evening rather deflated at the way our progress had melted away again.

There is nothing like a new morning, however, to put the bounce back in one's step, especially when the day is bright and breezy, with a blue sky and a promise of warmth in the afternoon if the clouds stay away.

On Sauchiehall Street, we arrived at the Locarno just in time to see Bert Bunyan – very much Bert Bunyan rather than Beau Montaigne, with his cap on the back of his head and a cigarette in the corner of his mouth – striding along the pavement looking cheerful and carefree. He tipped his hat when he saw us and went inside, taking the stairs at a bound and flicking his cigarette away at the last minute before he entered.

I was rather horrified to see one of our tame urchins, the little boy, pounce on the stub and put it to his lips.

'Here!' I said, climbing down. 'Throw that down again before you burn your mouth. How old are you?'

'Eight,' said the boy stoutly and he went to take another puff. 'There's no need to worry yourself about me, missus. I know how to smoke.'

'It's nothing to be proud of,' I said. 'But have it your own way. You can choose between the fag and the sixpence for being our garage-man again.'

Without a moment's pause he positioned the stub between his fingers and sent it in a great wheeling arc into the middle of the street far beyond the tramlines. His sister, watching from the doorway, cheered him.

As I was handing over the coins, however (I paid upfront since they had proved themselves already), I could not help but wonder that they were there again.

'Shouldn't you be at school?' I said.

'I'm too wee,' said the girl.

I gave a pointed look at her brother.

'And I've been sent home for fighting,' he said, without a trace of shame.

'And do you live near here?' I said, belatedly questioning why they were huddled outside the Locarno day after day without a policeman sending them packing. Both children hooted and chortled at the idea that they, barefoot and in their rags, might live amid the glitter of Sauchiehall Street.

'Naw, the Gorbals,' said the boy, naming one of Glasgow's worst slums, rivalling anything that the East End of London could offer. 'But the money's better up the town.' He bit on the sixpence and gave Alec and me a look so perfectly balanced between wisdom and innocence that it rather broke one's heart.

'Well make sure and be here tomorrow,' said Alec. 'This place will be packed out with people and lots of them might have motorcars.'

'Oh aye, it's always a good day when the Champs are on,' said the little girl cheerfully. I was appalled at one so young – not even old enough for school! – being quite so mercenary until she went on: 'I like seeing their frocks and the mennies in the penguin suits.' And she clapped her grubby little hands with glee.

★   ★   ★

Her excitement was shared, perhaps outdone, by that inside the ballroom. The Locarno was, quite simply, thrumming with nervous hilarity. Alicia and Jamesie were there, looking from their damp hair and limp clothes as though they had run a marathon, Bert had joined Beryl and was leading her through a set of steps so fast and sharp their feet almost blurred as one watched them, while Beryl, red-faced and panting, struggled to keep up with him. The biggest surprise was the jazz song being pounded out upon Miss Thwaite's piano by an enormously fat man in a striped collarless shirt and thick braces, who twitched his elbows and stamped his feet as though he were a one-man band but had forgotten to attach his cymbals. Mr Lorrison stood in the doorway to the office corridor and watched with his usual reptilian stillness, a stillness which deserted him instantly as he caught sight of Alec and me.

'Oh no,' he said, marching over to us. 'No, no, no. She's not here so you've no business here either.'

'Mr Lorrison,' said Alec, 'we've been learning a great deal since we last saw you and we have some questions.'

I was aware that the piano, although the music went on, was much quieter. Both couples continued to move around the floor but all eyes were upon us and all ears were straining too I am sure.

'How did you keep it out of the papers?' I asked under my breath and was rewarded by seeing Lorrison's eyes flash in anger and fear.

'Get away through,' he said. 'Youse can have five minutes.'

'I do not understand your demeanour,' I said once we were sitting on either side of his cluttered desk in that grimy little office. 'We're trying to help.'

Lorrison made an ugly sound to show his scorn.

'To prevent a reoccurrence of the same trouble,' Alec added. 'You can't really imagine that if there's another death at this year's competition you'll be so lucky as to sweep it under the carpet again?'

'Another death?' said Lorrison, looking sickly. 'Why would—'

'Foxy Trotter was sent a note and then a card and then that ghastly fur,' I said. 'Presumably you saw them?'

He nodded, paler if anything, and swallowing hard.

'And then on the day of the competition, Leonard Mayne was killed.'

'He tripped and fell down the stairs!' said Lorrison.

'He certainly fell downstairs,' said Alec. 'But he didn't trip.' Lorrison started to interrupt but Alec only spoke louder. 'He fainted because someone had doused his handkerchief with chloroform.'

Lorrison's clamouring was cut off as though someone had flicked an electric switch and taken the power of speech from him. He simply stared. Then he swallowed hard again and when he spoke it was without any of his bluster.

'Where did you hear that?' he breathed. 'Chloroform?'

'The handkerchief has been saved and stored in a good tight tin,' I said. 'The smell is gone but I'm sure that a chemist would be able to detect traces of it still. So you can understand our concern. For Tweetie, and frankly even more so for Roly.'

'This is not good,' said Lorrison, with what I thought to be considerable understatement. 'This is going too far.'

'Do you know who's behind it, Mr Lorrison?' I asked.

He gave me a hunted look and shook his head.

'Is there any way you can stop it?' said Alec innocently. 'Even though you don't know who's responsible? Or should we go to the police?'

Lorrison shot an arm out and grabbed Alec by the wrist. The movement was as quick as a lizard's tongue catching a fly and Alec had no chance to flinch away from it. I half stood, ready then and there to go outside and call for a bobby, but at a second glance there was no threat about the way Lorrison was hanging on; just desperation, matching the pleading look in his eyes.

'Don't do that,' he said. 'For my sake as well as your own. Please don't kick up any trouble. There's still time for the federation to pull the Champs away and have them some-where else and then I'll lose my job and my house and be ruined.'

'That would indeed be a misfortune, Mr Lorrison,' I said. 'But Leonard Mayne lost his life. If taking the competition to a different dance-hall would get rid of the threat of another death then it's well worth it.'

'Aye, but would it?' he said. 'Wouldn't the killer just kill at the Palais or the Roxy?'

'You know exactly who it is, don't you?' I said. 'Why are you protecting her?'

Lorrison, shocked by the pronoun I think, dropped Alec's wrist and only seemed to realise that he had grabbed it at all when he saw the way Alec rubbed it, unfastening his cufflink to get at the sore spot.

'I beg your pardon,' he said. 'I wasn't thinking.'

Alec shrugged and gave him a friendly smile. 'Don't give it a thought, old man,' he said. 'Save your worries for where they belong. Can you really contemplate being responsible for another dancer losing his life at the Locarno?'

'Could you not just get her told?' said Lorrison. 'Just tell that Tweetie Stott to sling her hook and leave us be? If she pulls out, what's lost? A spoiled wee besom has to give up dancing and get on with her ladies' luncheons and her soirées. And them that's left get a crack at a title. I can't stick the way she's just dabbling, just for fun, and taking away a prize that would mean the world to them that's losing it.'

'So it's one of the other dancers?' I said. 'We believed that jealousy was behind the threats too but we did wonder whether Jeanne McNab was the one.'

Lorrison, who had been hunched forward as though his worries were causing physical pain, suddenly unbent and sat tall in his chair again.

145

'Jeannie McNab?' he said. 'Aye, aye, it could well be.'

'But what on earth would she have against Foxy and Leo?' I said. 'Why would Miss McNab have tried to spoil things for *them*?'

Lorrison now had a grin spreading over his face. His thin lips stretched wide and revealed long, yellow, tobacco-stained teeth.

'Are youse really trying to tell me youse don't know?' he said. 'Some detectives!'

'This, Mr Lorrison, is how detection is done,' said Alec, clearly stung by the man's scoffing. 'We have just found out that there is something to be learned and now, if you'd be so kind, we shall learn it.'

But Lorrison would not budge. He grinned and hugged his secret knowledge to him like a teddy bear. So I saved myself the time and trouble of pestering him and came at it from another quarter.

'Who won last year, Mr Lorrison?' I said. 'Once Foxy and Leo were out of the way?' Of course I knew; I had read it in the press clippings at the Mitchell Library. Lorrison, however, was unaware of that.

Alec nodded; I could just see him from the corner of my eye.

'That's neither here nor there,' said Lorrison, all his glee gone in an instant and the old watchful look back in his eye.

'On the contrary,' said Alec, rather triumphantly for him; I guessed he had disliked being jeered at by this man just about as much as I had. '"Who benefits?" is always the first question.'

'Because it was our understanding that they were in with a real chance until the "accident",' I said.

'Never,' said Lorrison. 'Foxy's fifty if she's a day and Len Munn was never a Latin dancer.'

'We can take soundings out there,' said Alec. 'Ask around.

And even if no one wants to say Leo might have won, we'll soon find out who did.'

At that Lorrison leapt to his feet again and jabbed a finger across the desk. 'Just leave it,' he said. 'It was Bert and Beryl, if you must know. They swept the board. Highest score of the night for their foxtrot. So there. There's no need to go asking.'

'All the same,' I said. 'Since Jamesie and Alicia strike me as the sort of youngsters who're without an ounce of ill-will to anyone, I think I shall go to them for a second opinion.'

'Aye,' said Lorrison, subsiding into his seat. 'You do that. Ask Jamesie and Alicia. See what they say.'

16

'In other words,' I muttered to Alec as we made our way back out to the floor, 'Jamesie and Alicia know nothing of any use to us or danger to him and it's Bert and Beryl he's trying to keep us away from.'

'Bert *or* Beryl anyway,' Alec said. 'So shall we tackle them together or take one each and pool our findings later?'

We were lucky enough to catch them at a good time. The pianist, who went by the unlikely name of Boris, had stepped outside to finish smoking a cigar which Beryl and Alicia had found unbearable inside even such a large room and so the dancers were taking a short rest and looking, to my eyes, as though they needed it. Bert was sitting in a chair turned backwards, his upper torso draped over it with his hands hanging down, while Beryl, at his side, worked to explain some point, with a great deal of gesturing and banging her foot hard on the floor to signify the timing. He listened, shook his head and ran a hand through his damp hair. Beryl blew upwards into her fringe, which had dropped out of its wave and was obscuring the top half of her face, and began gesturing and stamping her foot again.

Jamesie and Alicia had gone right off the floor to sit in the front row of spectators' seats and share sweet nothings and it occurred to me that if Beryl and Bert did win again this year it was no more than they deserved for their dedication. Still, it was easier to interrupt a lecture, which it was draining one of the pair to deliver and which showed no sign of doing the other any good, than it was to break into the cooing of the lovebirds. I strode forward and hailed them.

'A minute of your time, Miss Bonnar?'

'We're up to our eyes, missus,' Beryl said.

'Oh, have a care,' said Bert to her. 'It's too late to be adding new steps anyway. The judges can tell a new step that's not bedded in right and they'll slam us for it.'

'I'm not giving you any more new steps than I ever have before,' said Beryl. 'It's not my fault if you're mixing them up. You're not usually a scatterbrain.'

I had been feeling impatient about what seemed like empty chatter, champing for my chance to cut in and start the interview, but Alec had seen something I had missed in all this.

'Is there anything in particular worrying you, Mr Bunyan?' he said. 'Beyond the usual anticipation, I mean. I find that I get terribly scatterbrained whenever something's preying on me.'

Beryl looked merely amused by this and, to be sure, Alec's attempt to be blokish and chummy was as unexpected as it was unsuccessful, but the expression on Bert's face turned her instantly sombre. His mouth was a thin line and the open collar of his shirt was trembling as a pulse in his neck raced, fast and high.

'Bert?' she said. As he turned to face her we could see a film of greasy-looking sweat on his brow, quite different from Beryl's high blush, got from exertion and not nerves.

'Whit?' he said, a mean bite of sound.

'Bert, what's wrong with you?' said Beryl.

'What's *wrong* with me?' he said, running his hands through his hair. 'It's nearly round to where somebody dropped dead last year. Our accompanist has got the sack, two of the professionals are not even here and Lorrison's like a bairn with a boil on his—'

Beryl was laughing again. 'You daftie,' she said. 'You don't think there's a curse on us, do you?'

149

'What's wrong with you that you don't?' said Bert. 'You never used to be such a cold-hearted woman, Beryl.'

I should not have been pleased to have such a verdict passed upon me and could not blame Beryl for the way her face darkened, as though a second flush, this of chagrin, joined the healthy bloom that her dancing had given her.

'I'm sorry about Len Munn,' she said. 'Of course I am. But the anniversary rolling round is nothing to fear. And the rest's just . . . Don't worry yourself about Billy Lorrison and Effie Thwaite. And as for Tweetie, don't you tell me life's not easier without all *her* nonsense.'

'I've no doubt,' came a voice, ringing out from the doorway. Theresa was making another of her dramatic entrances. 'But since we have a pianist again, I rather thought I'd make use of the ballroom, just like the other hopeful entrants. Sorry, Beryl. You won't be having it all your own way after all.'

'Who told you?' Beryl said. 'He's not been here more than an hour or two.'

'I have my allies,' said Theresa, so darkly that I expected Beryl, once more, to laugh.

In this instance, however, she narrowed her eyes and shot a look of great interest around the room. Bert did not meet her gaze. Jamesie and Alicia, still giggling together over at the side of the room, picked up enough of the atmosphere to raise their heads and glance over.

'Oh, there!' Jamesie said. 'Here we're all back together again like one big happy family. Now we can really get our last bit of polishing done and give them a right good show tomorrow, can't we?'

Alicia clapped her hands, delighted, and his words raised a grin from Beryl and a faint smile from Roly, who was skulking at Theresa's back, but Bert looked glummer than ever and Theresa shot such a withering look at Jamesie that all his happy chatter died in his throat. I could hardly bring myself to blame her, for there comes a point when cheerfulness shades into inanity and young Jamesie had found it and set up his stall there.

Beryl stood up and addressed Alec and me. I had all but forgotten our request for an interview.

'Youse can have five minutes while I get a wash,' she said, striding off the floor towards the ladies' cloakroom. 'Then I'll be back out whether you've done pestering me or not.' She lowered her voice. 'I'm not letting that Tweetie get in about Boris and flatter him.'

'A wash?' said Alec warily as we followed her in, clearly hoping that the word was being used in some heretofore unknown northern sense.

The fact that Beryl took a fresh cotton shirt from a bag on her coat hook and unrolled a towel from beside her outdoor shoes in the cubby-hole underneath suggested otherwise. As we watched, she retied the girdle of her pinafore, the better to stop it from sliding down, and then wriggled out of the shoulder straps and began unbuttoning the limp shirt she was wearing.

'Dandy, I think I'll—' said Alec, and almost wrenched the cloakroom door off its hinges while escaping.

Beryl laughed richly, rolled the discarded shirt into a ball and stuffed it in beside her shoes. 'It's well seen he's not Glasgow,' she said. 'I'm decent, am I not? I'm more covered now than many's a woman he'll see tomorrow at the Champs.'

It was a point of some validity; her chemise was made of sturdy linen, almost tough enough to be called canvas, and the straps were an inch across. I had appeared at balls and in opera boxes much more naked in my day. Still, I found it disconcerting to watch her run a basinful of warm water and begin scrubbing at her arms with a bar of green soap. If it was a tactic designed to distract and get rid of me the way it had seen off Alec, I was determined that she would not prevail.

'Tweetie won't "get in about" Boris any more than you have in the last hour, will she?' I began, reminding Beryl that she had had the advantage and that losing it was fairer play.

She grinned at me. 'I never tried,' she said. 'Bert and me just dance. It's Tweetie that wants thon blessed "jazz phrasings" as she cries them.'

'What?' I said.

'Ocht, every note hanging like a widow's tears while she's shaping.'

The first part of this so perfectly summed up the overly dramatic sort of rendition currently in vogue that I could not help smiling. As to Tweetie's 'shaping' I was at sea until Beryl obliged with a dumb show, clasping an imaginary partner around the shoulder with her left arm and dropping into something between a curtsey and the crouch of a serious athlete before the starting pistol of a sprint race while her right arm described an arch above her head. Then, as it occurred to me that once again she had managed to deflect my attention from its target, I deliberately withdrew my gaze from her nakedness, her posing and her friendly face – most distracting of all – and studied my notebook, screwing a good purposeful inch of lead out of my propelling pencil.

'You won the Championship last year, Miss Bonnar,' I said. 'Might I give you congratulations, even this late in the day?'

'Just in time!' said Beryl. She pulled the plug out of the basin and let the water go but did not reach for her towel.

'Were you happy with your score? I believe forty is the aim, is it not?'

'Aye, forty's the magic number,' she said. She was running the tap again, just the hot this time and the steam rolled up and obscured her reflection in the mirror.

'Did you achieve a forty that day?' I asked.

'A thirty-nine for the foxtrot was as close as we got.'

'And do you blame the upset for that?' I said. The entire surface of the mirror was fogged now and I could not see so much as a shadow of her expression but she had grown very still. A last drop of water plinked into the basin as I waited for her to speak.

'Naw,' she said and the silence resumed. She was gripping the edge of the sink and her knuckles were white.

'You don't think Foxy and Leo withdrawing and then Leo's fall might have knocked the rest of you off your game?' Another drip fell into the filled basin. Beryl glanced down at it and then turned to face me.

'It was our best ever score in a competition yet,' she said. 'I never even thought of that before. That's awfy.' She ran a hand over her mouth, keeping her eyes locked on mine with a searching gaze as though I could unravel some mystery for her.

'I'm not sure I—' I began but as she turned back to face herself in the mirror, she interrupted me.

'I just carried on as if nothing had happened,' she said. 'I got my best score and won the cup and was happy. Mrs Gilver, I honestly thought I was kinder than that. I don't half give myself airs.' She swiped at the steam on the mirror and stared at her own reflection. If she were acting then she was an actress of distinction, giving a performance easily worth a perfect score. I struggled for a few moments, torn between pressing my advantage and reassuring her, then with a jolt I saw an unmissable opening.

'Nonsense,' I began. 'Being a professional does not make you hard-hearted, Miss Bonnar. And dancing badly would hardly have helped poor Leo.' Then I paused, gave a little laugh I hoped sounded rueful and carried on in a vein I hoped sounded sincere. 'It is a great deal harder to forgive oneself unkindness – even if only imaginary – than it is to seek absolution, Miss Bonnar. My husband is your country-man, you know, but I've never been tempted to join his Church and lose the comforts of the confessional.'

As I had expected they might, her eyebrows shot up under her fringe.

'You're a pape, Mrs Gilver,' she said. 'Ma faither would have a fit if he knew I was getting this chummy with you.'

'Anglican,' I said. 'But rather high. Heavens, no! I'm not an RC. My own father would have plenty to say about that, I assure you.'

She bowed down and sluiced her face with the hot water and I could not help feeling that she did so to cover her confusion, but as to what had confused her, what misstep she felt she had taken, I could not say. When she stood up again, she was smiling and mistress of herself once more.

'Thank you for saying that,' she said, 'about letting myself off with it. That was nice of you.'

'Not as nice as all that,' I said, smiling back. 'I'm just about to ask you to repay me with information, or at least to ask you to search your memory in case you can find some.'

She was rubbing the green soap briskly in her hands again, working up a lather, apparently about to wash her face with it. Grant would have had fifty fits if she could have seen this, being strict to the point of turning rather peculiar on the evils of soap applied to a lady's complexion.

'It's about Leo's handkerchief,' I said. 'I want you to cast your mind back a year and ask yourself if you saw anyone tamper with it, if you saw anyone going through his pockets, or messing about at his spot in the cloakroom – I suppose that's hardly likely, mind you.'

'His hankie?' said Beryl, with her eyes screwed tight shut against the soap as she scrubbed at her face and neck. 'What's his hankie got to do with anything?'

'I wondered if you knew,' I said. 'I mean, I know that the incident was kept out of the papers but I did wonder if the dancers knew. Leo's hankie was doused in chloroform that day. That's why he felt faint and left the dance floor. That's why he fell down the stairs. It was another piece of sabotage like the fox fur and the other nasty things. Someone killed him, Miss Bonnar. Whoever it was might only have meant to nobble him, might never have meant it to go so far, but someone did it.'

She finished rinsing her face and applied the towel, wiping herself dry. When she turned to face me she was calmer than I had ever seen her. But I did not miss the redness around her eyes and the single fat tear rolling down one of her cheeks. I had shocked her badly enough to make her open her eyes when that horrid green soap was all over her face. Most certainly, I had shocked her.

'I thought it was an accident,' she whispered. 'I knew about the threats but I never put two and two together, except maybe to think they'd made Len nervous enough to get dizzy. Are you sure?'

'We have the handkerchief in our possession,' I lied, but only slightly. 'We shall be sending it for analysis shortly to make doubly certain, but yes I am sure.'

'And it never got as far as the police?' she went on. Her voice was a little louder and indescribably grim. 'It's been put down as an accident and nothing in the papers, eh?'

I nodded, watching.

'Right,' she said. She snapped out her fresh shirt, put it on and without even pausing to fasten the buttons she shrugged herself back into the top half of her pinafore and stalked out of the cloakroom before I could properly gather myself to follow her.

She was already talking by the time I got back to the dance floor.

'. . . was no accident,' she was saying. 'Mrs Gilver here told me and I believe her for she's no reason to be lying. Some wicked devil put chloroform on his hankie and guddled him that badly he fell down and died.'

Bert, Jamesie and Alicia stood frozen in their tracks. Alec, who had been dancing the gentleman's steps to Bert's lady again, stepped away from him and raised his eyebrows at me. Before either one of us could speak Beryl went on.

'Theresa, this is a piece of damned nonsense now, hen.'

Theresa stuck her chin in the air and stared at Beryl down the length of her nose.

'You can't risk it,' Beryl said. 'You've got to pull out – naw, listen to me. Listen, will you? For God's sake, you're an only one and your mammy and daddy would break their two hearts.'

'If you think for one minute I'm going to step aside and leave the way clear for your triumph,' said Tweetie.

Roly shifted his feet and spoke up. 'It wasn't Foxy that died, Tweet,' he said. 'Do you not think maybe you should ask me what I think?'

'It's a trick, Roly,' Tweetie said. 'Of course she's telling us to pull out, from the kindness of her heart I don't think.'

'She's being a sight kinder than you,' Roly said.

'Oh, for heaven's sake!' said Tweetie. 'Just don't sniff your wretched handkerchief then. Or keep it under lock and key if you're really so frightened. I am *not* pulling out.'

As quietly as a man of his size could possibly manage, Boris rose from the piano stool and slipped out of the room in the direction of Lorrison's office.

'I'll pull out too,' said Beryl. 'I'm not wanting to win again from somebody else's black luck. Me and Bert'll take our names off the list right now if you and Ron'll do the same.'

'Eh now, wait a minute there, Beryl,' said Bert. 'This is the first I've heard of this.'

Beryl, her chest heaving, turned on him. 'He died,' she said. 'A good man's dead and a good woman's a widow. How can you be thinking of anything except stopping it happening again?'

'Twenty pound prize money and a raise in my weekly wage is how,' said Bert. 'I never killed him. Why should the cup and the money go to somebody else just 'cos we're working at the same ballroom? See sense, Beryl, will you?'

Boris returned with Lorrison in tow, just in time to hear Jamesie Hodge pipe up.

'If it's all right with you, Alicia,' he said. 'I think I'll do what Beryl's saying.'

Alicia, her eyes wide with fear, nodded and took his hand.

'I'm out, Mr L,' Jamesie went on. 'If I'd have kent Len was killed I'd never have stayed and I'd never have let Alicia within a mile of the place.'

Beryl, on hearing these words, gave a long cold look at Bert, a look that I could not begin to decipher. I filed it away for later study and turned to Tweetie.

'There,' I said. 'That is exactly what your parents have been telling you, Miss Stott. And what Mr Armour would tell you too if he could. Now, why not take Miss Bonnar up on her very kind offer and withdraw before anyone else is harmed.'

'Now just you see here,' said Lorrison, striding forward. 'This is exactly what I said would happen. This is exactly the sort of bliddy nonsense I knew was coming when you two characters showed your faces. I don't know where you've got this story from – Foxy Trotter herself more than likely – but if youse think you're gonny throw your weight about and make the Locarno look bad, you've another think coming. This ballroom has got good business out of having the Champs and we're set fair to make it the double this year. Ronald Watt – if you pull out, you're finished here. Same with you, Tweetie, and you too, Bert. And youse know I mean it.'

I waited for one of them to protest that Beryl had been missed out of this shower of ultimata, but although each of them looked ready to kill Lorrison or Beryl or perhaps both, no one said a word. We all stood in some manner of silence, either glum or seething, while Jamesie and Alicia scurried away to the cloakroom, their hats and coats and a life without danger or glory. So keen were they to leave that I did, at that moment, begin to wonder if they were really as innocent as they appeared after all. I gazed after them, musing.

Thus it was that we heard what might have been missed under the usual sounds of the piano and the soft thump of dancing slippers upon the wooden floor. We were all still standing, silently, when the main door downstairs opened and was let bang shut and two pairs of feet, one female in narrow heels and one male in steel-rimmed soles, mounted the stairs.

'Aw, fling it to hell!' said Lorrison. 'They're early.'

'Let's see how quickly you drop out now,' murmured Tweetie in a sly little voice.

'I'm ready to put the whole thing in his hands,' said Beryl stoutly.

The door squeaked on its hinges and we turned in time to see a trim woman of middle years holding the door open for one of the most elegant young men I had ever seen in my life, including the romantic leads in repertory company plays and the tennis and golf chaps in the swishest hotels in Monte Carlo. From his hair, which was slicked back with such precision that it looked polished, to the shoes whose soles had ascended the stairs with such bright clicks of their silver tips, he was a vision of dapper perfection.

'My, my,' he said in tones of the wildest gentility overlaying a foundation of grocer's boy, 'I hardly expected to see you standing still and sweet silence from the pianoforte. Where is the feverish frenzy of final practising?'

'You might well ask,' said Beryl. 'We've got something to tell you.'

'I'll deal with this, Miss Bonnar,' said Lorrison. 'Welcome back to the Locarno, Mr Silvester. I have a bottle of your favourite through in my office and I can send out for a bite to eat just as soon as you tell me what you fancy. Come this way.'

17

By the end of the day, I was heartily sick of Mr Victor Silvester, head of the Imperial Institute of Dancing Masters, founding father of the Scottish Professional Ballroom Dancing Championships and, at least in his own estimation, great chief Pooh-Bah of dancing wherever dancing was done. If he had been dropped from a hot-air balloon into the jungles of Borneo and found six natives stamping around a fire he would have told three of them to work on their foot placement and sent them a bill for his time.

Grant had made a hero and a heart-throb of him by the end of the same day and Barrow was as close to unbending as was possible for him. These two developments occurred because, to my intense and reasonable annoyance, the verdict following a hurried conference in Lorrison's office between the great man, Alec and me was that the Champs would proceed with the addition of an extra couple planted in the dressing room and on the floor who would follow Tweetie and Roly closely and watch over them for possible interference and harm.

It took Silvester roughly a minute of watching Alec and me to determine that we were not the men for the job and roughly another minute, after I had summoned them via a call from the telephone kiosk outside, to decide that Grant and Barrow – suitably briefed by himself, naturally – would do.

At least half of my disgust with the great man was owing to his flat refusal to throw Tweetie out of the contest. I explained to him that her solicitor fiancé was unaware of her connection to the Locarno and the Championship and would not sue Mr Silvester or any of his strings of initials if he simply showed her the door.

One would have thought I was telling Dick Whittington to put down poison for the cat.

'The matter has been dealt with, Mrs Gilver,' he informed us, as lofty as he was surely mistaken. 'There is no need to pay any heed to such silly little pranks. None at all. Now then, let's see what these youngsters are made of.'

He turned to where Grant and Barrow stood waiting in the middle of the floor. Barrow clasped Grant to his bosom, so close I expected her to step away and slap his cheek for the effrontery, but she fixed a beatific smile upon her face, looked over his shoulder as though at a heavenly vision in the distance, and took his free hand in hers. Silvester beat time with the end of his ivory-topped walking cane until Boris at the piano came in with a waltz tune. Barrow assumed a smile to match Grant's and they set off, one-two-three, one-two-three, spinning around the room like tops. I noticed that Grant's skirt, which had looked perfectly unremarkable while she walked about, now swung out in a bell behind her and I concluded that she had, at some free moment, unpicked the seams and added gussets against just such an eventuality as this one. I shook my head more in wonder than anything else and pursed my lips at her blank angelic face as she and Barrow passed by where I was standing.

When they had made two full circuits of the room, Mr Silvester banged his cane on the floor again.

'Not bad,' he said. 'Not bad at all, although we could be up all night. Of course, it's a bit of a worry that no one's going to know who you are. But we can always say you've come down from Inverness or somewhere outlandish like that.'

'Alonzo and Alana are from Inverness,' said Beryl.

160

Mr Silvester saw off these details with a wave of his gloved hand. 'We must also come up with a pair of names,' he went on.

'Cordelia Grace,' said Grant, 'and Pierre Barreaux.'

She rolled the Rs so enthusiastically when she delivered this that she had to clear her throat surreptitiously when she had finished speaking.

'Is his Christian name Peter?' I asked Alec in a mutter.

'I seem to remember so,' said Alec. 'That was very quick thinking, wasn't it?'

It must have appeared so, but I knew Grant and I would have wagered that while she stitched extra panels into her skirt and sewed whatever had been in those extra cases she had brought with her, she had also been thinking up suitable dancing names.

'Those will be fine,' said Silvester, whom I was beginning to suspect of being christened Tom Smith. 'Now let's see your whisk, your chassé and a hesitation change if you know how to do one.'

Boris struck up again and Grant and Barrow launched into a string of those ludicrous dance steps, lurching first one way and then another before stopping dead, which ruin all the enjoyment of a party for everyone: the couple themselves because they are concentrating too fiercely for conversation and the couples around them because they have to keep their wits honed to jump out of the way.

'Stop,' shouted Silvester after Grant and Barrow had darted in every possible direction and Grant had rippled once or twice around her partner like the ribbon on a maypole. 'I've seen enough. You'll do. It won't be beyond the stretch of imagination that you would spend the ten shillings to enter. Of course, it's easy to tell that you are not really a couple. There's no short cut to that perfect sympathy that only comes from months if not years of dancing together until not only your bodies but your minds and hearts and souls are . . .'

He had lost sight of the beginning of the sentence in his fervour and he fell back on an airy gesture instead of trying to pin it down. 'But as I say, you'll do. You'll have to take part in all four dances, mind. Can you tango?'

Barrow and Grant both preened a little while Boris found the sheet music and embarked upon a throbbing Latin number.

We left them to it. Beryl agreed with Alec and me. Tweetie, enthusiastically, and Roly, reluctantly, were against us. Lorrison and Silvester were no help at all, and so there was only one thing for it. We went to Balmoral to try the Stotts again.

Jeanne let us in, it being Mary the maid's free afternoon, and a ghost of an idea, or at least the shadow of one, flitted over me when I saw her. It was gone before I could grasp it but it left me staring at her in a marked enough way to cause her to squirm and ask me if there was something wrong.

'There certainly is, Miss McNab,' I said, and I could hear how sharp I sounded. 'Matters have deteriorated steeply since we last met.'

'Did you give Miss Thwaite the sewing?' she said and, just as I had when she was bending over the dead wren, I thought to myself that she was a cold young woman; colder than could be explained away merely by the indignities of living as a poor relation, cold enough so that I started to wonder about her early life and the mother and father she championed so fiercely.

There it was again! She had said something or something had been said about her which touched on her family and which would have rung bells in me if I had been cleverer or had been paying sufficient attention. I certainly could not run it to ground now, because Lady Stott had come to the library door when she heard us arriving and was beckoning us even now.

'Theresa's away back to the dance-hall,' she said. 'Where have you been? You're supposed to be watching out for her, but she's skipping off here, there and yonder and you're nowhere to be found. We're very dissatisfied, aren't we, Bounce?' This with a glance over her shoulder.

'My dear Lady Stott,' said Alec, striding forward and taking her clasped hands in his own. 'We have been detecting as we told you we would. Being detectives rather than bodyguards. But you will be delighted to hear that we have drafted re-inforcements and that Miss Stott and Mr Watt are being very closely watched right now.'

'I hope you're not charging us extra,' came Sir Percy's voice from inside the library.

As was her wont, Lady Stott swiftly realigned herself with us and rounded on him. 'How can you talk about money when your own daughter's safety is at stake?' she said, marching back inside and standing over him.

He was sitting close to the fire in a smoking jacket and carpet slippers with his feet up on a little stool and a glass of something comforting on a small table beside him. Lady Stott shook her head and tutted with her hands planted firmly on her well-corseted hips.

'Look at him,' she said. 'Look at you! Sitting there as if you haven't a care in the world.'

I thought she was wrong about that; it was not that Sir Percy was without care, rather that he was beyond his capacity to stay alarmed. He had given up and was waiting to let be what would be. It is a dangerous state of mind, especially for a client who might decide while in it to save his money rather than squander it on our fees.

'If Tweetie can dance, why can I not sit quietly and have a whisky?' said Sir Percy.

'We've come to try to stop her dancing,' I said. I knew we were about to alarm them but saw nothing for it. 'Is there anything you could do, threaten her with, withdraw from her, that would prevail? An allowance perhaps? Is there anything in your gift that she values enough?'

Lady Stott tottered over to the armchair on the other side of the fireplace and sank into it.

'What's happened?' she said. 'Why is it so much more desperate all of a sudden?'

Alec and I glanced at one another, deciding which one of us should attempt to tell the news without sending the Stotts into a frenzy, but even the glance was too much for Lady Stott to bear.

'What? What?' she said. 'What do you know? What's happened?'

'It's about Leo Mayne,' I said, thinking that the truth could not be worse than the suspense for the poor woman. I was astonished to see a glance, the twin of Alec's and mine, shoot between the two Stotts.

When Lady Stott spoke again she sounded wary. 'What about him?' she said. 'What have you found out?'

'We don't think his death was an accident,' said Alec. 'At least not entirely. His dancing partner was threatened in much the same way as Tweetie has been and we think that the devil who threatened her caused Leo's death too.'

Was it my imagination, I wondered, that Lady Stott sat back in her chair a little – as far as her corsets would allow – as though relieved? I could not for the life of me fathom which part of Alec's report might have been a relief to her and before I could question her my attention was claimed in its entirety by Sir Percy.

'Do you mean to tell me,' he said, and his voice was low and cold, like the growl of a large dog when a stranger comes just near enough to the end of its chain for it to form a view of him, 'do you mean to tell me that Margaret went through this last year and this is the first I'm hearing of it?'

'Who's Margaret?' said Alec, not unreasonably.

'Foxy Trotter,' spat Sir Percy.

'Now, Percy,' said Lady Stott.

He raised his hand like a policeman stopping traffic and quelled her. 'What do you mean, not an accident?' he said.

'He was nobbled,' said Alec. 'And we fear it might happen again. We'd like to examine Miss Stott's costume.'

'Her costume?' said Lady Stott, weakly swallowing.

'Yes,' I said. 'Is it here?'

'She keeps everything in her room,' said Sir Percy. 'But I don't understand.'

'Nor do we,' said Alec.

'But *you* do, don't you?' said Sir Percy, fixing his wife with such a fierce glare that she shrank backwards, cringing. 'You knew about last year.'

'No!' she said. 'That is, not at first. I had no idea when Tweetie started being threatened. I don't think Tweetie knew herself.'

'Or if she did she was careful to keep it quiet,' said Sir Percy.

'Why are you always so determined to see the worst in her?' cried his wife.

'Oh, let me see!' said Sir Percy. 'Maybe because she's turned her back on all the advantages we worked so hard to give her and gone slumming in the gutter with the very dregs of humanity—'

'How dare you!' said Lady Stott, back in booming voice again.

'Oh! Oh!' said Sir Percy. He was really beginning to work himself up now. 'It's well seen where your loyalties are when you get right down to it. How *dare* I? How dare *I*?'

'Yes. How dare you be so high and mighty when if it wasn't for your precious rubber underwear buttons you'd be in the self-same gutter with the self-same dre—'

'A respectable professional man like Julian who cares for her and is willing to—'

'And not a word from me about any of it. Ten years I was living in that two room and kitchen scrimping and scraping every penny while you poured money into that blessed factory—'

'I've given you a fur coat, a set of jewels or an oil painting for your birthday and Christmas presents every year since I've had the brass to buy them—'

'I didn't know they were grudged!' shouted Lady Stott. 'I suppose you've got the cost all tallied up. And Tweetie's presents too.'

'Nothing's grudged,' shouted Sir Percy back at her. 'Not her car, not her diamond tiara, not the new house, nothing. But when it's flung back in my face for a night out at a dance-hall—'

'You're certainly listing them quick enough for someone who's not grudging,' said Lady Stott with a sneer.

'It didn't take you long to count up the years and get to ten!' he sneered back.

'House?' said Alec. He is a marvel sometimes. 'Do you mean to say Miss Stott and Mr Armour are expecting the gift of a new house when they marry? That could surely get their attention.'

'Oh no,' said Lady Stott. 'Don't you dare, Bounce!'

'An excellent notion, young man,' said Sir Percy. 'I'll lay that choice in front of the wee madam as soon as she decides to come home tonight and we'll see what happens.'

'You'll do nothing of the kind!' said his wife. 'What on earth would we tell Julian?'

'Why do you need to tell him anything?' I said. 'If he knows nothing of Miss Stott's dancing, why should he ever find out?'

Lady Stott searched my face for a while, thinking furiously, then all the fight went out of her.

'Because it won't work,' she said. 'If Bounce threatens to take the house away she'll just let it go and keep dancing and then Julian will have to find out, won't he?'

'But what makes you think she'll choose dancing over the house?' I said.

Lady Stott groaned and put her face in her hands. When she spoke her voice was muffled. 'Because I've tried already,' she said. 'As soon as I heard about Len Munn and the fox fur and all of it I went straight to Tweetie and told her. She just laughed in my face.'

'Oh, Eunice,' said Sir Percy, kicking his little footstool away and struggling to his feet. 'Oh, my hennie. Don't you fret yourself.'

'How did you hear about that, Lady Stott?' I asked, as Sir Percy brushed past me.

'Oh, Bounce,' she wailed, throwing her short little arms as far as they would go around her husband.

'Oh, Eunice,' he crooned, throwing his slightly longer arms as far as they would go around the considerable bulk of his wife.

Alec and I withdrew, first to the hall but then, when we realised that we could still hear them, to Tweetie's bedroom, finding it by trial and error.

The new costume was still with Miss Thwaite, but on a hook on the back of her door there hung a soft velvet bag, containing her shoes, stockings, bracelets and, crucially, her headband.

We subjected the thing to close scrutiny, running our fingers around it to feel for sharp protrusions and even, gingerly, trying it on. There was nothing to be learned: it was a simple band of stitched silver cloth, edged in spangled droplets, two inches wide and rather thick as though lined with some kind of cushioning or stiffening.

'Perhaps it was a slip of the tongue,' I said. 'Foxy said headdress when she meant hankie.'

'But she said "my headdress",' Alec reminded me. 'No one's tongue slips and says "my headdress" instead of "Leo's handkerchief".'

'True,' I said. 'And on the subject of the hankie: we need to brief Barrow. Tell him to keep a close eye on Roly in the men's cloakroom. And press upon Roly himself that he shouldn't leave his things unattended.'

'So, it's back to the bally Locarno again, is it?' Alec said.

I considered it for a moment: duty and thoroughness and how much Sir Percy was paying.

'Let's ring him,' I said.

But Alec was made of stouter stuff and insisted. So it was that we spent the rest of the day in the shabby armchairs of the withdrawing room, briefing and warning and grilling and testing each of the dancers whenever they took a minute's break from their feverish last-ditch practising.

That and listening to Victor Silvester coaching Grant and Barrow until I could have screamed and suspected that, on my deathbed, I would still be hearing his voice shouting: 'In line, in line, outside! Toe, toe, *heel*!' and the tip of his cane striking the floor.

18

Alec faced an evening and morning sans valet with perfect equanimity and so it behoved me to do the same about Grant, especially since I complained so loud and long when she was with me. When I arrived at the Locarno on Friday, however, I wished I was less dishevelled, for not only the competing couples but many of the ticket-holders come to view the spectacle were dressed up to the nines in true Glasgow fashion, prinked and polished like ponies on their way to a gymkhana and painted with not only rouge and lipstick and lash black but with blue above the eyes and red tips to their fingers.

I had celebrated being free of Grant's attentions by washing my face, paddling on some cold cream once it was dry and letting the fresh air at it for once. Now, though, I felt like a milkman's dray delivering at the gymkhana tea-tent. I prayed she would not see me or, at least, would be too busy to lose her temper if she did. Alec looked exactly the same as ever, his suit brushed, his shoes shined, his face shaved and his hair nicely smoothed back in wings, a perfect middle way between the rough curls of a working man like Jamesie and the oily slick of Mr Silvester.

Grant and Barrow were not the only of our servants to desert us that day. When we drew up on Sauchiehall Street it was to find our tame street urchins already employed guarding another motorcar and unwilling to add my Cowley to their beat.

'Aw, we daren't, missus,' said the boy. 'We've been told to

keep a right good eye on this one and we're gonny. They're in the pub the now but they're going to the dancing later.'

'How much is he paying you?' I asked, rootling around in my bag for the shillings I had planned to give them today.

'He's not paying us,' said the child. 'We're doing it out of the goodness of our hearts.'

'For a friend of yours?' asked Alec. It was hard to imagine this pair having a friend of such exalted style – the motorcar was a Phantom and a very new one.

'A better friend than an enemy,' said the child and his sister nodded soberly. It made no sense to me but I did not stop to argue, merely handed the shillings over anyway as a bonus for past service and told myself that the Cowley would come to no harm.

'Wonder who it belongs to,' said Alec. 'There was the couple from Inverness who sounded rather grand, but they'd hardly stop in for a pint of beer beforehand.'

We could not discuss it any further however, because as soon as we stepped towards the door of the Locarno we were swept up in a great surging crowd of spectators, all clutching their tickets aloft and all jostling to get to a ringside seat before the fun commenced. When Alec and I were spotted by Lorrison – resplendent today in whitish tie and greenish tails – and were taken in ahead of all those around us, a loud chorus of jeers and whistles accompanied us on our way.

'Special guests,' Lorrison shouted over his shoulder. 'Honoured guests of Mr Silvester himself. So youse can shut up and stop moaning.'

Inside, the Locarno was quite transformed, like a church for a wedding, with urns of flowers and ribbon banners hanging in swags from lamp to lamp along the corridor walls. Of course, the flowers were hideous – gladioli and lilies of elephantine proportion – and the banners were art-silk so shiny that they dazzled as one looked at them. Still, the overall effect was festive and added to the sense of bubbling excitement produced by the crowd surging along the corridor and the hubbub from the ballroom beyond. Lorrison elbowed his way between the bodies and managed to get us through the double doors at top speed. Neither did he break stride as he set out across the floor to empty seats on the other side but I was struck by untypical bashfulness at the thought of plodding across that gleaming floor in my coat and hat under the gaze of more and more spectators every minute, for the seats were rapidly filling. Alec seemed no more keen to make the trip, for he had stopped dead at my side and looked at me with an expression of alarm. Lorrison, our protector, was now a good five yards away and unappealing as it was to contemplate the walk at his heels, it was far worse a prospect without him. Accordingly, we scuttled after him and caught up just as he was turning, with a flourish belonging to a collection of manners he had assumed for the day. All around us there was a ripple of comment as the audience asked themselves who we were and why – I could not help hearing this – I had made so little effort to dress properly.

Alec was unremarkable, for the Glasgow citizenry en masse did not run to dinner jackets, much less to tails, and what few men there were in the little gilt seats had done no more than change to clean collars and choose their gaudiest ties. The women, though, under their cloth coats, wore an extraordinary assortment of finery: tea gowns with opera gloves, ball gowns with leather lace-up shoes, even one or two cocktail dresses looking very peculiar without the jewels one is used to seeing with them. One girl in her twenties had a frock of black and silver fringes and wore nothing with them but a gold cross on a chain and wool stockings. They had, I decided, simply worn the best they owned without worrying about what they did not. It was touching in its way although, if one were heartless, rather amusing.

The speeches to be got through were rather less so. Mr Lorrison, bellowing into a speaking trumpet, introduced all six members of the dance band collectively, individually and then collectively again, before beginning on the judges. Two of them got the merest of nods, but he fell over himself lauding Mr Silvester, droning on and on about his school, his medals and the transformation he had wrought in the world of dancing. The little woman I had taken to be his assistant was introduced as Alice Astoria, a fellow judge, but it seemed she had no comparable cartload of solid achievements, since the speech waxed on her elegance and poise and the way she graced the Locarno 'like a flower', which made me think only of a daisy on a dung heap. Judging by the way Miss Astoria's face tightened, exactly as a daisy closes when the sun goes down, the same allusion might well have occurred to her.

Eventually, however, Lorrison moved on to introducing the competing couples and there was a rustle of anticipation around the packed ballroom which I could not deny sharing. They were brought out from the cloakroom corridor in order of descending odds, beginning with a couple of rather plain puddings who even I could see were unlikely to go home with a trophy and for whom there was only a polite smattering as well as a few muffled titters. The next were no better, consisting of an enormously tall fellow with a lot of knees and elbows, giving him the look of an umbrella outwitted by a high wind. It did not help that his partner was fully a foot shorter and round withal, her skinny legs protruding from the bottom of a short, bouffant red frock and making her rather too reminiscent of a toffee apple with two sticks.

Then matters began to improve. The next few couples were clearly not going to win. Some of them were past their prime, rather creaky and arthritic-looking, with a good deal of brocade on the ladies' gowns and an old-fashioned cut to the gentlemen's tails. These did however have an air of tremendous confidence, moving together like two parts of the same creature, even when they were only parading across the floor.

The other group in this middle lot were at the opposite end of their careers, raw and unformed, very much still two separate beings trying to find a way to step in time. They would have done well to study the elderly pairs for tips, but instead with the insouciance of youth they ignored the treasure before their eyes, the way the elderly gentlemen inclined a chivalrous head towards their partners and the way the ladies tilted their chins just so to give an air of whimsy to their stately progress across the floor. The young are ever so; unable to believe that the decrepitude before it was ever firm young flesh or that they themselves will ever crumble.

Lorrison gave a marked pause after the end of these young hopefuls and old faithfuls and I felt the audience lift into a higher gear in some ineffable way.

'Couple number eleven, Alana and Alonzo Arabia,' he announced and the crowd, who had been clapping perfectly politely for everyone, now applauded with some fervour as a pair of terrifically glamorous black-haired individuals came stalking on to the floor dressed as though for a flamenco.

'From Inverness?' muttered Alec in my ear, sounding rather incredulous. And to be fair, it was hard to imagine such a pencil-thin moustache, like two anchovies laid on a boiled egg, or such bright gold earrings, so gold they might be brass, appearing on the streets of that town without a great deal of comment.

When the applause had quietened, Lorrison piped up again.

'And introducing couple number seven, lucky number seven, Miss Delicia Grace and Monsieur Pierre Barreaux.'

The audience was a-flutter. One supposed that hardened dance fans knew the names of the likely professionals and the sudden introduction of a new pair had thrown them. I noticed with wry interest that Grant had embellished her original choice of Christian name, probably in the changing room and probably in response to Alana Arabia, for she has an unslakable thirst for the theatrical and does not care to be bettered at it.

When Grant and Barrow finally appeared, after an unconscionable pause to build expectations, even I felt a little gasp escape me. Barrow of course looked much the same as usual, for a valet-cum-butler spends his days dressed for the ballroom in most particulars, although he had added some revoltingly shiny dancing slippers and there was a suspicious winking down the front of his waistcoat which hinted at jewelled buttons. Grant, though, was quite simply staggering. Her frock was a pale pearly pink, gleaming gold in the folds, and it clung to her like a second skin. There was plenty of her first skin on show too, since the pink and gold affair was essentially backless and surely nearer to frontless than the Locarno had often seen before. She looked beautiful; I had no idea that my maid, under her serge, possessed such a pair of milky white shoulders and such a long white neck. A neck made for diamonds and decorated this minute by a good lot of them. I sat up sharply.

'She's wearing my mother's jewels,' I said. I sat back. 'And looking better in them than I ever have.'

Alec snorted. 'How old is Miss Grant?' he said. 'I had no idea that we had had a swan in our midst all this time. Barrow looks quite smitten.'

'She's forty,' I said. 'Barrow is safe enough and you shouldn't get any ideas either, for she has a gentleman in Northumberland, a publican, with first refusal. The poor man has been writing to her for ten years and dropping hints like anvils.'

'Sshh,' said Alec, for Boris was tinkling his piano keys again and Lorrison was clearing his throat.

'And now,' he said, 'put your hands together for last year's winners and the reigning champions! Ladies and gentlemen, the Scottish Professional Ballroom and Latin trophy-holders for another two hours only! Couple number three, Miss Beryl Bonnar and Mr Beau Montaigne.'

The spectators, reaching fever pitch one supposed, not only clapped but also cheered and drummed their feet. There were a few hip hip hip hurrahs too and the noise as Bert and Beryl actually appeared was deafening.

'Tweetie has pulled out!' I screamed into Alec's ear, through the din. 'She must have or she'd have been before Beryl.'

'Just like Grant to carry on anyway!' screamed Alec back at me, then he turned to watch the entrance of the champions.

Beryl, workaday Beryl in her pinafore, had been transformed. She was not as dashing as Alana and thankfully not as naked as Grant, but she glowed as though lit from within. Her frock was every little girl's dream, sugar pink and white, and as frothy as a bottle of warm champagne. Her hair was elaborately dressed in a style which must have taken hours. In fact, I thought I detected the hand of Grant in the architectural masterwork that had been wrought on her head. It was just the sort of thing Grant loves and does not get to perpetrate on me any more since fashions have changed and I have become bold enough to forbid her.

'Bert looks terrified,' Alec said.

I flicked a glance at him but only for a moment. I simply could not tear my eyes away from Beryl. She looked, I had decided, like an empress, utterly transfixing.

Lorrison cleared his throat again.

'Oh, my Lord,' I said, understanding. 'Tweetie *is* here, Alec. Beryl let her go last.'

'Why?' said Alec, a mere man, unschooled in the wiles of womankind.

'To upstage her,' I said. 'Wait and see.'

'And finally,' said Lorrison. 'Couple number four, Miss Tweetie Bird and Mr Roland Wentworth.' There was no fol-de-rol, no string of titles and trophies and the applause, while enthusiastic enough, had no cheers or stamping. Poor Tweetie knew it too. She paused in the doorway with Roly hovering behind her and shot a look of pure venom at Beryl, who was clapping politely.

Tweetie glittered and dazzled as she stood there, despite the scowl. The headband was worn not low and straight across her forehead but high at the front and down to her nape at the back, so that it made one think of the Statue of Liberty, but apart from that curious detail she was quite lovely. If she had come before Grant and Beryl, she would have caused a sensation.

I should have expected her to realise as much and be upset but, after that one glare, the other dancers and certainly the spectators ceased to exist for her. She fixed her gaze on the far wall and stalked across the floor with great purpose and concentration.

I caught Grant's eye and saw her shrug, meaning that she had watched and seen nothing. Barrow patted his breast pocket, which I took to mean that he had kept watch over Roly's belongings and that no one had tampered with anything.

'Ladies and,' began Lorrison again. Then his voice died in his throat.

The street door had opened and four men stood there. They had such an air of authority that for a second I wondered if they might be policemen, if perhaps the Stotts had thrown caution – or at least Julian – to the wind and put the entire matter in the hands of the law.

'Have the Stotts engaged another firm to come and help us?' asked Alec. 'Or are they with Silvester, do you think?'

They did seem at home here, very sure of their welcome. In fact, as Alec spoke, four spectators, two men and two women, rose out of their front row seats and shuffled away, letting the four latecomers take their place.

I shook my head. Two of the men looked like – there is no other word for it – thugs. I could not imagine why two such lumpen creatures, rough-hewn and dour-faced, had come to see ballroom dancing. The other two were not quite so remarkable. One was neat, slight and bored-looking and I rather thought from the way he kept himself turned slightly towards the fourth of the group, that he was accompanying this last man, that the last man was where we should direct our gaze.

There was, I decided after doing so, nothing to see. He might have been a schoolmaster or a lawyer's clerk.

'They're not gentlemen of the press,' said Alec.

'They're not gentlemen at all,' I murmured.

The woman in the row behind leaned forward then and spoke in an undertone.

'Do youse really not know who that is?' she said. Alec and I both turned round more fully to see who was talking. 'Don't,' she said. 'Don't draw attention. He'll know we're talking about him.'

'But who—' I began. I was cut off by Lorrison and his speaking trumpet before I could finish my question.

'Now that we are all here,' he said, and I thought he glanced at the four men, 'let us begin. The first round will be that most beautiful and romantic of all the ballroom dances, everyone's favourite, the Quick Waltz.'

The four men were forgotten in the rustle of appreciation and delight as the dance band struck up and the eleven couples spaced themselves out around the floor. The house lights were snapped off as though we were at the theatre and one by one, as gently as dandelion seeds taking flight in a breeze, all the couples began to eddy around the room to the swell of the music. It was breathtaking.

'Dandy,' said Alec, after a while, 'who are you watching?'

I snapped back to attention with a guilty start, for it had been one of the elderly couples whose twirling and whirling circuit of the floor had been mesmerising me. I retrained my eyes on Tweetie and Roland. They were dancing with great gusto, spinning so fast that one imagined they must be dizzy, and changing directions apparently as if communing by some sort of telepathic magic. Grant and Barrow were looking rather ragged as they tried to keep up and Tweetie threw a look of irritation over Roly's shoulder as Grant and Barrow bungled a corner and prevented the other couple from haring off again as they clearly wanted to.

'It's like watching a flat race,' said Alec. 'I'm not surprised Leo fainted, doctored hankie or no.'

'And Grant isn't the best sailor I've ever met,' I said. 'I don't know how much more of that spinning she'll be able to do.'

At last, once the spectators were reeling with dizziness and one could only marvel that any of the dancers were still on their feet, the music swelled to a final flourish and the band fell silent.

The judges sat stony-faced for a full minute staring at the couples, who stood on the floor looking like condemned men waiting for the axe to fall. And fall it did. Once the other three had passed slips of paper to Mr Silvester and he had scribbled and shuffled for a while, he fixed his gimlet eye just above the dancers' heads and barked out a series of numbers. The message made no sense to me but the crowd sighed with relief or groaned with disappointment and one of the also-ran couples took a deep, grave bow and left the floor, trailing disconsolately towards the cloakroom to take off their costumes and try to cast their minds towards next year and greater glory.

The remaining couples gave their comrades looks which comprised a veneer of sympathy thrown over a smile of glee, then turned their attention back to Lorrison. He called for a quickstep and then skipped into the front row of seats as the elderly couple, as spry as spring lambs, bore down on him quite ruthlessly and obviously with no intention of swerving to avoid him.

Grant and Barrow did better this time, I thought. For in the quickstep one could decide for oneself where to go and how fast to get there, marching like centurions from one end of the ballroom to the other if it so pleased one. And then, once in place, there were endless fidgety little steps that could be used to stay there. They stuck to Tweetie and Roly like wasps to a jampot lid and stared hard over one another's shoulders at all the other dancers too. Such a marvellous job did they do that at the end of the dance, after Silvester and the other vultures had culled the toffee-apple woman and her broken umbrella, he spoke a whispered word in Lorrison's ear. Lorrison raised his eyebrows but delivered the message anyway, through his speaking trumpet.

'Couple number three have received a first warning for obstruction,' he said.

Tweetie nodded vehemently, glaring at Grant who flushed in deep patches all over her milky décolletage. I had never known her suffer from embarrassment before, but perhaps she had become swept up in the competition or perhaps she judged that her task was only possible if she stayed on the dance floor and would be dealt a knock-out blow by her being sent off. In any case, she and Barrow stayed well away from Tweetie during the first half of the tango that followed.

The second half of the tango was never danced. We failed, Alec and I. We failed more badly than ever in our detecting careers before. We sat in our little gilt chairs and watched a murder.

19

It happened quietly when the time came.

For a couple of minutes, the nine remaining couples stalked around the room, haughty expressions on their faces, stamping like lunatics – it really was the most ludicrous display I had ever seen and I suspect that my amusement distracted me. Tweetie and Roly were cheek-to-cheek, or temple to jaw anyway given the disparity in their heights, and they prowled around with their joined hands stuck out in front of them like two people trying to reach the top note on the same trombone. She was clutching him so tightly that probably he stayed on his feet for quite some time longer than he might have done without her. I noted his distress at the same time as Alec did.

'He's swaying,' was the first thing he said.

Roly certainly did not look fierce and jagged any more as one must in that silly dance. He was softening, his knees beginning to bow outwards. Tweetie, grim-faced, held him against her, and took a couple of faltering steps. I could see the cords standing out on her arms from the strain and the wild look in her eyes. At last, Grant noticed and she broke out of Barrow's arms and ran over. At that, the other couples all hesitated and half of the band members stopped playing, leaving just the piano and the trumpet blaring.

All of a sudden Tweetie was screaming. She let go of Roly and he slumped to the ground and lay in a huddled heap. Then she started yelling at the top of her lungs, taking huge mustering breaths before screaming again like a factory whistle. I wanted to slap her; her panic was panicking other people now, a good third of the women watching starting to sob or whimper. I leapt up and started towards her but before I could reach her, the rest of the dancers converged and made a barrier, shouting and jostling. Some of the crowd too started to surge on to the floor to see. Lorrison was bellowing through his trumpet, causing even more upset with his harsh voice and harsh words.

'Keep in your bloody seats, for the love of God,' he said. 'Keep away or you'll get what's coming!' It did not work. No one was left on the sidelines now except the four men in the front row, all of whom were watching the uproar with a calm lack of interest. They had stood up for a better view, but no more. I stared at them, transfixed, for it is not often that one sees utter cold-heartedness not troubling to hide itself. They saw me looking and even then did not muster a frown. Then my attention was hooked away by the sight of someone opening the door to the hallway and slipping out. As I shook my head thinking my eyes were playing tricks on me, Alec grabbed my arm.

'Never mind him now,' he said. 'Help me break through this lot, will you?'

Together, as determined as the tango dancers, we bludgeoned through the wall of tailcoats and ball gowns and reached Tweetie. She was crouching beside Roly, who lay face down and quite still, and she was rummaging in his top pocket. She pulled out his handkerchief, put it to her face and breathed in deeply.

'Theresa!' I said, horrified by her recklessness, but she took the handkerchief away and gave me a wobbly smile.

'It's fine,' she said. 'It's fine. He's only fainted. He was so anxious. He's just fainted.'

Alec, beside me, took hold of Roly's shoulders and turned him over. Then the crowd, those close enough to see, drew back with a collective gasp of horror. Whatever was wrong with Roland Wentworth, he had certainly not just fainted. His face was contorted in agony and was a deep livid colour unlike anything I had ever seen. He was struggling to breathe, his chest hitching and catching and his mouth wide open in a silent scream. He had been nobbled, like Leo before him, but it was something much worse than chloroform this time. Theresa stood like a pillar, her breathing very fast and shallow, staring down, unable to move.

'Roland?' said Alec. 'Roly? Can you hear me?' The poor man's eyes were closed but at the voice he waved a hand, clawing desperately at the air, until Alec grabbed hold of him and held him fast. 'Hang on, old chap,' he said. 'Help is on its way.'

'Can someone ring for an ambulance?' I shouted, staring around at the ring of faces. 'Mr Lorrison?' Lorrison was standing with his speaking trumpet hanging down at his side.

'Aye,' he said. 'Mick?' He nodded at one of the bandsmen, who trotted to the back of the stage and through the door, dodging Bert who was, at that moment, returning from somewhere in the back regions.

Roly was beginning to make a dreadful gurgling noise and his heels were drumming on the floor.

'Steady on, old man,' said Alec. 'It won't be long now.' Then over his shoulder: 'Dandy, can't you get rid of some of these people, for God's sake? Give him some bloody room and stop gawking.'

Where Lorrison had failed, Alec succeeded. Whether his voice was more commanding or the pain in it touched an answering humanity in others was hard to say but, in dribs and drabs, the watchers shuffled back until they were near the edges of the room again, some of them taking their seats. Only the dancers were left on the dance floor. Grant and Barrow stood stricken among them, their faces deathly pale.

'Is there a doctor in the house?' said Alec, but his voice

held no urgency, almost as though it were a benediction he was giving.

In fact, it served as such. After he had spoken Roly gave a strangled sound as though his whole throat were clenching and then his body went rigid until it seemed as if only his heels and the back of his head touched the floor. He held that dreadful pose for an impossible silent stretch of time and then he sank down and his head lolled sideways, a small trickle of blood running from the corner of his mouth and pooling on the floor.

We were all silent except for some weeping from among the women. Lorrison ran his hand over his mouth and gave a glance to the four men still sitting in the front row. At last, one of them spoke. It was the mild man.

'Where's Beryl?' he said.

Bert started into action, looked over and mumbled an answer. 'She ran out,' he said. 'I went after her but she kept on going.'

'Sensible lass,' said the mild man and he got to his feet, his supporters scrambling up as he did.

'Perhaps she went to telephone for help,' I said.

'Naw, she'll have got herself away out of this like I will too,' said the man.

I was puzzled by him. He seemed interested in Beryl but not at all concerned for her, which was an odd combination. As to why he denied my assumption of her helpful impulse, I could not imagine.

'Sir?' said Alec. He had laid his handkerchief over Roly's face and now stood up. He looked rather yellow – with his colouring he never goes white exactly – but steady enough. 'I don't think anyone should leave. The police will want to speak to all witnesses to this murder.'

'Murder?' said the man. 'It looks like a heart attack to me.'

I boggled at him. It looked about as much like a heart attack as it did a case of measles. The poor man had been poisoned, perhaps not in his hankie and not with chloroform this time, but certainly there was foul play. I searched around the gathered faces of the dancers. Most were simply shocked and miserable. Had one of them really killed two men? Tweetie was hugging herself, her arms wrapped tightly, rocking to and fro. Bert stumbled over to her and put a friendly arm around her but she shrugged him off, stepping away out of his reach.

The four men were leaving. In a row they walked across the floor and one of the thugs held the door open for the others.

'Mr Lorrison,' I cried. 'Are you really going to let them leave? The police—'

'The police'll find them,' Lorrison said.

I swung round to face the little dais where the judges were sitting. 'Mr Silvester?' I said. 'Since Lorrison has turned into a jellyfish, that leaves you in charge. Will you run after those people and detain them?'

'I think I should let the police handle this,' said Silvester. 'I shall leave my card. I can be contacted if they need me.' With that he rose and started to pluck at his cuffs and waistcoat to return himself to the pitch of dapper perfection.

'You're not leaving!' said Tweetie, looking horrified.

'I'm very happy to help the police with any questions they might have,' said Silvester, 'but this kind of unpleasantness is very—'

'But what about the Champs?' said Tweetie. 'You're the head judge.'

A horrified murmur rippled through the crowd.

'Miss Stott,' said Alec gently, but he was unable to go on for there was no way to say it without risking hysteria.

'I can dance with Bert,' said Tweetie. 'If Beryl's taken off and Roly isn't fit to go on.'

I could not help glancing at the still form which lay at our feet, his face covered with Alec's handkerchief. 'Not fit to go on' was something of an understatement.

'Tweetie,' I said. 'The competition can't continue. There has been a crime and it must be investigated.'

'He fell,' said Tweetie. 'He fainted and hit his head.'

Her voice was taut with desperation and as I took a closer look at her she seemed suddenly to be not quite in what one could call a normal state of mind. Her eyes were very round and staring and not only her limbs but her jaw also were trembling. Her skin was pouring with streams of sweat too, the cloth of silver clinging to her and growing dark.

'Theresa, my dear,' I said. 'You are in shock. You don't know what you're saying. We need to get you home or perhaps even to a doctor. At least come and sit quietly until help arrives, hmm?'

At that moment, though, we heard footsteps, heavy and hurried, coming along the corridor and all of us, as though our chins were hooked to a line, turned to see. It was not a doctor, however. Nor was it a pair of ambulance men with a stretcher which would have been even better. It was three policemen, burly and grim-faced, who burst in at the door with their truncheons held at the ready.

'Const—' Alec began, but before he could finish, Tweetie – still looking utterly crazed and running with rivers of perspiration now – was screaming at the top of her voice.

'They're going to arrest us all,' she shrieked. 'We'll all be flung in jail. You can't do that. We're innocent. They're letting the murderer get away to kill again. Run! Run! Save yourselves.'

I could have smacked her. In a second flat, the scene in the Locarno changed from horrified calm with everyone in their seats and poor Roly on the floor, to one of sheer chaos, spectators up and running, barging into each other, swarming the stage to escape that way, and all of them shouting. Tweetie went down in the midst of a particularly determined front of young women who barrelled past her with linked arms, kicking at Roly's body until it was turned on its side and the handkerchief floated away. Alec, horrified, dropped to his knees and gathered up the young man into his arms to protect him from further atrocities. At the same time, I struggled over to the main doors to try to close them or to somehow make a shield of myself to prevent all these witnesses from escaping.

Then my nerve failed. I could not understand it but these people, dressed to the nines, out to watch the dancing, had turned into a mob, easily capable of pulling me to pieces if I obstructed them. Thankfully, before my resolve was forced to do battle with my common sense, one of the policemen sounded his whistle, a painful, piercing shrill which brought everyone back to their senses.

'Anybody that sits down quiet now and answers our questions can get home to their own fireside just as soon as we're done,' he said. 'Any bloody eejit that keeps running about and yelling'll get three nights in the cells till a magistrate gets a wee look at them on Monday morning. It's up to youse!'

It was an unanswerable argument and the crowd subsided, jostling back into their seats, shaken and muttering.

'And as for you!' said another policeman to Tweetie, taking out his little book and snapping it open with a resounding thwack of its elastic.

'I am Miss Theresa Stott,' said Tweetie, full of dignity, even though she was sitting on the floor with one shoe off and her feathered dress in tatters. She had lost her headdress too and her hair was a tangle of pins and spangles, like the nest of a magpie with a taste for glitter. 'I am the daughter of Sir Percy Stott and he will have plenty to say if you are mean to me.'

'I couldn't care if you're the Princess Elizabeth and your faither's the king,' said the policeman. 'I've never seen such a display of—'

'Constable,' said Alec. 'That's all very well and I agree that Miss Stott did not help matters but the thing is that matters have changed for the worse since Miss Bonnar rang you. This man is dead. And it looks very much like murder.'

'Miss Bonnar?' said the third policeman, exchanging a glance with his colleagues. 'Beryl Bonnar? She's never said peep. It was a man that called this in. What's Beryl Bonnar got to do with it?'

I should not have pegged him as a ballroom dancing aficionado, but he certainly knew who Beryl was and seemed struck enough by the mention of her name that he was sidetracked from the matter in hand.

'Look,' said Alec, finally letting go of Roly's shoulders and letting him drop back to the floor. His face had relaxed into death in the minutes that had passed and the look of anguish had faded, leaving only the cherry-coloured flush on his skin and the trickle of blood from the corner of his mouth. There was a small rusty spot on Alec's shirt front where it had soaked in.

A memory was bubbling up inside me of sitting in the library at home leafing through a book, while Donald and Teddy played draughts with Hugh's chess set. Hugh thoroughly disapproves, for when Teddy was tiny he had once snapped off the ivory spear of one of the knights and it had to be sent to London to be mended. On the day I was remembering, though, I wanted them quietly occupied, so engrossed that they would not come to pester me and see what I was seeing, which was the pictorial section of *Gray's Anatomy*, dreadful enough to make me light-headed and sure to terrify them, unless it riveted them as did dead animals and skinned orphan lambs and every other grisly truth about life.

In my memory, I was staring at a page which alone of all the black and white photographs in the book had been tinted, like the pictures of Tweetie and Beryl in the windows downstairs. 'The effects perdure for up to an hour after death,' I had read, 'before slowly fading.'

187

'It's cyanide,' I said to Alec over Roly's body.

Tweetie shrieked and clapped both her hands to her face in the same gesture she had used the first time we had met her.

'She killed him!' she said. 'Beryl killed him! And she got away. Bert? Bert?'

Bert and Lorrison came pounding back through the office passage doorway.

'Is Beryl in here?' Bert said. 'She's disappeared.'

'I'll just bet she has,' said Tweetie. 'She's done it again. She's killed Roly and run away.'

20

It made no sense but I would have sworn that Tweetie's ringing accusation caused more of a stir in that crowded room than had the moment of Roland's death itself. All eyes were fixed on the ringleader of the three policemen, all breaths held. He frowned, pulled at the ends of his moustache and then glowered around at everyone.

'Beryl Bonnar?' he said. 'You're seriously telling me that Beryl Bonnar did this?'

No one spoke. It seemed possible that no one would ever speak again and so I cleared my throat and began.

'I wouldn't jump to conclusions,' I said. 'But it certainly doesn't look good. If she really didn't ring you then she must have had some other reason to flee.' I was struck by the curious stillness that crept over the audience as I spoke. Hardly any of them were looking at me or at Alec and Roly, even at Tweetie who was putting on such a show. They were all looking down into their laps, like schoolchildren avoiding a scolding. It was Grant's eye I caught as I cast mine around the room and when I did she gave a tiny, almost imperceptible shake of her head.

'Right,' said a policeman. They were all three of them constables as far as I could tell from their uniforms but he was definitely the boss. 'You all in the seats can go. Form an orderly queue and give your names and addresses to Constable Watson on your way out the door. Findlay? Go into the office there and ring the sergeant. We need a mortuary van and maybe an inspector.' The spectators nearest the door immediately began to shuffle out of their seats towards the main doors. 'You lot,' he went on, looking at the dancers still marooned on the floor in singles and pairs. 'You'll have to wait, but go and put some different clothes on, will you?'

'Er,' said Alec. 'Constable? I wonder if that's a good idea. The cloakroom is surely where the poison was given, you know. I wonder if perhaps we should all stay out of there until after it's been examined. Perhaps the inspector would—'

I had seen it before and could not mistake the signs of it happening again. The policeman drew himself up and stared Alec into silence.

'And who might you be?' he said.

'Alec Osborne,' said Alec, standing and stepping over to shake hands. He spoke softly, hoping to keep his words from the ears of the spectators who were passing close to him on their way to the end of the queue. 'I'm a private detective, working in association with Mrs Gilver here. And Miss Grant and Mr Barrow are our assistants. We have a great deal to tell you.'

'Private detectives, eh?' said the policeman. 'And no doubt you think we can't get by without your help. I've met your sort before.'

Alec thought very hard before he spoke again, searching for a way to impart the deluge of information we held without causing a loss of face which would set the policeman against him and us for ever. He made a valiant effort and failed.

'Shall we just wait with the dancers until the inspector gets here?' he said, as meekly as anyone could say anything.

'Oho!' said the constable. 'You want to go over my head, eh? Straight to the inspector? Sure you wouldn't rather speak to the Chief Constable?'

Alec gaped. 'I had no intent—'

'Leave your names and addresses with Watson like the others and get on your way,' he said, with a dismissive flick of his wrist.

'But, sir,' I protested since we appeared to have nothing to lose, 'we have a great many very important clues. Surely we should tell you. There's been a campaign of threats and it's not the first time.'

The look that ricocheted back and forth between the two policemen who heard this reminded me of nothing so much as the crazed flight of a bluebottle stuck inside a jar. Neither of the men said anything.

'And I think I have some new evidence to share,' said Grant, stepping forward rather awkwardly. I wondered if some part of the foundation of her extraordinary frock had let her down and she was worried about the whole thing falling to the floor.

'You can share it when we get as far as interviewing you,' said the policeman. 'It might be later today and it might not be till tomorrow.'

There was simply no talking to the man. All four of us together realised as much and decided to take him at his word and reap the benefit. We were about to get out of the ballroom with a chance to leap straight into solving a murder case instead of sitting around while the trails went cold and the perpetrator got away.

'Very well,' I said. I turned to Tweetie. 'Miss Stott, you can't drive in such a state of shock. When you are released, please telephone home and we shall come back and fetch you. Meanwhile we shall talk to your parents and let them know you are well, in case they see a line in the late edition before your return.'

Grant limped off to the cloakroom and returned, still in the extraordinary frock, but walking normally again and carrying her little case of outdoor clothes. Barrow too joined us in his tails, looking even more dashing with his white tie undone and his collar stud open, like a gigolo after hours at a casino. I could see a few of the dance enthusiasts giving him an appreciative eye as we passed them but he affected indifference.

'Idiots,' Alec muttered, as we descended the stairs to the street. 'Of all the putty-headed nincompoops. You just handed them a cause of death apart from anything else.'

'I rather think the police surgeon would have done that anyway as soon as he took a squint at the corpse,' I said. 'Cyanide. He must have drunk coffee, mustn't he? It's too bitter to pass in a cup of tea or chocolate. Barrow? Did anyone hand a flask of coffee around in the men's cloakroom before the start of the show?'

'Not that I can think of,' Barrow said. 'There were bottles of beer and Alonzo had a flask of whisky but he didn't share it that I saw.'

'And I don't suppose there were any deliveries,' Alec said. 'Chocolates or what have you?'

'Hardly, darling,' I said. 'It's not Covent Garden, with presents in the dressing room. What are you thinking?'

'How about visitors?' said Alec. 'Any young men with no business there who dropped in anyway?'

I stopped dead on the stairs, causing a pair of women to walk into the back of me. I apologised and started moving again.

'Of course!' I said. 'You saw him too. He slipped out the door and with all that happened afterwards I forgot.' I half turned and looked back up towards the ballroom. 'We should go and tell them, shouldn't we?'

'They had their chance,' said Alec, going as far as to put his hand in the small of my back to keep me moving.

'No visitors,' said Barrow, very properly waiting for silence before he answered, since a good servant would never do anything that smacked of interruption or interference.

'Who was it?' said Grant, with no such qualms.

'Julian Armour,' said Alec and I in chorus.

'The Stotts assured us repeatedly that he knew nothing of her hobby,' I said, 'and yet there he was, watching.'

'And slipping out as soon as things got sticky,' Alec said. 'We shall have to pay a visit to Mr Armour.'

We emerged blinking on to the street and, just as when one goes to watch a particularly melodramatic matinee at the cinema, it was shocking to see the daylight of an ordinary Friday afternoon and hear snippets of conversation from the passers-by.

'We've tooken good care of your motor,' said our little barefoot friend, standing up from where he had been playing jacks with a collection of pebbles. His sister gathered the stones and put them in her dress pocket. The Phantom was gone and it seemed that our watchmen had switched midshift to the Cowley, hoping for double pay.

I smiled and crouched down to talk to them but all their attention, at least that of the girl, was fixed on Barrow and Grant, and especially Grant, in her costume.

'Wait in the motorcar,' I said to the glamorous pair and turned back to the children, kneeling right down on the ground beside them. Alec joined me, pulling his coat closed over the bloodstain on his shirt front.

'What's going on?' said the girl. 'We saw three polis go running in. Why's everybody leaving?'

'There's been an accident,' I said. 'Nothing for you to worry about but you might be able to help us.'

She nodded solemnly but her brother got a sharp look in his eye. 'Worth a lot, is it? Our help?'

I shook my head in a mixture of disgust and awe. He was starting from nowhere but I imagined that if it depended on cheek alone he would go far.

'Worth a shilling each,' said Alec, rummaging in a pocket. 'Now, before the police came, what did you see?'

'We saw a gent come running out,' said the little girl.

Julian Armour, I thought, nodding at Alec.

'Which way did he go?' I said.

'He went to the telephone box,' said her brother, pointing at a kiosk nearby.

'And was he . . .' Alec said. 'Did he seem scared or upset in any way? Could you tell?'

'He was shaking like a jelly and as white as a ghost,' said the boy.

'He must have telephoned to the police station,' Alec said.

'Then what?' I said.

Both children shuffled their feet a little, coughing and looking down. Eventually the boy spoke up.

'Then them in the big car came out and drived away,' he said.

The four odd men in the front row, I thought. Of course. And these children did not want to remind us of them and of the fact that they were turning such a profit today, in case we saw fit to reduce our contribution in light of it.

'Anyone else?' I said, smiling at the girl.

She thought hard and shook her head.

'Are you sure?' I asked her. 'You didn't see a pretty lady in a pink dress?'

She looked interested in this possibility, but once again she shook her head. 'Naw,' she said. 'No women come out till you two. Her in the goldie frock with the necklace. That's lovely.'

I frowned at her. Beryl was certainly not inside the Locarno if one believed Bert.

'Is there another way out?' I said to Alec.

He shrugged.

'There's the side lane,' said the little boy, pointing. 'And a back door.'

'But no one came out that way?' I asked.

'The pretty lady in a pink dress?' said the girl.

'Did she?' said Alec.

'No,' said the child. 'Just a van.'

'Can you describe it?' said Alec. She looked rather panicked so he tried again. 'What sort of van, my dear?'

'A black one with gold writing on the side,' she said. 'And fancies.'

'Fancies?' I asked, but my frown of puzzlement upset her and she grew truculent.

'I can't read,' she said, 'and Wullie was looking at the big car.'

'Did you see who was driving it?' I said. I turned to Alec. 'No reason Beryl Bonnar couldn't drive a van, is there?' When I turned back to face the children their eyes were wide and their mouths were open.

'Beryl Bonnar?' said the girl. 'Her?' She pointed between the bodies of the dispersing crowd to the photograph in the foyer. 'It wasn't her. It was a mannie.'

'In a uniform?' I asked, hoping to hear that the child recognised the livery if not the writing.

She shook her head. 'Just a mannie in a cap and a jersey.'

'And we never saw Beryl Bonnar at all,' said the boy. 'We never saw nothing.'

'Very well,' I said. 'Don't upset yourselves. Now you've been a tremendous help to us and so here is a little something for you to take home to your mother. Promise you'll take this straight home and hand it over. No stopping at the sweetie shop.'

From the looks on their faces I do not think they had ever seen a half-crown before, much less held one in their hands.

With a wave at Grant and Barrow who were sitting back in the motorcar looking quite worn out, Alec and I dutifully trotted up the lane a few doors along from the Locarno and into a gloomy yard full of dustbins and coal bunkers.

Alec shook his head. 'A van parked here must have been connected to some other place,' he said. 'We're nowhere near the back of the ballroom.'

'Well, let's see if we can get there,' I said, scanning the roofline. 'Since we've come this far.'

We slipped through a gateway into a second yard, this one cluttered with barrels and orange boxes, and then along a narrow path between high brick walls until we came to what was unmistakably the side of the Locarno, soaring and featureless except for one blue-painted metal door, very chipped and with no handle on the outside. A further short path opened on to the next street to the north, which was a bustling thoroughfare to rival Sauchiehall Street.

'She must have gone off this way,' I said. 'But surely not on foot. That dress would have caused a sensation. She must have been picked up.'

'A get-away car they call them in the penny dreadfuls from America,' said Alec, as we made our way back again, along the path to the side door of the Locarno, through the yard of barrels and along the path to the yard of dustbins.

'Pennies dreadful,' I said automatically, for it is one of Hugh's bugbears along with procurators fiscal and mothers-in-law.

'Undoubtedly,' Alec said. Then he stopped and crouched down. 'Look at this, Dandy.' He took his pipe out of his mouth and pointed to the ground with the stem.

I bent down beside him and peered.

In the weeds growing up along the side of the yard, there was a scrap of sugar-pink fabric about three inches long and an inch wide with long threads trailing from either end where it had been wrenched off the frock it had been stitched to. Staring at it, I could feel my heart begin to beat a little faster inside me.

'She was in the van,' Alec said. 'Look – the tyre marks stop right here and look at *that*!'

Sure enough, the dust was scuffled and the weeds flattened just where the tyre prints ended and one could easily imagine a van, parked here waiting, and people shifting their feet as they opened and closed its doors.

'She must have been in the back,' Alec said, 'or the little one would have seen her.'

I thought it over and then nodded. 'She was driven away by the mannie.'

Alec was patting his pockets in the way which usually signals that he is looking for his pipe tobacco, but in this instance he took an envelope out of his coat instead of his baccy pouch, gingerly picked up the scrap of pink frill with his fingertips and dropped it inside.

'To take to the policemen and be bawled out for disturbing the evidence?' I asked him.

'The same policemen who let half the witnesses go and the chief witnesses go back to the scene of the crime to change?' said Alec. 'No fear.'

'I can't say I don't agree,' I said. 'But I am surprised at you. I've never known you quite so determined to take over from policemen before, Alec.'

'I shall tell all later,' he said. 'Suffice to say for now that I sense they wouldn't do their best for Roly any more than they did for Leo before him. Now let's get out of here before the inspector arrives and catches us.'

The stream of spectators leaving the Locarno had thinned to a trickle and no one paid us any attention as we emerged from the mouth of the lane and headed for the Cowley.

Certainly not our servants. I was surprised that Barrow did not leap out of his place in the front seat to open the door for me and, although I was not surprised exactly – for she had been getting rather spoiled ever since she first began to help with cases – still it was annoying to see Grant leaning back with her head lolling, taking her ease, paying no heed to my approach. A wave of missing Bunty washed over me as I drew near. At least, with a dog, one is always assured of a welcome.

It was not until I had the motorcar door open that I realised something was wrong.

21

Grant blinked slowly and regarded me with heavy-lidded eyes. Barrow in the front seat did not even do that much. His head nodded twice and then fell forward until his chin was resting on his chest. I gasped and it was as I breathed in that gasp that the full horror of what had happened grew clear. I met Alec's eyes, as terrified as mine, on the other side of the motorcar and then leapt in and started the engine.

'Where are you going?' Alec cried, only just getting into his seat and closing the door before the pavement whipped away from under his feet.

'Hospital,' I said. 'Open the windows, Alec, and let's see if we can't get them round with some fresh air on the way.'

Alec scrambled this way and that, unbuttoning the side flaps and setting about the window winders like a demented lock-keeper. He ended up practically straddling Grant at one point in a way which would have scandalised her if she had been in full possession of her faculties. In fact, that was when I began to hope she and Barrow were recovering. She blinked at Alec's face inches from her own and roused herself enough to cross her arms over her front and move her ankles tidily to one side instead of sprawling as she had been. A minute later, Barrow sat forward and coughed politely into his handkerchief.

'I must offer my sincerest apologies, sir,' he said.

Alec, finished at last with the windows and flaps, dropped into the seat beside Grant with a great puff of exhaled breath.

'Where are we going?' Grant said. 'Aren't you getting a

draught, madam? I didn't dress your hair for this today. Could you pull over to the side and let me tie a scarf over it?'

I started laughing for sheer relief and, finding a side street, I turned down it and drew into the edge of the road.

'I haven't the foggiest notion where the nearest hospital is anyway,' I said. 'Grant? Barrow? How are you feeling?'

'Perfectly well, thank you for asking, madam,' said Barrow, as he would if both his legs were hanging off.

'I've felt better,' said Grant. 'I won't lie. What happened?'

'You were poisoned,' said Alec. 'Gaspers, Dandy.' He took my cigarettes, lit two and handed one each to Grant and Barrow. Such was Barrow's state of shock at the news that he took it.

'Poisoned?' he said.

'Oh,' said Grant.

'I'm sure of it,' said Alec. 'I don't quite understand why it took so long to act or why fresh air might have stopped it, but—'

'Ah,' said Grant.

'What is it?' I asked her.

She took a deep puff on the cigarette and extinguished it in the little brass ashtray attached to the back of the driver's seat. Then she bent down and opened the clasp of her capacious handbag. I peered over to see what she was up to and caught sight of something winking and gleaming in the dark down there.

'It's Tweetie's headdress,' she said. 'I pinched it.'

Alec whistled, long and low, in admiration and although I already had fears that Grant's head would swell to such a size that living with her might become unbearable I could not help adding my voice in approbation.

'Bravo,' I said. 'Jolly well done. Did you snatch it right off her head?'

Grant wrung every possible scrap of drama out of the moment. She lifted the headdress reverently out of her bag and slid it onto the seat between Alec and her, arranging it in a circle and tucking in portions of the fastening which were not supposed to be on show.

'I didn't have to do any snatching,' she said. 'Miss Stott had wrenched it off already. She tore it off as if it were scalding her and threw it down so hard it shot away under the stage. I had to fish it out again. I remembered what you said about Mrs Munn's slip-up, you see. She said "head-dress" instead of "hankie", didn't she? And so I just thought . . . To be on the safe side . . .'

'Good grief!' I said. 'I *thought* Tweetie seemed odd. Even given the shock and distress. She was boiling hot and shaking. Good God above! The poison was in her headdress?'

'If she hadn't realised something was wrong and ripped it off her head,' said Grant, 'she might be as dead as Roly.'

'I can't quite believe she isn't anyway,' I said. 'Although, I suppose . . . she was wearing it awfully far back so perhaps none of it reached her nose.'

'Clearly,' said Alec. 'Now, let's see how it was done.'

But I put my foot down. 'No!' I said. 'I absolutely forbid it. We have no idea whether that thing has any more surprises in store.'

He looked as crestfallen as a child whose paper boat is sinking.

'I suppose you're right,' he said. 'But shall we take it to the police or to a chemist at the university?'

'I'm not so much of a killjoy as all that,' I said. 'I only meant we should get out and examine it on the bonnet instead of here inside in case it goes off again or however it was done.'

He missed the end of this because he was scrambling down, holding the headdress very lightly with a handkerchief over his bare hand. Barrow slipped out too.

'I thought it was a peculiar design the minute I saw it,' Grant said. 'Hardly flattering.'

This was a joke, for some of the more outré modes into which Grant has tried to coax me over the years have been so hideous that one cannot help believing the whole of Paris fashion is one enormous hoax perpetrated upon the gullible rich. Tweetie's headdress had not struck me (or Grant either, I should wager) as anything out of the ordinary in that regard. I said nothing and climbed out of the motorcar.

It would have looked like the adoration of the Magi to a casual observer but thankfully this was a very quiet little side street lined with warehouse buildings and so we were unseen as we all bent over the object.

'It's changed since yesterday,' Alec said.

It certainly had. As well as the droplets at the edge, the headband now had a row of large paste diamonds along its middle, sitting slightly proud. Alec, appointing himself surgeon general, grasped one of them and pulled. It came out very easily, rather too easily; looking closely, we could all see that it really was no more and no less than a long tack or short hatpin attached merely by being stuck in.

'That's an odd way to do it,' said Grant, but it was the band itself which, on a second viewing, now struck me as peculiar. It really must have been horribly uncomfortable to wear such a sturdy one while dancing energetically in a crowded room. And the puffed appearance was its oddest feature. Without the stuffing under the cloth it would have been both cooler to wear and prettier to look at. I pulled another of the tacks out and then jabbed it in again, feeling the resistance and then the give as it poked through the cloth.

'Do you have your penknife, Alec?' I said. 'Can you slit it and see what's under there?'

Alec rummaged and patted and eventually tracked down his little knife. He opened it, selected a blade with maddening deliberation and then carefully made a short slit in the cloth. Inside was what looked like a layer of thick fleecy interlining.

Alec's shoulders drooped with disappointment, but Grant and I huddled even closer. I was not privy to Grant's inner emotion but for my part I felt my pulse begin to bang in my throat. There was no reason whatsoever to interline a dancing cap. I caught Grant's eye and knew that she thought the same.

Gingerly – really, one would have thought that we were snipping the fuse of a ticking bomb, but having just seen poor Roly breathe his last I was not inclined to be braver than I had to be – I took off one of my gloves, reached out, poked the flannel and then rubbed my thumb and finger together.

'It's still wet,' I said.

Grant flipped the thing over and together we peered inside the pale lining.

'Oiled backing cloth,' she said. 'Someone soaked the whole thing. Put a syringe into the seams probably. Cloth of silver doesn't show the wet and this waxed cotton kept Tweetie from feeling it damp on her hair, but look at the stains here along the stitching. It's sopping wet still. What poison is it, madam? Do you know?'

'Cyanide,' I said.

Grant's eyes opened very wide and she immediately began to unbutton her gloves, before pulling them off and dropping them on the pavement beside her. She sniffed her fingertips and then relaxed a little.

'I saw her poking the pins in,' she said. 'She was chattering on. Saying what a good idea the extra rhinestones were. She said thank you. I didn't know which of the others she was talking to.' Grant's eyes filled with tears. 'Someone soaked her little headband in cyanide and gave her those pins and the poor girl did the last of it with her own hand. She pierced the pockets and let the poison out into the air.'

Alec was nodding very slowly and steadily as the story began to come together in his memory.

'It was that dratted tango,' he said. 'They were pressed so closely together you couldn't have slid a piece of paper between them. Roly must have been breathing in lungfuls of the stuff.'

'If the poison was strong enough to discommode Miss Grant and myself half an hour later through the walls of a carpet bag,' said Barrow, 'I don't doubt that the gentleman succumbed when it was fresh and it was right under his nose.'

We stood in glum silence for a moment contemplating this until Grant broke in.

'It's not a carpet bag,' she said. 'It's a vanity.'

At times before that day in Glasgow, Alec and I had found ourselves closer to the action in a murder case than any policeman would want a private detective to be. There was always, however, an innocent path to get us there; perhaps the case was cold or the police had missed a clue and could not, in conscience, blame us for uncovering evidence or even villains, much as they might want to. But we had never before been put in such an awkward spot as to have the murder weapon in our hands on the very day of the crime, faced with trying to explain ourselves as we trooped back to the scene to hand it over to them.

'We might be arrested,' I said.

'*I* might,' said Grant. 'You've done nothing wrong. Madam.'

'Do you think you could dream up a reason for having the headdress in your possession, Grant?' Alec said. 'If we help you.'

Grant regarded him with withering scorn and began to talk, as fluently and convincingly as though she were reading a part in a play.

'I saw it being trampled and thought it was such a shame if poor Miss Stott lost a memento of what's going to be her last happy day as a dancer, you see,' she said. 'So I popped it in my bag to return to her and then blow me down if we weren't hustled out of there without so much as a by your leave and I didn't get the chance to.'

'Splendid,' I said, climbing back inside the motorcar. 'And shall we try to impart some of what we think to that crew of Glasgow's finest or shall we just hand the bandeau back over and keep our own counsel?'

'What *do* we think?' Alec said, not unreasonably.

I was glad of the need to negotiate a turn in that narrow street and to avoid a flurry of carts as I emerged back on to the road, for it gave me time to think of something to say.

'We think, don't we, that either Jeanne or Miss Thwaite made that monstrous thing,' I said. 'But Julian, we now discover, had a motive and was on the scene.'

'And Beryl, although she had no means to manufacture the cap,' said Alec, 'certainly had the opportunity to set about it with a syringe in the cloakroom, and the same motive as last year, and she has scarpered which speaks rather loudly to her guilt.'

'Begging your pardon, madam,' said Grant, 'but it can't be Julian or Jeanne because why would either Julian Armour or Jeanne McNab want to threaten Foxy or kill her partner? It's only Beryl that has a motive for both.'

'And Miss Thwaite surely has a motive for neither,' Alec said. 'Unless it's just a sort of mania.'

'There must be mania in it somewhere,' I said. 'Simply because it's so . . . it's so very . . . poisoned headdresses? It's like something from a fairy tale. It's hardly an efficient way to do away with people.'

'It's melodramatic in the extreme,' said Alec. 'You're right. And neither Miss Thwaite nor Jeanne strike one as having an ounce of melodrama in them.'

We were almost back at the Locarno again and, whatever view the others might take of matters, I looked forward to seeing that stubborn policeman squirm when he was forced to accept that we had helped him. I drew into the side of the street and pulled on the handbrake.

'Who's all coming up?' said Grant, thus staking her own claim to part of the fun.

'Wait here, Barrow,' Alec said. 'You still don't look too jolly. Open the windows and take it easy.'

So it was only Grant, Alec and I who traipsed up the stairs to the ballroom, balanced perfectly between anticipatory glee and trepidation in case the policemen found a way to cause unpleasantness for us after all. It was very quiet; clearly all the spectators had long gone, but still I was surprised when we opened the doors to the dance floor itself to see it utterly empty. There were a few disarranged chairs and the bandsmen had left without covering the piano or tidying away their music stands, but of policemen, pathologists and witnesses there was not a one.

'Perhaps they're through in the office,' Alec said and so thither we went but there was complete silence in the corridor too and when I knocked on Lorrison's door no one answered.

'He must be around somewhere,' I said, 'or the place would be locked.' I opened the door and entered.

Lorrison, all alone, sat at his desk, barely looking up at us as we filed in. His tailcoat was nowhere to be seen and his white tie was loose around his neck. He puffed steadily on a noxious cigarette and the air, blue and shifting in clouds, told us that it was not his first one.

'Mr Lorrison?' I said. 'Where is everyone?'

At last he lifted his head. 'Who you looking for?' he said.

'Surely the police haven't finished already?' said Alec. 'The inspector hadn't even arrived when we left and that was hardly half an hour ago.'

'The inspector never came,' said Lorrison. 'He told his men to get back to the station as soon as the body was moved. It's Friday night coming. We'll be stretched.'

I watched as Alec's jaw dropped open.

Lorrison stubbed out his cigarette and coughed violently, so violently that he reconsidered lighting another before it was out of the packet.

'Don't look like that,' he said. Inspector Todd reckoned that Ronnie Watt can't get any deader so he can wait till everyone's home safe and sound after closing time.'

It made some sort of sense but it did not explain why there was no bobby stationed at the Locarno's door to keep out sightseers until the place could be gone over properly for clues.

'Aye,' said Lorrison again, 'that's their story and they're sticking to it.'

'What on earth does that mean?' I said.

Lorrison heaved a sigh up from the middle of the earth's core and regarded me with bleary eyes and as hangdog an expression as any I had ever seen upon his face.

'Truth is,' he said, 'nobody wants to risk looking for Beryl until they can be bloody sure they won't find her. Nobody wants to stir that wasp's nest and you can't blame them.' He huffed out a laugh as he said these words and it was then that I caught a whiff of the whisky, sharp and fresh, on his breath and realised that although he was not slurring his words, he was profoundly drunk and was saying things that his sober self would not so much have whispered in an empty room.

'You suspect Miss Bonnar then?' said Alec.

'Not me,' Lorrison said, swinging round and giving him a dreadful grin, almost a leer. 'I wouldn't dare. I suspect an unfortunate accident which no one could have foreseen or prevented. Aye, that's right, a terrible accident.' He paused. 'Another one.'

22

It was one of those moments, all too rare and much to be cherished, when one thing suddenly becomes very clear and lights up a great many others. Beryl's amusement at the notion of our interviewing her was explained; and Miss Thwaite's sudden dismissal too when she dragged up the firmly forgotten story of Leo's death; now, I knew what was frightening Foxy Trotter and why Lorrison was so defeated, not to mention the reason that everyone from the blustering policemen all the way down to our ragged little friends outside on the pavement seemed to know Beryl Bonnar's name. Also, I understood at last who the four men in the front row were – or at least who one of them was, the one who spoke and took charge without raising his voice or so much as waving a hand, although I was more puzzled than ever by his calm.

When the realisations had finished washing over me, I was left with a sense of profound irritation. Hugh, drat him, was right again.

'Gangsters?' said Grant as we hurried back downstairs. 'I can't believe it. Those men were honest-to-goodness gangsters? Right here in Glasgow like something off the pictures!' She held the bag with its noisome contents at arm's length as though it had become more dangerous by its distant association with such men. Of course, we had decided without discussion not to leave the headdress with Lorrison and it was without further discussion that we went straight back to the Grand Central with it still in our possession instead of finding a police station and handing it in there.

207

If the case was going to proceed in a cloud of favours, denials and backroom deals then we would jolly well hang on to it and use it to solve the murder ourselves.

'I think,' I said, once the bally thing was locked safely in Alec's dressing-table drawer along with the vulpine and ornithological objects, 'that I might telephone to Inspector Hutchinson in Perth and sound him out about all this. Gangsters and the like. It's hard to believe one is really discussing such things. Later tonight perhaps when he's off-duty and has had his whisky and soda.'

Alec nodded uncertainly. We had assisted Mr Hutchinson of the Perthshire Constabulary on a case a few years back and by its end we had both come to regard him as a man of great honour and intelligence. I understood Alec's qualms, though. Hutchinson had been intractable about the fingerprints and this was even more ticklish. One could not be sure where his native integrity and his loyalty to his brethren might meet at their border and one would hate to witness a man who had served as a shining example of rectitude reveal his feet of clay.

'You never know, Dan,' Alec said with rather hollow bonhomie, 'if we're lucky we might have solved the case by then and only be asking Hutchinson who we should ring up with the name of the guilty party.'

I raised my eyebrows at him in the glass, where I was standing affixing my hat, a black one, preparatory to setting off for Balmoral to interview Tweetie. We had allowed Grant and Barrow the rest of the day off in recompense for their nasty experience and had bade them ring up a doctor if they should begin to feel woozy.

'The name of the guilty party?' I echoed, jabbing at my hat with a pin and wincing at the memory of those tacks. 'You don't think it's Beryl?'

'I don't think it's Beryl alone,' said Alec. 'It can't be. Beryl can't have made that silly headband – that must have been either Jeanne or Miss Thwaite – and if Grant's right about its entire design being geared towards a drenching in cyanide then whoever made it is in this up to her neck. And then there's Julian.'

'He surely didn't stitch the band,' I said. 'But he did practically faint when he realised who I was and he was in the ballroom today until he slipped out again. Do you think we could get his home address out of Tweetie and beard him tonight or must we wait until Monday and catch him at work?'

'It's going to be a long night anyway without a visit to Julian,' said Alec. 'As well as grilling Jeanne and Miss Thwaite, I want to go back to Foxy and ask about her headdress.'

It began to feel like a long night about fifteen minutes after we arrived at Balmoral.

'You!' cried Lady Stott as she caught sight of Alec and me in the sitting room doorway. 'You're sacked.'

'I'm not at all surprised that you feel so,' said Alec.

'Well, I am,' boomed her husband. 'Tweetie is here alive and well at the end of that blessed competition and that's all we asked of you. You shall have a bonus and it's me who writes the cheques, Eunice, I'll thank you to remember.'

'*Well?*' said Lady Stott on such a high pitch that she was almost squealing. 'Alive and *well?* Look at her, Bounce – she's ragged. She has seen something no young lady should ever have to see. I'd be astounded if her nerves aren't frayed till the end of her days. Oh poor Roly, poor, poor Roly.'

'You're not making it any better, Mother,' murmured Tweetie in a weak voice, from where she was draped on a couch like a mermaid on a rock. Then she turned to us and managed a brave if rather watery smile. 'Have they caught her yet, Mr Osborne?'

If we had told the truth – that they had not even started looking – I think both of the elder Stotts would have burst into flames with indignation. So I simply shook my head and Alec made do with a regretful grimace.

'Poor Roly,' said Lady Stott again. 'He was such a nice boy. So attentive and such a good listener. And so young!'

'How are you feeling, Miss Stott?' I said, taking the liberty of settling on a low stool drawn up close to her side and peering at her. Her pupils were normal sized again and although she had that deathly pallor, there was no sheen upon her skin now. I took her hand and chafed it in my own. 'We were terribly upset about having to leave you. That stupid policeman.'

'And that's another thing,' thundered Lady Stott. 'What's the point of all those luncheons and fund drives and games of golf if when something like this happens you can't go straight to the Chief Constable and get him *told*?'

Sir Percy fidgeted a little on his plush armchair and smoothed his hair before speaking.

'Matters are rather more complicated than you – in your protected innocence, Eunice – can possibly understand.' If he had doused her in petrol and lobbed a lit match he could not have produced a more violent reaction.

'My what?' she said in a very low and wavering voice. 'My protected innocence, is it? Who do you think you're talking to, Bounce Stott? Do you think I came up the Clyde on a biscuit? I've forgotten more about what goes on in this city than you'll ever know and I don't care *who* she is. I want you to tell the Chief Constable and the Fiscal and Lord Burrell and the editor of the *Herald* and anyone else you can think of to tell, that she's on the run and she must be found. This is your own family, for the love of God.'

'Ronald Watt was no member of my family,' said Sir Percy with a warning look. 'Nor even of yours.'

Lady Stott subsided a little, fluttering her hand at her neck, tidying her pearls as she always did when she was discomfited.

'Too close for comfort,' she said. 'And this pair might as well have been chocolate soldiers.'

'We've discovered how it was done,' I said, unable to sit through another tirade on the subject of our inadequacy. 'Tweetie's headdress was soaked in cyanide and Roly breathed it in until he collapsed.'

All eyes, unsurprisingly, were suddenly upon me. Sir Percy's face had fallen, all his bluster wiped away and replaced by a dull gaping shock. His wife, in contrast, seemed to have added all his lost fervour to her own and was breathing like a bull, swelling over the top of her corsets. Tweetie was staring with wide eyes, aquiver in a way I had not seen except when a hare is sitting up in a field. Jeanne was the only one whose expression puzzled me. She was sitting forward, staring at Tweetie and looked, if one had to choose a word, annoyed. And annoyance was a most peculiar response to what she was hearing. I glanced at Alec to see if he had noticed it, but he was exchanging some silent masculine message with Sir Percy.

'Now, Miss Stott,' I said, 'we need you to try very hard and remember everything you can about what happened in the cloakroom today. Was anyone alone with your things at any moment?'

Tweetie ignored me. 'Cyanide?' she whispered. 'On my headdress? You mean it was *me*? *I* killed Roly?'

'You did nothing of the sort,' snorted Lady Stott. 'You were in grave danger yourself. You did nothing wrong. You killed no one. Tell her, Bounce.'

'You were the instrument of death, Tweet,' said Sir Percy. 'Not the agent.'

Unsurprisingly, Tweetie took this characterisation of her part in the tragedy rather badly. Her eyes filled with tears and her bottom lip began to quiver. Lady Stott formed an even dimmer view but expressed it more forcefully.

'Instru—' she said, so aghast that she could not say any more without another deep breath to gather strength to speak. 'Instrument of death? What the merry blazes is wrong with you, Percy Stott? How can you say such a thing to your own darling girl? I'll instrument of death you!'

Sir Percy gobbled and spluttered but could not break into his wife's flow to mount a defence. And even Alec, to whom he extended a supplicatory hand, could not help him. Alec looked as shocked as Lady Stott, actually.

'Beryl,' said Tweetie when at last her mother drew breath.

'Exactly,' said Lady Stott. 'Beryl blooming Bonnar is the instrument and agent and everything else of death. So put that in your pipe, Percival, and smoke yourself blue.'

'Beryl was alone with my things,' said Tweetie. 'It was about an hour before the doors opened, we were all in our costumes but I hadn't put my head ornament on. We went out on to the floor to get our pep talk from Mr Silvester, but Beryl hung back.'

'Why?' I said. 'What reason did she give?'

Tweetie laughed and shook her head. 'Beryl Bonnar doesn't have to explain herself to anyone,' she said. 'If anyone else had kept Mr Silvester waiting there'd have been hell to pay, but—'

'Theresa!' said Sir Percy. 'Will you mind your language? See what hanging around with those rough sorts has done to her, Eunice? Six years at the best school that money can buy and it's all undone.'

'Your father's quite right,' said Lady Stott. 'Julian wouldn't care to hear that sort of word on your lips, Tweetie.'

'Julian isn't the cherub you think he is,' Tweetie said, in a sort of sly drawl.

I caught Alec's eye, wondering if we should press her on what she might mean, but he shook his head.

'Miss Stott,' he said gently, 'how long was Miss Bonnar alone in the cloakroom?'

'Ten minutes perhaps,' said Tweetie uncertainly. 'I mean, I can't be sure. I was in my gown and had put my wristwatch away with my other things. Roly still had his pocket watch though. You could ask him.' As she finished this speech her voice died in her throat and with a huge gasp, she began to weep, tears pouring down her face and sobs tearing at her.

Both her parents converged on her then, fussing like a pair of hens, shushing and patting and tucking the blanket tighter around her shoulders. Then Sir Percy sat on the edge of the couch and rocked her with his stout arms clasped firmly around her shoulders and Lady Stott, outwitting her corsets by the power of overwhelming maternal devotion, managed to bend double over the back of the couch and plant kiss after smacking kiss on Tweetie's head like the priest of some flamboyant Church performing his rituals.

I caught Jeanne's eye and nodded towards the hallway then the three of us left as quietly as we could, fain to disturb the pietà, this precious moment when all three Stotts were one.

We retired to the library, where Jeanne went straight to a tantalus of brandy and a soda siphon, poured herself a respectable snifter and drank it down like medicine before turning to face us.

'My father will be spinning in his grave,' she said, with an apologetic grin. 'But I started to feel quite giddy in there. How many shocks can there be in one day?'

I gave a polite smile, one I learned from my mother, designed to acknowledge that one has understood the confidence just shared but give not even a shred of encouragement to the sharing of any more. Alec, in contrast, was listening.

'How many shocks have there been?' he said. 'Roly's death makes one.'

Jeanne smiled uncertainly at Alec and her eyes strayed to the tantalus again before she answered.

'Roly's death is the biggest shock, naturally,' she said, putting her head slightly on one side in the way that some men find winsome. She practically fluttered her eyelashes too and I wished there was a way to tell her that Alec is immune to such wiles; it makes uncomfortable viewing for a third party who knows how thoroughly it is bound to fail. 'But Beryl getting away with it is another – actually getting to leave the building and escape. And hearing the details of how it was done makes difficult listening.'

'Was your father a teetotaller?' I asked her.

She blinked, surprised at the change of subject, and turned to me. 'He was a lay preacher,' she said. 'Very low church as they say in your part of the world. Of course, the whole Church of Scotland is quite low.'

'Which church did he preach at?' I asked.

She gave the uncertain smile again and even briefly re-tilted her head, before realising that there was no point flirting with me and straightening it again.

'Why do you ask?' she said.

'Oh, gosh, no reason at all,' I said. 'I was merely trying to talk of other things to soothe you after the upsets.' She did not believe me and I did not blame her. 'But if you feel equal to a few questions, then we can crack on, can't we?'

'Fire away,' she said. 'I have nothing to hide.'

'Well, of course not,' said Alec in his most innocent voice. 'That surely goes without saying.' And so the fact that it had *not* gone so was there like a huge gaseous cloud between us throughout the rest of the very short interview.

'Which means there's no need to look so scared,' he went on. He smiled at her again and the venomous look she shot back was almost too blatant to go unremarked. I muttered a quiet 'touché' to myself and waited to hear what would come next.

It is not often that Alec arrives at the state of mind my sons describe in their slangy way as 'having it in for someone' but when some unfortunate individual does ruffle him badly, then he is positively biblical in his dealings.

'What we really need to find out from you, Miss McNab,' he said, 'is who made her headdress.'

'Tweetie's?' said Jeanne, which was intensely interesting. If

214

she knew about Foxy's headdress it was news to me and I regarded her with even more attention than before, which had been plenty.

'Tweetie's naturally,' said Alec and once again Jeanne realised that she had slipped.

'Well, you should know,' She said. 'You delivered it yourself, all ready for stitching.'

'It wasn't in the parcel we took to Miss Thwaite, I said. 'It was left behind here with her shoes? 'Oh,' said Jeanne. 'Then she must have finished it earlier than I thought.'

'But she did do it?' I said.

'Who else?' said Jeanne. It was an insolent riposte rather than a true question but I decided to take it at face value.

'Well, you, of course,' I said. 'Up there in your little sewing room, unsupervised. Unseen.'

'Are you accusing me of trying to kill Tweetie and of actually killing Roly?' she said, gaping at me.

'Neither,' I said, with a breezy cheerfulness which made me feel quite proud. 'I'm not accusing you of killing Roly – why on earth would you? – and I don't think anyone else at all has considered that Tweetie was the target. That's yours alone, Miss McNab. Whatever suggested it to you?'

She stared, aghast, for a long empty moment before she answered, then all the fight went out of her and she slumped back in her seat.

'Get me another brandy, won't you?' she said. Once she had it in her hand – in fact had half of it already down the hatch, and it was no small measure – she went on. 'Wishful thinking, I suppose,' she said, then she shook her head. 'No, not as bad as all that. Just that Roly is—' She gasped. '*Was*, gosh it's horrid, isn't it? Roly was a simple soul – ordinary, even – and Theresa is anything but. I can't for the life of me imagine why anyone would want Roly dead. But since the day Theresa joined the happy band at the Locarno she's been lording it over them all, or trying to, with her motorcar and her education and her address. I couldn't blame any of them, that's all.'

Her voice had grown quite bitter, for of course it was not only Tweetie's fellow dancers to whom she showed off, shoving her advantages at them and sickening them.

'The dancers don't seem to care about anything except dancing itself,' I said. 'I can't imagine Tweetie gets far patronising Beryl, for instance.'

Jeanne knocked back another fair-sized slosh of brandy and gave a mirthless laugh. 'I can't believe it,' she said. 'I just cannot believe for a minute that Beryl is mixed up in this. She's . . .'

'We've met her,' I said, 'and I agree. She is. But the world she moves in . . .'

'The world her father moves in, I'll grant you,' Jeanne said. 'But the world Beryl moves in is practice, lessons, costumes, choreography, music, competitions and trophies. And her father has nothing to do with any of it.'

'He didn't get her the job at the Locarno?' said Alec.

Jeanne shook her head. 'Beryl does have her father wound around her little finger,' she said. 'She has that much in common with Tweetie if nothing else. So of course, if she chose, she could have every treasure fall into her lap, for no one in this city would dare refuse her, but she is made of finer stuff and doesn't trade on her father when it comes to dancing. Look, if you're finished with me, I'm going to go and lie down. I'm terribly tired.'

Not to mention, I thought to myself, rather the worse for two enormous brandies.

'What an unhappy young woman,' Alec said when Jeanne was gone.

'But we finally broke through the crust and got some good solid information out of her,' I said.

Alec paused in his pipe-filling and gave me a hard stare.

'You should hear yourself sometimes, Dandy,' he said, for all the world as though he had not just been grilling Jeanne to a crisp himself. 'You really should just jolly well hear yourself.'

'It was Miss Thwaite who made the headdress,' I said, ignoring him.

'But it can't have been her who drenched it in poison. If she had, why would she open the toffee tin and show us the hankie? Even if her hints were rather vague.'

'That is a very good question,' I said. 'And it suggests that she's not a poisoner. I'm glad, because if we're going to visit I want a scone and a cup of tea.'

23

Miss Thwaite was already in her nightcap and gown with vanishing cream making her worried face gleam as she looked around the door to see who was knocking.

'Oh!' she said, letting it fall open and gesturing us inside. 'It's you. What a to-do. What a to-do. I can't believe it.'

'Has it been in the evening editions then?' I said, glad in a way for perhaps the most disturbing part of the story of Leo Mayne was the way the whole affair had been swept under the carpet. At least if Roly's death had been reported there was something working as it ought to, no matter how far short the police might be falling in their duties.

'No, nothing like that,' said Miss Thwaite. 'Someone came round asking.'

We were back in the kitchen which was cosier than ever with the fire well banked for the night. The door was open to a little cupboard-bed such as one finds in many lowly Scottish dwellings. One or two of the more modest cottages at Gilverton still have them, although Hugh tried hard to have them dismantled after the great influenza outbreak, feeling that such close air could not be healthy. He succeeded with most of his tenants, but a few who had known him as a child held firm, one fearsome pensioner who had worked in the nurseries and so had undoubtedly seen Hugh in his bath once upon a time had asked him how he'd like to have a brass bed sitting in the middle of his living room like a boil on the nose and if he wanted her alcove bed off her he could build a new room on to her cottage and she'd be glad of it.

Miss Thwaite, showing great delicacy, closed the door to her bed before she sat down.

'Has someone come from the police?' said Alec with more hope than certainty. 'What did they ask you?'

'Great merciful heavens, no,' Miss Thwaite said. 'It was someone from the club came round. Asked me if I'd seen anything of Beryl after the Champs. I hadn't the first idea what had happened till then. I spent a quiet day in the steamie getting my washing done and I've been ironing all night, see.' She gestured at the dolly above her head where a collection of very fine lawn nightgowns and bed caps, with their lace meticulously ironed, was hanging.

'What club?' I asked. 'Do you mean the dancing class?'

'I mean . . . you know,' said Miss Thwaite. 'Surely you must know by now. Mr Bonnar thought maybe Beryl would have come to me. We've been close for years, ever since her mother died, and I suppose the idea was that, in a pinch, it might be me she turned to.'

'Ah,' said Alec. 'The club. That's one way of describing it, I suppose.'

Miss Thwaite coloured and began fidgeting with the end of the long plait in her hair. 'I'm not saying he's an angel,' she said. 'I couldn't convince you of that, when he got me sacked last week for talking out of turn. But that was only a slap on the wrist. I'd have been back as soon as Beryl got her feet clear of the Champs and had time to get to work on him.'

'That's extremely understanding of you, Miss Thwaite,' I said.

'He's taken care of me,' she said. 'It's not just because Beryl has a soft spot. He keeps things quiet.'

'Miss Thwaite,' Alec said gently, 'we're not here to debate any of that, although, if we were we would start by asking what things and by what means, but let's not be sidetracked. I don't suppose you've seen Beryl, have you?'

Miss Thwaite shook her head, still worrying at the end of her plait with her busy fingers. 'I have not,' she said. 'But I don't need to have seen her to tell you that she didn't poison anyone. She had no reason to want Roland dead and she certainly had no reason to wish harm to Len Munn.'

'Let's concentrate on how it was done,' I said, hoping that her new mood of expansive communication would survive the change of topic. 'Tweetie's headdress. Now. What sort of state was it in when it left your hands?' I took out my notebook and pencil and gave her a look of friendly enquiry. 'If you can remember. Any little detail might help us.'

'Her headdress?' said Miss Thwaite and her face was blank and still. She had dropped the tassel of hair and let her hands fall into her lap.

'I know it sounds outlandish,' I said, 'but you, of all people, know that you don't have to drink poison for it to harm you.'

'Leo's hankie,' said Miss Thwaite. 'I didn't think you believed me.'

'We didn't understand you,' said Alec. 'Not at first. But we understand and believe you now. What was it? Do you know?'

'Chloroform,' said Miss Thwaite. 'It's gone now but it was as clear as anything the night Leo died.'

'Well, it wasn't chloroform this time,' I said. 'Tweetie's headdress was soaked in cyanide and Roly inhaled more of it than he could withstand.'

'But Tweetie's all right?' said Miss Thwaite.

'Thankfully,' I told her, shuddering to remember the way Tweetie had buried her face in Roly's handkerchief, with no thought to her safety.

'Cyanide,' said Miss Thwaite. 'Poor Roly.'

'I know,' I said. 'It's terribly upsetting, but the point is that the construction of the thing was geared to just that purpose. And we wondered when it was done, you see. After it left your hands?'

'It was never *in* my hands,' said Miss Thwaite. 'The sketch

Tweetie sent had just a ribbon with a spangled plume. I thought it was a little bit old-fashioned, if I'm honest. But . . . that's not the trouble.'

Alec flicked a glance at me and I knew what he was thinking. Jeanne said Tweetie got Miss Thwaite to make it and now Miss Thwaite denied all knowledge of the thing.

'I need to tell you something,' she said in a tiny voice. 'About last year. About Leo.'

'My dear Miss Thwaite,' I said, making a guess at what she was skirting. 'That's exactly why we came. We want to hear anything you can tell us about Foxy's head ornament.'

'What did it look like, Miss Thwaite?' said Alec. 'If you can remember.'

She was silent for a moment, then she nodded and sniffed. 'I can do better than describing it,' she said. 'I can show it to you.' She leapt to her feet and bustled over to the alcove bed, then dropped to her knees and pulled out a deep drawer fitted under the bed itself. It scraped along the floorboards with a dreadful dry screech. Clearly it was not often opened.

Miss Thwaite began lifting out bundles wrapped in brown paper and tied with wool, speaking as she busied herself. 'She'd ripped it off her head in all the to-do,' she said and the echo of Grant's words from earlier was eerie. 'It was getting trampled. And for all it was a funny-looking thing, I didn't want to see it ruined. So I put it with my bundles, meaning to give it to Foxy later. Then of course poor Leo died and after that I didn't like to bring back memories, so I just left it packed away. I didn't ever touch it the way I touched the hankie. So I can't tell you if there was anything poured on it. Ah, here it is now! See what you make of that then.'

She plucked a brown-paper parcel from deep inside the drawer and handed it to Alec. He slit the knots with his penknife in that way that men do, not having the patience to unpick them, then opened the crackling paper and gazed upon what it contained.

'Bingo,' he said quietly. 'Bull's eye. It's another one.'

It certainly seemed to be. It was not actually made of fox, for no one could have danced in that crowded ballroom with a fur hat on. It was made of rust-red velvet and the front part was fashioned in a point like a fox's snout with two black beads glittering away for the eyes. The tail was made like a giant pipe-cleaner and stood up at the back at a jaunty angle, even more so when Miss Thwaite had fussed over it and pulled it back into shape after its long incarceration in the bundle at the bottom of the drawer. When she was finished, Alec applied the smallest and sharpest blade and as soon as he made a slit we could all see the same thick flannel lining as in Tweetie's.

I lifted it very carefully and gave it a sniff. Of course there was nothing to be smelled after all this time but the padding was lumpy and wadded up as though it had been wetted and then dried very badly.

'It was certainly drenched in something,' I said to Miss Thwaite.

'Cyanide?' said Alec, poking at the wadded lining.

I thought it over, then shook my head. 'Chloroform,' I said. 'Like the hanky. Leo was faint, by all accounts and Roly was anything but faint.'

'Whoever it was has stepped it up then,' Alec said. 'Chloroform to cyanide strikes me as moving from mischief to murder.'

'But who would do such a thing?' said Miss Thwaite. Standing there agape in her nightgown and shawl she looked tinier than ever and so dreadfully old and tired too as the shock settled into her. Then her frown deepened. 'Who would choose such a strange way to kill a man?'

'We have no answer for either question yet,' I said. 'But perhaps you can help us. I suppose you had no hand in the fashioning of this?'

It roused no indignation, which was a testament to her innocence as nothing else would be. She simply shook her head and, as she mumbled her reply, she sounded quite faint.

'Foxy did it all,' she said. 'A beautiful seamstress. I never had a hand in her costumes.'

'Are you sure?' said Alec. 'What about Beryl? Is she . . . what's the phrase, Dan?'

'Good with her needle,' said Miss Thwaite and I in unison. Even this did not raise a smile.

'She gets by,' said Miss Thwaite. 'Those blessed pinafore dresses she runs up for herself. Her sewing is sturdy and she can follow a pattern. She'd help her fellow dancers to get ready for the Champs for she's kind that way.'

'So it's possible?' Alec persisted.

Miss Thwaite nodded. 'I suppose so.'

'Never forgetting that she's skipped off,' I said. 'And since her father's people are searching for her, it really does seem that it was her decision to go. It's not as though she was bundled away by someone to get her out of trouble.'

'But there's no way Beryl would ever have done such a thing,' said Miss Thwaite. She saw my look and bristled. 'The sins of the father, eh?' she said. 'But she is *not* her father and for all the advantages she could have had if she used him she always preferred to make her own way under her own steam.'

I could not let such an enormity pass unchallenged. I was almost spluttering as I spoke. 'Her own steam?' I said. 'Her father has Lorrison in his pocket and Silvester too, not to mention the police who should have investigated Leo's death and the same policemen or their compadres anyway who should be cracking right on with Roly's and aren't. And not to mention you, Miss Thwaite!'

She was shaking her head. 'That's all just fripperies,' she said. 'I'm not talking about Silvester refusing to shut down the Champs nor even of those policemen – they know what side their bread's buttered and no mistake – I'm talking about the scores. The judges. Beryl was always absolutely adamant that Mr Silvester and Miss Astoria and the other two judges subject her routines to Association Rules same as everyone else. She wants to win fair and square or not at all.'

'But she didn't win fair and square last year!' Alec cried out. 'She won because Leo and Foxy were out of the running. Tell the truth and shame the devil, Miss Thwaite, who would have won if Leo hadn't fainted?'

Miss Thwaite bit her lip and bowed her head which said more than any words might have. 'You didn't hear it from me,' was all she said.

'Agreed,' said Alec. 'And we'll take this out of your hands, if you don't mind.' Carefully he rewrapped the fox bandeau in the paper although, having snipped the string into bits, he could not secure it again.

'Where do you suppose she is?' I asked him as we clattered back down the tenement stairs.

'Spirited away by her father or his henchmen, of course,' said Alec, 'as soon as they realised that she'd gone too far this year.'

'And then he went around his circle asking after her as a double bluff?'

'Which doesn't augur well for us, does it?' said Alec. 'If an organised ring of gangsters have her hidden and even the police are too scared to challenge them, what chance have we?'

'Of finding her, none,' I said. 'Of proving that it was her and shaming the police into agreeing, I feel quite hopeful actually. There are plenty little loose ends. I just need to sit down and have a jolly good think about them. Review my notes, you know. No matter how much you laugh at me.'

'Not this time, Dan,' said Alec, as he climbed back into the Cowley and sat staring out through the windscreen as though at a distant view. 'If you and your little notebook can shine a light on all this you shall have nothing but my praise. Straight back home to crack on with it, shall we?'

I started the engine and pulled on my driving gloves.

'Not a bit of it,' I said. 'One of the strangest things of all is the fact that Julian Armour was at the Locarno and took off when the trouble started. Let's go and see what he has to say.'

Unfortunately for us, after such a long and exhausting day, Julian Armour lived even further than the Stotts from smoke and smells, out on the moors to the south of the city, and it took us half an hour and two stops for directions to get there from Springburn. At least when we did arrive, though, at a pleasant villa set back from a broad road through the village, the light had failed and we could be sure he was at home, for there were lamps lit in the windows and too many for servants alone.

Our knock was answered by a harried-looking housekeeper in her middle years. She gave us a peremptory look up and down and then folded her arms firmly over her considerable bosom.

'Mr Armour is discommoded,' she said. 'I'll tell him you called.'

'We know he is,' I said boldly. 'That's what we want to talk to him about.'

'We are old friends,' said Alec.

She gave us a sharp look, me especially. 'London friends, are you?' she said. 'For I'm sure I've never clapped eyes on either of you.' She unfolded her arms. 'And I must say you don't look much like London friends to me but if you can do anything to help him I suppose I'm not the one to stop you.'

On that intriguing note she turned and made her way, ponderous even when hurrying, to a door on the far side of the hall.

'Friends to see you, sir,' she said and then left us to make our entrance.

'Mr Armour,' I said, sweeping in. I stopped so suddenly

that Alec walked up my heels, taking a long scrape off the calfskin of my left boot which was sure to enrage Grant when she saw it.

Julian Armour was sitting in an armchair drawn close to the fire with a drink on a small table at his side, just like Sir Percy had been. Unlike Sir Percy, however, he was calamitously drunk. He was still dressed in the lounge suit he had been wearing when we saw him slipping out of the Locarno, but his tie was gone and his collar unbuttoned. His shoes were kicked off too and his hair was sticking up in spouts around his head as though he had been tearing at it. I glanced at the whisky bottle standing behind the empty tumbler and hoped that he had not opened it today for more than half of it was gone. And apparently he had not eaten enough to stop it hitting him like a hammer because, on the tray at his feet, half shoved under the armchair, there was only a single bite out of a sandwich and not so much as a dent in a dish of mousse beside it.

He looked up at us out of a face bleary not only from whisky but also from tears and, as he tried to focus on us, another rolled down from each eye and dripped off his chin.

'You,' he said. 'Do your worst. I don't care any more.' Then he bowed his head and went back to staring at something he held in his lap.

'Mr Armour?' said Alec gently. 'We are here to help you.'

I raised an eyebrow, helpless not to, for that was news to me.

'There's no help for me now,' he said and then he started to sob in earnest, bowing his head until it touched his hands.

I squinted to see what he was holding and felt a flare of fear to see that it was a card, another little round-cornered card with a printer's name stamped on the back. What monstrous thing could someone have sent to Julian Armour to have brought him to this wretched state? I eased it out of his hand and, although a moment later we were to learn that it was bad enough in its way, at that moment I was relieved to see that it was not a third round of threats.

In fact, it was a small copy of the photograph in the Locarno's plate-glass window: Tweetie and Roly holding one another at that frozen, eternal moment in the midst of their tango. I showed it to Alec and he only just managed not to look pleased, for it was also, of course, an excellent opening.

'We had been rather under the impression that you didn't know about Miss Stott's dancing,' Alec said.

'She didn't know I knew,' said Armour. He reached out and took the photograph back, nursing it against his breast. 'She knows now and she's sacked me.'

'She's broken off the engagement?' I said. 'Are you sure?'

'She telephoned an hour ago,' said Mr Armour. He hiccupped painfully, making me cast a fearful eye towards the whisky bottle. If he had drunk all that in an hour he needed at least a cup of broth if not a plate of stovies before it felled him like a dart gun.

'Wait until tomorrow,' I said, going to the side of the chimneypiece and pulling on the bell rope to summon the housekeeper. 'Miss Stott is terribly upset by what happened today. And it must have flustered her somewhat, finding out her secret was no such thing.'

Mr Armour was shaking his head, and rather too violently than was wise in his condition. 'It's over,' he said. 'She said she always meant to tell me tonight that the wedding was off, only it was supposed to happen after she and Ronnie won the tr-tr-troph . . .' Unable, between sobs and renewed hiccups, to finish the word, he buried his face in the photograph again and gave way to every ounce of his emotion.

'I don't think I understand,' I said softly to Alec, under the wails and snorts of Julian Armour's distress. 'I don't understand what either of them is playing at; why Tweetie would keep him stringing along, and why on earth he went to the Locarno.'

Before Alec could answer, the housekeeper arrived and I saw that she had been thinking along the same lines as had I, for she brought with her a fair-sized tureen of some hearty soup and quite half a loaf of bread, thickly sliced and slathered in butter.

She swiped the whisky bottle while putting the tray down in an admirable display of dexterity and, as she left the room again, I heard the cork being jammed back into the top of it most decidedly. She got away with it too because Mr Armour had cried himself out and now appeared to be beyond the need for whisky, although also beyond the reach of soup. He had fallen asleep or perhaps lapsed in unconsciousness. Either way, it was clear that there was no more to be got from him tonight and we took our leave.

'Perhaps,' said Alec when we were once more under way, creeping along the dark road back to the city, 'Tweetie knew that if she broke off her illustrious engagement before the Champs her parents would be angry enough to stop all the dancing immediately. So she strung them and Julian along.'

'But that doesn't explain why she was going to break it off at all,' I said. At last, I could see streetlamps ahead and the lights of another motorcar.

'Well, perhaps she thought if she won the competition her parents would change their minds and countenance her dancing on,' said Alec. 'If so, she was whistling in the wind, wouldn't you say?'

I did not answer, for the headlights of the approaching motorist were dazzling me and it was a narrow road with rough verges to either side. I slowed down and pulled as far as I could to the left, while it slowed down and pulled as far as it could to the right. Then, just before we were going to pass one another, suddenly the other driver appeared to decide there was plenty of room after all for he shot forward and, almost skimming the side of the Cowley, roared past me.

Once I was sure we were not going to collide, I looked

back over my shoulder at the other vehicle disappearing into the distance as if all the hounds of hell were on its tail.

'Alec!' I said. 'That was a black van with gold writing on the side. I'm sure it was. I saw it gleaming.'

'Dandy, there must be a hundred black vans with gold livery in Glasgow,' Alec said.

'And it had Prince of Wales feathers painted on it too.'

'What on earth are you talking about?'

'Fancies!' I cried, but Alec only shook his head and puffed out his cheeks. 'Well, why did he slow down and then hare off like that?'

'Because he's not a very good driver,' said Alec. 'No one was hurt.'

'But—'

'Beryl disappeared hours and hours ago, Dandy. You're tilting at windmills. Now face the front before you kill us both.'

'But why would a tradesman's van be out and about at this time of night?' I said. 'I'm going to turn around at the next gate and follow it.'

'It was an undertaker's van, darling,' Alec said. 'And they do tend to keep odd hours.'

At that, even I had to admit that I was clutching at straws and, since I was more exhausted than I can often remember being in my life, I agreed to call this dreadful day over and go back to the Grand Central to hope for sweet sleep and illumination, or at least a clear sign of the way forward, in the morning.

24

Grant met me at the door to my room, her eyes as round as buttons and her mouth as round as her eyes.

'You're back, madam!' she said, her voice a shriek which was somehow both suppressed and still wild around the edges. 'And Mr Osborne too! Come in! Come inside, both of you!'

'Thank you, Grant,' I said. 'That was the general idea.'

She shook her head furiously at me as we brushed past her to enter the room.

'There's someone here to see you,' she hissed, then she plastered an entirely unconvincing smile on to her face and turned back into the room. 'Here they are!' she said, again in the tamped-down shriek. 'I told you they would be!' With that, she withdrew and fairly trotted along the corridor and around a corner.

The room was dim, just one lamp lit by the fireplace, so that the figure in the armchair was silhouetted and I might not have recognised him despite squinting, since he was so very unassuming. The figure behind the chair, however, could not be mistaken. It was one of the henchmen, the larger of the two, and he stood with his arms folded and his feet planted wide apart, glaring at us.

'Mr Bonnar,' I said. 'You should have rung to let us know you were coming and you wouldn't have had such a wait. Still, we're here now. What can we do for you?'

'I'll ring down for a little something, shall I?' said Alec, crossing to the telephone. 'Whisky perhaps. Or cocoa, Dan?'

The henchman stirred himself and took a step towards Alec, unfolding his arms as he did so.

'There's no need to go lifting the phone,' said his boss, in a quiet voice with some amusement in it. '*Whoever* you had thought to call. Billy here can go down and order whatever it is you fancy.'

'Very well,' said Alec, changing direction smoothly. As he approached Billy, fishing in his jacket for his wallet, I was astonished and perturbed to see the man take a half-step away and to one side, slipping his own hand into his pocket as he did so.

'Good grief,' said Alec, visibly rattled. 'No need to box shy of me, old chap. I'm only getting a spot of cash for the barman. You are our guests, after all, and the drinks are therefore on me.'

Mr Bonnar gave a soft laugh and re-crossed his legs.

'Nobody in this hotel's going to let Simon Bonnar pay for a drink,' he said. 'I could see my way to a dram, Billy. So two large whiskies and something for the lady?'

I had sat myself opposite him and was behaving with the greatest composure. But something in me baulked at the idea of extorted cocoa and I shook my head, murmuring that I needed no refreshment. When Billy had left the room, Alec brought over the upright chair from the writing desk and sat down between us.

'Beryl is missing,' said Mr Bonnar after a short pause. The amusement in his voice was quite gone, replaced by a cold anger which made the back of my neck prickle.

'You were unconcerned at first,' I said, remembering his calmness at the Locarno. 'What's changed?'

'I thought she'd stepped away,' said Bonnar. 'Away out of trouble like I always told her to. But I've scoured the city for her and she's nowhere to be found.'

'It's rather a large city,' Alec said. Mr Bonnar made a sudden movement, small but very quick, and Alec stopped talking immediately.

'This is my city,' he said, with dreadful emphasis. 'It's no size at all when you know every ward of it, every pub and backroom, every corner shop and games hall. I've had all my boys out asking anyone who's ever crossed our path and no one has seen her.'

'Did you try the station?' I said.

He stared at me for a moment before answering, a glazed look upon his face. 'You think she ran away?' he said. 'Why would my Beryl run away?'

I thought it best to fiddle with my gloves rather than answer him, but even though I made heavy work of undoing the buttons and then pulled them off finger by finger without turning the cuffs, just the way Grant is always telling me to, still no one had spoken by the time I was done.

'We seem to be at cross-purposes, Mr Bonnar,' I said at last. 'Although I'm not sure I understand why. Haven't you just been telling us as much?'

'I said she was missing,' he replied. 'I think she's been kidnapped. I pray to God that she hasn't been harmed, but if she has then someone is going to pay.'

It was quite extraordinary. There had been a murder and one of those present had slipped out, and yet this man seemed not even to entertain the obvious connection.

'Kidnapped,' I said, deciding that nothing would be lost by taking his words at face value. 'Has someone been in touch with you?'

He made that curious sudden movement again, a sweeping away of some imaginary object before him, and again it struck me that I could not account for how violent it seemed. I did not want to cause him to do it a third time.

'I don't suppose Beryl gave any sign of being worried about anything in the last few days, did she?' said Alec.

Bonnar shook his head. 'She was excited for the Champs but not worried, no. It's just the two of us, has been for years since her dear mother died and she would have turned to me first if anything was troubling her.'

Not, I thought, if what was troubling her were the inevitable trials of planning a second murder. The man had an absolute blind spot as far as his daughter was concerned.

'Have you spoken to Bert, Mr Bonnar?' I said. 'He might know if something were amiss.'

Bonnar turned slightly in his seat and regarded me with another of the cold stares.

'He better not know anything,' he said.

I caught my lip in my teeth, dreading to plant an idea in this man's mind for which he might decide to exact revenge. As I thought this, though, I did remember Bert briefly chasing after Beryl and then slipping back into the ballroom as Lorrison's man went to the telephone. It was surely worth trying to find out whether she had spoken to him as she scurried away.

'He seems like a nice chap,' I said, backpedalling desperately. 'And fond of your daughter.'

'Fond!' said Bonnar. 'If that left-footer's got "fond" of Beryl he'll feel my boot. I only put up with them dancing because I can't tell her no when she smiles at me.'

'Well, if you're sure that Bert can't help you,' said Alec, 'and none of your usual associates have turned anything up, there's only one thing for it. You must go to the police.'

It was at that moment that Billy reappeared, with a tray bearing a whole bottle of rather good malt whisky, a soda siphon and a plate of biscuits. He shot a sharp look at his boss and Bonnar replied with an almost imperceptible nod. One wondered what the man might have done if it had been a shake instead, but as it was he simply put the tray down within Alec's reach and went back to his sentry duty behind Bonnar's chair.

'Well, now, me and the polis have a wee agreement,' Bonnar said. 'They keep out my way and I keep out theirs. That's why I've come to you two.'

'But surely when you are so very worried, they are the obvious port of call,' I said. 'They can pound on doors and demand admittance. We can only ask politely and leave if refused.'

'The Glasgow police wouldn't pound on doors to help me,' Bonnar said. 'I wish you'd take my word for it, Mrs Gilver. I've lived by the sword and nothing would give Inspector Todd greater satisfaction than watching me die by the sword too. But I must find her. I can't stand thinking of her out there somewhere, alone and friendless. I must find her and I'll pay you handsomely to help me.'

Once again, I did not know what to say. I imagined Hugh's face if he heard that I was in the pay of a mobster and it was not a comfortable notion. Alec, thankfully, saved me from having to reply.

'We shall certainly do our best to find her, Mr Bonnar,' he said. 'But we cannot take your money. Our clients are the Stotts and we cannot allow ourselves to serve two masters.'

'But how can you be working for me, looking for Beryl, if Eunice and her man are paying you?' Bonnar said, showing a nicety about financial matters that one would not have suspected, not to mention a familiarity with Lady Stott which would have raised eyebrows in Sir Percy's clubhouse and laid his origins quite bare, despite Balmoral and the paintings and his daughter's rise.

'Nothing we do to find Beryl will work against solving Roly's murder,' Alec said. 'It can't possibly be a coincidence that he was killed and she disappeared on the same day. It's the same case, no doubt of that at all.'

If Simon Bonnar had been still before, now he looked like a waxwork of himself, especially because his face paled, the late-night shadow on his jaw showing up suddenly. I shot a fearful look at Billy and was thankful that he was behind his master and could not see what Bonnar made of this, the

234

merest suggestion that Beryl might be guilty of more than upsetting her beloved papa.

There followed a long and intensely uncomfortable moment during which Alec and I held our breaths expecting an explosion and Bonnar stared at each of us in turn. At its end he rose to leave, without another word.

'How shall we contact you, Mr Bonnar?' I asked as he was on his way to the door Billy was holding open.

'No need,' he said. 'I'll be watching you.'

When we closed the door behind him Alec headed straight back to the whisky bottle.

'I'll join you this time,' I said. 'Good grief, Alec. What have we got ourselves into?'

Alec knocked back a stiff drink, poured another for each of us and then settled himself with a soothing pipe.

'Do you think there's any chance she really was kidnapped?' he said.

'From under the nose of her father and all his men? Hardly. Who would dare?'

'Anyone who knew Bonnar had trained her to leave a scene at the first hint of trouble.'

'That would be taking audacity a little too far,' I persisted.

'Not if it worked,' Alec said. 'I was glad you didn't mention the pink lace and the black van by the way. I was having kittens in case you piped up in that way of yours.'

'I'm not quite as ingenuous as all that,' I said. 'Why did *you* want it kept quiet?'

Alec coughed in surprise at an inopportune moment and spluttered a little on a sudden lungful of pipe smoke.

'How can you ask? Because that man would have set his "boys" on every tradesman with a black van in the whole of the city. He'd have gone chasing after that undertaker on the country road and had Billy go to wakes to crack heads and search the very coffins for Beryl.'

'Not wakes,' I said mildly. 'Far too popish for a man who

talks of "left-footers" that way. Such a nasty expression. And golly, who'd be Bert, eh? With a man like that breathing down your neck and you knowing all the time you were on sufferance.'

'Talk about dedication to one's art,' Alec agreed.

'And to one's job!' I said. 'You were very impressive, the way you assured him that you would solve a murder and find his daughter. Are you really so confident?'

Alec took his time and three long puffs before he answered.

'I think so,' he said. 'I'm far from sure about how all the pieces fit together but there are enough pieces that I can hardly help believing I'll be able to make something of them.'

'How very mysterious,' I said, gently mocking him. 'It's usually me who waxes metaphorical when we're deep in a case. It must be rubbing off on you.'

Alec clicked his fingers and sat up straight. 'That reminds me,' he said, 'and it's worth the teasing. I meant to ask you to go back through your little notebook and read out all the names.'

'All what names?' I said. I was already rummaging, for the occasion of Alec honouring my notebook and pencil this way was just about unique.

'I'm not sure,' he said, 'but I think we've heard something that we should have remarked upon but missed.'

'Is that how I sound to you when I go off on one of my flights of fancy?' I said, flipping through the pages. 'If so, I can only apologise and promise not to in the future. Here we are: dramatis personae.' And I proceeded to list them, the plain workaday names and the ballroom affectations. He sat up when I got to Foxy Trotter and Leo Mayne, Mr and Mrs Len Munn, but then he sank back again and by the time I was listing the names of the also-ran dancers from that day's competition he was barely listening.

'It's gone,' he said at last, when I was done. 'I don't know what it was I thought I had noticed but it's gone now.'

'In my experience,' I said, 'if you stop trying to think of it, it will come back to you. Sleep on it, Alec dear. In fact, let's sleep on all of it.'

'And start afresh in the morning,' he agreed. 'Can we start at Balmoral? I'd like to know why Tweetie broke it off with Julian Armour. And I'd very much like to have another crack at cousin Jeanne. She's in this somehow, I'm sure of it.'

'But she had no motive to kill poor Leo,' I said. 'And anyway, Beryl Bonnar's guilt is surely unarguable. She left by the back door and sped off in a van parked in the alley. How much more suspicious could someone be?'

Alec nodded, but it was more resigned than anything.

'If that's what happened,' he said at last. 'Something went wrong, didn't it?'

'I should say it did,' I said. 'Especially for Roly.'

'No,' said Alec, 'you misunderstand me. If it was Beryl – and I agree, it certainly looks that way – then surely she meant to do the same as last year. Do away with the competition and carry on to glory. But instead she ran off. The question we must ask ourselves is, why? What happened to change her plan?'

'But if she didn't mean to run off, then what was the van doing there?' I said. 'It would have been rather convenient for her to rush out into the alley and just happen to find a helpful van driver to get her out of hot water.'

'The only thing I can think of that was unexpected,' said Alec, 'was that you and I were present.'

'But she knew that for days beforehand,' I said.

'And Grant and Barrow,' said Alec. 'If they saw something . . .'

'But they didn't,' I reminded him. 'Or they would have told us about it.'

'Grant picked up the headdress,' Alec said. 'Perhaps Beryl saw it in Grant's possession and panicked.'

'And ran off in a van she couldn't have arranged for?'

Alec gave a sigh that might have blown the fire out if he had been facing the chimneypiece head-on.

'You're right,' he said. 'Let's sleep on it.' He stood, stretched, gave me a peck on the cheek and made his way to the door, stopping to pour himself a fourth whisky on the way.

'I suppose she knew her father was coming,' I said.

'If they're as close as Bonnar thinks they are, I suppose so too,' Alec said. 'You think he might have surprised her by turning up when she didn't expect him t—' He stopped, stared at me and we spoke in chorus.

'Julian Armour!' we said. For of course *that* was who was where no one expected him to be.

'But what might his connection be to Beryl?' I said.

'No more mysterious than Len Munn's,' said Alec. 'We should go back and see Mr Armour anyway, for the sake of common humanity. And now let's *really* try to sleep on it, shall we? There's plenty to be sleeping on. One feather bed and twenty peas.'

25

It is unsurprising that, after such a day, my sleep was torrid with nightmares. Countless times, I fell deep into a pit of sleep with such steep sides that I could not climb out and with such horrors at its bottom that I could not bear being there. I woke over and over again, damply hot and twisted up in my bedding, with the last of the monsters still reaching out for me. Beryl was there, her pink frills sloughing off like a mummy's wrappings, and the black van with the gold writing and feathers was always there somewhere too, nosing around the corner of some dim street of tenements as I drove faster and ever faster, trying to get away. Tweetie was there, glittering and twinkling and quite dead, lying on the sofa as her parents wailed and rent their garments and Jeanne and Miss Thwaite stitched and smirked in a corner. Upstairs someone was dancing; I could hear them through the floor. Downstairs Mr Bonnar and his men waited for me to do something unstated and impossible. The only one missing, and the one who could have saved me, nudging me awake with her cold nose in the crook of my neck when I started tossing, was Bunty. I missed her with as sharp a pang and as dull a weight as on the first night she was gone. I turned my pillow, fanned my sheets and blankets into place and closed my eyes yet again.

It was Foxy Trotter who was waiting for me now; Foxy wheeling round a dance floor all alone with a fox upon her head. I tried to call out to her but my voice was a puny thing struggling and failing in my throat and I could only watch as the creature opened its impossibly red and gleaming jaw and ran its tongue over its rough yellow teeth.

I sat up, turned on the lamp and reached for my notebook. Perhaps if I concentrated on the sense of the case the horrors would let me alone. Alec had thought there was some little loose thread somewhere around Foxy Trotter; if I could find it perhaps the rest of the puzzles would fall into place and I would get some sleep before morning.

Why did Foxy suspect that we were referring to her headdress?

How did Tweetie come to feel like a daughter to her?

Why did she not take Leo to hospital?

What does Sir Percy hold over his wife?

Why did Tweetie break the engagement?

Why did Tweetie ever *make* the engagement?

Why did Julian go to the dance-hall?

Why did Julian pretend not to know?

Why did Julian blanch when I met him?

Why wouldn't Tweetie stop dancing when the threats began?

Why did Tweetie *start* dancing in the first place?

If Beryl got away with one murder why did she run the second time?

If not Beryl, then who?

Did Jeanne have a motive to kill Leonard Munn?

Did Miss Thwaite have a motive to kill either of them?

Why did Bert start to follow Beryl and then give up?

There were so many of them. So many secrets stubbornly hidden, so many unaccountable decisions. In fact, the only person I had met since taking up this case who had *not* puzzled me, the only little pocket of reason and clarity, was Simon Bonnar. He frightened everyone because he was frightening. Fright made everyone pander to his daughter, overlook his and her transgressions and smooth his path, even if it meant turning a blind eye to murder. He made perfect sense, but the rest of them were a hopeless tangle. I told myself that even organising matters into a list of questions was no mean feat and I should count it as progress. Then I turned out the light and returned to my dreams again.

'You look dreadful,' said Alec the next morning at breakfast. 'Are you ill?'

'Alec, dear,' I said, 'just in case you were wondering, it is never a good idea to tell a woman she looks dreadful. Never.'

'Very well, then,' Alec said. 'I retract it. Dandy, you look almost ethereal enough to call it "wan". It's utterly captivating, of course, but one worries that perhaps you are ill.'

'Oh shut up,' I said. 'I'd rather listen to insults than that tripe. And I'm not ill; just tired. I was awake half the night trying to make head or tail of this dratted case, of course. Weren't you?'

'I fell asleep like a baby after all that whisky,' he said. 'But I do need my eggs and bacon to see off its effects.' He craned around the dining room for a waitress and, seeing one, summoned her with a smile.

I could never get used to ordering breakfast instead of peering under the covers to see what looked tempting and so, although I was sure I would regret it before luncheon, I asked only for toast and made up the deficit by putting rather a lot of sugar in my coffee.

'Where did you get to after all your deliberations?' Alec said, but, before I could reply, he sailed on. 'I've only had my shaving time of course, so all I've come up with is that we needed an explanation for why Tweetie started dancing. And I was thinking about the fact that Foxy Trotter said she was like a daughter. And then there's the fact of Tweetie picking a very similar name to Foxy's – the same template, sort of thing – and in short I think there's a connection there that we've missed so far.'

'Does it explain anything?' I said, rather brusquely, for it was irritating to hear that Alec had made more sense of things during his morning shave than I had managed to, sitting up half the night, furiously scribbling.

'It must,' Alec said. 'If something's being kept secret, then necessarily it's something we should know about.'

I was so very tired and he sounded so very confident that I found myself nodding my head dumbly for a moment or two. Then, finally, roused to something like my full capacity by the sweet strong coffee, I began shaking it instead.

'Rot,' I said. 'If I've learned something in the last decade, Alec, it's that everyone is hiding something and it's usually nothing that's of the slightest interest to you and me. There very likely is something between Foxy and Tweetie that we don't know and they don't want us to know but unless it leads to Beryl then we can leave that stone unturned.'

'Of course it could lead to Beryl!' Alec said. 'A connection between them might very well reveal a better motive than mere professional jealousy.'

'I suppose so,' I said. 'And the same goes for Julian too. We're just assuming that he was at the Locarno to watch Tweetie but if whatever it is *he's* hiding leads to Beryl then we should know it.'

'It doesn't,' Alec said. 'Remember what the urchins told us? Julian summoned the police. He'd hardly do that if he were in cahoots with Beryl, now would he?'

'He still troubles me,' I said. 'He was terrified when he met me. And Tweetie gave him the sack. And he was where he didn't belong. Those are three puzzles I'd like to have solved.'

The waitress arrived then with our breakfast plates and Alec made a great business of making space on the little table, and thanking her and making sure I had butter to hand and generally fussing around so much that the moment passed and the subject of Julian Armour was dropped.

When we arrived at Balmoral half an hour later, we had no particular plan beyond knowing that we should have to press Tweetie harder than would feel kind the day after her ordeal.

'Miss Stott,' I said, once we had been shown in. I suppressed a shudder, finding the scene a little too reminiscent of the worst of my nightmares, what with Tweetie reclining, the elder Stotts close by with knitted brows and Jeanne off to the side with her mending basket.

'Do you have news?' said Tweetie.

I felt my breath catch as I got a good look at her in the strong morning light. If she faded any more she would be positively transparent and I did not wonder at her parents' looks of anxious concern.

'We have news of Mr Armour,' said Alec. 'We saw him last night and he's utterly heartbroken. Quite undone.'

Tweetie snorted, rather a robust noise to come out of one so frail-looking.

'I'll bet he is!' she said.

It was an extremely puzzling remark and I looked to her parents' faces, sure that I would find there the same frown that had twitched at mine. How could a girl feel such scorn for the misery she had caused? It was not only callous; it was senseless too. Sir Percy and Lady Stott however gazed at Tweetie with a sort of diffident appeal on their faces, looking like naughty children or perhaps dogs who have chewed a slipper. Most puzzling.

'But I'm afraid that it's questions we've come with rather than news,' Alec went on.

'Well,' I said, cutting in. 'We do have the news that Beryl has fled the city.'

Tweetie looked up quickly at that and once again her demeanour seemed quite at odds with what the moment required. Her eyes – just for a second – danced in her pale face. I could not for the life of me see how such an expression of mischief and delight fitted into this sorry mess.

'They've let her skip off then, have they?' said Sir Percy.

243

'Glasgow's fine constabulary. It's come to a pretty pass when a man can hold a town to ransom that way.'

It appeared that the more indelicate ramifications of Tweetie's dancing – the falling in with gangsters – were now to be spoken of freely. I could not help a flash of irritation that, had matters been so from the start, we should have found our task easier and a young life might have been spared.

'She got away before the police were ever called,' I said to Sir Percy. 'She left in a van waiting for her in the back lane.'

Tweetie gaped at me and swallowed hard. 'Gosh,' she said. 'I've rather scorned you, up until now. "Private detectives", you know. It all seemed pretty silly, but how on earth do you know that?'

'She was seen by a pair of witnesses and we found them,' said Alec. 'Now we must decide the best way to proceed. Sir Percy, if you are correct in your view of the local police, do you think perhaps we should put the information in the hands of a different force? We have connections in both Edinburgh and Perthshire who might be more willing to press matters. And since Beryl is no longer in Glasgow, if her father is to be believed, it's going to be another force who tracks her down anyway.'

'No police,' said Lady Stott. 'We've told you that from the start.'

'But it's a murder case now,' I said. 'And with the greatest respect, it's no longer your place to decide.'

'My place?' said Lady Stott. 'My place? Bounce, are you going to sit there and let this woman talk to me that way?'

'But she's right, my dear,' said Sir Percy. 'In fact, it's probably been a murder case all along, hasn't it? What with Munn last time.'

'What is it you need to ask?' said Lady Stott, turning like a bird in mid-flight.

'It's about Mr Armour,' I said.

Tweetie snorted again and both her parents shot her an anxious look.

'He was there yesterday,' said Alec. 'At the Locarno. Did you know?'

'I knew,' said Tweetie. 'I saw him, as no doubt I was supposed to. It wasn't very subtle.'

'Now, darling, don't upset yourself again,' said her mother.

I was tussling with it and I thought it began to make a little sense at last. 'He came to display his knowledge of your secret, is that right?' She nodded. 'With a view to what, though?'

'With a view to making a great show out of forgiving me,' said Tweetie. 'If I made it worth his while, naturally.'

'Blackmail,' said Sir Percy. 'An ugly word for an ugly deed. We were sorely taken in by Julian Armour, I'm afraid to say. And we're glad to see the back of him.'

'Do you mean he hoped to get a better settlement out of you?' I asked.

'He hoped to rob our darling girl of her life and all her happiness!' said Lady Stott. 'He's a devil. He's a monster.'

'Oh, Mother,' said Tweetie.

'That is rather conniving of him certainly,' I said. 'But if you could have seen him last night, Miss Stott, you wouldn't doubt for a moment that he really does care for you.'

There was a silence then and all four of them, the three Stotts and Alec, shifted their gaze around the room in a very fidgety fashion. Sir Percy even explored the inside of his mouth with the tip of his tongue in an attempt to look nonchalant. They did everything but whistle. Clearly, they all knew something that I did not, but I had better prospects of discovering it from Alec and so I decided to leave it until I could tackle him alone.

'Miss Stott,' I said, 'if you are able to, do you think you could go over the events of yesterday with us? Who was where when, and what you saw. Every little detail might be of help, you see.'

'She's far too tired,' said Lady Stott, just as Sir Percy said, 'Of course she'll help.'

'I can't really remember anything,' said Tweetie. 'I felt so dizzy and ill.'

'But before that,' I said. 'Perhaps you could just run through everything you remember.'

'But why?' said Lady Stott. 'If Beryl Bonnar has killed twice and got away with it, what good will it do to torment Tweetie and make her relive her ordeal?'

'I do understand your concern,' I said. 'Gosh, of course I do. I'm a mother myself. But the more complete a theory we can place in the hands of the police the better. And the plain fact of the matter is that this deed can't possibly have been carried out by one person, working alone. There was an accomplice and that person must be found just as Miss Bonnar must be.'

'An accomplice?' said Tweetie.

I was aware, out of the corner of my eye, that Jeanne had lifted her head from her sewing for the first time and was looking over.

'Someone to drive the motor she left in,' I said.

'But then that person wasn't inside,' said Lady Stott. 'And Tweetie can't have seen him.'

What I did not say was that someone must also have stitched the ludicrously absorbent headband and that there was a candidate sitting in this very room, and sitting with an unnatural stillness, just watching. Thankfully, before I was forced to fill the silence, we all heard the telephone bell out in the hall and listened as the baize door was opened and Mary trotted across the hall. She answered politely and then approached the open door of the morning room.

'It's your sister, madam,' she said. 'Ringing up to ask after Miss Stott.'

'Really, Mary,' drawled Tweetie. '"Your sister" is not how you refer to a member of the family. You should—'

'Tweet!' said Lady Stott. 'That's quite enough. Tell her I'll be there directly, Mary.' She stood and bustled out.

'There now,' said Alec. 'There's nothing like one's family, is there? To rally round in troubled times.'

It was a sentiment of extraordinary banality for him and I could not help wondering what lay beneath his decision to give voice to it. He was standing, I noticed, and before I had the chance to gather myself and stand under my own steam he had grabbed me by the elbow and hauled me to my feet.

'We must dash,' he said, dragging me towards the door. 'Not to be rude, but once a case really begins to move we need to keep pace with it, you see.'

Mary hardly had time to give Alec back his hat and certainly none to open the door. We were out on the gravel again while she was still crossing the hallway.

'I've got it, Dandy,' he said. 'I have got it at last.'

'Splendid,' I said. 'Got what? And where are we haring off to? I need to know, if I'm to drive there.'

'Just round the corner out of sight,' said Alec. 'I had to get out and get this off my chest for fear I'd explode or forget it again.'

Obedient as ever, and also agog, I drove around the nearest corner and parked the motorcar on another of the quiet streets with which this suburb was so plentifully endowed.

'I know why Tweetie started dancing,' Alec said. 'Roly almost told us the truth when he said it was down to Jeanne's mother. In other words, her aunt. He was lying but only just. It really was Tweetie's aunt.'

'Who?' I said.

'Foxy Trotter,' said Alec triumphantly. 'There were three of them – Foxy, the dashing fair-haired brother who was called Goldie to the end of his life, and Puddy, the little round dumpling who goes by the name of Eunice these days, which is not much better. We already knew that Foxy and Tweetie are close – like a daughter, she said. And at last it explains how two people we thought were quite separate can each have one of those ridiculous headdresses. And we don't need to twist ourselves into a knot to suspect poor little Miss Thwaite.'

'It fits . . .' I said doubtfully.

'Listen,' said Alec. 'I've hardly started. When Foxy heard about the threats to Tweetie, "Lady Stott's sister" telephoned Balmoral. It was the same day! And Sir Percy reminded his wife pretty sternly that Leonard wasn't part of their family. Do you remember that? And Jeanne said that Lady Stott's sister was a respectable widow living alone.'

'Jeanne!' I said.

'Exactly,' said Alec, with deep relish. 'We couldn't imagine why Jeanne would have a motive to threaten Foxy and kill her partner. But now we know—' He broke off midstream and sat back. 'Huh,' he said. 'Actually, what do we know? There's still no motive.'

'But there's a connection,' I said. 'There's somewhere to search for a motive. Foxy is Jeanne's aunt and Tweetie is Jeanne's cousin and oh!'

'What?' said Alec, still looking a little crestfallen.

'The printer with the golden tresses!' I said. 'Jeanne's father was a lay preacher, wasn't he? And her sainted mother was a Sunday school teacher. Just exactly the sort of people who'd have those sentimental little prayer cards lying around. And they were a bookish family who'd have *Cock Robin* too, weren't they? You really have cracked it wide open, Alec. It might very well be Jeanne.'

If anything he looked further deflated. 'My first proper epiphany and you thought of at least half of it,' he said. 'It's awfully dispiriting to be outdone all the time, Dandy.'

'Oh, nonsense,' I said. 'You've picked up every ball I've ever found and run further with it than I ever could have.' I had no idea if that were true but I had got used to delivering such flattery from years of being the mother of two boys who had been rivals their whole lives and now, with Alec as it always did with Donald and Teddy, it was working.

'Really?' he said, cheering up. 'One hardly notices when one's doing it, I suppose. Very well, then. Pats on the back for both of us.'

'What I don't understand,' I said, 'is the connection between *Beryl* and Jeanne. Beryl was on the spot to do the actual deed with the cyanide, as she was last year with the chloroform, and Jeanne might have done the preparatory sewing. But, why would those two be in cahoots?'

'No idea,' said Alec. 'Let's go and ask Foxy. She must know something. She probably suspects Jeanne already, don't you think? Or at least she knows without knowing and just needs a nudge.'

'Ah, now,' I said, when we were under way, 'speaking of who knows what. What is it that everyone in that morning room knew about Julian Armour and his blackmail, but which eluded me?'

Alec drew his pipe out of his pocket, filled it, tamped it and lit it. I wound down the window ostentatiously, although the truth is that I do not mind Alec's pipe smoke as much as Hugh's for it is a sweeter blend and he is a great deal more fastidious about cleaning out the bowl while refilling.

'Yes,' said Alec. 'Well, you see the thing is, I rather suspected this but the Stotts' demeanour this morning confirmed it for me. Tweetie, we know, met Roly first and through him, Julian.'

'When she went to meet Roly from his office, yes,' I said. 'And presumably she met Roly through Aunt Foxy who was Tweetie's introduction to the world of dancing, much to Sir Percy's chagrin.'

'That's not really important,' said Alec. 'The point is I think Tweetie was invited to the office specifically to meet Julian,' said Alec. 'Roly – far from playing a dangerous game in dancing with his boss's fiancée – actually provided a fiancée for his boss.'

'A rich one, you mean?'

'Not necessarily,' said Alec. 'It wasn't the money, no.'

'Well what then?' I asked. 'And why would Julian pretend he didn't know about the dancing?'

Alec sighed. 'Tweetie wanted to dance. Julian wanted to marry a respectable young woman. I think the plan was for Julian to "find out" that Tweetie was not respectable – capering at the Locarno in the arms of another! – and for him to agree to go ahead anyway then hold his magnanimity over Tweetie for ever. In effect, to blackmail her into going ahead with the wedding – or staying in the marriage, depending on when he faced her – if she showed signs of not wanting to.'

'I still don't understand,' I said. 'Why *wouldn't* she go ahead with it, or stay in it, having agreed to it? He clearly loves her. He was inconsolable that she broke it off. I'm perhaps being very stupid, but I really don't see.'

'He wasn't inconsolable because she broke it off,' Alec said. 'She broke it off because he was inconsolable.'

'About what?' I said.

'Really, Dan,' said Alec, 'how can you be such an innocent? About Roly, of course. About losing Roly.'

I was negotiating the busy junction on to the Great Western Road and it saved me from having to answer for a minute. For that reason, and that reason alone, I did not blurt out the opinion that no boss in the world glugs down half a bottle of whisky because one of his employees has died. Thankfully, waiting for an omnibus and a grocer's cart with a very flighty pony to get out of the way, and then concentrating on getting across the tramlines, I had time to catch up and spare myself any guffaws.

'Ah,' I said. 'I see. The tears were all for Roly. Yes, I see. That's why he turned pale green when he realised I was a detective.' I finished executing the corner and shifted up a gear again. 'So Roly procured a suitable bride,' I said. 'But why would Roly – or Julian come to that – foresee her agreeing to a sham marriage? Why should she?'

'Because she's only concerned about two things,' Alec said. 'She's a dancer and she's a snob. If she married a suitable man for real he'd never let her keep dancing. If she married a man who would, she'd plummet down the social scale. This way she gets a position and a comfortable home and can keep dancing with clerks and baker boys.'

'But what about . . . ?' I began. 'What about . . . children?'

Alec snorted and I flushed.

'Presumably Julian would turn a blind eye to however she got them. It really should have been a neat arrangement.'

'But Roly and Julian grossly miscalculated Tweetie, didn't they?' I said. 'And you are too. When she found out she was to be duped into a loveless marriage she broke it off that very day.'

'I wonder how she *did* find out?' said Alec.

'Presumably she rang him up,' I said. 'He'll be lucky if she doesn't call the police. In fact, I'm very surprised that Sir Percy hasn't insisted on calling them already.'

'I am too, a little,' said Alec. 'One would expect a man of his sort to go harrumphing off to his golf chums covered in rectitude.'

'Except that it would be rather embarrassing, wouldn't it?' I said. 'Rather humiliating to admit that he was so roundly taken in.'

'Or,' said Alec, 'and this is a very interesting possibility, Dan. Maybe Sir Percy doesn't want the police looking too closely at the affair in its entirety.'

'Why not?'

'Well, the truth about Lady Stott's low relations – who they seem to have left behind them – would come out, and the truth about his daughter frequenting a dance-hall and associating with gangsters. Or even . . .'

'The fact that his niece is an accessory to two murders?' I said. 'But he can't possibly know that. If he knew it was Jeanne he would have thrown her out of the house and he wouldn't have employed us.'

'True,' Alec said. 'It must just be the embarrassment and the prospect of becoming a social pariah. No more hobnobbing with Lord Burrell and the Fiscal once *that* story got around.'

I grunted. Hugh is the gossip in our family and loves nothing more than sucking away at some morsel of another's disgrace, he and George at his club like two old women in shawls on market day. I have never developed a taste for it. In fact, the accidental uncovering of other people's shabby secrets is one of the least welcome corollaries of digging into crime.

'Poor chap,' said Alec presently.

'Sir Percy?' I said. I could not see it that way. He still had his wife and his daughter and his dignity and surely another suitor could not be long in coming.

'I was thinking of Julian,' Alec said.

'You are kindness made flesh,' I replied. 'I could cheerfully smack him.' Alec said nothing and even I could hear the briskness in my voice and decided to keep quiet rather than unleash any more of it. We are supposed, one always hears, to turn into our mothers but something had gone wrong with me. My mother grew more artistic and less worldly the older she got until at the end she was completely daffy. I sometimes thought I was turning into Nanny Palmer, who in her later years could fairly be called a battle-axe.

'The question we must ask ourselves is this,' Alec said, after we had turned off and were back in Partick, creeping along those tunnels of tenements, 'was it one way or was it reciprocated? Julian and Roly, I mean.'

'Reciprocated,' I said, without even having to think. 'If Roly hadn't shared Julian's . . .'

'Proclivities?' said Alec.

'Ugh,' I said. 'I've always hated that word. It reeks of both sanctimony and glee and I can't say which is worse. Let's say Roly must have been in a similar predicament, otherwise Julian would have been opening himself up to all sorts of trouble. Blackmail, indeed.'

'Very well then,' Alec said. 'I agree. Then the second question we must ask ourselves is this: was it Roly's nature that got him killed?'

'By whom?' I said, as we finally drew into the kerb at Foxy's tenement. 'And if we're entertaining that as a motive for Roly, where does that leave Leo?'

'Leo was a young man, devoted to dancing, happy to marry a woman many years his senior,' said Alec. 'And they didn't have any children, despite Foxy's obvious maternal feelings, which instead she spent on her niece.'

'Oh nonsense,' I said. 'Alec, she *adored* him.'

Alec only shrugged. 'Let's go up and see what she has to say on the matter,' he said.

'You can't mean to ask her *that*.'

'It's the sort of question that might be better coming from another—'

'Oh no,' I told him, going as far as to wag my finger in his face. 'You have inveigled me into many things over the years, darling, but not this one. And anyway, can you see Beryl and Jeanne banding together to murder two young men quite unconnected with either of them, simply because of their nature?'

Alec screwed up his face and squeezed shut his eyes, but after a minute he was forced to let his pent-up breath go and shake his head.

'I can't,' he said. 'Unless it were some sort of obsession. Unless they were on a kind of crusade.'

'A crusade?' I said. 'There's nothing holy about poisoning people. I shouldn't call it a crusade.'

'I don't suppose the crusaded ever find it that holy when it befalls them,' Alec said, opening his door and stepping down. 'Let's go in. And if the conversation takes a turn in an opportune direction I shall take care of the question myself and shall never berate you for not helping.'

Of course, this was a skilled move and I could only sigh. Now, he should have all the glory of asking the hellish question and all the extra glory of never casting it up to me. It was almost enough to make me try. But not quite, I thought, as I followed him.

26

It was a very different Foxy Trotter who opened the door to us today. Gone were the chandelier-like earrings, the silk wrap with the dragon on its back and the great confection of red hair piled above the painted face. Today she was the very picture of what Jeanne had called her: a respectable widowed woman living alone. Her hair was pinned in a bun, her face was bare and her clothes would not have been out of place at any of the city's churches.

'Oh!' she said, making the word into a sigh of exhaustion. 'It's you again. Well, you can come in for I haven't the strength to stop you but I can't go answering a hundred questions because something's happened and I'm tired out from it.'

'We know,' said Alec. 'We were there.'

'Roland dying is not even the half of it,' said Foxy.

'We've just come from your sister's house, Mrs Munn,' I said. 'We know *everything*. But you mustn't blame anyone because we worked out your part in the drama for ourselves without being told.'

She turned away from the door and walked back into the flat, leaving us to follow her. When we got to the kitchen door it was just in time to see her drop into her armchair and lean her head back.

'So you know, do you?' she said. 'And are you come to take me away to the police station with you? I'm so tired I dare say I'd go.'

Since her eyes were shut she did not see the look that ricocheted between Alec and me. We had not meant to do it but somehow we had pulled off the oldest trick in the book. We had told her we knew everything and she had believed us. If we played our next hand very carefully we might yet make our claim come true.

'I don't see any reason for that,' I said. 'But we would like to hear your side of it, naturally.'

Alec nodded vigorously and urged me to carry on.

'It was an accident,' Foxy said.

'Of course,' Alec murmured. 'We didn't doubt that for a moment.'

'The thing is,' I went on gently, 'that we don't understand the reason for it. We'd be very glad to know why.'

'Beryl,' said Foxy, causing my heart to leap inside me. I saw Alec's eyes light up too. It truly did seem as though if we sat there quietly and did not say anything foolish, we might be about to have the case solved for us. I could hardly breathe.

'You know who she is, of course,' Foxy went on. 'Who her father is. And, you see, I knew we were going to win, Leo and me. I think Beryl knew it too and she kept on joking about fair play and how much it meant for her to go by the rules, win or lose. She even said once that she must be a disappointment to her father, throwing back in his face all he had worked for because she wanted to do it her own way.'

'I see,' I said, which was no more than the truth. It must have been a horrid prospect to think that one was going to win a competition and beat into second place the beloved only child of a ruthless man who might exact whatever revenge pleased him.

Foxy opened her eyes and lifted her head. 'Really?' she said. 'Do you?'

I nodded but wished she would close her eyes again for I was sure that Alec and I looked like startled fauns under her gaze.

'But if we withdrew it would be as good as telling Beryl we were scared of her. And even if she won she wouldn't have won fair and square. Then she might get angry enough to complain to her father and we'd be in trouble anyway. You don't know this man, and if you're lucky you don't know anyone like him.'

'We've met him,' I said. 'He seemed rather unassuming, and yet I know what you mean.'

'He's the quiet sort, right enough,' Foxy said. 'He doesn't do his own dirty work, but by God it gets done.'

'His quietness is more disturbing than a lot of bluster, if you ask me,' said Alec.

'And so I decided to take matters into my own hands,' said Foxy. 'To make it seem as if someone was threatening me and that was why I was withdrawing from the Champs. So Beryl would know it was nothing to do with her. If she saw the threats – and we made sure she did – then she'd never think twice about us leaving.'

'You did it yourself,' I said, unable to help it.

Once again, Foxy sat up and looked at me. 'What?' she said. 'I thought you knew.'

I could only blink but Alec was quicker.

'We had formed the opinion that it was *Mr* Munn,' he said. I nodded dumbly. 'Because of the fainting act.'

Foxy leaned all the way forward then and put her head in her hands, groaning. 'It wasn't an act,' she said. 'He really did faint. At least he passed out, if that's different. We agreed on it together. We wanted it to be convincing. He tried to act a faint but it never looked right. So we used chloroform. Some in my headdress as if it was another prank like the fox and all that. And some extra in his hankie in case the stuff in the headdress didn't work.'

It was no longer difficult to keep quiet; I could not have spoken for a pension. She had not only sent herself the notes and threats. She had actually killed her own husband. And with his foolish collusion. Alec's face was the mirror of my own, eyes wide and mouth hanging open.

'He was supposed to sink to the ground,' said Foxy, 'and we'd have to leave the floor and be disqualified. Then he'd go out and get some air and if anyone asked why he was so anxious we'd have the story of the threats. And if anyone suspected the chloroform we'd say it was put in my headdress by the threatener. We thought we were so clever, stories and back-up stories and everything. But I think I overdid the chloroform because he fainted again at the top of the stairs and oh! Oh, Leo!'

She fished out a handkerchief from her sleeve, buried her face in it and gave way to a storm of weeping. Alec eyed the kettle on the range and nodded at me. I sighed and got to my feet. I had never made tea in my life before I began detecting. That is to say, I had filled a little pot from a hot kettle on a tea-table but I had never worked a pump or a sink tap and boiled a great iron monster on a stove. I had never searched a kitchen for a packet of tea nor a cold larder for a bottle of milk. But since Gilver and Osborne opened its doors I had become a master. I could have donned a kimono and knelt before samurai. Alec, naturally, wanted nothing to do with this little sideline of the detecting life and after having once tasted his coffee I did not insist.

As to the weeping, I could dimly remember a time when it would have discomfited both of us. I should have squirmed and Alec should have left the room. Now it was barely note-worthy. I ignored it entirely and Alec stood by her chair patting her shoulder and shushing her absent-mindedly while he thought of other things.

'Did he speak to you, Mrs Munn?' he said at length. It sounded like solicitude but I knew better. Alec was gently trying to find out whether we could let well alone or whether honour required us to turn this revelation into an official report to the authorities.

'He did,' she said, raising her eyes and giving her nose a thorough blowing. 'He begged me to take him home. Of course, I was adamant that he should go to the hospital but he was scared – well we both were – that the doctors would be able to tell, you know, and that we might get into trouble. Take me home and let me rest, Foxy, he said, and I-I-I'll never forgive myself to the end of my days. I let him persuade me. I didn't call for the doctor until I was sure it was out of his system. If I hadn't listened he'd be here today and whether I was in the jail or not I couldn't have cared less for he'd be here and walking around and going to the dogs and the dancing like he should be.'

'Shush, shush,' said Alec, with relief flooding his voice. 'There, there now.'

'I was going to call the doctor in the morning,' Foxy went on. The worst of the storm had subsided and she spoke musingly now, as though merely reminiscing. 'I thought I'd let it all flush through, and then make sure he was well the next day. I never got the chance. Never even got the chance to say sorry. He slept like a baby right round the clock and while he was sleeping he just slipped away.'

'Tea,' I said, holding a cup and saucer close to her so that she had to reach out and take it from me. It was brusque but I feared that Alec was about to tell her what she clearly did not know: that after a bang on the head one should keep the patient awake, not watch him sleep like a baby. It was he who had told me, recounting a dreadful night in the trenches with a friend who, in the end, did not survive. 'With some sugar to help bolster you up a bit,' I went on.

We waited, sipping at our own cups of tea and just about managing not to grimace, for I had made it, with Foxy in mind, the colour of teak. When she began to revive a little I sat forward and, in my kindest voice, asked the crucial question.

'Now Mrs Munn, what we must try to establish is who knew about what happened. Who knew enough to be copying it all again this year.'

'No one knew what I did,' she said. 'No one. I've kept it locked away inside me for a whole year. You two are the first I've breathed a word to.'

'Of course,' I said. 'We didn't mean that you had told the tru— That is, we didn't mean to suggest that you had come cl—'

'You mean, who heard my tall tales about the threats?' said Foxy, with much less crippling nicety than I had been trying to juggle.

'For a start,' said Alec.

'Beryl, of course,' Foxy said. 'It was her I was trying to convince. But there's no secrets in a dance-hall and the others were around too. They were all kindness itself. Every one of them. And there was me making it look as if one of them was threatening me!'

She gulped and looked fair to begin another bout of grief and remorse.

'So anyone might have copied the three threats,' said Alec. 'The next question is who might have copied the headdress. Forgive us pestering you, Mrs Munn, but it's still hard to see how Beryl could have brought about a second one of just the right design and construction.'

'We've looked at both the headdresses now, you see,' I said. 'Miss Thwaite has kept yours all this time. And they are identical except for the decoration.'

'Well, mine lay about the cloakroom for anyone to see,' said Foxy.

'But for someone to make such a close copy she would have needed a reason to look,' I said. 'Might Beryl or another of the dancers have witnessed your actions on the day of the competition?'

'I'll never forgive myself,' Foxy said. 'I should have gone

and put myself off a bridge into the Clyde the very next day, only I didn't want to shame my family.'

She was showing a great deal of consideration for a family which, almost in its entirety, scorned her.

'Where did you go to carry out the procedure?' Alec asked, perhaps thinking that speaking plainly was best. 'Did you do it at home before arriving?'

Foxy shook her head. 'One of the cubicles in the cloak-room,' she whispered. 'With a syringe.'

'But no one saw you?' I said.

It was hard to imagine how someone might and she shook her head as I had expected her to.

'Well, I can't make sense of it,' I said. 'You didn't make Tweetie's headdress and she didn't make yours and yet they are strikingly similar to one another.'

'I suppose Jeanne might have noticed mine lying round while I was so busy with costumes in the run-up to the Champs,' she said. 'She was with Tweetie a lot, acting as a chaperone, and so she spent some time in my sewing room through there.' She nodded towards the front of the flat.

'Jeanne,' I said.

'And it was probably Jeanne who made Tweetie's band too,' said Foxy.

It was hard to credit that an aunt, and hardly a beloved aunt at that, would have such unshakable faith in a niece as not to feel the slightest suspicion when she related this. She must have been witness to at least a little of Jeanne's envy. We were strangers and we had seen plenty of it.

We sat in silence for a while, each of us thinking. My thoughts led nowhere. Only Jeanne could have made the second bandeau to match the first but Beryl had run away. There was nothing to connect them. Yet they must be connected. After a while Foxy sighed and began speaking again.

'Jeanne was kind to me when Leo died,' she said. 'She

stayed with me those first few weeks after the funeral and I couldn't have got through it without her. In fact, I went as far as to ask her if she'd care to stay here permanently.' She laughed, shaking her head. 'Daft of me. Who'd want to stay here in my room and kitchen instead of at Puddy's with all that splendour.'

I did not say that that bare little sewing room upstairs at Balmoral where Jeanne spent her days was a good deal more spartan than either of the rooms which made up Foxy's abode.

'But as I say,' Foxy went on, 'she was very good to me. I was beside myself that first month. Couldn't sleep and then the powders the doctor gave me were worse than not sleeping at all. Nightmares and terrors, and Jeanne sat with me, so patient, calming me and quieting me, and never complained.'

'What a blessing,' said Alec in his soupiest voice. 'Does she often visit you now?'

'She looks in,' said Foxy. 'Just to see that I'm doing away.'

'A blessing indeed,' I echoed. I would have put a sovereign on it that Alec and I were thinking exactly the same thing. Jeanne had noticed the peculiar headband while she was poking around her aunt's house over a year ago. And then in those early days of new widowhood, while she shushed and comforted and sat in the night listening to whatever ramblings the sleeping powders had produced, she heard a story – disordered and fragmented perhaps, but revisited often enough to be pieced together eventually – which interested her greatly.

We still could not say why she might have conspired with Beryl, or what either of them had against poor Roly, but we now had a clear indication that Jeanne had made that horrid silver pincushion, sitting there in her little room, and that Beryl, on the spot on the day, had soaked it in cyanide and, between them, they had murdered him.

'But why did Beryl leave and Jeanne stay?' I asked Alec when we were on our way back downstairs again.

'I have no idea,' Alec said. 'Perhaps one of them had to stay behind to see that the plan worked. Perhaps Jeanne was supposed to snatch the headdress back when Tweetie brought it home. She must be going crazy, trying to work out where it's got to.'

I clutched him, causing him to take an extra step on the steep stone stairs and clutch me back to save himself from falling.

'What?' he said.

'She must have worked out that we've got it,' I said. 'How else could we know how the thing was done? I think we need to go to the police now, Alec. Bonnars be damned.'

27

We failed. Seldom can two detectives have failed so summarily to interest the members of a constabulary in such clear evidence of a crime. Seldom, even in our chequered history of dealings with the police, have we come away so convinced of the stupidity and venality of a body of men.

We even had the foresight to leave Beryl's name out of it and simply tell the inspector that Jeanne McNab was guilty. Much good it did us too.

'Ah yes, the unfortunate accident at the ballroom,' said the inspector to whom we spoke. We had deliberately made a beeline for a police station at some distance from the Locarno, hoping not to run into the particular bobbies we had met on Friday or any of their friends. It seemed, though, that the death of Ronald Watt had gained notoriety across the city.

'The second unfortunate accident in a row,' I said crisply. 'Following the one last year.'

'Has a post-mortem been completed yet?' said Alec. 'Cyanide poisoning must surely be a fairly unusual happening.'

'You seem to know a great deal about it,' said the inspector. He patted his breast pocket, where he was carrying a fountain pen and looked about his desk as though for a pad of paper to begin taking notes.

'We were there,' I said. 'And we are detectives. We tried to tell your colleague that but, shall we say, there was little interest.'

'Look,' Alec said, sitting forward, man-to-man. 'We understand your predicament, sir. But we are not here to talk about

Miss Bonnar.' The inspector pursed his lips as though to shush Alec and looked swiftly around, although we were in his private office with the door closed and quite safe from overhearing. 'We are convinced that Miss McNab, a niece who lives with the Stott family at Balmoral in Bearsden, is guilty of the murder.'

At these words the inspector looked somewhat mollified. At least he sat back in his chair.

'A member of Sir Percy Stott's family murdered the dancing partner of the daughter of the house?' he said, betraying an extraordinary familiarity with the cast of characters, if anyone was asking me. 'Why?'

'We don't know,' said Alec. 'Jealousy perhaps.' I noticed that he looked troubled as he said this and I understood perfectly, for jealousy as a motive made admirable sense if Jeanne could be accused of working alone. It was the matter of collusion between her and Beryl that muddled things. And yet we needed Beryl as a puzzle piece because she had been there on the day to do the deed and, more to the point, because she had fled the scene.

'Jealousy,' said the inspector. 'Is this Miss McNab another dancer?'

He was not, I surmised, a man of great imagination. I was hardly the most imaginative woman born but I could see that Jeanne would hardly have to be a dancer to feel that she was living in Tweetie's shade.

'Motive aside,' Alec said, 'she sent threats. A card, a book and a dead bird, all very cleverly chosen to unsettle and frighten a young woman for whom a bird was a kind of mascot. And then, on Friday, she added cyanide to a part of Miss Stott's costume and poisoned her dancing partner.'

The inspector frowned, then shook his head and sat forward again. 'A part of her costume?' he said. 'What do you mean? How can he have eaten part of her costume?'

'He didn't eat it,' said Alec. 'It was in her headdress and he inhaled it. That's why it's of the utmost urgency that the post-mortem should be carried out. There will be no cyanide in his stomach and if you know how long the effects of it might last in his lungs then you know a great deal more about it than I do.'

'A poisoned hat,' said the inspector and I could tell that we were losing him. Of course we were. Foxy had never meant the chloroform to be a murder weapon and Jeanne had only copied it – with the nasty added twist of using cyanide instead – to cover her tracks. No one in his right mind would have set out to murder someone that way. 'And it wasn't even on the victim's own head,' he added.

'Well, obviously not,' I put in. 'One doesn't breathe the air from above one's own head. His partner was shorter than him and her head was close to his face. But actually she was affected to some extent. She was extremely woozy and . . .' I was seeing the scene passing in front of my eyes again. Tweetie had plucked Roly's handkerchief out of his breast pocket and inhaled its folds deeply. I remember shrieking at her not to be so reckless and after a minute she did assume a look of horror and throw the thing away from her. In all the commotion and distress I had only had time to thank God it was not poisoned and that she did not grow worse from breathing through it, but now another thought struck me. She had not only not worsened; she had improved. She was anything *but* woozy when I spoke to her; she was feverish and jangled with nerves. I had taken it to be the result of the shock and yet now, thinking it over calmly, I had never seen shock affect someone that way. A theory was forming in my mind.

'Dandy?' said Alec, shaking my arm. 'You're wool-gathering.'

The inspector was now regarding me with more than a little scorn.

'As I was saying,' he resumed. 'Didn't she find it strange that her head was dripping wet?'

'It was lined with oilcloth,' I told him.

'And didn't she find *that* strange?'

'No,' I said. 'She didn't. She can't have noticed.' I was aware of a creak as Alec shifted sharply round in his seat to look at me, finding this notion suddenly as odd as did I.

'Well, it's an interesting tale, I must admit,' the inspector said. 'But I don't think I shall take it to the Fiscal just yet. It was my understanding, you see, that the unfortunate young man had a heart condition. And—' He broke off and once again looked over his shoulder, checking for spies. 'Since we are men of the world' – here he inclined his head to show me that I was most graciously included in the scope of his words – 'if I was going to go poking around where Beryl Bonnar lives, it wouldn't be with a story of poisoned hats and wee girls all upset because they don't get to go dancing.'

Alec looked ready to argue but I sent him a silent signal, hardly even a signal, actually, but these days I merely have to think something hard enough and Alec seems to hear me. He closed his mouth without a word, stood, put his hat on after tipping it and bade the inspector good day.

'What is it?' he asked as we trooped back outside again.

'Roly's handkerchief,' I said. 'It wasn't soaked in cyanide. It was soaked in something else. Is there an antidote?'

'There certainly is,' said Alec. 'A kind of smelling salt, I believe.'

'Does it have any peculiar side effects?'

'I have no idea,' said Alec. 'Where are we going, Dandy?'

'The Locarno,' I said. 'To ask who swept up and tidied yesterday. Tweetie threw the handkerchief away from her and it was caught in the stampeding feet.'

After that we drove in silence, each of us trying desperately to make sense of the thing. I got nowhere. Jeanne alone, Jeanne and Beryl, Beryl alone; no matter how I shuffled them I could not get the means and opportunity and motive divided between the two.

★   ★   ★

'Now what on earth are you doing here today?' I said to our friends the urchins when we arrived. 'There'll be no business for you, surely.'

'How d'you mean, missus?' said the little girl. 'They're all in there. It's busier than ever 'cos there's a vacancy and everyone's trying to get the job before anybody else comes along and swipes it.'

Alec stared at the two of them open-mouthed. 'In there right now?' he said. 'Vying to take Beryl's place and Roly's?'

'Aye,' said her brother. 'How not?'

There were the arguments of a decent interval and a period of mourning, let alone the small matter of becoming a third couple to dance at the Locarno where two couples' careers had been cut short by sudden death. Glasgow was, really and truly, dance-mad. I saw it then more clearly than ever before: a nicely brought-up girl like Tweetie risking her position to dance; a strangely brought-up girl like Beryl turning her back on all her illicit privileges to dance; and now, apparently, hordes of hopefuls flocking to the scene of a murder, not from the usual ghoulishness, but with utter indifference to everything except dancing.

It *was* a horde too; one could hear them – a veritable babble – as soon as one opened the door. The ballroom was almost as full as it had been when the spectators had been gathered to watch the show.

I even thought I recognised some of them. Indeed, I knew for a fact that I recognised two of them. Tweetie and Bert were there in the front row, in the very spot where Mr Bonnar and his associates had been sitting, smoking cigarettes and watching a pair of youngsters going through their paces, while Miss Thwaite, evidently forgiven, pounded out a waltz on the upright piano. Alec did not hesitate; he walked straight across the dance floor towards them, causing the whirling couples to change direction or halt to keep out of his way. I scurried after him, smiling my apologies.

'Auditioning for a replacement already, Miss Stott?' said Alec, as he sat down in an empty seat beside Tweetie. There was a ring of empty seats all around them as though the young hopefuls did not dare to encroach too closely upon the great ones.

'My replacement?' said Tweetie. 'I'm not going anywhere. Why should I look for a replacement?'

'I meant a replacement partner,' Alec said.

My attention was taken as Jamesie and Alicia wheeled past where we were sitting. They had clearly overcome their worries about the Locarno since bowing out of the competition.

'Bert is my new partner,' said Tweetie blithely. 'We don't need to replace Roly or Beryl with any of these.'

I turned to Bert to see what he thought of this rather imperious young woman talking for him and I was shocked to see what a change had come over him in just a day. He was as cleanly shaven and as slickly pomaded as ever but his complexion was grey and he had dark purple shadows under his red-rimmed eyes. He was smoking determinedly too, with a small scattering of cigarette ends at his feet, suggesting he had been doing so all the time he had been sitting there. When he noticed me looking at him, he turned slightly and stared miserably back at me, causing the light social smile I had been wearing to die upon my lips.

'Isn't it rather soon?' I said.

'For what?' said Tweetie. 'The ballroom must be back up and running properly by tomorrow no matter what fiasco has been made of the Champs. In fact, this rigmarole is wasting time that we could make use of. But Lorrison is so stubborn.'

'What do you mean?' Alec said. His voice was cold; clearly he was disgusted with her and I could hardly blame him. Roland had died in her arms not twenty-four hours before and yet she called it not a 'tragedy' nor even an 'ordeal' but a 'fiasco'.

'This silly audition is solely to punish Jamesie and Alicia by making them wonder if they'll get the job of the other professional pair,' said Tweetie. 'And of course they will. I've told Lorrison that I insist upon it, but he wanted to make them squirm a little first for their desertion the other day and so here we sit.'

'You insist,' I said.

She turned to me with a smile. 'I am the senior dancer now,' she said.

'But what if Beryl comes back?' I asked her. 'Or if the investigation disrupts things so much that—'

'There will be no investigation,' said Tweetie. 'Simon Bonnar won't allow it.'

'Simon Bonnar isn't here,' said Alec, and I have never heard him sound grimmer. He turned away from Tweetie and fixed Bert with a hard stare. 'Mr Bunyan,' he said. 'When you followed Beryl yesterday, I presume you spoke to her.'

'What?' said Bert.

'Did she answer you?' Alec went on. 'Surely she did. What did she say?'

'What are youse on about?' said Bert. 'She went banging out and I went after her. I asked her where she was going and . . .' He shrugged.

'And what?' I said. 'What did she say to make you give up and return to the ballroom?'

Bert looked at the floor and was silent.

'Didn't you think it very odd?' I asked. 'It's not what one expects in the midst of such a scene: that one of the principals would rush off without a word and then vanish.'

'Is that why you followed her, Bert?' said Tweetie. She spoke quite kindly to him and was watching him closely.

'I don't know why I followed her,' Bert said. 'I was too het up to know *what* I was doing.' Tweetie nodded and even gave him a small smile. 'And I came back because she shouted at me to leave her alone. I'm surprised you didn't hear her. Screaming like a fishwife.'

Tweetie nodded again. Then she stood suddenly and waved to Miss Thwaite. 'Enough of this,' she said. 'Foxtrot please, Effie.'

Bert stubbed out his latest cigarette on the sole of his dancing shoe and got to his feet.

'Peppermint, Bert,' said Tweetie. 'Until you give up those filthy things like I told you.'

I had expected the auditioning couples to be disgruntled at her sudden interruption of their efforts, but quite the reverse. There was a flutter of excitement amongst them as it became clear that Tweetie Bird was about to take to the floor. They all backed away to the edges as Miss Thwaite struck up a different tune.

Tweetie spread a smile of monstrous insincerity upon her beautiful face and raised her arms, waiting for Bert to step into them. Then on a loudly played note they were off. They looked rather wooden, truth be told, holding one another at arm's length and jabbing at the floor with their pointed feet as though they were stamping on ants. I saw a few of the spectators exchange doubtful looks. Then slowly, although it is hard to say which happened first, Miss Thwaite began to change from her percussive practising music to a more melodic rendition of the tune. Perhaps it was a favourite of hers and she could not help it or perhaps she felt for Tweetie and Bert displaying their halting first attempt to dance together in front of such a knowledgeable crowd. Perhaps it was that, but I noticed that she was watching Tweetie and Bert very closely and so perhaps she began to play differently because she was so caught up in the slow budding and blossoming of their dance.

For their dance was certainly changing: they held one another closer and Tweetie's smile was dream-like and secret instead of frozen on to her face like a mask. They began to sway from side to side in perfect harmony as though the same breeze were gently blowing both of them and they rose to their tiptoes and down on to the flats of their feet again as though dancing on a rolling hilltop instead of a flat wooden floor. But it was more than that. All these points were technicalities, as I knew after an interminable day of listening to Victor Silvester instructing Grant and Barrow. Rise and fall, heel and toe, and sway were part of the esoteric rule-bound ways of the ballroom. What Tweetie and Bert were beginning to display was something that could not be taught. The elderly couple from Saturday had had it despite their creaky joints and their hesitancy; the bouncing young couple had not a whisker of it. Here, whatever it was, they had it to spare, and as they swept around, Tweetie's practice frock hugging the front of her slender body and streaming out behind her and Bert's simple shirt and slim trousers doing nothing to conceal the willowy strength beneath them, I was not the only one to forget all else and simply drink them in.

'Simpatico,' someone behind me said. Perhaps the oddness of the word in a Glasgow accent brought me to my senses.

'It's a miracle,' breathed another.

I did not believe in miracles. As easily as that I was out from under their spell and memories began to assail me. Roly had said there was no time to break in a new partner and look like a couple, no matter how talented the girl. Foxy had said she had not the heart to dance again now that her true partner was gone. And then Beryl's voice echoed in my mind, laughing with Bert, saying she didn't understand how he could forget a step they had been dancing for years and asking what had muddled him. What had muddled him was his new partner and their preparations to begin dancing as a couple once the loose ends had been tidied away.

The music subsided and the room around me broke into spontaneous applause. I alone did not join in with it; even

Alec put his pipe in his mouth to free both hands and clapped heartily.

'They're jolly good, Dandy,' he said, then, catching my expression, he lowered his voice. 'What is it?'

'They're *too* jolly good,' I murmured. 'Look at Tweetie. She knows she's given away her secret.'

Indeed, Tweetie's expression of romantic bliss had curdled into something ugly and she was glowering at Bert, who flashed his eyes at her and nodded to the audience, still clapping.

'What's wrong with them?' said Alec. 'They might have made a mistake in their footwork, but if they're going to be so grumpy with one another after a measly little practice session they shan't do very well in competitions when the pressure's on. Where are you going?'

I had stood and now made my way towards the door across the yards of empty dance floor, aware but uncaring that Tweetie was watching me. I knew I was raising her suspicions but I could not help the feeling that there was not a moment to spare. Besides, if I had stayed my face would have betrayed me.

'We've had it all wrong,' I said, hurrying downstairs with Alec close behind me. 'It was Tweetie.' I stopped in the foyer and laid it all out as quickly and plainly as I could. 'She sent the threats herself, just as Foxy did. And Foxy said, didn't she, that Jeanne came along with Tweetie. *With her.* Meaning that Tweetie was just as well placed to see the headdress under construction.'

'But why would Beryl help Tweetie?' Alec said.

I shook my head. 'We've had it *all* wrong. Not just the villain but the victim too. All that rot about Bert following and Beryl roaring at him. I don't believe a word of it. We need to try to find Simon Bonnar, Alec. I think Beryl's dead.'

28

Of course our urchins, once they got used to the idea, were simply thrilled.

'The big car you were looking after on Friday,' I said to them, crouching down and taking a hand of each of them in each of mine. The girl looked delighted by the caress and I could feel her rubbing the soft leather of my glove appreciatively. The little boy, a couple of years more canny, instinctively pulled away from an adult laying hands on him. Probably he had had too many hidings from the adults in his life to be confident that one would grab hold of him for any other reason.

'What about it?' he said, crossing his arms across his grubby little jersey and staring me down.

'It was Simon Bonnar's motorcar, wasn't it?' I said.

He stuck his chin in the air to look brave and tough but his sister sidled in closer to me, scared even by the sound of the name.

'Aye,' said the boy. 'How?'

'We need to see him,' I said. 'Do you know where he lives?'

'Everybody knows where Mr Bonnar lives,' said the girl.

'And where is that?' I asked.

'The Gorbals, of course,' said her brother. 'Our bit.'

'Could you show us?' I said. 'Would you come for a drive in my motorcar and point it out?'

Now the boy stepped closer again. 'A hurl in your car?' he said. 'Can I drive it?'

'Certainly not,' I told him. 'But you can toot the horn.'

'I'm feart,' said the girl.

'You don't need to come into the house,' I assured her. 'You just need to point it out to us.'

'Naw, I'm feart for the car,' she said. 'Can I sit on your knee?'

So it was that Alec drove, ably assisted by a great many tootings and honkings of the horn from the passenger seat, while I sat in the back with a lapful of rather grubby little girl, breathing in the sharp scent of her long-unwashed hair and yet not quite able to despise the experience, for it had been many years since either of my sons submitted to such a thing and even then they were wont to squirm and kick their heels against my legs and usually had some boat or pop gun in their hands with which to jab me. This little one simply sat cuddled close with her head tucked under my chin and stroked the fur collar of my coat with her free hand, while she sucked her other thumb.

'Do you know, my dear,' I said to her presently, 'I don't know what your name is.'

'Elsie,' she said. 'What's yours?'

'Mrs Gilver,' I told her but, finding that rather ridiculous since she was attached to me like a baby koala bear, I amended it according to the custom common amongst the Scotch working people regarding how children address adults who were not parents, teachers or clergy. 'Auntie Dandy,' I said. 'And Uncle Alec.'

I had thought the boy was not listening, but after another few minutes he gave a particularly strenuous blast of the horn and cried, 'We're here, Uncle Alec! And look at all they weans. Gonny drive right up the street and back again and I'll wave.'

We did the lap of honour as requested but we had not missed the door halfway along the street where, instead of the usual clutch of housewives or lounging group of unemployed men, we could see a pair of brawny lads standing to attention, one on each side. They turned and called up the close as they saw us and a window halfway up the tenement face was opened, although we could not see by whom.

It was not at all what I should have expected, I thought, stepping down, for it was meaner by far than Foxy's street, meaner even than Miss Thwaite's, a place of broken kerb-stones and missing cobbles, the tenements not the red sandstone which can lend a kind of grandeur nor even the plain yellow stone, quick to blacken in the city's smoke it is true but still solid; these were brick, faced with a skim of stone on one side only, hastily built for the last great expansion, left behind now that the shipyards were beginning to close again and, from the look of them, given over to the slum lords who did not trouble themselves with paint and nails. Above the very close door where the two heavies stood on sentry duty there was even a window tacked over with cloth where the glass had been broken and not replaced. Judging by the way the cloth had bleached in the daylight it had been like that for some time too.

After a nod from one of the men, who showed no surprise at our arrival nor curiosity about who we might be, we passed through into the darkness and began to climb the stairs. I was forced to put my hand up to my face and try to breathe through my glove, because the acrid smell of unswept chimneys over cooking ranges did not quite choke out the engulfing smell of 'inadequate plumbing', as the planners describe this sort of close-pressed humanity. It was the smell of poverty and urban poverty at that, as far from the cottages of Gilverton with their wells and gardens as a hansom cab from a hay cart.

On the second storey there was another young man standing guard outside the middle of three doors on the landing. He too nodded, and reaching back over his shoulder with his fist, he rapped hard on the door then stepped aside and opened it for us to enter.

I had not prepared my expression, expecting to be able to do so in the hall before joining our host, but the Bonnar residence, we discovered, was what is known as a single-end: one room, comprising living room, dining room, kitchen and bedroom, right behind the front door. There was a box bed with the door open, a table with four chairs, two low chairs by the range and a couple of chests, one with drawers and one just a box with a hinged lid. This, along with some shelves above the sink and a cupboard set into the wall beyond the range, was the whole of Simon Bonnar's home.

He sat alone at the table while his inner cabinet, one assumed, or at least the three men who had come with him to the Locarno on Friday, stood leaning against the walls and windowsill.

He looked up at us out of a haggard face and when he spoke, his voice had a tremor in it. 'Have you found her?'

'We haven't, sir,' said Alec.

Simon Bonnar sat back and let his shoulders drop.

'We need to speak to you,' I said and, at a flick of his head, all three men filed out and closed the door behind them.

Then there was silence. Neither Alec nor I knew how to broach the news without revealing our earlier suspicions and neither of us knew how angered he might be by them, even now they were behind us. As we sat quietly, I became aware of a curious sound coming from the open door of the box bed. It sounded as though there were a flock of little birds in there, chirping and peeping, and I could not help glancing that way.

'Puppies, Mrs Gilver,' said Simon Bonnar. 'I run Glasgow but a bitch pups where she chooses. So I've been in Beryl's wee hurly bed there for two nights.'

At that Alec could not prevent his thoughts from showing on his face and Simon Bonnar not only saw them but answered them, unspoken as they were.

'There's nothing unusual about it, Mr Osborne,' he said.

'There's plenty a family bigger than mine lives decently in a single-end, even though it wouldn't suit you.'

'Of course,' said Alec, quite sincerely, for it was not over-crowding that concerned him. It was the matter of a widowed father and his grown daughter which struck him as strange.

'Of course, he says!' Simon Bonnar scoffed. 'I know what you're thinking. But listen to me. These are my people and I get a sight more loyalty living in among them than if I was out and away to some swanky villa in a suburb somewhere and pretending I was born last week at the golf club.'

'Do you mean Sir Percy?' I said. 'Are you saying that Percy Stott used to be a—'

'Him!' said Simon Bonnar. 'Not him. He was born with a rubber spoon in his mouth, didn't you hear? But those McNabs never had two ha'pennies to rub when we were all bairns together. And their faither worked with my faither more than once to get a bit of business done.'

I took this in as quickly as I could, but still it left me reeling. We had thought Sir Percy's disdain for his wife's family sprang from Foxy's dancing. Now, it appeared that all three siblings had done rather well, starting somewhere similar to the circumstances surrounding us now: one snaring an industrialist, one a church-leaning printer, and one ending up in a comfortable flat with happy memories and enough to live on.

'But never mind Eunice McNab,' Bonnar went on. 'What is it you need to say to me?'

Again we faltered, just as the chirping from inside the box bed grew in volume. Bonnar looked over towards the source of the sound and I was astonished to see his eyes filling with tears.

'She was that excited about the pups,' he said thickly. 'Getting ready for them. Getting homes lined up for them. I told her it was her job to look after them all, but here if she hasn't got me doing it after all. Eh? Eh? She's pulled a

278

fast one, hasn't she? She'll come swanning back once all the work and trouble's done – the besom.'

I could not bear it any longer and spoke over him. 'Mr Bonnar, we greatly fear that Beryl has come to harm.'

It took no more than that for his false cheer to crumble. 'Aye, well I know it,' he said. 'But that can't be what you needed to tell me. *I* told *you* that much.'

'We didn't believe you,' said Alec. 'We thought if a murder had been done and someone had disappeared then that person was the murderer.'

'She'd never—' he began hotly.

'We know that now,' I said, much relieved that his mind was running to the goodness of his daughter and not just the temerity of her accusers. 'We believe now that Beryl has been got out of the way, just as Roly was. We don't understand why, but we have reason to believe that is what happened.'

'Got out of the way of what?' said Simon Bonnar.

We fell silent again then, for to tell him was surely to sign a death warrant for Bert and Tweetie.

'Rivals,' said Alec at last, and rather ingeniously.

'Dancers?' said Bonnar. 'Who was it?'

'We can't tell you that,' said Alec, which was also very nicely judged. 'But three of the Locarno's professional couples have been broken up now, you see. And Roly's dying in such a dramatic way allowed Beryl to be bundled away with no one noticing.'

When he put it like that it was so obvious that I blushed to think how long it had taken us to see it.

'But you don't know who took her?' said Bonnar.

It was no more than the truth when Alec answered him. 'We do not, sir,' he said. 'We have no idea. But we mean to find out. Of that you can be sure.'

He nodded, accepting our vow and even smiling faintly. Then, without any warning at all, he took the baccy tin he was clutching and threw it against the wall with such force that it broke open and showered flakes of tobacco all over the floor.

'Three years!' he bellowed. 'Three years I've being playing nice to that dirty tink, watching him pawing her, watching her walk out of this house knowing she's going to meet him, talk and laugh and have her picture taken with him, six feet tall and right in the window in Sauchiehall Street for all the world to see. And I never said a word about it. A bloody Fenian bastard and I put up with it. And now some black-hearted devil that wanted the couples broke up has passed him over and killed her! Killed my Beryl! Why in the name of Christ could he not have killed Herbert bloody Bunyan and left my Beryl alone. Eh? Eh?'

We had no answer.

'I tell you this, it can't be a Glasgow man,' Bonnar went on, calming down a little, at least enough to notice the squealing and whining coming from the box bed where the bitch and pups were registering their displeasure at his outburst. 'No Glasgow man would go after my daughter – *my daughter* – when he could just as easy get what he wanted from killing that useless article that no one would miss and leaving my girl alone.' He had gone over to the opening and now reached in and pulled out one of the puppies, a wriggling greyish-pink little grub, almost hairless and still with its ears flattened in folds against its head.

'Shush, shush now,' he said, taking another one in his other hand and walking across the room towards us. 'Beryl wasn't a week old when her mother died,' he said. 'And there was me, Big Man Bonnar, boiling milk and washing bottles. Beryl in her cradle in one corner and her mother in her coffin in the other. Looks like I'll be doing the same again now, doesn't it? Weaning pups and burying my girl. If you'll just find her and bring her home to me.'

The squealing of the other puppies rose to a frenzy and

all three of us turned to see why. Their mother had got to her feet and looked out of the opening into the room worried for the missing two. I gasped when I saw the long white snout, the quivering black nose and the dappled ears.

'A Dalmatian?' I said. It is far from a common breed in Perthshire and I had not seen one since Bunty died.

'Beryl's choice,' said Bonnar. 'Daft kind of dog.'

'We shall find her, Mr Bonnar,' I said to him. 'I feel it in my bones that we shall. We shall bring her home.'

29

'Here's what I don't understand,' said Alec, when we were back at the Grand Central, making a very late luncheon out of two bowls of soup and a round each of ham sandwiches.

Grant and Barrow were nowhere to be seen and I rather thought she must be leading him astray, for that young man was normally just beyond a guardsman for correctness and rigidity.

'What?' I said.

'The sledgehammer of murder to crack the walnut of a change in dancing partner,' Alec said. 'Why couldn't Bert and Tweetie just tell Beryl and Roly that they were moving on to pastures new and wish them good luck?'

'Well,' I said. 'You saw Simon Bonnar this morning. Would you fancy upsetting his daughter and him asking her why she was weeping?'

'I'd fancy it a lot more than killing her and seeing what he made of that.'

'But he must have hoped – and has succeeded so far – in making sure that no one blamed him for the murder. If he had sacked Beryl there'd have been no denying it.'

'But even so,' Alec insisted, 'by all accounts, Beryl was scrupulous in keeping her father's way of doing things quite separate from her triumphs and disasters in the ballroom.'

'As long as it was honest effort in open competition,' I said.

'It might have been a different story if Bert gave her the push?' said Alec.

'I think so. Humiliation and rejection at the hands of someone she'd had to fight so hard to get her father to accept.'

'He was pretty well deranged on that topic, wasn't he?'

'From where you're looking,' I agreed. 'But to listen to Hugh it was nothing out of the ordinary. Glasgow's sectarianism is only just behind Belfast's in his view. So it's a case of local custom rather than derangement, really.'

Alec nodded, chewing thoughtfully on his sandwich, which if it were anything like mine, took quite a bit of chewing.

'I daresay it's the same for the dancing couples,' he put in at last. 'We can't see the trouble but there must *be* some because no one in his right mind would murder over it otherwise.' He took a great draught of water and then pushed the remains of his sandwich away from him, since it was mostly crusts. I had cut mine off but still it was heavy going. 'And I know who to ask too,' he said, wiggling his eyebrows at me. 'Jamesie and Alicia. They're innocents in all this. They couldn't get away fast enough when it looked as though trouble was in store. I reckon they'll tell us, without stirring up another hornet's nest.'

We could not have been more wrong, although we were only wrong because we were so very right. It was just that we got to them second. Once before, as we were about to discover, Jamesie and Alicia had been chosen for their innocence and their disinterest and that would give us the last break in this toughest of cases, like a woodcutter's wedge hammered in hard which will at last break apart even the knottiest knuckle of oak and allow it to be stacked in the basket like all the others.

The tricky bit was finding them. We were both agreed that we wanted to stay away from the Locarno, but we had no addresses for them. All we had to go on was that Jamesie Hodge was a baker, but a quick perusal of the *Post Office Directory* in the residents' lounge showed almost a page of bakers and not one of them with a telephone.

'We could ring up Balmoral and ask for Tweetie,' Alec said, 'then if she's safely at home we could go and beard Lorrison.'

'We could try again with the police,' I said doubtfully.

'And tell them that we're sticking to the notion of a poisoned hat – and I have to say it does sound silly when you say it like that – but that we've got two victims rather than just the one.'

'What's this?' said a voice behind us, making us both jump. It was Grant, still in her outdoor things, with Barrow at her side.

'Where have you been?' I demanded, the fright making me short with her.

'We went for a walk along the river,' she said. 'Very pleasant although you meet some funny sorts under the bridges. And it's been quite useful because it's given us a perspective on things, hasn't it, Mr Barrow? And we've come to the conclusion that Beryl Bonnar is innocent.'

'Oh really?'

'And very likely dead too,' Grant went on.

'And what led you to this conclusion?' I said. 'I agree, I should say. But Mr Osborne and I arrived at the conclusion because of observations in the Locarno this morning. How about you?'

'The pink frill,' said Grant. 'We didn't get a chance to examine the back alley on Friday, seeing as how we were lolling around like Chinese opium smokers with our eyeballs on backwards.'

I am used to Grant and so is Alec but it was causing Barrow considerable distress to be included in the 'we' she spoke of so unguardedly.

'So we went back there on our way to the riverside,' Grant went on. 'And we think there's a problem. Is it still locked in your dressing-table drawer, sir?' she asked Alec. 'Might we all repair up there? It'll be easier to see what I mean if we're looking at it.'

Minutes later we were gathered in Alec's room with the envelope opened out flat and the pink frill lying on it.

'Now,' Grant began, like a lecturer beginning a talk from a podium. 'As you see, the frill is in perfect condition, except that for some reason it's been wrenched off its backing cloth. It's not torn in and of itself. Do you see what that means?'

'No,' I said.

'I'm afraid not, Grant,' said Alec, rather more diplomatically.

'It wasn't caught on anything. If it had been it would have been pulled out of shape, if not actually ripped. It's cheap stuff and it would show the marks of a force strong enough to break the stitching.'

'It might not have been caught on anything,' I said, 'but that's not to say it wasn't caught *in* something. In the door to be precise. That would cause only compression, and compression, once released, wouldn't show.'

'Ah,' said Grant, 'but if she had caught it in the door it would have been on the other side. Inside the building.'

'I meant the van door,' I said. 'I'm not quibbling,' I added as she shot me a rather poisonous look, 'just trying to understand.'

'If she'd caught it in the van door she'd have driven off with it sticking out of the van door,' said Grant. 'She'd hardly care about such a trivial matter if she was speeding away from the scene of a crime she had committed, would she?'

'It's very bright,' I said. 'Quite noticeable. Perhaps she wouldn't want it waving from the door as she drove away.'

'Well, then she'd have reopened the door and pulled it in,' said Grant. 'If she was worried about it being seen she wouldn't have left it behind her.'

'That's an excellent point,' said Alec which, to be fair, it was.

'No, the only way for a frill to come unstitched like that

– and remember I've seen the quality of Beryl Bonnar's sewing at close quarters; she might have no flair but the sewing itself is very sturdy – the only way for a frill to come unstuck that way was if the wearer of the dress was pulling in one direction and some other person was pulling in the other. We couldn't imagine, Mr Barrow and me, why the getaway driver and Miss Bonnar would be pulling in opposite directions. They'd both want to be going the same way.'

'And from that' – I pointed to the scrap of pink lace – 'from that alone you surmise a complete new theory?'

'Not complete,' said Grant. 'We still have no idea why they wanted her dead.'

'They being?'

'Tweetie Stott and Bert Bunyan,' said Grant. 'Stands to reason. Two partners have been got rid of. Who else would have done it but the pair who're now free to team up. But we've no clue why they didn't just switch. Why they had to go killing people.'

'No more have we,' said Alec. 'In fact we've hit something of a brick wall. We'd like to speak to young Alicia and Jamesie to press them on it, if we can lay hands on them.'

Grant was rewrapping the lace in the remains of the envelope but she looked up at that. 'I don't mind slipping along to Alicia's work and asking her to drop in here at teatime,' she said.

'Would you?' I said casually, but Alec ruined it.

'You're a marvel, Grant,' he said. 'How did you find out where she works?'

'I don't know what you mean, sir,' said Grant. 'We were in that dressing room for nearly two hours getting ready. I know she works at the City Dairies in the packing room and lives in Dennistoun with her parents and two brothers. One of them is apprenticed to a riveter at Brown's Works and the other—'

'All right,' I said. 'That's plenty to be going on with. Yes, please, Grant, just you slip along to the City Dairies and ask young Alicia to come and see us at the end of the day.'

She brought Jamesie with her in the end, which was even better. He had gone to meet her at the end of her shift and, whether from a protective instinct or sheer nosiness, he came to see what we wanted.

It took a while to settle them when they got into my room, so diverted were they by its luxury.

'Look at the bedspread, Jamesie!' Alicia exclaimed, running a hand over its tasselled edge. 'And curtains to match. Look at the curtains! There must be ten yards of velvet in them and all that braid. Have you got— Pardon me, Mrs Gilver, but does that door go to a bathroom?'

'You're showing me up, girl,' Jamesie said.

'It does,' I said. 'Would you like to use it?'

Grant squeaked and Alicia squeaked a little too as she answered.

'Oh no,' she said. 'But I'd love to have a wee keek at it, just to say I had. When am I going to be back in a hotel bedroom with its very own private bathroom right next door? Can you imagine, Jamesie?'

When she got back her eyes were shining. 'Beautiful,' she said. 'Just like something off the pictures.'

I could not quite see what aspect of the chilly, white-tiled and green-linoleumed bathroom might have struck her that way but I did not argue.

'If we're all settled then,' said Grant stiffly.

'Thank you, Grant,' I said. 'I'll take it from here.'

Grant subsided, but she was quite unbowed. She derives almost as much pleasure from watching me make a mess of things as she does from getting to do them herself. If the one can be followed by the other she is usually deeply thrilled.

'I'm hoping, my dears,' I began, trying hard for a grandeur which comes easier every year, 'that we can speak to you in complete confidence. It's us or the police and we thought you'd prefer us.'

This wiped away the last of the sparkle from Alicia's face; the delights of the bedroom curtains and bathroom tiles were nothing to her now. Jamesie folded his arms firmly across his chest and narrowed his eyes. Grant smirked faintly.

'The thing is,' said Alec, taking over, 'we don't believe Beryl killed Roly.' Now Alicia folded her arms too. 'And we think Beryl has been killed too.'

Because of the folded arms, it was very easy to see that their chests had begun moving rapidly, their breath to quicken.

'We can't have any part of this,' said Jamesie. 'And you wouldn't either if youse had any idea what youse were getting into.'

'We have met Mr Bonnar and come to an understanding with him,' Alec said. 'You are in no danger.'

'Aye well, if you've got an "understanding" with Simon Bonnar maybe we should watch ourselves with you too,' said Jamesie.

Alicia looked rather shocked at his impertinence, but she could not stop herself from nodding. I sighed and looked over at Alec to see if he had a way through this impasse. How to explain to two such youngsters the pangs of Bonnar's fatherly grief and to make them understand that all he cared about were his own worries and that all other considerations had faded for him. Then I thought of something.

'And we know who did it,' I said. 'It was Tweetie and Bert. If you help us bring them to justice then not only will you be a professional couple at the Locarno but you'll be the senior couple.'

'Without Tweetie flexing her new muscles,' said Alec, catching on quickly.

'Tweetie and Bert?' said Alicia, her voice as filled with

wonder as a child on Christmas morning. 'Killed Beryl and Roly? Killed them both?'

'But the one thing we can't work out and where we need your help,' said Alec, 'is *why*. Clearly they wanted a change of partner. But why, we've been asking ourselves, did they not just *change* partners?'

Alicia and Jamesie continued to look back at us wide-eyed and open-mouthed, but a transformation had come over them. There was a fixity now about Jamesie's gaze and after a minute Alicia glanced at him and raised her eyebrows, asking a silent question.

'Ah,' said Alec, sitting forward until he was perched right on the edge of his seat. 'You know something, don't you?'

Both shook their heads and Alicia moved further back in her chair to put a safer distance between her and this advancing threat.

'You can tell us,' I added, 'and we shan't ever breathe a word.'

'He'll know,' said Alicia.

'Simon?' said Alec.

'He'll *tell* Simon,' said Jamesie. 'Then we'll be for it.'

'I promise we'll think of a way to keep you out of it,' I said. 'I promise you.' Of course this was beyond rash as I was just about to discover. 'We shall say we found out whatever it is some other way.'

'You couldn't have,' said Jamesie. 'There's only Bert, Beryl, Alicia and me knows in the whole of Glasgow.'

'And it gives a motive for the murders?' said Alec. 'Well, as Mrs Gilver said before, it's either us or the police.'

'Aye, but then she said she'd keep our names out of it,' said Jamesie, pointing at me. 'That's not fair, going back on the deal.'

'My dear fellow,' Alec said. 'You refused the deal.'

'Aye but,' Jamesie said. He ran a hand through his hair,

ruffling it up out of its neat waves. 'What will we do?' he said, twisting in his seat and searching Alicia's face.

'Tell them,' said Alicia. 'I'm not lying to the police. My mammy would kill me just for being in the station. Just tell them, Jamesie, eh?'

It took him a couple of good gulps to pluck up his nerve but when he spoke at last it was a succinct and orderly report, which covered all the necessary points.

'We were the witnesses at their wedding, Alicia and me.'

And just like that, the whole case fell together with a click.

'Oh my good lord,' I said. 'They're not just dancing partners. They're man and wife.'

'I couldn't for the life of me see why any man would risk the wrath of Simon Bonnar by murdering his daughter,' Alec said. 'But once he had married her, his life was over already, wasn't it? Bonnar would have killed him anyway.'

'Beryl said she'd work on him,' said Alicia. 'Bring him round. But it's been a year and nothing's changed.'

'I still don't understand why Roly had to die,' I said.

'I do,' said Alec.

'So do I,' said Grant. 'And it's wickedness beyond reckoning.'

I waited and for once she did not make a dramatic performance out of delivering the news. Perhaps in her disgust she was beyond it.

'If Beryl disappeared the whole of the city police would be falling over themselves. But if there was a murder and Beryl disappeared the police wouldn't touch it with a barge pole. They think she did it and they're letting her get away with it. They must believe her father's grief is an act.'

'Are you really saying what I think you're saying?' I said. 'That Roly was just a means to an end?'

'He was part of the method of killing Beryl,' Alec said. 'Nothing more.'

We shared a moment's quiet reflection then, each of us

trying in our own ways to come to terms with the sheer arrogant waste of his poor young life. Of course, it was dreadful to think of Beryl done away with to set her husband free, but somehow the killing of poor Roly was the true horror for me. I could not forget the sound of the ragged sobs being torn from Julian Armour's throat and I hoped that somehow he could be spared knowing why Roly had died.

'Very well then,' I said, after a while. 'You two can go on your way with our grateful thanks. In fact, when is your wedding?'

'September,' said Alicia. 'We're saving up for it.'

'And how would you like to spend your wedding night here?' I said. 'As a present from Mr Osborne and me, to say thank you.'

'Oh! That would be lovely,' said Alicia, clapping her hands and bouncing out of her seat with the joy of it.

'And when Mrs Gilver says "here",' said Alec, 'she means the honeymoon suite, of course. If they have one.'

'Will they let us?' said Jamesie. 'They'll not come over all snooty when we get off the bus and haven't a set of suitcases and hatboxes and all that?'

He had a very exalted idea of the Grand Central's clientele and I could not help but smile.

'We shall make sure you are welcomed as their treasured guests,' I said.

I was salving my conscience because, when the news of Bert and Beryl's marriage came out, someone – police, lawyer, or Bonnar himself – would want to see the certificate and there their witnessing signatures would be. If Bonnar then wanted to wreak his revenge for their part in it, nothing we could do would stop him.

30

'And finally to the police,' Alec said, once the youngsters were gone. 'To lay the entire thing down in front of them. Culprits, victims, means, opportunity and, most important of all, motive.'

'I'm not sure I'd go quite that far,' I said. 'We have no idea who drove the van and we can't account for how Tweetie or Bert got hold of cyanide. I don't suppose he's a chemist's assistant or anything quite so handy.'

'He's not,' said Grant. 'He's something far worse. If I were Miss Bonnar's dad it wouldn't have been the religion I baulked at. I mean, who'd want their only daughter married to an undertaker? Think of him coming home and chucking her under the chin with those hands.'

'An undertaker,' said Alec, squeezing my arm really quite hard. 'I don't suppose you know the name of the firm, do you?'

'Certainly I do,' said Grant. 'Haddings. They're a fine old family firm. My Uncle Timothy's funeral was handled by them, him being a Glasgow man, and I'll never forget what a send-off they gave him. Of course that was in the days of horse-drawn hearses but their livery is just as smart now they use motor-vans.'

'Smart livery?' I said, clutching Alec back.

Grant spread a hand in front of her as though tracing the elegant coach lines in her mind. 'A fine gold line on patent black,' she said, 'and "Haddings for Service" written in copperplate in a lozenge. With painted plumes.'

I felt the room move a little as the dizzying shock of it hit me.

'We passed him on the road, Alec,' I whispered in a sort of moan. 'The driver recognised us and sped away! We were that close and we let him go.'

'*I* let him get away,' Alec said. 'You were all for giving chase, so don't berate yourself.'

'Who?' said Grant. 'You saw the van driver? Who was it?'

'Well, it must have been Bert by then,' I said. 'Getting the body out of the city to dump it somewhere. And how perfect! An undertaker would have half a dozen places to hide a body.'

'But it wasn't Bert driving away from the alley,' said Alec. 'He obviously bundled her out of the ballroom but he must have handed her over pretty much immediately.'

'He couldn't possibly have got one of his colleagues in on it,' I said. 'Too dangerous.'

'Can Miss McNab drive?' said Barrow. 'With her hair tucked under a cap maybe.'

I jumped. He had been so perfectly silent for so very long that I had forgotten he was there.

'Excellent, Barrow!' said Alec, making the young man smirk with pleasure. 'That's how it must have been done.'

'Let's stop at the telephone kiosk on our way out,' I said, 'and just make entirely sure.'

Mary answered and I should have preferred to ask her the questions, but she really was an excellent maid and she was having none of it.

'I'm sure I couldn't say, madam,' she told me in reproving tones. 'I'll just run and fetch my mistress for you.'

So it was Lady Stott with whom I had to deal, picking my way across the delicate ground and trying to tease the useful grains from the cloud of chaff she sent up. She was even more volubly displeased than ever and wanted me to know.

'Are you determined to blacken the names of my entire

family?' she barked down the line at me. 'I've had my sister on the phone to me, weeping. Tweetie came home all upset from the Locarno saying you've got some nonsense in your head about *her* and now you're making nasty insinuations about my niece!'

'I merely asked where she was on Fri—'

'Merely!' shrieked Lady Stott. 'Oh, you *merely asked* where someone was when a murder was being committed. Is that all?'

She took her mouth away from the machine but there was no significant reduction in decibels. 'Bounce?' she shouted. 'Bounce! It should be you here listening to this. It's those detectives you were so clever as to invite into my home and you'll never guess what they're saying now!'

'For pity's sake, woman,' came Sir Percy's voice.

'Don't you dare "woman" me, Percival Stott,' his wife screeched. 'It's not you having to hear wicked lies about your nearest and dearest.'

'*I* should be your nearest and dearest,' said Sir Percy, bellowing in an extremely unendearing way, unlikely to draw anyone nearer to him. 'If you had cleaved unto your husband like you should have, Theresa wouldn't have been hanging round that flighty piece in the first place.'

'That flighty piece is my sister!' Lady Stott shouted. 'How dare you!'

'Lady Stott,' I said, thinking that at least a woman so angry could not be guarded and if I just asked she might, without thinking, just answer. 'Does Jeanne know how to drive a motorcar?'

'Jeanne?' she said. And suddenly she was speaking so quietly and in a voice so puzzled that I could not understand what she was asking me. Then I realised that she was not asking me anything; was not in fact talking to me at all. 'Jeanne, what are you doing?' she said. 'Why are you— *No!*'

I was frozen for one second and then I crashed down the

earpiece, leapt out of the kiosk and streaked across the lobby to the front door, then I was out of the door and into the Cowley where Alec was waiting.

'Stotts', as fast you can get there,' I said and Alec, revving the engine vigorously, nipped out into a tiny space between a brewer's cart and an omnibus, causing cursing all around. Then he shot straight across to the other side of the road and put his foot down until the pedal touched the floor. I held on hard to the top of the glove box and tried not to see the narrowness of the gap between two trams that we were about to squeeze through. I certainly did not notice that we were not alone, that another car was squeezing through it right on our heels.

'I think I've done something very stupid,' I said. 'Lady Stott wasn't very self-contained when I asked her about Jeanne's movements on Friday and Jeanne overheard enough to put the wind up her. I think she's either skipping out – I hope she's skipping out – or she's . . . I don't know what she's doing. Alec, hurry.'

We made it to Balmoral in record time, screeched up and stopped in a spray of gravel. The house looked so very ordered and peaceful, with the flowers newly watered and the step newly swept that I could not imagine anything untoward happening there. It was only when no one answered our ring that I truly began to believe, and moreover to face, how badly wrong this day might have gone. I opened the letterbox and bent down, listening.

It was faint but it was definite. Someone inside was weeping. I gestured to Alec to try the door. Locked. I could not imagine what he was doing when he started to rummage about around the pots of begonias, but Alec is a young man of the world. I have never lived in a house where everyone went out at once and there might be no one to answer the door. In my childhood home as well as Gilverton and the London place when we owned it there was always at least a footman. But

Balmoral, for all its comforts, was a Glasgow villa run by a maid or two and so the Stotts, like thousands of others, had a latchkey under a flowerpot at the front door. Alec held it up and grinned at me, then fitted it and opened the door.

We entered practically on tiptoe and followed the sound of the quiet weeping across the hallway and into the morning room. What a change had been wrought from our first sight of it less than a week ago. Sir Percy and Lady Stott, along with Mary the maid, were together on the floor, clutching one another closely, their faces white and streaked with tears, while on the other side of the room Jeanne McNab stood with Tweetie held in front of her, an enormous knife at the girl's throat, so close that it made a dent in the skin of her smooth young neck.

'You took your time,' Jeanne said.

'But,' I began. She must have tightened her grip or pressed with the knife because a small moan escaped Tweetie and her mother's weeping grew louder. Sir Percy pulled his wife closer to him, burying her face in his chest and shushing her.

'This is a bluff,' I said. 'They're in it together, Lady Stott. I'm sorry to upset you but it's the truth.'

'Shut up before you get me killed,' hissed Tweetie.

'Please, Mrs Gilver,' said Sir Percy, emotion catching at his voice. 'You've got it wrong.'

'We *were* in it together,' said Jeanne, 'but she double-crossed me.'

'I didn't,' said Tweetie. 'I keep telling you. I didn't *mean* to.'

'What happened?' said Alec.

'It was the perfect plan,' Jeanne said. 'Beryl and Roly out of the way and the police too scared of what they'd find to go looking. That left Tweetie and Bert free for each other and to cap it all, I was supposed to get Julian.'

'Get him how?' said Alec.

Jeanne blinked, confused. 'Get him by telling him I was having him,' she said. 'He could hardly say no given what I know about him, could he? I was going to get married and get out of this house. No more sleeping curled up beside the chimney, you know. No more yes you ridiculous old harridan, no you pathetic old fool, three bags bloody full you spoiled selfish filthy little tart.'

'But he won't have her,' said Tweetie. 'I can't imagine why.'

'How do you know?' I asked her.

'He told me when I broke it off. I hadn't imagined it would make much difference to him which one of us it was, but with Roly gone he said he didn't care any more. He's going to live like a monk, I gather.'

'Tweetie,' said Lady Stott, with a faint echo of her old mustard. 'Don't be coarse, dear.'

'So,' I said, 'for you to get Julian and you, Miss Stott, to get Bert, two innocents have died?'

'Not quite,' said Jeanne.

'What do you mean?' Alec demanded.

She turned her amused face to him and gave him a veiled look. 'Well, what do you think I mean?' she said. 'What could I possibly mean? They're not innocent, are they? Ronald Watt was an unspeakable creature, quite prepared to deliver my cousin into a sham marriage and carry on regardless under her nose.'

'How can you be so lofty about a sham marriage you were happy to enter instead?' I asked Jeanne. She shook her hair back and stared me down.

'On my terms,' she said. 'And by my choice. That's quite a different thing.'

'How did you find out about the sham?' asked Alec. He was looking at Tweetie. 'We thought you twigged after Roly's death but we were wrong, weren't we?'

Tweetie's anger rose again as she remembered.

'I *saw* them,' she said. 'At the office one day. I was this close to marching in and confronting them, but then an idea just landed in my head. Like a dandelion seed.'

'A dandelion seed,' I echoed flatly. 'The idea to keep going along with Julian until you could kill Roly and Beryl and blame one for the other.'

'N—' Tweetie began, but Jeanne tightened her grip.

'Do shut up, Theresa dearest,' she said.

'And what *of* Beryl?' said Alec. 'What did she do to you?'

I happened to glance at the Stotts as he spoke and was astonished to see guilty looks upon both their faces. Only young Mary still appeared to be simply terrified and miserable. Sir Percy and his wife were looking decidedly shifty.

'Her father killed mine,' said Jeanne, in a voice thrilling with self-righteous anger.

'And once again I shall ask the question,' said Alec. 'What did Beryl do to you?'

'Her father killed my father!' shouted Jeanne.

Tweetie, feeling the knife bite into her as Jeanne's hand shook, let out a whimper and begged me with her eyes to make Alec stop the goading. I laid a hand on his arm and shushed him gently.

'Why?' I asked.

'Because he was going to the police,' said Sir Percy. 'Butter wouldn't melt, that was my dear brother-in-law. He found out this and that about a matter of private business, no concern of his at all, and he wouldn't rest.'

'Are you telling me you knew about it?' said Jeanne. 'I never told you of my own suspicions because I feared I wouldn't be able to convince you of anything so outlandish. And you knew all along?'

'Of course I didn't know,' Sir Percy said, but then he added, 'not the details.'

His wife struggled out of his grasp then and stared at him in horror. 'Not the details?' she said, the ghost of her old self a little less faint now.

'Not even the facts,' said Sir Percy. 'Just that he knew what he shouldn't and before he could act on it, he was dead.'

'He went to warn Bonnar,' Jeanne said. 'He gave him a chance to do the right thing.'

I could imagine it. The lay preacher, wrapped in sanctimony, marching into the gangster's lair to tick him off. Such foolishness when he had a wife and child depending on him.

'Aye, that sounds like Goldie,' said Lady Stott. 'He was too good for this world. *You* fit right in to it,' she added, with a look of pure poison fired at her husband. 'You suspected him of killing my brother and yet you carried on taking his protection and giving him your money?'

'Your blessed sister went rubbing shoulders with his daughter and took our girl along,' Sir Percy shot back.

'Don't try to tell me Foxy knew a thing about it!' said his wife stoutly. 'You're the only one here who turned a blind eye.'

'And kept you in the style to which you and our daughter—'

'Don't you dare,' said Lady Stott. 'Don't you blame me for this. I would have gone back to a room and kitchen in Meadowpark Street to have Goldie alive again. Him and his girl and me and mine; we'd have been quite happy.'

There was no chorus of agreement from the two girls. I rather thought they were more attached to the easy living at Balmoral than Lady Stott gave them credit for.

'And what about you, Theresa?' I said. 'What was your excuse for killing Beryl? Were you such a devoted niece to your uncle as all that?'

'I had no choice,' said Tweetie. 'It was either her or Bert.' She was undoubtedly a selfish and spoiled girl but at that moment I could see that she truly loved him: as she spoke of him her voice softened and she seemed almost to forget the knife at her throat. 'Beryl coaxed him into the marriage,' she went on, 'saying her father would come round to it.'

'He must have loved her,' I said.

299

Tweetie's face clouded. I guessed she preferred to gloss over that in her reckoning.

'He knows what love is now,' she said, preening rather. 'And don't glower at me; even if Bert and I hadn't found one another, he would have seen through Beryl's tricks soon enough. She promised to work on her father, but after nearly a year she was still sleeping in that ludicrous little hovel and acting as an unpaid housekeeper. She'd just started breeding from her silly dog, for goodness' sake; she'd clearly settled for life. And, every day, she knew that if her father found out he would put Bert at the bottom of the Clyde in a minute.'

'But—'

'That's enough talk,' said Jeanne. 'You.' She nodded at me. 'Go and sit over there with them. And you.' She glared at Alec. 'You are going to go to wherever you've got your little hoard of clues and you're going to bring them back here to me. How long will it take you?'

'Thirty minutes,' said Alec.

'So in thirty-one minutes, if you're not back, you'll be sorry.' She thrust Tweetie forward. 'Take a good look at her and ask if you want her death on your conscience. I want both the notes, both the books, the bird and the fox, but most of all I want the headdresses back. Because no one who hasn't seen them would ever believe it, would they?'

After Alec's and my efforts to make that inspector listen, I could only agree. Especially, I thought, since we would be the only ones saying any of it. Sir Percy, Lady Stott, Foxy and Tweetie all had far too much to hide and the Glasgow police would rather pretend the Bonnars did not exist at all than get anywhere near a scandal surrounding them. And then there was poor Roly, whose family would no doubt let his death go unexplained rather than have his reputation suffer as it must should the truth come about how he had lived and died.

Alec was drilling into me with his eyes, but I could not tell what he meant to convey.

'And make sure there's plenty petrol in the tank and two canisters besides,' Jeanne said. 'I have a very long way to go.'

Alec turned on his heel and walked away, his footsteps ringing on the marble floor. I heard the front door open and then a long, long pause. My heart leapt; he had thought of something! He had thought of a way to stop this and was just about to turn around and come back again. I heard the door close and waited for his feet approaching, then I felt a sickening drop inside myself as the engine started up. He really was driving off and, as the sound grew fainter, a little knot of fear began to smoulder in my chest.

'Where will you go?' I said to Jeanne when all around us was silent again.

'No talking,' she barked at me. Then she looked past the four of us huddled on the floor, over towards the door which led to the dining room at the back of the house, and said, 'Oh.'

'That's right, Miss McNab,' said Simon Bonnar's voice, sending a jolt through all of us. 'Now, throw the knife away and let Miss Stott go.'

Jeanne hesitated for just a second and that was all the time it took. A shot rang out, deafening in the close confines of the room.

Tweetie crumpled to the floor first and Lady Stott shrieked a pure peal of rage and despair, but it was only shock and the sudden relaxing of Jeanne's arm from around her. She was back up on all fours in time to see Jeanne let the knife fall, begin to sway, then sink to her knees and fall softly sideways, looking so much like Tweetie that first day that I could not bear to see it.

I scrambled up and rushed over, getting to her just as Simon Bonnar did. He was tucking something away into his pocket – a gun, one supposed – and his men, the same three men, were helping the Stotts and Mary to their feet and guiding them to chairs.

I bent over Jeanne, ripping her coat open, hoping to staunch the wound, but falling back in hopeless horror at the way the blood poured and bubbled as though it were as endless as water from a spring.

'You . . . you . . .' I said. 'You *shot* her!'

'Think she wasn't going to kill the lot of you if she could manage it?' Bonnar said.

I gazed at Jeanne, unable to believe his words and unable to believe what was happening.

She looked beyond me into Simon Bonnar's face. 'Fool,' she said, her voice somewhere between a gurgle and a croak. 'I was coming to talk to you.'

'What does—' said Bonnar, dropping to his knees at her side, but she coughed and made a hideous bubbling sound, then, halfway through a second cough, she stilled.

'What did that mean?' he said.

But I barely heard him. Before I had even caught my breath from the shock of watching her die, I heard Alec's footsteps ringing out again as he sprinted across the hall then across the morning room and dropped down beside me.

'I thought you'd gone!' I said. 'I mean of course it was the right thing what with Tweetie, but I thought you'd driven off and left me.'

'Don't be a goose,' said Alec, giving me a bone-crushing hug as though we were team-mates after a winning game of rugger. 'I saw Bonnar's man out in the garden looking through the window and reckoned the quietest way to let them in was for me to open the front door.'

'But how did you get here?' I said to Bonnar, struggling out of Alec's arms.

'I've been following you,' he said. 'I told you that already.'

I knelt up on my heels, thinking fast. 'Since when?' I said.

'All day.'

'You didn't follow us last night then?' I said, slumping.

'I was still looking for Beryl last night,' said Bonnar. 'I hadn't quite given up hope then. Why?'

I could not bear to tell him that we had probably passed the van carrying his daughter's body, that if he had been following us then he could have got her back again.

All around the room, there was a great bustle going on. One of the large men came and draped a rug over Jeanne. The other was pouring brandy for the Stotts and Mary, putting cushions at their back and stools under their feet. The third had left and minutes later I heard an engine and saw a small motorcar come up the drive, pass the front door, then reverse slowly towards it again. I shuddered. She was going to be tidied away and they were doing it so efficiently one knew it was not the first time or the tenth time they had done such tidying.

'Do you know how she died?' said Simon Bonnar. 'I know what the plan was. Make it look as if she'd killed a rival and run away. And I know why, of course. I killed the girl's father. It was years ago but I did it all the same.'

I had to tense every muscle in my body to keep myself from turning to look at Tweetie. He knew nothing of Bert's place in his daughter's life, nothing of Tweetie's role in all this. He thought Jeanne had done it alone.

'Do you know if it was quick?' he said, reaching out and taking hold of my hand. Later that day I would put it to my face and smell the cordite on my fingers. 'Did she suffer?'

I thought of the pink frill and how loudly it spoke of a struggle and wondered how to tell him that I didn't know how his daughter died or where or even when.

Then a great light broke over me. A struggle meant that Beryl was alive when she left the Locarno. When I said two innocents had died, Jeanne said, 'Not quite,' and smirked about how clever she was. I assumed she meant that Roly was no innocent, but now I saw more clearly.

And then her last words were that Simon Bonnar was a fool to shoot her before she had the chance to speak to him. Numb with shock as I was, I staggered to my feet and reached out to grab him by the arms.

'I think she's alive, Mr Bonnar, but she's hidden away.'

'Where?' said Bonnar. He broke free and grabbed me instead, shaking me.

'Steady on,' said Alec. 'If Mrs Gilver is right, she was driven away in a van and she's somewhere out of town beyond the village of Eaglesham. Bert drove her there late in the evening.'

'I'd believe anything of that devil,' said Bonnar, 'but he didn't. He went home and stayed put. We were watching him.'

'Jeanne went out,' said Tweetie. Her colour was high and her eyes were very wide.

'Theresa!' said her father.

'It was after you'd gone, Mrs Gilver,' Tweetie went on. 'She went out again.'

I stared at her. Was she really looking me straight in the face and telling lies, with Bonnar and his men right there listening? It was a reckless move, but then the stakes could hardly be higher. And it was not the first time Tweetie had thought this fast. I remembered her sudden shrieks, which caused all the panic in the Locarno and neatly stopped the police from doing anything so useful as sealing off the exits before Beryl could be got away, or corralling the witnesses before Tweetie managed to ditch her headdress.

I exchanged a look with Alec and saw him nod slightly. He knew that Tweetie was lying as well as I did but if we played along we might learn something useful. If we challenged her, she would shut like a clam.

'What time did Jeanne get back?' Alec said.

Sir Percy moaned and tears sprang up in his eyes. 'She's lying there dead on the floor, for pity's sake,' he said.

I was more sure than I had ever been about anything that

it was *Tweetie* who had gone out, *Tweetie* whom we had passed on the road. I turned to her mother.

'Lady Stott,' I said, staring hard. 'What time did "Jeanne" get in last night?'

'She wasn't—'

'Mother, for God's sake,' said Tweetie, her voice wire-taut.

'Half past nine or thereabouts,' said Lady Stott, without meeting my eye. 'She came home in a taxi. No matter how many times I tell her.'

'Told her,' said Sir Percy, with a break in his voice, pointing at the wrapped bundle on the floor.

His wife subsided and said it again. 'About half past nine.'

'If we're right about this van – and I think we are – then we know where Beryl was at quarter past eight,' I said, 'going south. And we should be able to work out where she is now, given the time for the driver to get back into town, drop off the van and pick up a taxi to get here by half past nine.'

'But from where?' said Simon. 'It's a big city. Where did she *go* to change from a van to a taxi? That might make all the difference in the world.'

'Haddings Undertaker's,' I said.

Tweetie moaned softly. Simon Bonnar's face grew thunderous and his eyes flashed. For the first time since I had met him, I could truly believe that he was what he was. In his cold rage, he was utterly terrifying.

'He knew,' he said. 'He helped.'

'Mr Bonnar, there is no time,' I said. 'Now, think. If you were on the road to Eaglesham at a quarter past eight at night and you came back from your destination to Haddings and took a cab back here, arriving at half past nine, where would you have been going?'

I saw the realisation hit him; his face lit up.

'Boyce, McEllon,' he said. 'You come with me. Billy.' He glared at the other man.

'Right, boss,' they all said in chorus and then he was flying out of the door with two of his henchmen at his side and Alec and me right behind him.

'Where are we going?' I asked as we roared through the suburban streets, tyres squealing and pedestrians scattering as we passed.

'Cemetery,' said Simon Bonnar, 'where my wife's buried. Except she's not.'

I made a determined effort not to wonder what that might mean but when we got there it was not so bad as all that after all. All he meant was that his wife, who he loved more than his loyalty to his Protestant ways, was in a mausoleum rather than a grave, an ostentatious little folly of sparkling pink granite with railings all round and pillars to either side of the door.

'The black devil,' said Simon Bonnar, watching as the sexton wrestled with the enormous key. 'He knew an under-taker's van wouldn't stick out and he could easily get into the wee office place and get the key to copy. Hurry up, man!' he shouted. 'It's been open last night. It can't be rusty.'

At last the key turned and Simon Bonnar pushed the sexton roughly aside and, grabbing the handle, shouldered the heavy door open on to darkness.

'Beryl?' he said, with a crack in his voice.

'Da?' came a quavering cry and all of us let out shouts of relief.

He was shrugging off his overcoat to cover her when I lit a match and got my first glimpse of them. The pink dress was streaked with dirt and she was shivering, and looked as if she had lost a stone in weight and most of it from her face. But she was awake, her eyes were bright and she was smiling.

'I'm as clarty as all get out,' she said. 'Don't touch me!'

But Simon Bonnar could not help showering her with kisses and hugging her over and over again and no one watching could help but beam at them.

306

'Da, I'm sorry,' Beryl said.

'You've done nothing to be sorry for, hen,' said Bonnar. 'It was Bert Bunyan and Jeanne McNab did this to you.'

'Jeanne?' said Beryl. '*Someone* knocked me out after Bert grabbed me away from the floor. Was it Jeanne?'

Simon Bonnar swept Beryl up into his arms. We stepped outside to let him pass through the door.

'And I did do something,' Beryl said. 'I married Bert.'

Her father staggered a little as the shock of the news hit him. 'Aye well,' he said. 'You're a widow now.'

Foolishly, I thought it was a threat, a promissory note to make it so.

'It was Jeanne who drove her out here, Mr Bonnar,' I said, hoping to change his mind.

'Must you punish Bert as well?' said Alec.

'Too late for arguments,' said Bonnar. 'I sent Billy to deal with him while we came here. He's away.'

At that, finally, Beryl began to cry.

Postscript

The puppy glared at the faded tassel on the corner of the cushion, growled in her throat and then pounced on it, shaking it so hard that she lost her balance and tumbled into a heap in the corner of the blue chair.

'She's ruining that,' said Alec.

'It's had its day,' I said. 'The whole place could do with a little something, in fact. I'll wait until she's a bit more civilised and then see about brightening things up.'

'I still can't believe you accepted her,' said Alec. 'Won't she remind you of it every single day?'

'I *want* to be reminded,' I said. 'I *want* to think of it every single day, because that way I shall keep asking myself if we did the right thing until I manage to come up with an answer.'

The trouble was that, even though Jeanne had brought punishment upon herself in a manner of speaking – for anyone who holds a knife to another's throat is inviting danger – and even though Bert had been dealt rough justice by Simon Bonnar's right-hand man, Tweetie was living at Balmoral with her mother and father and no matter how I tried to convince myself of it, I could not find a way to call that fair.

'She got off scot-free,' I had said to Alec many times. The official version was that Jeanne killed all three men, Leo and Roly and Bert too, so jealous of the dancing girls around her that she stole their partners away. Of course, it was not a story which would have been swallowed in any other city but, in dance-enthralled Glasgow and with Simon Bonnar endorsing it, it held sway. Besides, it had the merit of being much easier to understand than the true story of Goldie McNab's naïveté, Percy Stott's venality, Foxy Trotter's misguided cunning, Julian's machinations, Tweetie's ruthlessness and Jeanne's slow descent into sheer evil.

'She did,' Alec always agreed when I laid it out before him. He was agreeing again at this very moment, but still arguing too. 'But that means Foxy is not tried for manslaughter in the death of her husband and Julian Armour is not sent away to do hard labour because of Roly either,' he said. 'I was convinced even before this latest development.' He pointed the stem of his pipe at the letter in my hand, which I had just been reading to him.

Beryl had written to tell me that her father was retiring; that was the blameless way she expressed his plan to stop running what Miss Thwaite had called 'the club' in Glasgow.

He says it'll be for the worse. He says within a year there'll be worse gangs and trouble than ever happened under him and the police themselves will be harking back to the good old days when at least somebody was in charge. But I've told him. I'm having none of it. If he'd not been 'in charge', I'd have told him about Bert and me and three lives that are lost would be saved. So he's retiring and we're moving to England, if you can believe it! Down to the south coast near Dartmouth, to a nice wee town with a big hotel that needs a dancer. It's the sort of place you can't imagine murders ever happen. I'll send you a Christmas card unless you ask me not to. Give the pup a wee clap from me. Have you decided what to call her yet? What about Tango?

Yours ever in gratitude,
Beryl Bonnar

'Tango,' said Alec, musing.

'I don't think so,' I said. 'For one thing people would ask me why and I'd have to lie to them.'

'You'll have to call her something if you're ever to start her training,' said Alec. 'Which can't, if you ask me, come a moment too soon.' He lifted the puppy away from a chair leg she was trying to subdue with all four paws and both rows of her tiny white teeth.

'Bunty,' I said firmly. I had decided and, despite Hugh delivering one of the finest snorts of a long snorting life, I was fixed upon it.

The puppy raised her head, gave a yip and came trotting over to me to see what I wanted.

'Bunty,' I said again.

She sat down in front of my feet and waited to hear more.

Facts and Fictions

The Locarno Ballroom in Sauchiehall St was indeed the venue for the first Scottish Professional Dancing Championships in 1928 but, usefully for my purposes, it was closed and for sale between 1929 and 1934.

Razor gangs had a period of lively activity in Glasgow in the 20s and 30s, but their heyday did not begin after the departure of an all-powerful restraining presence. Simon Bonnar isn't a fictionalisation of a real gangster; he's totally imaginary.

It has to be said, though, that this story could not have been set much later than the summer of 1931 because, in the December of that year, the esteemable Percy Sillitoe became the Chief Constable in Glasgow and set about some ruthless and effective gang-busting. I've named Sir Percy Storr in his honour.